SEE NO EVIL

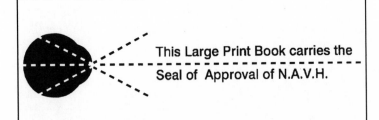

This Large Print Book carries the Seal of Approval of N.A.V.H.

SEE NO EVIL

ALLISON BRENNAN

THORNDIKE PRESS

An imprint of Thomson Gale, a part of The Thomson Corporation

Detroit • New York • San Francisco • New Haven, Conn. • Waterville, Maine • London

THOMSON

GALE

Thorndike Press® Large Print Basic.

The text of this Large Print edition is unabridged.

Other aspects of the book may vary from the original edition.

Set in 16 pt. Plantin.

LIBRARY OF CONGRESS CATALOGING-IN-PUBLICATION DATA

Brennan, Allison.
    See no evil / by Allison Brennan.
      p. cm. — (Thorndike Press large print basic)
    ISBN-13: 978-0-7862-9404-6 (alk. paper)
    ISBN-10: 0-7862-9404-3 (alk. paper)
    1. Teenage girls — Fiction. 2. Stepfathers — Crimes against — Fiction.
3. Serial murders — Fiction. 4. Online chat groups — Fiction. 5. Public prosecutors — Fiction. 6. Large type books. 7. Psychological fiction. I. Title.
PS3602.R4495S44 2007
813'.6—dc22   2007008043

Published in 2007 by arrangement with The Ballantine Publishing Group, a division of Random House, Inc.

Printed in the United States of America on permanent paper
10 9 8 7 6 5 4 3 2 1

For Gary & Karin Tabke

ACKNOWLEDGMENTS

Thank you to everyone who helped with the details of this book, especially Candy Calvert, CJ Lyons, Gary "Officer Friendly" Tabke, Donna Thompson, Wally Lind, and most particularly, a special thanks to Mary Kennedy for her insight into the minds of teen killers.

Because sometimes I need to get out of the house to find my muse, a special thanks to Starbucks #5557 and the Elk Grove Brewery.

And the usual suspects: Kimberly Whalen, Charlotte Herscher, and Dana Isaacson; Dan and the kids; and always my mom.

I invite you to visit my website at allison brennan.com to read exclusive content, deleted scenes, and view book trailers for this and my other books.

PROLOGUE

The teenaged girl had the gun in her hand. Paul Judson was supposed to be her first kill.

Robbie was the driver. He was parked two houses up where it was dark. He'd removed the plates from his new black truck. Cami was the lookout. If anyone approached, she'd take care of it. What that meant, Faye didn't know. She trusted Cami knew what she was doing. Supposedly it had all been Cami's idea in the first place.

But Faye suspected Cami wasn't the brains behind the plan. She felt as if they were all puppets, just pieces in someone else's game. If they managed to get away with this, Faye would find out exactly *who* was pulling their strings.

"It'll be easy," Cami had told her earlier. "Shoot him between the eyes."

Faye hated guns.

Now Skip walked Faye to the door, stood

right there next to her on the porch when she knocked.

"I can't," she said.

"What?"

Skip had a panicked look on his face. He nervously shifted his weight, looking about the neighborhood. Worried. He'd been the most confident of the plan, arrogant, sure of himself, like so many guys in her school. "You can't back out now, Faye."

"I don't like guns."

"What's that got to do with it?"

She handed the gun to Skip and pulled her knife from her pocket. Its shiny stainless-steel blade winked under the porch light as she turned it over and over in her palm. "I'll use this."

"Don't be stupid," said Skip.

The door opened.

Faye tightened her grip around the handle and stared into the eyes of the man they had been sent to kill.

"Who are you?" Judson squinted. "I don't recognize you. You're not from the school."

He didn't move.

Faye raised the knife.

They knew from their research that Judson was severely nearsighted. He didn't see the knife right away, but followed the movement of her arm.

Realization hit his eyes just before Skip pumped two bullets, one after another, into his brain.

"Move it, Faye!" Skip pocketed the gun. *"Now."*

She pocketed her knife as she ran back to the car, into the backseat, to safety. But her heart didn't stop racing as Robbie drove away. Casually, so as not to attract attention.

The kill had been too fast, too easy. *Bang, bang,* a man was dead. A bullet in each eye, his brains splattered into the room behind.

She had wanted to feel his blood. Touch it. Taste it.

She hated guns.

Someday Faye would use her knife on someone other than herself.

ONE

How would you kill him?

I don't know.

Think about it. He hurt you. He made you touch him. He humiliated you. You must want him to pay.

Yeah, but . . .

You would never *really* kill him. I know that. But you need to get over your anger, release the rage. The only way to be free of him is to picture him without any power over you. Visualize the one person you hate the most in the world dead. Can you?

Yes.

What does he look like?

He's sitting at his desk.

And you walk in . . . what does he say to you?

"Come here. Kneel. *Now.*"

What do you do?

I go. I have no choice. They'll send me away . . . I've lived on the streets. I've been to juvie.

13

It's worse than sucking his dick.

Picture yourself walking toward the desk. This time, you're going to say no. This time, you're going to pay him back for touching you. For making you touch him. How?

I want him to know exactly what it feels like. And?

I want to cut his dick off and shove it down his throat. Let *him* suck on it.

Good. Very good. Picture him choking on his penis whenever you get angry or upset. That's the first step to getting rid of the rage, the anger. To heal and become normal.

I'll never be normal.

Emily Chandler Montgomery would never be normal.

She sat in her idling Volkswagen Bug and stared at the looming house in front of her. She didn't even want to pull into the garage, as if it would swallow her and she'd never escape. She hated coming home.

Home. What a joke. She had no home. It had disappeared when her father died. All she had was a house of many rooms, none of which welcomed her, except for her tiny sanctuary upstairs.

But where else could she go? She'd run away, and that hadn't worked. Living on the streets was impossible, especially for a pampered, spoiled rich kid like her.

At least that's what her shrink had told her.

And in many ways — *most* ways — it was true. She didn't want to live on the street and sell her body. Because out there these were her choices: whore or gutter rat. Emily liked her bedroom, her spa, the Olympic-size swimming pool where she could swim laps until her arms ached and her lungs gasped for air. The clothes, the food, the roof.

If only Victor was gone, she could live in the castle without fear. Why had her mother married Judge Victor Montgomery? He was a creep back when they were dating, and he was worse now. A fake. A hypocrite.

I hate you I hate you I hate you!

She pounded her fists on the steering wheel until her hands ached. The rage circulating in her blood made her ears hot, her sight dim. She wanted to break something, but the words of her shrink battled against the anger.

Take a deep breath. Again. Let it out slowly. Focus on your calm place. Picture a blank canvas. Now paint your oasis, the place you feel safe. Paint that in the canvas of your mind. Put yourself there, in the picture.

Emily released the car's clutch and slowly

drove into the garage. She pretended she floated in the middle of the sea, nothing around her. The ocean was calm, peaceful, the water a brilliant blue, the sky orange, red, violet in the setting sun.

Her oasis.

As Emily parked her car next to Victor's Jaguar, her safe place disappeared. She held her keys in her hand and considered running them along the side of his precious sports car. But they'd know she did it and find a way to punish her. Make her spend another weekend in juvie. She could hear her mother's cold, disapproving tone. "It's for your own good, Emily. Your antics have embarrassed the family yet again."

When you get angry, you let your enemies have control. Take a deep breath. Picture those who torment you getting what's coming to them. Justice for you and everyone like you. Write about it. Talk about it. Get it out of your system. When you keep your feelings inside, anger wins. Your enemy wins.

Don't let him win.

Emily took a deep breath, then another. Through the windows on the far side of the garage, the quality of light seemed to have changed. How long had she been sitting in her car? She looked at the time on the dashboard. *Five-thirty?* A full hour? That couldn't be right.

She picked up her cell phone to check the time. Five-thirty.

This wasn't the first time she'd worked on controlling the rage only to discover that she'd blanked out on the passage of time.

She grabbed her backpack and reluctantly left the safe haven of her Bug. It was Wednesday, which meant her mother would be home late. Wednesday, Wednesday . . . right, planning for her annual charity auction. This year it was puppies and kitties. Last year it was children. Every year a new cause, a cause that came first. A cause more important than her daughter.

The one year Emily thought her mother had actually cared was the year she raised money for runaway children. Spent time with her, but it was all for show. She had been the poster child. The tears and forgiveness were all an act. It was for the cameras and society page, and to help Judge Victor Montgomery win reelection.

Crystal Montgomery didn't care about her daughter, and Emily had almost given up caring about that sad fact. But she couldn't. She sometimes wondered if she'd ever really *had* a mom. Maybe the memories of them walking on the beach, playing with Barbies, making cookies was all a dream.

Those good times seemed so far in the past that Emily wasn't sure if she'd made up some of the details to get herself through the nights when her mother wasn't home. To get through the days when Victor was.

Thirteen months and she would legally be able to walk out the door and live on her own. Her trust fund would be hers. She would no longer be dependent on her mother and Victor.

Thirteen months. She prayed she survived that long. It wasn't that she was worried about Victor killing her. She feared her own hand.

She closed the large, overhead garage door with the remote and walked to the side door that led to a covered walk. Their house was huge, far bigger than the three of them needed, but Crystal and Victor *entertained,* and that meant they needed a big house with huge rooms to fill with people as phony as they.

It struck her as sad that when her dad had been alive the house hadn't seemed as big and scary, even though she'd been smaller. And there'd only been the three of them then, too. But with her dad, everything was a game. They raced Matchbox cars down the long marble halls, played hide-and-seek in the maze of rooms, slid down the banister of the great center staircase.

The fun died with her dad.

Emily entered the house through the secondary entrance, the one Victor ordered the hired help to use. None of the outside doors used a key. That would be *common.* Emily typed in the security code on the keypad next to the door and the lock sprung. The atmosphere was cool, in both temperature and aesthetics. Her mother had the downstairs professionally redecorated every two years. Last year, she wanted the feeling of the ocean, everything in blues and greens. The sound system piped in canned ocean waves whenever her mother was home.

No music, no mother.

She waited for the intercom's grating *buzz,* every cell in her body on alert. Victor was home, his Jaguar was in the garage. Of course he was home, it was Wednesday. Her mother was gone, the housekeeping staff had the night off, and Emily *had* to be home. Every day by six p.m. by order of the court.

Damn curfew. Damn the police. Damn the whole fucking system.

And damn *her* for being so stupid. Vandalizing the courthouse. What had she been thinking? Of course, she hadn't been. Just like when she'd run away. All emotions, no plan. Emily couldn't see anything beyond her anger. And she was paying for it now. Maybe she deserved it.

The intercom didn't beep, her stepdad didn't summon her to his office. She slipped off her sandals to tread soundlessly across the marble floors. Slowly, she walked down the long, wide hall to the center foyer, waiting for the telltale *click* of the intercom and Judge Montgomery's deep and disgusting voice.

Emily, please come to my office.

Nothing. Silence.

Maybe he was on the phone. Maybe he hadn't been watching the security system and was unaware she'd come home. Maybe he'd hung himself. She could only hope.

She started up the grand staircase, her heart racing. As Emily ascended, she began to run. Free. She was free. She'd lock herself in her room, because he didn't dare come after her in there. It was always his office, his desk. His domain.

She closed and locked the door behind her, grinning. She leaped onto her bed and jumped up and down like a little kid. Then she went into her bathroom and started the water in her bathtub. Hot, with bubbles.

She wasn't supposed to drink. In addition

to being underage, it was a term of her plea bargain last year since she'd been intoxicated when she'd vandalized the courthouse. But she had a flask of dark rum hidden in her dresser, which she refilled periodically from Victor's bar.

She had to have something to wash the foul taste of him out of her mouth and mind.

Now she drank in celebration. Locked in her room. Alone. At peace.

Downstairs, Victor Montgomery sat in his desk chair, dead, his bloody body horribly mutilated.

TWO

A murder, as well as a possible attempted suicide.

Detective Will Hooper was working the case alone. His partner, Carina Kincaid, was on a well-deserved vacation with her fiancé, but he missed having her here to bounce around ideas and theories. They made a good team.

But murder doesn't take a vacation.

He arrived at the crime scene at the same time as the crime lab director, Dr. Jim Gage. The high-profile crime brought out the big guns in the department.

The murder vic was a judge, Victor Montgomery, which meant that right away they had politics and brass in the middle of the case. As soon as the press got wind of it, they'd be slithering all over the crime scene. But for now it was only the responding officers, Gage and his two techs, and Will.

A female teen, Emily Montgomery, had

been taken to the hospital, an apparent attempted suicide. Will didn't want to make any assumptions, though she'd obviously been drinking — a lot — and the responding officers found a half-empty bottle of Xanax. Her stomach would be pumped and the doctor would formally determine whether she had, in fact, tried to kill herself.

The fact that Judge Montgomery had just sentenced Herman Santos — the closest thing San Diego had to a Mafia don — to death by lethal injection for his role in a three-year-old execution-style murder of two cops also couldn't be overlooked.

"Why didn't we know about the girl when the nine-one-one call came in?" Gage asked Will as they met outside on the circular driveway at the base of the wide front stairs that led to large double doors, now open and guarded by two uniformed officers. Though late, the evening was warm enough to leave his jacket in the car.

"The wife found her husband's body when she returned from a meeting. She ran to the neighbors to call and never said anything about her daughter. Diaz found the girl upstairs when he did a walkthrough." Will motioned for Diaz to approach. "Good to have you on the job."

Officer Diaz gave a half smile. "Two days

back and I feel human again." Last month he'd been shot in the line of duty in a gang initiation stunt, but made it through and recently received medical clearance for duty.

"What happened with the girl?" Gage asked, glancing at an upstairs window.

Diaz checked his notes, cleared his throat. "We arrived on scene at ten-fourteen, nine minutes after the nine-one-one call came in. We checked the perimeter, attempted entry, but the door was secure. Mrs. Crystal Montgomery then approached from her neighbor's house" — he gestured north — "and let us in with her security code. She remained in the living room while we inspected the ground floor and verified the deceased." He looked up, a little pale. "It wasn't pretty."

Gage motioned for him to continue. Will and Gage certainly weren't expecting a pretty crime scene.

Diaz said, "We asked if anyone else was home and she then told us her sixteen-year-old daughter, Emily, was supposed to be home."

Will interrupted. "What was Mrs. Montgomery's demeanor when she informed you of her daughter's presence?"

"It was an afterthought."

Her daughter, an afterthought. "Go on."

"We called in the homicide and searched the house. Knocked on her bedroom door, which was locked, and when there was no answer we broke in. She was lying next to her bed in a robe, unconscious. We ascertained that she was alive, called for an ambulance, monitored her vitals. Weak. The room smelled of alcohol and we found an empty pint flask in the bathroom next to the bathtub. The tub was wet, there were damp towels, and a bottle of some prescription medication on the floor."

"What did you touch?"

"Other than Emily Montgomery — we pulled a blanket from her bed to keep her warm — we didn't touch anything else. There was blood in the girl's room, but no visible wounds on her."

Gage said, "I'll send one of my people over to the hospital to collect evidence."

"Where's Mrs. Montgomery now?" Will asked.

"In the living room."

"Thanks, Diaz."

After Will and Gage entered the house, Gage instructed a tech to inspect every entrance and window. Another tech followed Will and Gage with a camera to photograph the crime scene.

Judge Montgomery had a large, high-ceilinged home office, dark and distinguished. Just the sort of understated elegance you'd expect from a respected jurist. A pen set, small clock, and a picture of his wife decorated a large desk otherwise devoid of clutter.

The thick white carpet was spattered with blood. Arterial spray covered Judge Montgomery's chest, but there was no visible evidence of a wound. His eyes were open, glassy, unfocused. Dried blood coated his swollen mouth and face, dotted his full head of graying blond hair, and peppered the bookshelves behind him.

Gage walked behind the desk and stopped short, staring down. Will looked over his shoulder and the blood drained from his face.

Montgomery's pants and boxers were pushed down to his ankles. His legs were spread, his groin a bloody mess. His penis had been removed in a brutal manner, resulting in severe muscle and tissue damage.

Gage said, "I'll send one of my people over to the hospital to collect evidence."

"Holy shit." Will instinctively put a hand over his crotch.

"Don't worry, dude, your package is still there," Gage said with a half smile. "It's only the judge who's missing his." Gage looked closer, motioning for the tech to take pictures from specific angles. "Look here. See this striation?"

Will swallowed uneasily and focused on the area Gage indicated.

"No." All Will saw was pulp.

"It looks like something sharp," said Gage. "Double edged, like heavy-duty scissors."

"Can you cut off a dick with scissors?" Will asked, incredulous.

"If they're sharp enough. But it looks like it took several cuts to remove it."

That was more information than Will wanted to know, especially staring at the result of the killer's handiwork.

Will looked around for the missing organ. "Did the killer take it with him?"

"Look in his mouth."

Montgomery's penis was shoved partly down his throat. His mouth wasn't swollen, it was filled.

"See the arterial spray?" Gage pointed out the long lines of blood that had splattered across the desk, floor, and victim. "To get the spatter this far indicates that blood was pumping. He was alive during the amputation. This is the kind of spray we'd see from a partial decapitation or a stabbing where a major artery was pierced."

27

"But he didn't have his throat slit or his heart stabbed."

"Right. I'd guess Judge Montgomery was in the act of sex or fellatio when someone snipped him. We'll know for sure during the autopsy — a flaccid penis would be cut like rubber — multiple incisions until the scissors tore through the muscle. An erect penis would show different marks."

Will could handle the most brutal of crime scenes with professionalism, but this one was particularly gruesome and unusual. He was glad his partner wasn't here to see it. Not because she couldn't handle the gore, but because she would be full of penis jokes for months.

"No guy is going to sit still while someone slices off his dick," Will said. The judge was physically fit, tall. There was no visible means of restraint.

Gage walked carefully around the back of the chair and looked at the bookshelves. "Blair," he ordered his assistant, who was still taking pictures, "grab my kit from the hall and get the black light and slow film out of the van. I'm going to Luminol this place. I think I know what happened."

"And?" Will prompted. "What do you think happened?"

"Come here."

Gage stood on the other side of the vic's chair. "Do you see what's different about the blood spatter on this side and the blood spatter on your side?"

"There's no blood on this side. Like someone was standing here."

"Exactly. And look at Montgomery's shirt."

It was open at the collar, which was virtually bloodless. "I see." Will stood behind the chair. "Someone was restraining the judge by wrapping his arms around the neck while another someone did the dirty deed."

"That's why we have this pattern. But why would he get aroused? If your life is on the line, sex is the furthest thing from it." Gage thought. "Maybe they restrained him, then pulled down his pants."

"Or maybe he was in the act of oral sex when the killer came in." Will frowned. "Then where's the woman? The killer wouldn't just let a potential witness go. She's either dead or an accomplice."

Gage didn't say anything but glanced at the ceiling. "Let's see how much blood is upstairs."

"The daughter? That's sick."

"*Step*daughter."

"It's still sick."

"Time of death?"

Gage inspected the body. "Less than seven hours, more than four."

"Three-thirty to six-thirty. That's a big window."

"The coroner is on his way. He'll narrow it down. We're still in the twelve-hour window." The sooner a body was discovered, the better the time-of-death estimate.

"Santos was sentenced last week," Will said. Just saying this cop-killer's name made him tense.

"I was thinking about that. Santos has enough people on his payroll to pull off something like this."

"But why the theatrics? Wouldn't a bullet in the back of the skull be more his style?"

"That's beyond my expertise. I'll collect the evidence, you figure out who did it. But," Gage continued, glancing at Will, "Santos might be sending a message of some sort."

"I'll talk to some beat cops and see if there's something personal in the delivery." Will frowned. "But I still don't see him going to this trouble."

When Gage's assistant came back, he instructed her to finish the photographs and start mapping out the crime scene. They had purchased a state-of-the-art forensics program last year when they had a onetime budget increase. It was amazing that the lab pinched pennies when ordering common supplies and couldn't hand out more than nominal pay raises, but could purchase a multimillion-dollar computer system simply on the whim of state politicians.

"I'll be back to work with the black light after we finish upstairs."

Gage and Will left, both carefully looking for potential evidence on the floors. "Where are the drops of blood?" Gage asked. "Being that close, the killer would have been slick with it."

"Maybe they had an extra layer of clothing and removed it."

"That would take planning."

"Premeditated murder makes for a much longer sentence," Will said.

At the base of the stairs, on the bleached wood railing, a bloody handprint stood out.

Will and Gage proceeded upstairs to Emily Montgomery's bedroom. They walked slowly, carefully observing. The marble stairs were carpeted with sea blue Berber, keeping with the ocean theme of the mansion. Where the carpet met the marble were several drops of dried blood. Two more drops were closer to the top. Another faint, dark red handprint was pressed into the carpet, left of center, this one smeared.

31

"There doesn't seem to be a lot of blood," Will said, "which holds with the idea that maybe the weapon and clothing were put in a bag or disposed of."

On the radio, Gage asked his second assistant to methodically go through every room looking for blood, no matter how small, and to start processing the garbage.

Gage said, "Logically, there was more than one person involved. The accomplice could have left with the weapon and clothing."

Will didn't know why it made him feel better to think that Emily Montgomery hadn't been the one to do her stepfather's amputation, though being an accessory was almost as bad.

"But they didn't make any effort to clean up the stairs."

"Panic? Fear? Diaz said the daughter's room smelled of alcohol."

Emily Montgomery's room was the first door on the right, as evidenced by the slight splintering of the doorjamb when Diaz had broken in earlier.

The room was in disarray, partly from the paramedics who had worked to stabilize Emily before transporting her to the hospital.

Nothing stood out to the cops. Again, the carpets were white, but the decorations were more in line with the tastes of a teenaged girl: dark purples, black, and red rather than the subdued, cool elegance of the main house.

But in the bathroom, one towel had blood smeared on it, and the sink faucet had another smear.

"I'm going to have to call in a larger team, or processing this house is going to take all night," Gage said, making the call.

Will noted the empty flask and the pill bottle. "What type of pills?"

Gage bent down and picked up the bottle with gloved hands. "Xanax. Prescribed to Emily Montgomery and refilled two weeks ago. Empty." He stood, pointed to pills all over the floor. "There are at least twenty on the floor. She could have had half a bottle, or almost full. The prescription reads *'Use as needed. No more than two in a twelve-hour period.'* " He opened the medicine cabinet.

"This kid's pharmacy is bigger than mine," Will commented.

Eight or nine prescriptions, all prescribed by Dr. Garrett Bowen, lined the top shelf. Two bottles were on their sides, and another three were unopened on the floor. "Another Xanax, but an older prescription. Anti-depressants. Tylenol."

"Tylenol in a prescription bottle?"

"Prescription strength. And here's Imitrex, primarily for migraines."

"Sixteen and has more legal drugs in her cabinet than I've taken in my entire life," Will muttered.

Gage frowned. "Some of these shouldn't be taken together. Someone needs to talk to this Bowen doc and see what's up."

Will made a note. "I'll talk to the mom first."

"Until we're done processing the evidence, there's nothing for you to do here. I'll let you know what we find."

"I'll be downstairs with Mrs. Montgomery." Will paused. "What's your best guess?"

"At this stage, I can't possibly guess."

Will stared at him. "I need something to go with."

Gage shook his head. "Theory, but only theory: at least two perpetrators, but I wouldn't be surprised if there were three. No sign of forced entry. Someone let them in. One or more known to the vic or to the stepdaughter."

"And this blood?"

"We have a lot of work to do tonight, both here and downstairs, but I'd say Emily Montgomery was in Judge Montgomery's office during or after he died. It's looking a lot like murder-suicide, only she failed in the latter."

"Or maybe Santos's men threatened her," Will offered as an alternative.

"Then why leave their witness alive?"

THREE

Julia Chandler was playing with fire. She didn't care, she was used to it. But this time it wasn't her job. Emily was in trouble and Julia would do anything to protect her niece.

She didn't have to show her identification to be let into the crime scene. While it was rare to have a deputy district attorney show up at the beginning of a murder investigation, it wasn't unheard of. Considering her take-no-prisoners reputation, no one wanted to cross her, cop or criminal.

Perhaps because of her high-profile background as a Chandler, where putting names to faces was required learning back in preschool, or because of her naturally sharp memory, or simply because she worked closely with law enforcement, Julia made it a point to recognize on sight those in uniform. Officer Diaz was manning the door, and her colleague was handling the prosecution of the gang member who shot him last month. The defense council was pushing for a plea, which the district attorney himself had refused. Andrew Stanton was not moved by the circumstances of the kid's tragic upbringing. Neither was Julia, not when innocent bystanders were hurt.

"How're you doing, Officer Diaz?" she asked. "Looks like you lost a few pounds."

"Hospital food. I just started exercising full-time last week. I'll bulk up."

"Glad you're back in form."

She brushed by him, hoping the small talk had distracted him from asking her purpose.

"Um, Ms. Chandler?"

She stopped as she was about to follow Dr. Gage's assistant down the hall to the presumed crime scene.

"I'll need to tell Detective Hooper you're here before you can go in." He fidgeted. "You understand."

She plastered a fake smile on her face. "Of course."

"No need." Will Hooper sauntered down the stairs, appearing laid-back and casual, but Julia knew better. The man was a shark, and she loved it when he took the witness stand. It was precisely because of his easygoing, flirtatious manner that he could turn a jury. She never had to spend much time prepping him for trial, which made her job a lot easier. And it was because of his testimony the other month in appellate court that she was able to keep a convicted murderer on death row. He held firm under fire.

"Hi, Will. Where's your partner?"

"Vacation." He pinned her with a curious blue-eyed stare and nodded toward the formal dining room off the main entrance. Her goose was cooked.

She closed the pocket doors behind her for privacy and turned to face the detective. "I know what you're thinking."

"You do?" He quirked his head.

"She's my niece. I heard through the grapevine that Judge Montgomery was killed, what would you do in my shoes? Think I'm going to sit on my ass and wait to find out if my niece is dead or alive? Suicide? I don't believe it."

"Shit, Chandler, don't mess with my case. Does Stanton know you're here?"

She didn't have to answer.

"Just because you're Stanton's shining star doesn't mean you can do whatever you want."

She rubbed her eyes, but when she pictured Emily she opened them. "I'm not going to jeopardize your case, Will. You know that. If anyone is a stickler for the rules, it's me."

He stared at her, and she stared right back. *Don't let him see you're scared. Don't let him see you have no power.*

"What do you want to know?"

"Everything. But right now, how's Emily?"

"Why don't you ask Crystal Montgomery? She's in the living room."

Julia bit her upper lip. "Crystal and I don't always see eye-to-eye." *On anything.*

"How close are you to your niece?"

"Not as close as I'd like."

"That's an evasive answer, Counselor." He stared her down.

Julia took a deep breath. Will Hooper was one of the good guys, she reminded herself. "When my brother Matt died, Crystal refused to let me see Emily. I sued for visitation and won. I have her every Sunday." And after school, whenever Julia could get free, but Will didn't have to know that. If Crystal knew Julia had broken the court agreement, she'd drag her back before a judge and try to take away her Sundays, just out of spite.

It had already cost her half her family's wealth — Matt's inheritance — to see Emily. Julia had dropped the probate lawsuit when Crystal consented to a one-day-a-week visitation. At least Emily had a secure trust fund that Crystal couldn't touch.

"Emily has a history of delinquency," Will said, the friendly good guy gone and the hard-nosed cop in his place. "Runaway, vandalism —"

"You don't have to quote her rap sheet to me, Detective," she snapped, angry with herself for losing her temper. "I know Emily has problems. She's been working hard to turn her life around. You don't know her mother —"

"No, I don't. But I'm about to go interview her."

"I have a question for you, Will," she said, trying but failing to keep the prosecutor out of her voice. "Why was there a lag time between the nine-one-one call and the call for an ambulance?"

Hooper's eyes narrowed. "I was just about to ask Crystal Montgomery."

"Why?"

"She didn't tell anyone her daughter was in the house."

Julia's chest tightened and for a moment she almost couldn't breathe. She whirled around, pushed the pocket doors into the wall, and strode across the hall to the living room. Will was behind her, but he didn't stop her. The back of her mind ran scenarios: Why was he baiting her? Was this a game to see what kind of reaction Crystal had? Was Emily in deeper trouble than she knew? Julia was almost blind with anger when she opened the living-room doors.

Poised and classy, Crystal Montgomery emanated old money, though it was *Chandler* old money that had bought her style. A forty-something former fashion model in a chic business suit, a petite version of Professional Barbie, Crystal Montgomery was a viper in disguise.

Crystal's mouth opened and closed, her eyes narrowed, and she glared at Julia. "What are you doing here?" she snarled.

"You found Victor dead and you didn't even check on Emily? What's wrong with you?"

"Don't talk to me."

"Answer my question!"

"I'm not on trial. I don't have to answer your questions, Julia."

Fists tightening, Julia whirled around to collect her temper. *Think about Emily.* Protecting her niece was the most important thing. She glanced at Detective Hooper, still standing by the door, a blank expression on his face.

Crystal saw Will at the same time. Her

41

voice turned softer, worried, a hint of a tremble. "Detective. She . . . she killed Victor, didn't she?"

"What?" Julia slowly turned to face her sister-in-law. "How can you even *think* such a thing?"

"The crime lab is on the premises and they have yet to make their report," Will said formally, closing the wide living-room double doors behind him. "I have a few questions, if you don't mind."

"I refuse to allow Julia to be involved with this investigation," Crystal said. "Isn't there some conflict of interest? She's related."

"The inner workings of the District Attorney's Office are far beyond my influence," Will said noncommittally, but Julia registered the concern in his eyes.

"I'll call Andrew Stanton myself."

Will hardened, and Julia couldn't help but feel a hint of glee that Crystal had shown her colors early on. No cop appreciated a threat to call any superior.

To avoid putting Will in a difficult position, primarily because she wanted him on her side, Julia said, "I'm leaving. But this isn't over, Crystal. Don't screw with Emily."

"You're blind, Julia. You always have been."

Julia firmly shut the door behind her and gathered her wits. How could she be so certain of Emily's innocence?

Beautiful, smart, destined for something wonderful, Emily wouldn't have killed anyone. She was just *sixteen,* dammit, and even with all her problems an honor student.

But what *were* Emily's problems? Running away three years ago had been a shock. Worse, Julia hadn't even known Emily had run. Crystal didn't tell her. It wasn't until she came by the following Sunday morning to pick her up that Crystal said her daughter hadn't come home from school on Tuesday. That had been five days previous. Emily could have been kidnapped, raped, or murdered. The prosecutor in Julia had envisioned every scenario with increasing dread.

Crystal had notified the police and filed a missing persons report forty-eight hours after Emily didn't return home from school, but there was no evidence of foul play, no ransom request, nothing.

That was when Julia took matters into her own hands and hired a private investigator.

She straightened and everything became clear. *Connor Kincaid.* She couldn't be involved in the investigation — she knew the DA would have a fit considering how politically charged this case promised to be — but Connor was a pit bull when he cared about something. And he cared about Emily. He'd tracked her down after three torturous months and brought her home.

He'd made it clear that finding Emily three years ago when she'd run away was the last time he planned on talking to Julia, but Connor wouldn't turn his back on Emily when she needed him.

And she needed him, now more than ever. There was no way Julia could trust Crystal with Emily's welfare. The police, though more than competent, had a multitude of cases on their plate. And the press . . . Julia didn't even want to think what was going to be in the newspapers and on television over the coming days. She'd managed to keep a low profile, especially after Matt died, but the vultures always circled around the money and tragedy that surrounded the Chandler name.

She pulled out her cell phone and looked up Connor's number in her electronic address book. She'd had to swallow her pride to call him three years ago to find Emily, but she still had his number. Just in case.

His voice mail picked up. "Kincaid here. Leave a message." *Beep.*

Why was her heart pounding? She cleared her throat. "Connor, it's Julia Chandler. I have a job for you. It's about Emily." She left her number and hung up. She hated using Em's name, but he'd never call back if he thought it would help *her.*

"Counselor?" Jim Gage came down the stairs and cocked his head. "What are you doing here?"

"I came to check on my niece, Emily."

Gage didn't look surprised. "She's at the hospital. Where's Hooper?"

"Talking to the victim's wife."

"Would that be your sister-in-law?"

"Unfortunately."

"You shouldn't be here."

"I haven't touched anything. Tell me what happened." When Gage didn't respond, she added, "I'm going to hear about it when I get to the office."

Detective Hooper stepped out of the living room, closed the doors behind him, and glanced from Julia to Gage. "Well, that didn't go over too well. Mrs. Montgomery's calling her lawyer."

"Why?" Julia asked. "Is she a suspect?"

"She has an alibi." He paused, uncertain.

"Will, I just told Gage that I'll hear all the details anyway. You know that. Just spill it."

"I can't imagine a mother not worried

45

about her teenaged daughter after she discovers her husband murdered," he said simply. "It just doesn't ring true."

"You don't know Crystal Montgomery. She's a sociopath," Julia said.

"What?"

"She's narcissistic and a pathological liar. My brother was married to her for ten years and I had to fight for visitation of my only niece after he died. She would never think of Emily first, second, or last. It's all Crystal, all the time. The phrase, 'it's all about me' could have been coined just for her."

Julia cleared her throat. "Look, I need to know what happened to Victor. Emily couldn't possibly have killed him. I know my niece."

Gage put up his hands. "Stop. This is a preliminary investigation and a crime scene, not a deposition."

"Are you done upstairs?" Will asked.

"Almost." He looked over Julia's shoulder at Will.

"I get it," she said, irritated. "You want me to leave. I will, right after you tell me what happened to Victor."

It was Will who spoke. "He was killed in his den. His, um, penis was removed."

She swallowed hard, unable to speak.

"Actually," Gage said, "he choked to

46

death. On his penis."

Julia blanched. "And you think a young girl is capable of *that?*"

"She couldn't have done it alone," Gage said. "At least two other people helped."

"So you think that a sixteen-year-old girl could convince two others to choke to death a fifty-year-old judge with his own dick? What did the killer use? A knife?" Julia's mind went through all the scenarios. "He'd have to have been drugged or restrained. Did you find rope, tape, or —"

"Ms. Chandler, we're in the middle of the investigation and the district attorney will be getting our report shortly." Gage suddenly looked tired and irritated.

"Did you know that Judge Montgomery just sentenced Herman Santos to death row?" Julia said. "He has enough people to pull off something like this, and —"

She mentally hit herself.

"Of course you know that." Julia released a breath she hadn't realized she was holding. "Okay. I understand. But don't you think it's odd that the wife of the victim didn't inform dispatch that there was possibly a second victim in the house? What would a normal person do if you walked in and found your spouse murdered?"

Will said, "I'd hunt through the house for

the culprit."

"Don't think like a cop."

Gage nodded. "If I were in her shoes, I might leave the house out of fear. Call nine-one-one."

"And tell them your daughter might be in the house."

"Maybe she was too distraught. In shock. It wasn't a pretty scene."

"Murder never is, Dr. Gage."

Will interjected, "Even if she was in shock, when the responding officers arrived, at the very least, she should have told them there was someone else inside. They searched the house per protocol, looking first for a culprit."

"Exactly." Julia nodded.

"Maybe the mother didn't think she was home?" Gage offered.

"Emily is on probation," Julia said. "She has to be at home from six p.m. through six a.m. every day unless she is with a parent or guardian."

"What did she do to land probation?"

Julia took a deep breath. "She vandalized the courthouse last year."

Recognition sparked in Gage's eyes. "I remember. Graffiti."

"She spray-painted 'hypocrites' all over the building," Will said. "Some sort of political statement?" He looked at Julia for answers she didn't have.

"Emily never talked about it. That's why she was sent to a psychiatrist. That was one of the court orders."

Will made note of that. "Dr. Garrett Bowen."

"Right."

"He prescribed a lot of medication for a teenager."

Julia tensed. Now she needed to get out. She knew too much about the medication, too much about what Emily was and was not doing with it.

She would not jeopardize her niece, but she couldn't lie to law enforcement. They were on the same side. She had to remember that.

"Emily did not kill Victor Montgomery," Julia said. "That much I know."

"But maybe she knows who did," Will said pointedly.

Julia ached for her niece. "I'm going to the hospital."

"Don't interview her," Will warned.

"I'm not," she snapped. "She needs someone who loves her right now, and I think I'm the only person in the world who does."

Will walked Julia to her car. "Julia."

She turned to look at him, swallowing the

fear and worry that rose in her throat. "What?"

"I have the utmost respect for you. You're one of the best we have in the DA's office. But I have to tell you something as a friend." He stared at her, his expression stern. "The only thing you can do for Emily right now is to get her an attorney. And you have the money to hire the best."

She put a hand on her stomach, feeling sucker-punched. "Is the evidence that damning?"

Will sighed. "It doesn't look good."

Julia slid into her car, then made the second call she didn't want to make. This time, the person called picked up the phone.

"Iris Jones."

"Iris, it's Julia Chandler."

Iris laughed, low and full of irony. At least, that's how it sounded to Julia. "I heard about Montgomery."

"News travels fast."

"Helps when you're listening. I knew you'd call me."

Julia almost hung up. She didn't like Iris Jones, attorney-at-law, or Iris Jones, the person. Oil versus water. Justice versus anarchy.

But Iris was as good at her job as Julia was at hers, and she had a grudging respect for the woman.

"Emily was taken to Scripps Memorial. Can you meet me tonight?"

"Give me an hour."

Will watched Julia drive off, wondering who she'd been talking to on the phone. He motioned to Diaz. "Hey, follow the counselor. I think she's going to the hospital to visit her niece. Relieve the guard we have on Ms. Montgomery's room and let me know what they say, okay?"

"Roger that." Diaz left.

Gage joined him on the drive. "Chandler is going to be pissed if she finds out," Gage said.

"She'd be doing the same thing if she were thinking straight," Will countered. "It's pretty obvious what's going on. Julia Chandler and Crystal Montgomery hate each other. Crystal was married to Julia's brother. He dies, and Crystal wants the Chandler money but not the Chandler family. I remember when Emily ran away."

"I don't," Gage said.

"Connor Kincaid was the PI who found her." As Carina Kincaid's partner, Will was an honorary member of the Kincaid family. He knew more than most about Connor's life since he'd been pushed off the police force.

51

"I've called the e-crimes unit to dismantle and check the computers and security system," Gage said. "They'll be here in an hour."

"By the book, that's all we can do right now."

One of the crime technicians entered the front door.

"Dr. Gage?"

"What?"

"We found shears with possible blood evidence."

"Shears?"

The assistant held up pruning shears sealed in a clear, thick plastic evidence bag. The curved blades made up half the ten-inch length. Except for the dried blood, they looked new and unused.

"Where'd you find them?"

"In the gardening shed behind the house. We have some foot impressions and other possible evidence. We're collecting molds right now."

"Keep me informed."

Will said, "If the killer put the shears back in the shed, it couldn't have been the stepdaughter, not in her condition."

"I never believed she acted alone."

FOUR

Justice? Revenge? Payback? Any way the police looked at it, his plan was working even better than he'd hoped. He smiled, confident he was in complete control of the operation.

He poured himself a Scotch straight up, a twenty-one-year-old Chivas, took it out on the balcony, taking in the cool midnight ocean breeze. The view of the brightly lit coastline, the ocean, black and endless, moved him. He observed the exquisite beauty of the moment, held it with his trained eye, imprinted the exact time and emotion in his soul.

This is how God must feel.

Victor Montgomery was dead. Not only dead, but killed in a manner that suited his lifestyle. He loved the irony of Montgomery's murder, just like he'd enjoyed the irony of how he picked his killing team, how he planned the executions, how everyone involved recognized and worshipped his brilliance.

His team leader had, of course, immediately reported the successful kill earlier that evening, so he didn't have to wait for newspaper and television reports to announce Montgomery's death. But it was only now, late at night, that he had time to sit alone in his beautiful home, with his favorite drink, and savor his triumph.

After the final kill, the circle would be complete. The police would scramble about with their theories, but they wouldn't be able to prove anything. The media would learn the secrets of the murdered and expose their reputations to humiliation and embarrassment. Through it all, he'd sit in his house and enjoy the product of his handiwork, all without getting a drop of blood on his own hands.

He'd been thinking a lot lately about the beginning. The real beginning. Not when they'd executed the first kill. Not when he recruited his team, not even when he came up with the plan in the name of "justice."

The real beginning was the day of his birth. Every day from then forward, his mother had told him he was destined for greatness. But again and again his decisions had been stolen from him. Life conspired to dominate him, control him.

Not anymore. He'd engaged in the battle and was winning.

He stared at his hands, the fingers with the Midas touch. His physique — strong, muscular, not an ounce of extra fat. He didn't need a mirror to know he was handsome. He didn't need a woman to tell him so.

Each step of his elaborate plan had been taken with extreme care. The test. The accident. The execution. Now for one more who would restore balance to the world. The one who really mattered.

He sighed, ran a hand over his face, and turned from his view. Poured himself another Chivas and ran through the scenarios. While the plan seemed under control, he had a wild card to worry about. She was always pushing, pushing, pushing toward the final kill. She didn't understand the setup, but few people would be capable of that. He'd explained it over and over and still she only saw the end.

Impatience could cost him his freedom.

Inside, he put his glass down. He wasn't worried about the kids — they toed the line. Quite easily, in fact. Cami was giving the boys what they needed, and Faye . . .

He sighed. *Faye.* She was really the only

one who understood him, who enjoyed his unrivaled brilliance and his physical beauty. She knew, in her heart, exactly who he was. She would do anything he wanted, just because he asked her. She never asked why, she never questioned him. She loved him unconditionally.

He'd never before had that type of love, and he found himself wanting it more and more, craving his time with Faye to bask in her unbridled need for him. He couldn't see her tonight, but he would soon.

It was the *other* one. The wild card. The one who almost blew everything eighteen months ago.

He was about to leave to visit her, make sure she stuck to the script, when his doorbell chimed.

Tense, he turned on the front-door security camera to see who was on his front porch.

It was her.

He opened the door. "What —"

"You fucked up!" she yelled.

He pulled her into the foyer and shut the door. "Don't —"

"Turn on the news. *Now.*"

When he did, he was as surprised as she was. But not upset. "The plan was designed for every contingency. Don't worry."

"How can I not be worried? If they arrest Emily Montgomery, it's only a matter of time —"

"They have no evidence."

"Since when does evidence matter to the police? They have evidence, they don't do anything. They don't have evidence, they'll make it up."

"You're exaggerating. Just calm down and —"

"Don't tell me to calm down!" She started pacing. She'd been pretty at one time, beautiful — he could still see it in her skin and lush hair — but the anger and grief had eaten away the light in her eyes. He was trained to observe, but still he was surprised no one else saw what he did in her face.

He poured her a Chivas and watched as she drained it in one long gulp. "I promise, there have been no mistakes. Everything is under control."

"How can you say that?"

"Don't you trust me?"

"Do you trust me?" she countered.

He laughed. "No, darling, you're the last person I trust. But you'll listen to me and do what I tell you because only then will we get what we've wanted for so long. Don't let the fear in. Sit tight and follow the course I laid out."

"I wish I'd done it my way at the beginning." But she had calmed down, poured herself another drink, and sat on his couch, staring at the amber liquid as if it were rare.

He sat next to her. "If we'd done it your way, you'd be dead or in jail by now."

"Being dead doesn't sound all that bad," she whispered. She slugged back the Scotch. "Better than living in Hell."

Death made her feel alive.

Holding something so delicate in her hand, something men treasured — their existence — and having the power to let him keep it, or take it.

Her choice. Her decision.

Some people didn't have choices. Some people couldn't make their own decisions.

Cami closed her eyes, remembering exactly how it had played out. The plan had been executed perfectly. Victor Montgomery was a creep, through and through, and she knew exactly how to play him. How she had played so many other men in her life. If only she could tell her friends everything, they would relish her genius.

But some things were safer kept secret. Especially now when the end was so near.

The bed shifted next to her and Skip sat up.

"Where are you going?" she asked, panic building.

"It's late. I need to go home."

"No. No, not now."

She reached for him, pulled him back down. He resisted for a brief minute and her panic turned to anger. That Skip would even think of walking away. *From her.* No man walked away. They all wanted her. Hadn't she proved that today? That she could seduce a man to his own death?

"Make love to me."

"I don't know if I can."

"Yes. You can."

Cami reached out, touched him, caressed him. Kissed him. Brought him down on top of her. She knew exactly what he liked, exactly what excited him. She knew everything about Skip, all the way down to his darkest needs. Those needs were what she played on now, knowing he would bend to her will.

He groaned and spread her legs. She was already wet, waiting to be fucked.

"Do it hard. Make it hurt."

"No —"

"Yes."

He liked to hurt her, and he hated himself for it. Cami played on that. Gave the pain up to him willingly. Made him crave more.

He bit her until she cried out, making him pump into her harder. Squeezed her breasts until she gasped; bruises would show later. He was getting closer, closer . . .

She wasn't. She closed her eyes and pictured putting her mouth on Victor Montgomery's cock, making her victim hard, making him want her.

He had quivered between her lips. He'd held her head down tight and she couldn't breathe. She let go of him.

"Don't stop."

"I want you to fuck me."

He had groaned, his eyes alight with sick desire. Desire she had put there.

The power flowed through her then. Knowing that now he was as alive as any man could be, and in two minutes he'd be dead.

Her lover dug his nails into her ass and pushed himself into her as he came.

When she remembered the moment of the judge's death, her breath quickened, her desire peaked, and she joined her occasional lover for the ride over the top.

The phone rang thirty minutes later. Skip continued snoring in her bed.

She glanced at caller ID. It was him.

"Hello," she said quietly.

"You're not alone."

"He's asleep."

"We have a change in plans."

"You said no —"

"This isn't up for discussion."

"But —"

He sighed and she tensed. "Who's kept your secret for nearly two years?" he said, his voice low, and she wondered if he was alone. "Good, you understand. She'd kill you and I wouldn't be able to stop her. I wouldn't want to, Cami, because that means you're being foolish. So listen to me. Meet me at my place, ten a.m., and I'll give you the details."

"All right."

He laughed. "Don't sound so concerned. You're great at improvisation. In fact, you're a damn good actress. If anyone can pull this off, it's you." He hung up.

She put the phone down. She wouldn't be able to sleep tonight. She wouldn't be able to get him out of her mind.

He was the only man she really wanted, but he refused to have sex with her. *Yet,* he'd said.

"Wait until we're done with the final execution. Then I can give you what you want."

Cami looked at Skip. He was a distant second, but he'd have to do.

She woke him. "Make it hurt, Skip."

FIVE

Emily was sleeping a deep, physically exhausted sleep.

Because Julia flashed her badge, recited her credentials, and acted like she had a right to ask questions, Emily's doctor spoke to her.

"Borderline alcohol poisoning — her blood was at .28 — and we pumped her stomach," Dr. Browne said. "Fifteen hundred milligrams of Xanax was recovered, which is approximately three pills. More may have been absorbed into her bloodstream depending on when she took them, but if she'd taken more than six or seven with that amount of alcohol she'd likely be in a coma. We've sent a blood sample to the lab and the report will come back tomorrow."

"Has she regained consciousness?"

"More or less. When her stomach was pumped she came to for a few minutes.

She's sleeping, but it's largely a drug-induced sleep from the pills her body absorbed."

"Did she say anything?"

"No."

"I'd like to sit with her."

"I can't allow any police interviews tonight. She's being monitored twenty-four/seven and the police have put a guard at her door."

"I just want to sit with her." Julia added softly, "She's my niece."

Dr. Browne nodded, her warm eyes suddenly sympathetic. "I don't think she'll wake up, but if she does I'll need to examine her in private."

"Of course."

"Where's her mother?"

Julia tensed. "Home."

Mother was just a word to Crystal Montgomery. The irony that Matt had married a woman so much like their own mother was not lost on Julia.

Julia left the doctor, nodded to the police guard outside Emily's room, and walked in.

Emily was in the psychiatric wing of the hospital. She couldn't wrap her mind around Emily trying to kill herself. She honestly didn't think her niece would do it, no matter how depressed she'd become.

Julia could see her accidentally overdosing. She'd talked to Emily about the drugs Dr. Bowen had prescribed and she thought she'd convinced her to stay off them, but Emily had so many problems with Crystal, then with Judge Montgomery after Crystal remarried three years ago, that Julia suspected the prescriptions were a comfortable fallback. A sanctioned escape.

Had Julia been wrong about the drugs? She wasn't a doctor. Maybe Emily really needed some of the many pills Bowen had prescribed.

Julia rubbed her forehead with her palm. What had she been thinking? What had she been doing? Trying to be a part-time mother to a disturbed teenager? She wasn't a mother, and at the rate her love life had been going she'd never be one unless she was artificially inseminated. Maybe childlessness was a good thing, because the one child in her life, the one kid she cared about, was suffering. And she might have had something to do with it.

Could a half-dozen prescriptions be good for a sixteen-year-old? Julia had never heard of most of them, though she'd researched a bit to understand. When she was depressed, take this one. When hyper, this. When she couldn't sleep, something else. Different pills for different moods, to regulate her temperament. What had Dr. Bowen hoped to accomplish? What had he hoped to fix? The fact that she'd run away, or that she'd vandalized the courthouse? And how could pills fix problems when all Emily really needed was someone nonjudgmental, someone she trusted, to talk to?

That was the crux of it: Emily had never talked about *why*. In court, Emily had said she'd been drinking and didn't know what she was doing. Julia hadn't fully believed her then, but Emily never expounded on her admission and Julia hadn't pressed.

She should have. She should have done a hell of a lot more than leave Emily in a house without love.

Julia had grown up in one of those. It was ego shattering.

She finally approached the hospital bed, her eyes wet with unshed tears, staring at the too skinny, fragile teen. Her blond hair was limp and tangled. Dark circles ringed her eyes. She had an IV and was hooked up to some sort of monitor — it tracked her vital signs. Julia couldn't look at Emily any longer without breaking down, so she watched the electronic heartbeat as she held her slender hand, the faint *beep beep* soothing her.

If her brother, Matt, were alive, none of this would have happened. Matt had adored Emily, worshipped Crystal. At least he had until about six months before his death. Julia made it a point to never criticize her sister-in-law — the one huge fight between her and Matt had been shortly after their marriage, and it was clear then that Matt would always choose his pregnant wife over Julia.

Julia couldn't, wouldn't, force him to make that choice. So she swallowed her pride and tapped down on her worry and fear that Matt had made a terrible mistake.

Crystal was a brilliant actress, but she couldn't keep the act going indefinitely. Cracks appeared in the marriage script. Eventually, Matt saw her for who she was: a money-worshipping narcissistic bitch who didn't care one iota about Emily or even Matt, beyond his ability to keep her in luxury.

If it weren't for that awful car accident, Matt would be divorced and Emily wouldn't be living in that loveless house with Crystal and Victor.

Julia couldn't fathom that Victor was dead. She'd sort of liked him. At least she thought he'd be a good influence on Crystal and provide stability for Emily. He was a respected jurist, a judge she'd always liked to draw for trial because he was tough on criminals while being compassionate to victims. In her experience, that was a rare combination.

But he also liked wealth and social position, and last summer he'd brought up in conversation the subject of Emily's trust, which put Julia on full alert. She'd dismissed him without comment, then just last month he'd asked her to come to his chambers, she thought to discuss a pending trial; instead, he'd handed her an analysis of Emily's trust fund that he'd hired a friend to produce.

"Ted is an established financial planner. He says Emily's trust is too conservative, that she could be seeing far more interest if she manages the stock more aggressively."

"As the executrix of Emily's trust, I'm comfortable with the firm we currently have managing it."

Victor attempted to sweet-talk her, but by the end of the conversation he was quietly angry. "You're making a mistake, Julia."

"No, I'm not."

That conversation made her realize that there was only one person looking out for Emily's interests, and that was Julia.

The door opened with a quiet *swoosh.* Julia startled and glanced over her shoulder, expecting a nurse or the doctor she'd spoken with earlier. Instead, it was Officer Diaz.

"You have a visitor," he said.

She glanced at her watch. Two in the morning. Where had the last two hours gone? Had she dozed off?

She kissed Emily on the cheek and quietly left. Emily was in the psychiatric observation ward. The nurses' station in the center of a larger room monitored all patients through windows looking into the individual rooms. It pained Julia that Emily was under suicide watch, but it was in her best interest.

Diaz nodded toward defense attorney Iris Jones, who stood beside him.

Iris didn't look like she'd been woken from a deep sleep. In fact, she was impeccably dressed in a gray Anne Klein suit and matching blouse. Her black hair was pulled into her customary ponytail, and her makeup had been sparingly applied. She could have been any age between thirty and fifty, but Julia knew that Iris was five years older than she was, thirty-nine. Iris's beauty and diminutive height were misleading — she was a force to be reckoned with, the only defense attorney Julia had lost a trial to.

"I have a room down the hall that's secure," Iris said, brushing by Diaz. Julia gave him an awkward smile as she followed, felt his disapproving glance. Consorting with the enemy, he probably thought. Julia couldn't let other people's opinions influence her. Emily needed her rights protected.

Iris closed the door behind them. "What do you know?"

Julia filled her in on everything she'd been told and observed at the Montgomery house. "Detective Hooper thinks the evidence is damning."

Iris waved a hand. "See, you look at things from the eyes of a prosecutor. All I see is a bunch of circumstantial evidence that means absolutely nothing. Did they find the murder weapon?"

"I don't know. But . . . the way Victor was killed. It would take more than one person."

"Which proves another point: Emily didn't have to be involved at all. Two or more people entered the house and killed Victor either before Emily got home from school, or while she was upstairs."

"They think she tried to kill herself."

"Conjecture. Do they have a doctor's report on that?" Iris glanced at her notes. "I was late because I was doing a little research. Emily was on probation, correct?"

"Yes."

"And seeing a shrink? Garrett Bowen?" Iris smiled. "Interesting guy. I don't trust him."

"You don't trust anyone, Iris."

Instead of being insulted, Iris grinned. She tapped her notes. "We need our own shrink, and we want our person to talk to Emily first. I'm going to petition the court first thing in the morning. And I'm going to ask that you be appointed as Emily's temporary guardian until the situation is resolved."

"Crystal will never agree —"

"She doesn't have to. She's on record as believing her daughter is guilty of murder. That's what you told me, correct?"

"Yes, but it was phrased in the form of a question, so —"

"Leave that up to me, Julia," Iris said, dismissing her. She put her pen down and stared at Julia, making her feel distinctly uncomfortable. But Julia refused to squirm. She stared right back.

"Okay, let's lay out the ground rules now. You don't like me because you think I work for the bad guys."

"You do."

Iris raised her hand to silence her. "Do

you think Emily is a bad guy?"

Julia felt tears spring to her eyes. She rubbed them. "No."

"Do you think she's guilty?"

Julia hesitated. "No."

"But?"

"No buts."

"You don't know, do you? But that's okay. You don't have to know. What you want is to protect her rights. She's a minor child who has a troubled past and she has rights. But because she's a minor, she needs a guardian and I'm confident I can prove Crystal Montgomery is unfit to make decisions on Emily's behalf during this time." Iris glared at Julia. "My question to you is, can *you* do it?"

"Of course I can," Julia snapped. "She's my niece. My brother is dead, I can't —" She stopped. There was no way she was going into detailed family history with this woman. Iris's job was to protect Emily's rights. That's it. "I love Emily. I will do what I have to do to protect her."

Iris nodded. "I'd like to retain Dr. Dillon Kincaid for the defense."

"Kincaid? He usually works for Stanton."

"Unfortunately." Iris fanned herself. "What a hottie. I've hired him for psychiatric evaluations and he's good at his job. His

71

credentials are impeccable. But I want him because he usually works for your people. If we hire him to evaluate Emily, they can't use him for their side. We want him on our team. We're building our case, Julia."

"Okay." Julia had worked with Dillon several times — for the prosecution. She respected him greatly, and if anyone had to probe Emily's psyche, she'd rather have Dillon do it.

"Good, because I already called him. He's meeting us here at nine this morning." She glanced at her watch. "Six hours. Glad I don't need a lot of sleep. Next step, we need to bring in a private investigator. We need to verify everything the police say and do, follow up on our own leads, interview friends, neighbors on our own. Our goal is to find holes in the prosecution."

"If it gets that far!" Julia had been pacing. She finally sat down, defeated. "They may not even charge Emily. They might not have a case against her."

"True, but when was the last time you heard of a detective telling someone to get an attorney? They know something we don't." Iris made a note. "I have Bruce Younger on retainer. He's a top investigator, the best I have —"

"I've already called Connor Kincaid."

Iris didn't hide the surprise in her eyes. "Yet another Kincaid? Isn't Connor the cop you screwed in the Crutcher case?"

"You don't know what you're talking about, Iris," Julia said, feeling weary. She explained the history. "Three years ago Emily ran away from home. I hired Connor to find her. He told me if Emily ever needed help again to call him."

"Why did he agree to help in the first place?"

Julia squirmed under Iris's scrutiny. "Emily was just a kid. Thirteen at the time. And —" She shrugged. She'd asked Connor because she trusted him and knew he was good. But she'd had to appeal to his sense of family and honor to get him to agree to work for her. She felt guilty she'd compared Emily to his own teenaged sister, but it worked and that's what counted.

And then he'd found Emily and brought her home and she hadn't spoken to him since.

Iris started with another question, then stopped. "Why didn't Emily's mother hire the investigator?" she asked.

Julia's jaw tightened. "She thought it was a stunt for attention and that Emily would come home on her own when she was hungry."

"Was it? A stunt?"

"No."

"Then why did she run away?"

"I don't know," Julia admitted. Emily had refused to talk about it.

"Well, we just nailed Crystal Montgomery's coffin shut. You're as good as in as Emily's guardian." Iris glanced at her watch. "I'm going home for a couple hours, make some calls, then come back here before nine. If you can bring in Connor Kincaid, more power to you. He knows cops, and we can use some inside information. But I'll admit, I'm surprised he's given you the time of day."

Six

"Late night?"

Connor Kincaid halted within arm's reach of his front door, keys in hand. He knew that voice. A low rumble, quiet, too damn sexy. Slowly, he turned and faced her.

Julia Chandler.

She leaned against the porch's support beam. As Connor stared Julia straightened, her casual manner all too brief, layering on the take-no-prisoners prosecutor image she had perfected. Top to bottom, she was a piece of work. Richly textured blond hair, put up tight on her head so no one knew how long it really was; aristocratic bones, long and elegant; a curvy figure hidden underneath sensible, expensive lawyer suits. And those legs. Those legs never ended.

She looked tired, and her makeup was less than perfect. Several strands of long, wavy hair had escaped, softening her pretty face. He put that aside. He didn't care about her,

75

her appearance, her life. She'd helped destroy his career, everything he believed in, everything he thought he was.

Yet Julia didn't have the decency to stay away. No, she'd called on him to find her niece three years ago — begged him, manipulated him. Used him and his family. *"What if it was your sister? What if Lucy ran away? Emily's even younger. I don't trust anyone else with her safety."*

Trust. Julia Chandler didn't know the meaning of the word. But she loved her niece and the comparison to Lucy worked. Family meant everything to him, and Julia knew it, used it. It wasn't the first time.

She stood here on his porch to try to manipulate him again. *Try* was the operative word, because Connor wasn't going to fall for her plea this time. He'd heard the hot news about Montgomery's murder driving back from the gym. If she thought he gave a shit, she was even stupider than he thought.

He should have said no the first time. He'd definitely say no now.

Tossing his keys back and forth, palm to palm, he stared down the prosecutor. He didn't care how many perps she put in prison, how many rapists she went after or murderers she convicted. Five years ago, as a hot new assistant district attorney, she'd had his balls in her brass palm. Julia forced Connor to do something he'd sworn he'd never do. Squeezed until he turned in his resignation.

"You're the last person I expected to be waiting on my doorstep."

"I need your help."

"Oh? I thought you were here to take me to bed." He let his eyes roam from her head to her full breasts, down to her narrow waist and long, long legs. He wished he didn't find her so damn attractive; it would be much easier to hate her.

She reddened at his obvious perusal and he gave a half smile. "There's at least five hundred certified dicks in San Diego, I'm sure one of them would be more than happy to take your money and do whatever *job* you have."

"May I come in for a minute?"

"No."

"Connor, please. This is important."

"It's always important with you."

"I don't want to have this conversation standing here."

"I don't want to have this conversation."

The change in her demeanor was almost imperceptible, but Connor watched carefully. Her left hand clutched her purse, her right flexed. "If it weren't for Emily, I wouldn't be here at all."

"Don't do that. Don't use Emily as a way to get to me." Why did he expect better from her?

"I'm not, it's just —"

"I heard about Montgomery's murder on the news. I have no desire to get involved in a police investigation. Missing person? Sure. Bring it on. Emily ran away? I'll find her. Write out the check and leave it in my mailbox. No need to show up here again."

He turned, put a hand on his doorknob, hating himself for wanting to know why Julia had come to him. He wanted to go inside, shower, eat breakfast, and head back to the gym to work with the high school dropouts who thought gangs were the answer to their problems. He didn't have a regular job, thanks to Julia Chandler, but damn if he was going to hide for the rest of his life.

"Judge Montgomery was murdered in his home office."

"Tell me something I don't know." He slid his key into the lock.

"Emily was found unconscious. The police think she tried to kill herself."

He stopped, glanced at Julia. Little could have surprised him more. He'd kept in touch with Emily. Irregularly, because she

78

was Julia's niece. But suicide? Against his better judgment he asked, "Is she okay?"

"She's in the hospital, but I don't think she tried to commit suicide. I don't have the doctor's report yet."

"Why do you need me?"

"The house was secure from the inside. She was apparently the only one home when Victor was murdered."

"They can't think Emily killed him."

"They do, and they think she had help. Detective Hooper is in charge and he knows about the threats Herman Santos made on Montgomery's life. Maybe someone threatened Emily, she had to let them in. I don't know what happened. All I know is that Emily didn't kill him. I know it. You know it. But I can't be involved in the investigation. Stanton warned me off right away. But I *am* Emily's aunt and no one can keep me away from her."

The bastard Stanton didn't know the meaning of the word *family*. Though Connor couldn't disagree with his reasoning on this case. Julia had to stand back. Something Connor knew would be virtually impossible for her to do. "And you want me to do *what* exactly?"

"Stay apprised on the investigation. Prove Emily didn't have anything to do with it."

She paused. "I hired Iris Jones."

"That bitch? She takes pleasure in keeping the bad guys out of prison."

"She's good at her job. Someone needs to protect Emily's rights. She's already retained Dillon to evaluate Emily."

Against his better judgment, he asked, "How did Montgomery die?"

"It wasn't on the news?"

Connor shook his head.

"His penis was amputated."

He shifted uncomfortably. "Amputated?" he repeated.

"It was shoved down his throat."

"Good God."

"Gage hasn't said it flat out, but I know what he's thinking. I've worked with him and Hooper enough. They think Emily had help, that she let people into the house to kill Victor."

"And you?"

"How can you even ask me that?"

"You're her aunt. You don't see her every day. She's a troubled, closed-mouth teenager. You don't really *know* her. Not anymore." As he said it, he didn't fully believe it. But Emily's involvement was a possibility. It would be better for Julia if she accepted at least that possibility early on.

Why did he even care about what was

good for Julia? Let her heart break.

Julia was angry but controlled it. She was the epitome of control, always keeping her emotions in check. Never rising to the bait. Always right, standing by her oh-so-perfect ethics. Everything was black-and-white in Julia Chandler's world.

Her next comment surprised him. "You're right. I saw Emily every week, but I don't really know her. I should have fought harder for custody. But I'm just her aunt. I know the law. It was stacked against me. Crystal is a bitch, but that doesn't mean a court will take her only child away from her. Being a bitch isn't a crime."

"I don't know what you think I can do. I'm not a cop anymore, which I'm sure you haven't forgotten."

The softness and pain that had crossed Julia's face when she spoke of Emily disappeared and the hard-nosed prosecutor was back.

"I don't have to tell *you* that this is a sensitive, politicized investigation and I can't have my fingers in the pie. But I'll do anything to protect Emily. She's my family. My *only* family. I want you to prove she couldn't have killed Victor. I want not only doubt but innocence."

"You hired Iris Jones. I'm sure she has

investigators on retainer. Use them. Don't manipulate me."

"I'm not trying to manipulate you." She stared at Connor, her dark emerald eyes full of emotion, imploring him. He hadn't noticed the resemblance to her niece until then, but he saw it now, could almost picture Julia as a young girl, getting what she wanted with that determined look, those piercing green eyes. She wasn't one to back down. He admired that trait as much as he despised it.

"You have contacts I don't have, you can go places I can't go. Please, Connor. You have to help."

"Shit, Julia," he whispered under his breath. "You're a bitch, you know that?"

Her eyes darkened. "That's what makes me so good at my job," she snapped.

"I'll think about it."

"Think about it at the hospital. Listen to Dillon interview Emily. Maybe that will convince you."

"Dammit." He raked a hand through his hair.

"Nine o'clock."

"That's twenty minutes from now."

"I know."

"Don't count on it."

She reddened. "I won't."

She turned on her heel and left.

Connor watched her walk down the stairs, head high, the queen in action. Damn, damn, damn. Working with Julia Chandler was the last thing he wanted or needed in his life. He'd finally been able to put aside the crap five years ago that had cost him his job, and she walks back into his life like a nineteen-forties femme fatale. Hot and sexy and too damn smart.

He wanted to say no. He wanted to throttle her. But in the end, could he live with himself if Emily Chandler Montgomery ended up in prison and there was a way he could have prevented it?

Besides, he was sick and tired of working for insurance companies chasing down fraud claims. Boring for one, but more than that, it was intensely disheartening that so many people in the world were out for the easy buck that lying had become second nature.

He went inside his small house and to the bathroom. Maybe a hot shower would clear his mind.

He pictured Julia's long legs and the body that came with them.

Make it a cold shower.

SEVEN

Julia drove back to the hospital from Connor's. Never had a man, friend or foe, infuriated her as much as Connor Kincaid did. Arrogant and with a chip on his shoulder a mile wide.

A tickle of guilt reminded her that she was partly responsible for the size of the chip. But five years ago she hadn't asked him to break the law, she'd only demanded that he do the right thing.

She walked into the room directly outside Emily's and into a tense situation.

"I have Emily under seventy-two-hour medical surveillance," Dillon was saying to a red-faced Detective Will Hooper.

"She may have crucial information about a murder investigation. You can't stop me from interviewing her."

Dillon raised an eyebrow. "My number one concern is the health of my patient. I will be running tests and speaking with her

84

today, and if I think she's strong enough to go through a police interrogation, I will let you in."

"I'm not going to interrogate her, Dillon."

Dillon just stared at him.

"Dammit." Will ran a hand through his hair and saw Julia standing in the doorway. "You work fast, Counselor. We're on the same side, you know."

"Not if you think Emily is guilty."

"I don't have an opinion yet."

"You can't bullshit me, Will. I'm a prosecutor. You have an idea and you're running with it until it pans out or proves to be wrong. I know what the situation looks like. And Emily is delicate right now."

"You certainly didn't think Yancy Inez was too delicate when you and I interrogated him after emergency surgery," Will remarked, glaring at her.

Julia fumed. "Don't you dare compare Emily to a man who raped and mutilated women!"

Dillon put a hand on Julia's arm but looked at Will. "Will, you know me, and you know I'm not going to play games with the investigation. I need time with Emily. You know as well as I do if you push this and her, and she gives something up under duress — against the advice of her doctor

— it's not going to hold up in court. You do your job, I'll do mine."

Will wanted to say something, his mouth working, but no sound came out. Finally, he left.

Dillon rubbed Julia's arm before dropping his hand. "You okay?"

She nodded. "Thank you for taking Emily's case."

"I read her charts. Do you know her current psychiatrist, Garrett Bowen?"

"I've met him in court a couple of times, and when Emily was put on probation last year."

"That was for vandalism, correct?"

"She sprayed graffiti on the courthouse."

"Where Victor worked."

"Yes, but she said that had nothing to do with it. She'd been drinking —" She stopped. "Everyone thought it was Emily's way of getting attention, acting out because her mother remarried."

"The graffiti was definitely a cry for help, but probably not for the obvious reasons." Dillon looked pointedly at Julia. "I'm going to ask some hard questions. You can observe through the window — you'll be able to hear everything through the one-way speaker at the nurses' station — but you have to promise me that no matter what, you won't come in until I tell you it's okay. No matter what she says, what she does, you must stay out."

Julia reluctantly agreed.

Dillon walked through the door. Emily didn't move and Dillon sat in the chair next to the bed and watched her. Sleeping, perhaps. Exhausted from a traumatic night, the drugs, the drinking. Julia ached to be in the room with Emily, holding her hand, telling her everything was going to be all right, but she had to trust that Dillon Kincaid knew what he was doing. She glanced behind her at the door, wondering if Connor would show. Both praying and fearing he would. He was the best at getting to the bottom of anything, but he played loose with the rules. Isn't that why he'd lost his job in the first place? How could she have turned her back on his flagrantly breaking the law, taking matters into his own hands?

But isn't that what she was asking him to do now? To get to the bottom of Victor's murder, and Emily's possible involvement, no matter what he had to do? Did that make her any better than him?

She rubbed her eyes, resigned that her history with Connor Kincaid was too much for either of them, and she would have to find some other way to help Emily.

Emily rolled over and opened her eyes, looked at Dillon. Dark circles framed Emily's pale green eyes that were so much like Matt's it was like looking into Julia's brother's soul. Tears clouded Julia's vision as she remembered how she and Matt had depended on each other for everything. Their parents had one social obligation after another. Chandlers needed to maintain the act. They hid grandpa's drinking and much, much worse. Image was more important than substance. Both her parents had affairs, but they were discreet. As long as the press didn't know, as long as the image was clean, they could do anything they wanted.

Matt had been the one who took care of the Chandler Foundation. He went into the business because *someone* in the family had to and he had a knack for numbers. Matt protected her when she shunned her heritage and decided to use her law degree for public service instead of protecting the family name. Her mother never forgave her, would have disowned her if the trust had allowed it.

Matt understood and made sacrifices for the family so Julia wouldn't have to. Julia needed to get away from the house, the money, the image and find herself and her own dreams. Julia accepted the good and the bad that came with forging her own path. She wasn't always happy, but she was free to make her own choices. She'd given up a lot to do so, maybe too much. Because if being free meant losing Emily, none of it was worth it.

Dillon gave Emily a half smile. "Hi, Emily. I'm Dr. Dillon Kincaid. We need to talk."

Julia unconsciously leaned forward, her left hand on the window, aching to touch her niece. She could hear everything, although the voices sounded slightly tinny through the small speaker.

Emily's eyes showed fear and skepticism. How could a person so young have so much negative emotion?

"Do you know where you are?" Dillon asked.

"Hospital." Her voice was rough and Dillon offered her some water through a straw. He adjusted her bed so she could sit up.

"How are you feeling?"

"Like shit." Her voice cracked. She was trying to put on a front, but Julia saw the pain in her eyes.

"You drank a lot last night."

"I guess." She drank some more water. "You're a doctor?" She was looking at Dillon suspiciously.

He nodded. "A psychiatrist."

89

"Great." She closed her eyes and whispered, "Just what I need, another shrink."

"I need to ask you some questions. It's important."

The door opened behind Julia and relief washed through her when Connor Kincaid walked into the ward.

Connor's collar-length black hair was damp from a recent shower, and along with the chip on his shoulder and bad attitude, he brought into the room a rich, clean fragrance of soap, raw masculinity, and a quick glance that saw everything. He caught Julia's eye and her pulse quickened.

She turned to focus on Emily. "Thank you," Julia said quietly.

"I'm here for her, not you," said Connor.

"I know." She told herself she didn't care.

Connor stood next to her, his presence almost overpowering. He was the biggest of the Kincaid brothers — broader, taller, darker. Dillon Kincaid had the Irish good looks of his father — brown hair, blue eyes, and fair skin — while Connor had the dark good looks of his Cuban mother — and the hot-blooded temper of his combined Irish and Latin genes.

It was all Julia could do to stand still. So she focused on Emily and reminded herself that Connor Kincaid hated her and was only here because Emily needed help.

Dillon was speaking in the adjoining room. "Emily, I'm here to help."

She shook her head. "No one can help me." How could she sound so full of anguish and defeat? Julia stepped closer to the window. Had Emily really tried to kill herself?

"I can help. Your aunt Julia hired an attorney to protect your rights and interests. I'm part of that. So anything you say to me is between you and me. And" — he motioned toward the window — "your aunt. If you want me to, I'll ask her to leave."

"Aunt Jules is here?"

Dillon nodded. "She's worried about you."

Tears rolled over her bottom lashes. "Can she come in?"

"Not right now. I think you and I need to talk first. Sometimes it's easier to talk to a stranger. I want you to know that you're safe here. No one can hurt you."

Emily's voice cracked. "Is . . . is he really dead? It wasn't a dream, was it?" She sounded hopeful.

"It wasn't a dream. Victor Montgomery is dead."

She squeezed her eyes shut. "It was so awful."

"What was awful?"

91

"I . . . I saw Victor. He was . . . dead."

"You walked in after he was killed?"

Emily took a deep breath. "Oh God, it's true. It's all my fault."

"Why do you say that?"

Julia tensed, touching the window with both hands. "No, Em. No." But she remembered that Dillon was on the side of the defense this time. He wouldn't be testifying against Emily. Still, she ran through all possible scenarios. Maybe having Emily committed, at least temporarily, would help. Protect her. Legal precedents churned in her head and she almost missed Emily's next words.

"I planned it. Exactly like that. I thought of it, I pictured it in my mind. But it was so much worse, so much blood."

"Oh God," Julia said, blinking back tears. She turned to Connor. "Don't let her confess."

"She's not," he said, not taking his eyes from Emily's face.

"How —"

"Shh."

Dillon looked Emily in the eye. "Did you kill Victor?"

She shook her head violently. "No, God no. No. But I wanted to! I wanted to so bad. You don't know what it was like living with him. And I thought about it, about killing him. About him being dead. About how it would feel to take away his power over me."

Dillon took Emily's hand and squeezed. "Emily, this is important. Did you ask someone to kill Victor for you?"

"No, of course not."

"Were you threatened in any way? Did someone threaten to hurt you or someone else if you didn't let them into the house?"

Her expression was confused. "You mean did I let someone in to kill Victor?" She shook her head vigorously. "No."

"If you were threatened, I promise around-the-clock police protection. No one can hurt you in here. We have a guard outside, this room is secure."

She kept shaking her head. In a small voice she said, "I didn't let anyone in yesterday. No one threatened me."

Julia's heart dropped. It would have been a good defense. No jury would convict a teenager who was scared and let in a killer. And as she thought it, she knew it couldn't have happened. Santos's men would never have left a witness alive.

"Did you try to kill yourself last night?" Dillon asked.

Emily's jaw dropped and she looked at Dillon directly for the first time. "Kill

myself? Absolutely not. Never. I didn't —
Why would you think that?"

"You took several Xanax on top of a
substantial amount of alcohol."

She shook her head. "No. I didn't — I
hate that crap. I took Tylenol." But she
averted her eyes. Why was she lying?

"Before or after you drank a pint of rum?"

"After."

"And?"

She closed her eyes, bit her lip. "I was
drunk. I didn't try to kill myself. Believe
me, I didn't . . . I didn't want to. I was — I
don't know. I just couldn't believe what I
saw. I was scared but numb. Like I wasn't
in my body, that everything was in my head,
but I knew it wasn't. I'm not explaining this
very well."

"What did you see?"

"I —" She stopped.

"Tell me from the beginning, if it's easier."

"Yesterday afternoon is so fuzzy."

"Tell me how you remember it."

"I got home from school, but I didn't go
into the house. I just sat in the garage. For
over an hour. Just sat there."

"Why didn't you want to go in?"

"Victor was home."

"But you have to be home because of your
probation, correct?"

She nodded. "I have to be inside by six p.m. And on Wednesdays my mother is out late and Victor is home early . . ."

Her voice trailed off and Julia knew what she was going to say. Her stomach dropped and her fists clenched. "That bastard!" She almost hit the window, but Connor's hand shot out and grabbed her fist. Held it. His hand was hot and dry.

Emily's lip quivered and Dillon asked quietly but firmly, "When Victor and you were alone at the house, what happened?"

"He —" She stopped, cleared her throat, her eyes rimmed with tears. "He made me give him oral sex." Her voice was flat.

"Did you tell anyone?"

She shook her head, averting her eyes. "I was scared."

"That's why you ran away three years ago?" Dillon asked.

"Y-yes."

"It's been going on for over three years?"

She nodded.

Dillon's voice was soothing. "What did your stepfather do to you?"

She didn't look at Dillon, but Julia knew she was telling the truth. Her cheeks were red from embarrassment, humiliation. Her hands twisted in the bedsheets. "Six months after he and Mother got married I saw him watching me swim. It freaked me out, but he went away. Then it happened again. And again. And I couldn't go in the pool anymore unless I knew for sure he wasn't at home.

"One day a couple months later, I was in the pool house showering. I thought I was alone, completely alone because it was a Wednesday and the servants had the day off. I opened the shower door to grab a towel and he was there. Naked. I screamed and he slapped me. He raped me. Right there on the bathroom floor."

Next to Julia, Connor squeezed her hand, his own anger radiating from his tight body. "I'd have killed him," he said, his voice a low, vicious rasp. "He deserved what he got."

Julia couldn't disagree, though she was the last person who believed that anyone should take justice into their own hands. She wondered what she would have done had she known Victor raped her niece.

Julia would have turned him in. Had Victor Montgomery prosecuted and thrown in prison, where maybe he would see what it was like to be raped. Three years ago, Emily had been under fourteen, which meant special circumstance sexual assault. Montgomery would have been locked up in maximum for ten-to-twenty and required to register as a sex offender.

But Julia knew what the victims went through. They were scared, true, but more than that they were deeply humiliated. The hurt didn't end with the physical pain. They suffered emotionally for the rest of their lives. On top of that, Emily would have had to talk to a judge, possibly take the stand and testify. Her word against a respected jurist. And now, three years later, any physical evidence was gone. No proof. Even a mediocre attorney could rip Emily's story apart.

"Why didn't you tell someone?" Dillon asked Emily quietly.

"I don't know. Who'd believe me? And . . . I tried to forget. I didn't want to think about it. Ever. And then, a month later, he was there, outside my bedroom when I was leaving for school. He told me I was a good girl because I kept my mouth shut, and so he knew I'd liked it." Tears streamed down Emily's face. "He said he'd have a surprise for me when I got home from school and not to be late. That's when I ran away."

Dillon said, "When you came home after you ran away, when did your stepfather start hurting you again?"

"He didn't touch me, not like that. Instead

he" — she drank more water, coughed — "he made me give him a blow job every Wednesday afternoon. I started drinking to get rid of the taste."

She had no more tears, her voice was a monotone.

"And one day I read a newspaper article about a rapist he put in prison. He was quoted. 'When a woman says no, she means no.' And I realized then, I'd never said no. I just did what he told me. It was all my fault. And I got drunk and spray-painted the courthouse."

Dillon tried to reassure Emily. "It wasn't your fault. You are not to blame for what he did to you."

"Goddamn bastard," Connor whispered, his body radiating the same tension building within Julia. He dropped her hand and paced.

Dillon reassured Emily, and steered her back to what happened yesterday at the house. The day Victor was murdered. "You said you came into the house but didn't hear your stepfather. I don't understand what you meant."

"Every Wednesday I come home as close to six as possible. Hoping he'd be busy. But he always heard me, like he was waiting. Watching through the security camera. He would call out for me. He now had something on me. He said if I didn't come and do what he wanted, he would call my probation officer and tell her I was habitually breaking curfew. I had no choice."

"But yesterday he didn't call for you."

She shook her head. "I thought he was on the phone. Maybe had company. I ran upstairs and was so happy. I locked my door. Safe. And stupid. I got some rum. I know I'm not supposed to drink, but it numbs me, makes the bad stuff go away. I can forget about him, forget everything."

"This is important, Emily. I want you to think hard. Why did you go downstairs?"

"My flask wasn't full, so I ran out of rum. I thought I could sneak down to the parlor and get a refill. So I did."

"What time was that?"

She thought, then gave a halfhearted shrug. "Six-thirty. Maybe later. I'd taken a bath when I got home. I put on my robe and went downstairs. Barefoot, so he couldn't hear me. Tiptoed. Filled the flask and put it in my pocket.

"Everything was weirdly quiet in the house. I was drunk, I knew it, but I was scared 'cause something was wrong or out of place, but I didn't know what. Then, out of the corner of my eye, I saw Victor's library door open. He never leaves it open when he's in there. And I had to know where he was. If he wasn't in his library, was he looking for me? I was very quiet. I walked down the hall and looked in the room.

"He was dead. I'd imagined it before in my head, just like this, but there was so much more blood. So much more."

On her bed, Emily began to rock back and forth, back and forth. Julia clasped her hands together to force herself to remain calm and not burst into the hospital room.

"It was like I was in a trance," Emily said. "It took forever to walk across the room, but I did. I had to look closer. He was dead. Just like I dreamed."

"Did you touch him?"

"I think . . . I think I did touch his desk, maybe his arm. It was unreal, seeing him dead. I thought I was hallucinating. This was a drunken nightmare, and I'd wake up in the morning and Victor would still be alive."

"What did you do next?"

"I ran, slammed the door shut — I don't know why. It's not like he could chase me. He was dead. I don't know what I was thinking, but I was scared. It was exactly like I'd planned. I'd wanted to kill him. I wanted to! But I didn't. I don't think I did. I don't know anymore. I just don't know." Emily rolled over and curled into a ball, sobbing.

Dillon soothed her, assuring her he would return and no one would hurt her. He left the weeping girl. Julia, too, felt comforted by Dillon's soft, rhythmic words. Her heart rate slowed, and she was better able to process the evidence without the cloud of too many emotions.

Julia turned to Dillon when he exited Emily's room. "Can I see her?"

"Yes, in a minute." He looked at his brother Connor. "What are you doing here, Con?" The three of them stood in the observation room outside Emily's room.

"Ms. Chandler hired me."

Dillon said, "Good. I'll need to talk to Emily again, and we need someone to follow up on what she tells me. She said she 'pictured' Victor's murder, that she planned it. I need to know exactly what she means by that. Maybe she did plan it, talk about it to someone else."

Julia shook her head. "The police will be all over her for it. She didn't mean that."

"We don't know what she meant until she tells us," Dillon reminded her.

"This is an obvious case of sexual abuse,"

Julia said, her voice cracking. "Stanton won't prosecute, even if she was somehow involved." She cleared her throat. "I need to be with her."

"Julia, we still don't know exactly what happened," Dillon cautioned her.

"Are you saying she's lying?" Julia exclaimed.

"No."

Connor interjected, "What Dillon means is that Emily was impaired yesterday. She might not have all her facts straight. We need to verify everything she says, find out exactly what she meant about 'planning' Victor's death."

"Whose side are you on?" Julia asked them. "I thought you were here to help her, not interrogate her —" Julia stopped herself, rubbed her face, and took a deep breath. "I'm sorry."

"You haven't slept, you're stressed, it's understandable that you're edgy. Go in, talk to her. What Emily really needs right now is family support." Dillon paused. "Where's her mother?"

Julia glanced at Emily through the observation room's window. She'd stopped crying, but her body was still curled into a ball. She looked so small. "Crystal . . . she has issues."

"Everyone has issues, Julia."

"Crystal is defined by her status. With men, with money, with society. Having a child didn't fit into that."

Reluctantly, Julia continued. She didn't like thinking about Crystal and her brother, Matt, and her problems with her brother before he died.

"Crystal and Matt were in college and she got pregnant. I'm convinced she deliberately got pregnant because of who Matt was. His connections, his money, his name. They married and everything seemed okay for a while."

"A while?"

"Matt adored Emily. Adored her more than Crystal, or so Crystal thought. She played all these mind games with him — pretending to be ill, pretending to have secret admirers — every game in the book. Eventually, Matt tired of it. I don't know the details. He knew I didn't like Crystal so we rarely talked about his marriage. It had been a sore point in our relationship, something I regret because we lost so much that we had before Crystal came into the picture. But I knew something was going on. Matt asked me to review all the legal documents that Emily was associated with, and he made me executrix of her trust. Then . . .

he died."

"A car accident, right?" Dillon asked.

It had been the worst night of Julia's life, and she couldn't go into the details for fear of cracking. The guilt scratched at her, trying to control her again. She pushed it back. "Six years ago. It was awful. Losing him, then battling Crystal just to see my niece. Very unpleasant." Unpleasant? Julia sounded like her mother. That entire year had been Hell.

"And what's Emily's relationship with her mother?"

"Crystal doesn't have real relationships. Unless you can do something for her. It's all about connections. Crystal's only connection to Emily is through my brother, a dead man she certainly never loved."

Dillon sighed, made some notes. "I don't think it's in Emily's best interest to go home," he said, "but circumstances may change in the next few days. Right now, the best thing for Emily is to keep her here. But I don't think she's suicidal. I'm going to put her under a nondisclosed medical observation for seventy-two hours. That should give you," he said to Connor, "some time to follow up on her comments."

"First place I'd go is to her shrink," Connor said.

"I'll talk to him," said Dillon. "He won't give you anything."

"And you'll share?" asked his brother.

"Of course."

Connor nodded. "The police have the house and Emily's possessions as evidence, but I'll follow up with her friends, her school, her affiliations, anyplace and anything to find out who she might have talked to about her feelings toward Victor. Verify her whereabouts yesterday, her state of mind. I'll call around to see what kind of evidence Will and Gage have. I still have a few friends on the force."

"We should regroup tonight and compare notes, go from there."

"Can I see her now?" Julia asked, only half-listening to Dillon and Connor's plans.

Dillon nodded. "Yes, but then go home and get some sleep."

She just shook her head, then glanced at Connor. "Thank you."

Connor watched Julia enter Emily's hospital room. The two men observed the young girl carefully. Her response to Julia was warm and tearful. They embraced and both women cried. Connor felt distinctly uncomfortable. He'd never thought Julia Chandler capable of real emotion. He knew she cared about Emily, though she'd played the runaway situation a lot differently than this.

"Emily has been very forthcoming," Dillon continued, "but there's something she knows and either can't remember or doesn't want to say."

"I think you're right."

Dillon said, "I was surprised to see you, considering your history with the counselor. Why are you doing this?"

"I like the kid." When Dillon didn't say anything, Connor added, "I found Emily when she ran away. I didn't know — she never let on what Victor had done to her."

"What was her state of mind back then?"

"She was living on the streets. She was scared, tired, and using drugs. She cleaned up, promised she wouldn't . . ." Connor sighed. "Maybe I just didn't see the signs. I knew she didn't want to go home. I should have found out why."

"Don't beat yourself up over it, Connor. Julia's guilt is enough for everyone." Dillon paused. "Tread carefully."

"Don't I always?" Connor smiled.

"Can you say that with a straight face?"

The outside door opened and Officer Diaz stepped into the observation room. Dillon asked, "What's wrong?"

"The press is all over the building. I just thought you'd want to know."

"Thanks," Dillon said. "We'll go out the doctors' garage. It's secure."

Connor watched Julia and Emily talking. He could barely make out what they were saying, but Julia was trying to convince the girl that she should have told her about the rape.

"I would have taken care of it, honey."

"I was scared, Jules."

Jules. He remembered Emily always called her that. Never "aunt." More like an older sister. Friend. Confidante.

But Emily hadn't confided in anyone, and the pretty teenager was now the prime suspect in a murder case.

EIGHT

Dr. Garrett Bowen was a renowned leader in anger management. Expert witness and oft-appointed court psychiatrist, he handled an array of celebrity and charity cases, from the rich to the poor and every stripe in between.

Dillon didn't have time to read Bowen's numerous publications in every major psychiatric journal, but he wasn't surprised to see Bowen was a minor celebrity in his own right with a two-book deal, the first of which was being published in three months: *Exploit Your Anger for Health, Wealth and Happiness.*

While Bowen handled some charity cases — and made a big deal about them — his client list favored the wealthy. Upon arriving at Bowen's suite of offices, Dillon took note of the opulence, the fine art and rare antiques complementing the predominately modern decor. The only personal effects on

Dr. Bowen's desk were several framed photographs of his family — a lovely wife with a teenaged son. Dillon remembered reading a while back that Bowen was a widower. Another picture was of a beautiful woman of about forty and Bowen on a yacht, another an older picture of Bowen as a very young man with who appeared to be his parents and sister.

Dr. Bowen himself looked the part of quiet wealth — in his midforties, manicured hands, expensive yet business-casual attire, hair graying perfectly at the temple. Dillon wondered if he dyed it to appear distinguished.

At that moment, Dillon completely understood why Emily didn't trust this man. Teenagers, as did most people, got their first impressions based on appearance, but unlike people with more experience, teenagers routinely stuck with that impression, good or bad. Emily hadn't said anything to that effect, but she certainly hadn't told Bowen about her stepfather's sexual abuse. Dillon made a mental note to check the judge's contributor reports and charity listings for cross-references between Bowen and the Montgomery family.

Crystal Montgomery was attracted to the trappings, the feeling of wealth and confidence. These same things repulsed Emily. If Emily had been allowed to pick her own psychiatrist, perhaps she wouldn't be in the position she was today.

Or perhaps not. Victor Montgomery was still a child predator and rapist, and Dillon couldn't muster a whole lot of sympathy for his death. The main thing that disturbed him was that someone had either taken justice into their own hands — never a good thing — or Montgomery's murder had nothing at all to do with Emily. That meant running through the judge's criminal court cases one by one.

"Thank you for taking the time to see me today, Dr. Bowen," Dillon said.

Bowen steepled his fingers. "I was on my way over to the hospital to talk with Emily when you called. I was . . . surprised, to say the least . . . when you told me you were her doctor."

Dillon didn't want to let on exactly what his role was. He didn't like Bowen's tone. "We both have Emily's best interest at heart."

"I didn't know you worked for the police department."

"I'm in private practice. A consultant, not on payroll. Much like yourself. I'm low profile."

"Don't be humble. You've handled several cases that garnered extensive media attention. The recent killer — the guy who glued his victims' mouths shut — wonderful profile and analysis. I saw that interview with Trinity Lange. And the Lorenzo case a year ago, the Steiner trial — your analysis there was particularly fascinating, by the way — then the Brooks suspected murder-suicide. Your testimony turned the case. You have a knack for speaking straight with the average person."

Dillon disliked the press attention he'd received, mostly because of the media's propensity to sensationalize every detail, often to the detriment of victims and survivors. "The press just made it seem that way."

"You're their golden child."

Dillon was becoming uncomfortable with this conversation, and couldn't help but think Bowen was intentionally baiting him. He was about to get the conversation back on track when Bowen said softly, "You're the only psychiatrist I know who can comfortably work for both the prosecution and the defense."

It was the passive-aggressive tone, trying to elicit a reaction from Dillon, to see what buttons might be pushed. If Bowen treated his clients like this, it's no wonder they grew to distrust him.

Dillon knew he'd waited too long to answer and had given Bowen some indication of his anger threshold. Wasn't that his specialty? Anger?

"I wanted to discuss Emily Montgomery with you, Dr. Bowen," Dillon said.

Bowen nodded, didn't say anything. He didn't take his eyes off Dillon. Did he think the scrutiny would unnerve him?

"When was the last time you saw Emily?"

Bowen turned to his computer screen, tapped a few keys, then responded, "A week ago Tuesday. I see her every Tuesday, but she missed her last appointment." He didn't sound like this was unusual. He'd already pulled her file; everything he did now was for show. Dillon couldn't help but wonder what he was trying to prove — or hide.

"Did she call?"

"She did. Spoke to my secretary and assured her that she'd be back next week."

"Is that allowed? Considering that her counseling is court-ordered."

"It is. She's required to take twenty-six sessions a year, every other week. Her mother insisted that it be weekly, and I accommodated that request. Considering that Emily is being counseled for anger management issues, the more often she can talk out her problems and inner anger, the better for her and less likely she'll get into trouble down the road." He sighed. "Can't say that it helped in this case."

"What do you mean by that?"

Dr. Bowen looked at him strangely, his eyebrows raised. "Considering she's being held for murder."

"I think you've been misinformed," Dillon said. "No charges have been filed."

Dr. Bowen waved his hand. "You know as well as I that the police are building their case as we speak, and they won't file any charges until you report back to the court. Seventy-two hours, correct?"

"She's under a seventy-two-hour assessment." He saw no reason to correct Bowen's misperception over which side he was working with.

"Suicide watch, according to her mother."

Again, Dillon didn't correct him. "Has Emily ever exhibited any signs of wanting to end her life?"

"Anyone filled with the rage she had when she vandalized the courthouse is capable of ending her life."

Dillon disagreed, but didn't argue with Bowen. However, people who were sexually abused, particularly as minors, were more likely to become clinically depressed and self-destructive. "Has she said anything to you?"

"Now we're getting into dangerous territory, Dr. Kincaid."

"Are we?"

Bowen straightened. Almost imperceptibly, but Dillon didn't miss the bristling of his back. "My reports are filed monthly with the court, as per the agreement. You can read my evaluations and assessment of Emily's progress in them."

Dillon had been prepared to ask about sexual abuse, but pulled back. He didn't want to give Bowen any information he didn't already know.

"I'd hoped I could get your general feelings about Emily, her state of mind, anything that might help me in making an assessment of her emotional strength."

Bowen sighed and glanced at the computer screen, but Dillon suspected he was thinking more than reading. "Emily Montgomery is a troubled young lady. Ran away from home — twice. Vandalized the courthouse to the tune of nearly a quarter million dollars. Serious damage. Hostility toward her mother, her stepfather, and deep-seated anger at everyone and everything in her life. I believe it stems from losing her father so suddenly, and having a

114

mother who is, for lack of a better word, emotionally immature. Crystal Montgomery wants everything in her life picture perfect — everything to look just fine for neighbors, friends, and anyone else she wants to impress. Emily acting out — undoubtedly to gain her mother's attention, if not her love — is the imperfect picture that Crystal abhors. But teenagers aren't perfect, they act up, they need attention, they need guidance."

Dillon was stunned at the seeming about-face in Dr. Bowen's attitude. One minute, reluctant, the next, espousing a textbook explanation of the Montgomery family. It had the ring of truth but it seemed too bland. And considering Bowen didn't know about Judge Montgomery's sexual abuse of his stepdaughter, Dillon couldn't help but wonder just how much Emily had lied and manipulated to avoid talking about what truly terrified her.

"One final question, if you don't mind," Dillon said.

Bowen nodded, leaned back in his chair, and clasped his hands across his flat stomach.

"Emily's relationship with her mother and stepfather was strained, but what about her aunt?"

"The prosecutor?" Bowen seemed surprised by the question and rubbed his chin in thought. "Emily never really discussed Julia Chandler. It seemed to me from the little she did say that they had some sort of cordial relationship, but Emily views her more as an authority figure. Considering Emily's delinquency problems, I can't imagine that they were all that close."

"But you don't know that with certainty."

Bowen tensed. "No. Emily rarely talked about her."

The doctor-patient relationship cleared for Dillon. Over a year of therapy and Emily told Bowen very little about her life, just enough to get by. Dillon wondered how detailed Bowen's reports to the court were, and whether their accuracy could be trusted.

As if sensing what Dillon was thinking, Bowen said, "Teens are naturally reticent when faced with authority. Close-mouthed. Especially troubled kids like Emily."

Sounded like an excuse to Dillon.

"Thank you, Dr. Bowen. I appreciate your assessment." Dillon stood to leave.

"Can I expect a copy of your report?" Bowen asked.

"It will be filed with the court." Dillon smiled.

"Of course."

"I'll review your court documents and get back to you."

"Please do." Bowen stood. Some sort of invisible line had been drawn. Dillon wasn't sure exactly what Bowen's game was, but something was off.

Dillon walked toward the door, stopping only when Bowen asked, "How did Judge Montgomery die?"

The information would be coming out sooner rather than later. "Penile amputation." He kept the rest of the details to himself.

Bowen blanched. "Sounds like a sexually motivated crime."

"Appears so, on the surface."

"You have a different opinion?"

"I have no opinion at this point."

"If that's the case, you have a stronger spine than I thought."

By the time fourth period ended and lunch began, La Jolla Academy was abuzz with rumors.

"Ohmigod! Did you hear about Emily *Montgomery?*"

"She killed herself."

"No, she *tried* to kill herself."

"No, she *pretended* suicide so she

117

wouldn't be thrown in jail. Her stepfather's dead."

"He was a senator."

"Dummy, he was a *judge*."

"Maybe one of those people he put in prison killed him."

"Hey, maybe it was the terrorists, you know, going after people in their homes."

"Shut up, dumbshit, they use bombs, not knives."

"Knives? How do you know?"

"I dunno."

Faye Kessler sat in the far corner of the gym, pretending to eat her lunch. Quiet, reticent, and known on campus as a geek, Faye had few friends at school. That she had been arrested for shoplifting would have surprised not only her teachers, who found her odd but extremely gifted, but her peers, too, who didn't care enough about her existence to even make note of the occurrence.

Much like her father. If Faye hadn't broken two display cases at the mall store she'd stolen from, he would have brushed the incident under the rug just like he'd done everything else in his life. She'd gotten his attention for about five minutes. Then he carted her off to a shrink, paid for the displays, and ignored her again.

Get over it.

Yeah, right, she'd been telling herself that for years, ever since her mother walked out, leaving both of them, in order to "find herself" in some country far from America. Faye got a card every August — for her birthday — and that was the only connection with the woman who'd given birth to her, then left seven years later without a second thought.

What Faye *knew* and what she *felt* were two completely different things. Sometimes her feelings bubbled up and she couldn't control her actions. It was both invigorating and terrifying. But most of the time Faye felt nothing. Except when she was angry. She knew this, understood it, but couldn't control it.

She spotted Mike Olson across the lunchroom. That fluttery feeling came back, starting in her chest and tingling out, down her spine, making her flush. The same feeling she'd had when Trent Payne had invited her to the movies last year. She thought he liked her because he'd told her she was "really sharp" and could get into whatever college she wanted. He'd seemed so impressed with her that she'd mistaken the attention for something more. When he'd kissed her, the same tingles were there, hot and exciting and forbidden, but then he started hurting

119

her and he wouldn't stop. He tore her new blouse, the one she'd bought just for their date, and tried to pull off her jeans. He was going to rape her, she knew it, while murmuring nice words in her ear, trying to get her to go along with it.

She'd seen then, in the Cadillac truck his parents bought him for his sixteenth birthday, that he had never liked her. He'd thought she'd be easy, an unattractive girl who never had dates, who no one looked at, who got straight A's in school but no one noticed, not even the teachers. A little attention from a cute football player and she'd be willing to spread her legs and let him fuck her.

She had more self-respect than that.

Not only did she stop him from humiliating her, she'd broken his nose, and a week later his precious truck got broken, too.

Payback.

Mike Olson glanced over at her. Their eyes met. She couldn't even swallow.

He turned away. Maybe he wasn't really looking at her. Maybe he didn't even know her name.

"Faye," Skip said.

She jumped, her thoughts so focused on Mike Olson that she didn't see Skip approach. He sat next to her at the lunch table. The tables sat eight, but she had this one all to herself. Faye always ate alone.

"We're meeting this afternoon," he said.

"Okay." She glanced at Skip, Mike's friend. Had he seen her staring at him? Her pulse quickened. She hoped not.

Skip leaned in. "Deep down Mike's a jerk like Trent."

Faye looked at her lunch, her appetite gone. How could Skip even bring up Trent? It was something she'd told them in anonymity. Even though, intellectually, she knew her secrets were no longer her own, no one had said it out loud.

"Hey, I'm sorry, kid."

Kid. She wasn't a kid.

"It's okay."

"No, it's not. I'm sorry." He touched her arm, made her look at him. She blinked back tears, tried to smile. "Men are bastards. Even me. But I don't want to hurt you. Life sucks and you don't need crap from your friends. You know I'm your friend, right?"

She nodded, unable to talk. She'd never noticed what beautiful eyes Skip had. Grayish blue, with little flecks of darker gray. Unusual. And long lashes. A small mole on his cheek. No wonder he was so popular.

And now they had a secret together. A

huge secret. A secret that bonded them forever.

She smiled a little. "This afternoon. I'll be there."

NINE

Connor pushed the guilt aside about his plan. Right now, he had to remember that Emily was his number one concern. And if Connor had to use his connections, even if one of them was his brother Patrick, in order to prove her innocence, he would.

Patrick's e-crimes division was in the far corner of the top floor. It took Connor fifteen minutes to get up there. Unless they were new to the force, those who still didn't hold a grudge against him for testifying against a fellow officer stopped to ask Connor how he was doing. He felt distinctly uncomfortable. After all, he'd left the force amid a huge scandal. Not his scandal, but he'd uncovered it. It just went higher than he'd thought and he'd been set up to blow.

Just remembering the last six months of his career as a cop made his blood boil with anger and regret. He had been right, but that meant shit when someone in power

wanted to destroy you. It was only margin-
ally satisfying that justice had been served
for those poor dead girls. Because in the
end, he'd lost his job, and the department
had been in turmoil for years after. And as
much as he was loath to admit it, his ex-
brother-in-law Andrew Stanton had done
more than his fair share to mend fences in
the three years he'd been district attorney.

If Julia Chandler had her way, he would
have sat in a prison cell for contempt a helluva lot longer than the three hours she'd
managed to keep him there.

Finally, he walked into Patrick's upstairs
work area, a large open room he shared with
four other cops, two males and two females.
They all looked fresh out of the academy,
though their quiet confidence told him
looks were deceiving as they worked on
eight different computers seemingly simultaneously. Where in the world had Patrick
got his technical skill? No one else in the
vast Kincaid family, except maybe their
baby sister Lucy, could do much more than
turn on a computer and check e-mail.

What a difference a few years make.

Patrick looked over, obviously surprised
to see Connor. It wasn't every day that he
came by the station. In fact, the last time
was when he was working a missing person's

case and needed to chat with Dean Robertson, nearly a year ago.

Connor nodded a greeting and sauntered over. Patrick was tall and skinny, almost gangly in appearance, as if he'd just gone through a growth spurt and his muscles hadn't caught up. Actually, Patrick was a marathon runner and ten years older than he looked.

Connor extended his hand. Patrick clasped it and slapped Connor on the back. "Hey, bro. Good to see you always. Let's go to my office." Patrick directed his team. "See if you can get the programmer on the phone. Call me if he'll talk. Threaten a warrant. If that doesn't work, I'll get the damn thing."

He led Connor into his cramped office. As division chief of the understaffed e-crimes department, Patrick's office would have been large if it weren't crammed with computer equipment in every available crevice. Patrick closed the door and leaned against his desk. "What makes me think your showing up here has to do with my current case?"

"You're a good cop."

"This case is politically hot. You don't want to get involved."

"Too late."

When Patrick didn't say anything, Connor leaned against the metal filing cabinet and said, "DDA Julia Chandler retained me."

"Aw, shit, shit, shit." Patrick slid a hand through his short-cropped hair and stared briefly at the ceiling, then caught Connor's eye. "Didn't you track down Emily Montgomery when she ran away?"

"Yes."

"This case is a mess."

"You've only had it for twelve hours."

"Dead judge, wealthy family, troubled teen. What do you know?"

"Not enough. I need information, Patrick."

"Connor, don't do this to me."

"What I don't know I'll find out. You can make it easy for me or hard."

"Just tell me what your interest is."

Damn, why did Will and Patrick want to know why? Because of his history with Julia Chandler? "I don't think Emily had anything to do with the murder and she needs an advocate."

"You think her aunt is going to let her go to prison?"

"I think her aunt is a prosecutor, not a cop. Doesn't matter if the kid goes to prison or not. What matters is clearing her name."

And that was the crux of it, Connor suddenly realized. He'd lived for years under a cast of suspicion. He didn't want a young, impressionable kid to suffer through the same. And from what he knew of Crystal Montgomery, he didn't see any support coming from her direction. And Julia? She might want to protect her niece, but did she think the kid was innocent or guilty?

"Aw, hell. If Carina were here she'd blab to you anyway. You always were her favorite." Patrick pushed away from his desk, walked around, and collapsed into his chair. "I'm really going out on a limb here, Connor."

"I know," he said quietly. "I'm going to tell you something off the record, okay? Montgomery raped his stepdaughter when she was thirteen years old. The kid has needed help, but no one saw it. Not me, not her aunt, and certainly not her mother. If I can help . . . dammit, I'm going to."

"I'll deny I said anything to you, not that anyone would believe me," Patrick mumbled. "This is what we have so far. The security system is state-of-the-art and I can't get anything out of it other than log-in and log-out times. I need the programmer to pull out more information. What we know is that Emily Montgomery's code opened the garage at four thirty-five yesterday afternoon. We know that she entered the house at five twenty-nine."

"Where was she for that hour?"

"Who knows? The garage door closed at five twenty-nine as well. What was she doing for nearly one hour in the garage? Or did she walk around the grounds of the house?"

"When did the judge arrive home?"

"Two-eighteen. Parked in the garage. Door closed at two-nineteen. Entered house at two twenty-one. What I can't get without help from the programmer is whether any other doors or windows — other than the two coded entrances — were opened between two twenty-one and five twenty-nine."

"Time of death?"

"Don't know, don't want to know. I'm looking at the technology. I'll give Will and Gage the facts. It's up to them to fit those facts into the puzzle of the investigation."

"What about security cameras?"

"No tape. Just live feed." Patrick paused. "I have one other thing, but I haven't told the investigative team yet, so keep this to yourself until I talk to Will after the autopsy. The judge logged onto his computer at two forty-three yesterday. Retrieved e-mail, responded to a couple of messages up until three thirty-nine when he opened a message and started to respond. He never finished. It was still on his screen when I retrieved the computers early this morning." He picked up a coffee mug, drank, grimaced, and put it back down. "Want some coffee?"

"No thanks."

"Yes you do." He stood, stared at his desk, then said, "The pot's downstairs. It might take me a few minutes."

Connor didn't miss his meaning.

When Patrick closed the door, Connor went through the folders on his desk. The case file was easy to find — it was labeled in Patrick's thick block letters: MONTGOMERY HOMICIDE.

He flipped open the file. The security logs were on top, the information Patrick had just given Connor. Connor wrote down the times and facts, flipped rapidly through the papers. Stopped when he saw a series of e-mails.

The content chilled Connor's blood.

FROM: em429
TO: wishlist
DATE: January 14
SUBJECT: RE: justice
I would cut off his dick and shove it

down his throat. Make him suck himself just like he made me do it.

>> How would you get back at the person who hurt you most?

Connor knew Patrick would have another copy of the e-mails stored on his computer, so he glanced at the window — the blinds were closed — and pulled the message from the file, folded the paper, and put it in his back pocket. He skimmed the other e-mails, all to and from the group "Wishlist" taken off Emily's computer. There were hundreds, most seemed innocuous and chatty. The "justice" thread was disturbing — several people wrote about killing.

As the messages continued, they became more corrupted with missing or odd characters. Patrick must have run an undelete program to extract them. Connor flipped quickly, looking for Emily's name, and found nothing else that would incriminate her. The first message was damning enough.

Near the bottom of the stack his eye caught one familiar word. *Judson.* He didn't know why it was familiar, and there was no date or name to give him a hint.

Jackass Judson ruined my life. He told the college recruiters that I 00000000000

00000 AP tests. It wasn't me, I'm a fuck-ing straight-A student. 0000000000 0000000 saw me coming out 0000000000 classroom after 0000000000000 and she couldn't find the tests. 000000000000 00000000000000 mom started crying. 0000000000 but Jackass 000000000 I lost my 0000000000. Now my mom 00000 000000 and it's fucking not fair. Jackass needs his eyesight checked.

He pulled the Judson message, pocketed it, and left Patrick's office.

Time to go to the library and search the newspaper archives. Who was Judson?

As soon as Connor saw the article about the high school principal's murder, he remembered the case. Paul Judson, fifty-seven, opened the front door of his house and was shot in the face with a nine millimeter. Dead after the first shot, but the killer hit him again in the other eye.

The cops had looked hard at Billy Thompson, a high school senior who'd lost his basketball scholarship after Judson accused him of cheating. But Billy ended up having a solid alibi. No arrest had been made, and the case was still open.

Connor drove out to the south end of the city, close to the Tijuana border, to talk to Billy at the auto repair shop where he worked. Connor knew Billy well from the youth center. The last thing Billy needed was the cops all over him. The kid was clean, but he didn't like authority, and after what happened with Judson, Connor couldn't blame him. Still, Connor had no doubt that Billy had written the message about "Jackass Judson." It sounded just like him.

Six feet five inches of lean black muscle, Billy Thompson looked older than a nineteen-year-old almost-basketball player. His head was shaved and his hands were huge. Connor waited while Billy finished with a customer before walking over to him.

"Hey, Billy." He stuck out his hand and Billy slapped it front, back, and then slammed his knuckles.

"What's up, Kincaid?" Billy asked. "Problem with your truck?"

"No, I just need to talk to you about something."

Billy narrowed his eyes. "You sound like a cop again."

"You can take the cop out of the precinct, but . . ." Connor smiled. Billy didn't. He crossed his arms.

"What do you want me for?"

Connor wasn't going to bullshit Billy. He'd been through enough crap in his life. "It's about Judson."

Billy's face froze, and his body seemed to double in size.

"I have nothing to say."

"I know. But this is important. Someone else is being railroaded for a murder they didn't commit, and I think there might be a connection."

That was enough to at least get Billy to relax a bit.

"Why should I?"

"Because you want to."

Billy blew out a long breath and led Connor into the back where he had a small office. A basketball rested on top of a filing cabinet, sandwiched between two trophies; a framed picture of Billy with his mom on the desk; and his high school diploma, honors certificates, and newspaper articles with photographs of Billy playing high school basketball were displayed on the walls.

Billy sat behind the desk, the chair pushed back to accommodate his long legs. "What?"

"How's school?"

"Fine."

"What happened with Texas?" Last Connor had heard, one of the top college basketball scouts was looking at Billy.

"Don't know anything yet. I'm not getting my hopes up. Can the small talk and spill it."

"You might have some information we could use to help us in a murder investigation."

"I didn't know you're a cop again."

"Nope, still a private investigator. But a friend of mine is in trouble and I want to help her."

"So what do you think I know?"

"It's about Judson's murder."

"You know I had nothing to do with that."

Billy sounded hurt that Connor might think bad of him, so Connor put his hands up. "I know. Judson screwed you big-time. This isn't about you."

"We all look the same to white folks. There were twenty-three brothers over six foot four in that school, but Judson was certain it was me."

It was well known on the force that witnesses whose race differed from the suspect were less than reliable in identification. Connor could easily see that happening with a vice principal in a school with over two thousand students. Judson, an older white man versus a school filled with boys and girls across all races.

Connor had gotten some of that himself. He looked far more like his mother's Cuban family than his father's Irish family. When he was in high school virtually every teacher made a comment about his last name. If he had a dime for every time someone said to him *you don't look Irish* . . . on occasion he'd wanted to deck someone.

One he had. He hadn't started it. He'd been thirteen and Brian Forster said, "Kincaid? What kind of spic name is that? Must be adopted, you don't look Irish."

"Funny, you don't look stupid."

He hadn't swung first, but he won the fight and as a result, he'd been suspended for a week. Still, it had been worth it to see the blood spurt from that asshole's nose. For about ten minutes. Then his father lectured him and his mother cried and that was the last time Connor hit someone out of anger.

He cleared his mind, focused on the task at hand, renewed empathy with the kid in front of him. Connor had been working with underprivileged youth since long before he left the force. When he had resigned, he spent even more time at the youth centers around town. Some kids were bad news. Others were trapped and ended up making the wrong choices. And others, like Billy, really tried to change their lot in life and sometimes got shit on by those who claimed to want to help.

"Billy, you know I understand where you're coming from. Don't give me shit."

Billy said nothing, but his physical demeanor relaxed. He shrugged, leaned back in his chair, crossed his arms. "What about Judson? Everyone thinks I killed him, you know."

"But you didn't. You have the truth on your side," Connor said softly.

"What do you want to know?"

"Have you heard of a group called 'Wishlist'?" Connor asked.

Billy straightened. "How do you know about that?"

Connor slid over the message he'd taken from Patrick's file.

"Do you recognize this?"

Billy didn't touch the paper, but he read it.

"Yeah. I wrote it. What's it to you?"

"What is 'Wishlist'?" Connor asked.

"Hell if I know. Just a bunch of whiny pricks. Life sucks, you know? Shit happens. But these people just whine and complain 'bout every fucking thing that happens to them."

"You were in the group and you don't know what it is?"

"It's just an online message group. You know, sign up and get e-mails from everyone in the group. It was supposed to be anger management or something — talk about your problems and they'll disappear, shit like that. But it wasn't for me, you know? I quit after a couple months."

"How did you get hooked up with them in the first place?"

"After Judson expelled me I was stupid, okay? I took a bat to his car. I had to pay for the damage and take this anger management class. So I did. The shrink told me about the group, said it was for people like me who just wanted to talk. Do I look like someone who needs to *talk* about my shit? But I did it because I thought I'd get points and get out of the stupid class. I dumped it as soon as my probation was up. Kept my nose clean since. You know that, Kincaid, don't you?"

"You have the cleanest nose down at the gym."

A half-smile turned Billy's lips up. "Damn straight."

"Did you save any of the e-mails?"

"Naw, and I never had a computer either. I used the computer at the library at school.

Haven't been online since I graduated last June."

So "Wishlist" was an online anger-management community, apparently aimed toward teenagers, considering that both Billy and Emily had been members. Billy's psychiatrist recommended it, and Connor wondered if the same had happened with Emily.

He was about to ask when Billy tapped the message and said, "Damn, I sounded like a lunatic when I wrote that. But it's easy to rant when it's anonymous. Now, I don't care. I've got a chance to go to Texas in the fall and the only thing I want to do is play basketball and take care of my ma. I'm not going to blow it." He looked at Connor, fidgeted. "Um, thanks for the recommendation letter. Appreciate it."

Connor nodded, stood. "By the way," he asked, "who was your shrink?"

"Dr. Bowen. Some rich-ass shrink. Nice enough guy, I guess, but he never understood. Though, to tell you the truth, talking about my frustration did help. Maybe not then, but now . . . well, I don't let things get me riled like they used to, if you know what I mean."

"A lot of people never realize that, Billy," Connor said. "You're already ahead of the game."

The bell over the main door rang and Billy said, "Look, Kincaid, I really can't help you. I wish I could, but I have a good job here." He stood up. When he looked through the door, he swore. "Fuck."

Connor stood, looked around Billy's shoulder. Will Hooper was standing at the counter, hand poised above the bell.

"Billy Thompson? I'm Detective —" He stopped when he saw Connor. His jaw clenched and Connor could feel his anger even fifteen feet away.

"Kincaid, can I talk to you?"

"I was just leaving," Connor said. He glanced at Billy and said quietly, "You have my number. Call me if you remember anything."

Billy grunted.

On the sidewalk, Will started in on Connor. "What are you doing here? I thought I saw you around the station, and now here? You interfere with a police investigation and I'll take action."

"Lighten up, Will."

"You're going to get Patrick fired."

"Saint Patrick? He does the work of three guys. He didn't tell me anything, anyway."

"I'm not stupid. He wouldn't have to say

anything."

"You think Emily is guilty?"

"What I think doesn't matter. I'm just looking at the evidence."

"And the evidence says?"

"I'm not talking about this case with you."

Connor leaned over. "I saw the e-mail. If I were still a cop, I'd be all over it."

"Don't go there."

"Go easy with Billy. He's a good kid."

"What did he tell you?"

"Ask him." Connor walked away. He wasn't going to make it easy for Will, especially not now when his gut told him Emily was on the verge of being arrested.

TEN

Faye Kessler sat in the papasan chair in Cami's ornate penthouse apartment. Faye yearned to have her own place, where she didn't have to hide, didn't have to be anyone but who she really was. Cami was brilliant. She had graduated from high school early and could have gone to any college she wanted, but she was tired of school. Genius-level IQ, but Faye knew having a high IQ was as much a curse as being ugly. Cami had connected with Faye in a way no other person ever had.

They were soul mates. Bound by something greater than life. *Blood.* There was no greater union.

"Do you think it's safe?" Skip asked. "Shouldn't we lay low for a while?"

Cami shook her pretty head. "It's perfect." She gave Skip that smile, the one that said, *I know what I'm doing and I love you for caring, but we're doing it my way.*

Faye marveled at Cami's ability to control men. Faye wanted that control, but she was destined to stand on the sidelines and observe.

"Where's Robbie?" she asked.

"He's coming," Skip said, winking at Faye. *He knew.* He knew that she and Robbie had had sex. The idea turned her on as much as it scared her. Maybe Skip had even watched. Seen her body, scars and all. Robbie didn't care about them, he had his own. It's why Faye let him touch her naked.

Even if Skip had watched that night, when Cami was doing her thing and she and Robbie were on the couch, he couldn't have seen anything. No lights, that was Faye's rule. And Robbie didn't care, he just wanted to screw her.

Only Cami had seen her marks.

They'd met last year after talking online for months.

They'd gone to different schools. Faye to a private high school; Cami, a year older, had graduated from high school early and was part of an independent study program with Stanford. They were from opposite ends of the same track — both smart, Cami pretty and poised while Faye was ugly and gangly. Rich single parents, only children, and one other thing in common:

Boredom.

They'd talked online about everything, but some of their cybertalk was dangerous. They were crossing a line and Faye's self-preservation kicked in.

"We should meet," she suggested to Cami.

"Where?"

"The club."

That was another thing they had in common. Cami's mother and Faye's dad had memberships to the most exclusive golf club in San Diego County.

At the end of their oh-so-formal lunch overlooking the dock, Faye asked, "Have you ever cut yourself?"

She knew Cami had, it was one of the first things they'd talked about online. It was the reason Cami had been sent to therapy.

Cami's pretty blue eyes glazed over. Excitement? She flushed. "I can't. My mom checks my arms all the time."

"Still?" Cami was eighteen and didn't even live with her mother anymore.

She frowned, nodded. "Not as often, but I never know when. She'll send me away. She said she'd commit me."

"Can she do that now?"

"Yes. She wants my trust fund. It's why I moved out, but I still have to go through the hoops until I'm twenty-one. God, I can't wait."

"Come on." Faye got up and they walked to the bathroom.

The bathroom at the club was opulent. There were no stalls, but complete rooms that housed a toilet, sink, and shower. Two private sitting areas and even a lounge, which Faye suspected some of the refined women used after purging. Doors that closed. Walls that were, almost, soundproof. Sometimes two women came out of a private room. Flushed. Doing the forbidden.

Cami followed Faye, who closed the door tight behind them. Without a word, Faye pushed up the sleeves of her shirt.

Cami gasped, took a finger and ran it over the rows and rows of raised scars. "Wow," she breathed heavily. Cami turned her left arm over, palm up, and Faye touched the old, faded scars, seven of them, on her forearm. They were shallow. Time would make them disappear to all who didn't know they were there.

Faye reached into her purse and extracted her favorite knife. Very thin, very sharp. She handed it to Cami.

"I can't," she whispered, though she held the knife, staring at the blade as if in a trance. She licked her lips.

Faye turned around, pulled up her shirt, and showed Cami her back. There were no scars there; a clean slate.

"Do me."

"You want me to cut you?"

"It will seal our friendship."

Faye almost thought she'd read Cami wrong. But then Cami's breath caressed her neck and she relaxed with anticipation, closed her eyes.

She inhaled sharply at the first sting of the cut, the familiar warmth, pain and heat blending to create a power she only felt at this moment, when blade sliced flesh and reminded her she could end it all if she chose. There was always the option, always the choice. She had the power. Just a matter of how deep, how long, how quiet she could be . . .

Cami was gentle, the cut was shallow, perfect, an inch long. Blood oozed over its edge, trailing slowly over her shoulder blade. A finger touched her back, along the slender line of blood. Faye closed her eyes. Lips touched the fresh wound, and she held her breath, squirming against her jeans, a rush of pleasure gliding through her body.

Cami's lips kept pressure on the cut until it stopped bleeding. Faye had many sexual fantasies, but they were all about boys.

None of her fantasies felt as good as Cami's lips on her back.

"Thank you," Cami whispered in her ear. "Can we meet here again sometime?"

Faye could only nod.

"I'll TM you."

Then she kissed her on the neck and left.

"So we're all in agreement?" Cami said. She looked at Faye, who nodded.

"Dammit, Faye, can't you talk some sense into her?" Skip was angry, but that wasn't unusual.

"You liked it, didn't you?" Cami countered.

Skip had. Faye had watched his expression when she killed Judge Victor Montgomery. Wide-eyed. Amazed. Empowered. Blood held a surprising attraction.

And there had been a lot of blood.

"It's justice," Cami said, using the one argument that always worked with Skip. "You know what he did to Emily. And do you really think anyone as *establishment* as a judge would be prosecuted?"

"I just didn't think Emily would get hurt."

Cami waved off the concern. "She'll be fine. She didn't kill him, they'll let her go. Now, we had a plan. I want to finish it."

Robbie entered then, clearly stoned. Cami

fumed. "You're doing drugs again."

Robbie shrugged, slumped on the floor up against the door. "Whatever."

"You *promised*." Cami despised drugs. Like some people hated gays and some people hated Christians; Cami hated drugs with an unusual fervor. When Robbie joined them ten months ago, right before they took care of the teacher, the rule was *no drugs*. Robbie had been fairly sober since.

"What happened?" Faye asked him as she knelt next to him.

He looked at her with glassy eyes. It wasn't just drugs she saw in them. It was pain. "What happened?" she asked again. When Cami tried to interrupt, Faye put up her hand.

She reached over and lifted up his shirt. Fresh bruises covered his chest. "Oh Robbie, you need to go to the hospital."

"Hell no." Robbie brushed off her hand. "I got three fucking months left. Three months and I get my money. I'm not doing shit until I get the money and then I'm going to kill him and disappear. Fucking bastard." He sniffed, rubbed his nose, and winced.

Skip helped him up. "I'll take care of him."

Cami was unmoved by Robbie's pain. "No drugs. That was the rule. You'll get no second chance."

"What are you going to do? Suck me dry and cut off my dick, too?"

Cami reddened and pointed at Skip. "Talk to him. Straighten him out. This is bigger than all of us. Don't you see? This is justice. This is payback for everyone who can't fight for themselves. Straighten Robbie out or he's gone. *Disappeared.*"

Skip glared at Cami, but nodded. He took Robbie into the bathroom.

"His old man really walloped him," Faye said, walking over to Cami.

Cami frowned. "Drugs are like drinking. Loose lips. You know that saying? It's like military or something. *Loose lips sink ships.* We can't let Robbie destroy everything we've been planning for over a year. I won't have it."

What she really meant is *he* wouldn't have it, but Faye didn't correct Cami. They never talked about him. Cami didn't even know that Faye knew about him. The less Cami knew about that the better.

"Robbie won't screw us," Faye assured her, though even she had her doubts.

She'd had early doubts about bringing in Skip, but he'd turned out to be immensely valuable. Cami could get him to do anything — *anything* — and Faye loved watching her in action. But at the beginning, when they first talked about this, it had just been the two of them. Cami and Faye.

"We're going through with this." Cami sat down heavily on her bed. "As soon as we know when. No backing out. It's the final act, the one we've been waiting for. And if Robbie and Skip are problems, you know what we have to do."

She did. "You know I'm there."

Cami smiled, touched her cheek. "I know. You understand better than anyone. I never have to explain anything to you." She reached over Faye and into her nightstand. "I have a treat for you."

Cami handed Faye a vibrator and a video. "Take them home. You'll know what to do."

Faye took them, both nervous and excited. She wanted to view the video before she shared it with *him.*

She started to leave when Cami spoke.

"It's only because of you that Robbie's made it this far, Faye. He's your responsibility. If he screws up again, you're going to have to take care of him."

Faye stared into Cami's dead eyes. She wondered if they mirrored her own.

"I will."

Julia didn't want to be in her office. She

should have taken the day, the week, off to take care of Emily. But she had a trial starting a week from Monday, a rape, and she needed to prepare. Talk to the victim, ready her for the stand. Talk to the detective. The witnesses. Julia had turned down a plea offer — six months, ridiculous for a forcible rape — and had to prove beyond a shadow of a doubt that Melanie Ruiz had said no and Juan Fuentes attacked. She had doctors' reports, a witness, and the victim had bruise marks around her neck.

Fuentes told police that Melanie liked it rough.

The best thing right now was to focus on her job. Try to keep her mind off Emily. Putting Fuentes in prison for five-to-seven would satisfy her need for justice.

Besides, being in the office gave her an excuse to keep her ears open. Pick up any details about Victor's murder.

She worked on her opening statement, but her mind was far from the case. She prided herself on always knowing what to do and when to do it, but right now she was so lost and she had no one to turn to, no one to talk with.

What few friends Julia had over the years had all left the San Diego area. They barely kept in touch via e-mail. Matt, her brother, had truly been her best friend, and he was dead. Maybe that's why she'd thrown herself into her job, her career.

But when she needed someone, anyone, to talk to, there was no one.

She'd never felt so alone except the day Matt died and she'd lived. But for the grace of God, Emily would have perished with Matt.

"Where's Em?" Julia asked when she opened her door to Matt that stormy Saturday night.

"She begged me to drop her at the movie theater with Jayne." He stepped in and shrugged off his wet jacket. Julia hung it in the closet.

"You left two ten-year-olds alone at the theater?"

"I walked them in, and the movie lets out at nine thirty-five. I'll be back long before." He smiled, though it was a sad expression. She was about to ask her brother what was troubling him when he asked, "Do you have a minute?"

"Of course."

Matt followed Julia into the kitchen.

Julia poured her brother some tea from the pot she had just made for herself. "Have you given any more thought to what we talked about?"

He sighed. "I've thought of nothing else. I just don't know anything anymore, Jules."

"I just want you to be happy."

"Do you know how many of Emily's friends have divorced parents? All but one."

"So she'll be in good company."

He didn't laugh. "Crystal wasn't always like this."

Julia disagreed, but didn't say anything.

"Or was I just so blind I couldn't see?" He was trying to convince himself.

"I don't know, Matt. I guess she had her moments. And I really thought Crystal loved you." For about five minutes, thought Julia, but she didn't add that.

"She did. I just don't know what happened."

They sat in silence sipping tea. "You and Em could come live with me for a while. Until things settle down."

"I appreciate that. Em adores you."

"You know I love her."

"I have something for you to sign. Guardianship papers. If anything ever happens to me, I want you to be her guardian."

Julia's eyes welled. "Don't talk that way."

"Seriously. You love my daughter unconditionally. That's what kids need."

"Something we never had."

"We turned out okay."

She smiled. "Because of you." She squeezed her brother's hand. "Hey, let's put all this depressing stuff behind us and go meet Emily for that movie. When did it start?"

"Ten minutes ago."

"Let's go."

Not only did they miss the movie, but Matt died before the movie was over and Emily heard about it from the media as she waited in the lobby of the theater for her father to pick her up, wondering why he was late.

And it had been Julia's fault. After all, she'd been driving.

A knock on the door startled Julia out of her reverie. She glanced at her watch. Six-thirty? Where had the time gone? "Come in."

Her boss, Andrew Stanton, entered and closed the door. He sat down across from her desk. Most prosecutors in her position didn't have their own office, but Julia's conviction on a high-profile rape-murder last year had earned her the door.

"Why did you hire Connor Kincaid?"

She knew it was bound to come up. "I need to protect Emily's interests," she said cautiously.

"You did. You retained Iris Jones."

Since Stanton didn't ask a question, Julia didn't answer.

"Julia," he said, his voice soft, "I know this is hard on you, especially in your position, but you need to know I'm also looking out for Emily. You don't need to —"

She put up her hand. "Don't. I appreciate your help, but you can't possibly be on Emily's side. If the roles were reversed I would have the interests of *this office* to protect. Just like you."

Stanton remained silent for several moments, then said, "You're on the fast track, Julia. You know it as well as I do. You can have a judgeship inside of five years, or anything else you want. Don't blow it by playing cop. Don't blow it by trusting Connor. You know better than anyone what a loose cannon he is."

"Andrew, if you think that I care about my career more than my niece, then you'll never understand any decision I make."

"I only meant —"

"Connor may be a loose cannon, but he's also committed to the truth. I can keep him reined in." She didn't wholly believe it, but she would damn well try.

Stanton raised an eyebrow, his face stern.

She felt like she was a hostile witness. "Oh? You think you can control Connor Kincaid? Then why was he interviewing a witness? Spending time at the police station?"

"He's looking out for Emily."

"He's interfering with a police investigation."

"No, he's not." Julia stood her ground. "Emily needs an advocate, and not just a defense attorney telling her to keep her mouth shut. She needs someone working overtime to prove her innocence."

"The police —"

"Are damn good. Will Hooper and Jim Gage are the best. But the evidence is what it is. I know in my heart that Emily didn't murder Judge Montgomery. But my heart means nothing when faced with the damning circumstances."

Stanton stood. "I hope you know what you're doing."

"I do."

"Then you'll take this the way that it's intended. You're hereby on administrative leave."

"What? I have a trial in eleven days, I have six depositions next week and a discovery hearing in a first degree —"

"You follow your heart, Julia, and you'll pay the price. Hand everything off to Hannah Peterson —"

"No, let me —"

"Or you can resign."

For the first time Julia had an inkling of what Connor Kincaid had felt five years ago when she had given him almost the same ultimatum. Except hers had not really been an ultimatum. It was testify or go to prison. What choice was that?

"Let me pass everything to Frisco Lorenz. He's better with rape victims."

Stanton agreed. "All right. I'm sorry, Julia."

She didn't believe it for a minute.

Revenge, justice, payback all led to one thing: control.

It was the lack of control — Emily's inability to stay away from her lecherous stepfather, Billy Thompson's inability to prove he hadn't stolen the tests — that created the need for justice.

A woman is raped, she has no control. All the power is in her rapist. She gains control when she fights back. But the system doesn't always work. Sometimes bad guys go free. Sometimes they're never found.

Sometimes no one knows a crime has even been committed.

Vengeance was such a powerful motive

because no one questioned it. Righting wrongs was human nature. What human being feels sympathy for a child molester who is raped in prison? Who hasn't had the fantasy of killing a serial killer or assassinating an evil despot in a foreign land? Thousands of years ago, human beings lived and died by their instincts and a crude sense of right and wrong. There were no courts, no men to stand in the way and talk about *feelings* or *rights* or *abuse.* Because life had been lived on the ancient principle of an eye for an eye, a tooth for a tooth.

He would never be discovered, but even if he were, he would be the hero in the eyes of everyone who had lost control of their lives. For the abused, the defeated, the downtrodden — he would be their knight in shining armor, a martyr, a vigilante. Thousands would march in the streets demanding his release. Anarchy would ensue, and it would be his lone voice that controlled the masses. The powers would beg him to speak, to bring order to the disorder.

He sank into his chair, eyes closed, sipped his evening Chivas and relished the future.

But he abandoned his fantasy. He wouldn't be caught, the police would never learn of his role in this game of vengeance. Playing out other people's vendettas, like in

157

Patricia Highsmith's classic novel *Strangers on a Train,* gave him the distance necessary to watch, assess, and move forward.

Like chess, he had to think several steps ahead. If his opponent moved one way, discerning his purpose wasn't always obvious. A wise man looked at every possible move and chose the one that would give him the greatest future gain, even if it meant sacrificing a piece. It was his vision that made him a genius. He saw the game board as one unit, all possible solutions clearly laid out. If his opponent did X, he already had his response at the ready. If his opponent did Y, he had another plan prepared.

In life, chess was three-dimensional. You had more than one opponent, and what one opponent did affected what every other opponent did. Seeing all the players' moves was crucial, and like God, he was the only one in this game who knew every player. He knew why they made their choices, what motivated them, how to defeat them.

He was the chess master.

He reached for his cell phone and dialed Cami. Time to give her a bone and make her perform.

Time for the next move.

Eleven

Connor grabbed two beer bottles from Dillon's refrigerator, slammed them down on his kitchen table, and turned the chair around so he could sit in it backward.

"Some things never change," Dillon mumbled as he twisted the top off his beer and swallowed.

Connor was trying to bribe Dillon with pizza and beer, though he knew his brother really couldn't be bought for any amount of food or money. Dillon was as straight as they came, and Connor admired him greatly for his ethics, even when they ran counter to his own interests. This time, however, they were on the same side.

Based on the evidence they had, Dillon was working up a profile of the killers. He was determined to prove Emily wasn't involved, perhaps using the information Connor had gleaned from Billy Thompson.

"I wish I had access to the crime lab on

159

this one," Dillon said. "I'd like a copy of Victor Montgomery's autopsy report."

"I'll get it for you tomorrow."

"Don't."

"I'm not going to break into the coroner's office," Connor said. "I'll get it legitimately." More or less, he thought.

"We don't want Emily's defense to be compromised."

"It won't be. It's all information Jones will get in discovery anyway. You know as well as I do that the prosecution will hold on to everything until the last possible minute. Most of the time, I'm glad. But when Emily's being dragged into a murder investigation? Nope, we need every in we can get."

Dillon stared at a blank legal pad, pen in hand, a faraway expression on his face. He was entering his "killer mindset," trying to go deep into the thoughts of someone capable of such a vicious crime.

At first, Connor just enjoyed his beer. Every few minutes, Dillon would write several sentences, draw arrows and lines, and then pause. After thirty minutes, Connor grew antsy. He hated sitting still. He wanted — needed — to be out *doing* something. He'd seen Emily earlier that evening, but she'd been sleeping.

If he could just see Will's notes on the case, he might have another direction to go. Right now, he had to wait until morning to check out Emily's school and talk to her friends. But he was no longer a cop. And it's not like he could go down to the precinct and beg for his job back. Like that would happen. He didn't take orders very well. And he didn't like traitors.

Neither did his former colleagues. It's just that they viewed *him* as the traitor, not his dead ex-partner. *Don't upset the apple cart. Crutcher is gone, we'll just forget all this happened.*

But how could he forget when Crutcher had left two dead girls behind and others in the department willingly looked the other way?

No, Connor couldn't go back. If only he'd done things differently . . . but when you catch your mentor, the man who trained you to be a cop, taking bribes to turn the other cheek in the importation of sex slaves from Mexico, what do you do? Confront him and get a hole in the back of your head for the effort? Or go to the boss?

He'd done the latter, and he ended up without a badge.

But he was still breathing — that was some consolation.

"There had to be three people, one of whom was a female," Dillon said, finally breaking the silence.

Connor started to peel off his beer label, leaving pieces of wet paper on Dillon's table. "Makes sense. That's what Julia said Hooper told her last night."

"Three people," Dillon mumbled to himself. "You need one person — a female — to sexually excite the victim —"

Connor interrupted. "But he wouldn't have dropped his pants for just any woman who walked into his office. And a woman with a couple of guys? Do you think Judge Montgomery would get off with an audience?"

"Some do."

Connor rolled his eyes. "Okay, we have a female, on her knees, giving the judge a blow job. Maybe or maybe not two males watching."

"But they'd have to be nearby. And if they were watching, it could mean the judge was participating in some fun and games."

"After raping a kid, I suppose anything is possible." Connor ripped the rest of the label off in one pull.

"If they weren't watching, maybe he was having an affair and his mistress wanted him dead," conjectured Dillon.

"Why?"

"You're thinking too much like a cop, bro."

"I am a cop," Connor said, before correcting himself. "Was a cop."

"You were a great cop, Connor."

"Hmm."

Dillon looked as if he was going to say something else, but then his brother changed the subject. "It takes a certain type of person to set up a man to be murdered. And a certain type of person to commit a particularly violent, premeditated crime."

"It's payback. Santos."

Dillon thought about that for a long minute. "Emily denied anyone threatened her."

"Maybe Santos's men didn't even realize she was home. Or maybe Montgomery was dead before Emily came in."

Dillon pulled out a sheet of paper. "Julia said that Will told her the preliminary time of death was three-thirty to nine-thirty. The autopsy report would be more specific."

"Emily could still have arrived after he was dead. Patrick said Montgomery had an unsent e-mail on his computer that he began writing at three-forty."

"True, but it still puts the TOD about the same time she arrived home. Picture this:

Emily comes home with friends. They walk in and Montgomery calls out for her like he always does. She goes in, gives him what he wants. Her friends quietly get into position and she severs his organ. They hold him down while she puts the penis in his mouth."

Connor could picture the scenario all too well. "But she'd have a lot more blood on her, certainly more than a few drops on her hands and feet. Emily's explanation also rings true."

"I agree, but it could have happened either way. She had the motivation. And she bathed that night. She could have bathed after the murder."

"You met Emily," said Connor. "Do you really think she's capable of a mutilation murder?"

"A lot of people are capable of terrible murders without showing any outward signs of depravity."

"Dammit, Dillon, you're not helping."

"You're the investigator, Connor. Look at the scene logically. You can't come in with a faulty assumption that Emily is innocent."

"She's not guilty either. The man brutalized her. Raped and humiliated her —"

"And the prosecutor will probably offer a decent plea because of that."

"*If* she did it. What about this Wishlist group?"

"It throws a completely new dynamic into the mix. Premeditation. Group dynamics. I'm going to talk to Emily again tomorrow, ask her about the message and what, if anything, she did about it."

"We need to find out whether the police have tracked down the group, the organizer, any other messages that may have been associated with a solved, or unsolved, murder. The Judson homicide is still open," Connor said. "I think it's not a coincidence that Billy wrote that Judson needed his eyes checked, and a couple months later the guy is killed by two bullets in the head. And then Emily's message."

"Patrick already went out on a limb by giving you access to those messages." Dillon looked at the two messages Connor had taken. "These are relatively anonymous. Did any of the other messages you saw have identifying names?"

"Not that I could see, but I was speed reading."

Dillon shook his head. "Doesn't mean anything, really. If it's a small group of people, they could all go to the same school. Were Emily and Billy at the same school?"

"No. Emily goes to a private school in La

Jolla; Billy went to a public school in the heart of the city."

"No connection there."

"Bowen."

"Excuse me?"

"Billy said that he'd been required to take anger management classes from Bowen after he was arrested for vandalism."

Connor's mind started connecting dots. "What if," he continued slowly, "Bowen had group therapy sessions? Isn't that something that's done?"

"Yes."

"So they meet in person in this group therapy, and then start this online group where they push the envelope. Someone in the group knew about Emily's wish, and knew who she was and who she was talking about even if her identity wasn't revealed online."

"Are you suggesting a vigilante?"

Connor nodded as his theory took shape. "Exactly. It fits in with the case of Paul Judson, who was murdered and had his eyes shot out when another Wishlist member, who we know was Billy, said Judson needed his eyesight examined. The only connection between Billy and Emily is Dr. Garrett Bowen."

A knock at the door interrupted what Dillon was about to say. He got up to answer, and came back in with Julia Chandler.

Connor tensed. Every time he saw her, he became angry and conflicted. With himself, with her. Five years was a long time to hold a grudge, but it was his career — his *life* — she had destroyed.

"Hi, Connor." She nodded stiffly.

She was tired, dark circles beginning to emerge under her eyes. Julia's makeup had worn off during the day, making her skin translucent, pale. She was still a beautiful woman, particularly now that she'd dumped her too-conservative Ms. Deputy DA suit and put on a long flowing skirt and simple peasant blouse. Connor had never seen her out of her professional attire. He liked it.

Her hair was down, the waves of dark blond falling halfway down her back, held away from her face by a haphazardly placed clip.

"I'm sorry to interrupt, but I couldn't relax and . . . I knew you'd be working on Emily's case." She looked at Connor with an expression that said: *But I didn't know he was going to be here.*

"Your insight into Emily may be helpful," Dillon said. "She trusts you more than anyone. Sit down."

Julia impatiently wiped a stray tear and

sat in the chair between the two men. "So what have you come up with? Anything?"

Dillon nodded. "There was one ringleader. One person who made the decisions, who came up with the plan."

"Why do you think that?" Julia asked

"It's the psychology of group killers." Dillon rose from his seat, retrieved two beers for Connor and Julia, and poured himself orange juice. "When you have a killing pair, there is almost always a submissive. Someone who takes orders, does what they are told. Doesn't matter if the submissive is male or female — though in the overwhelming majority of killing pairs, the dominant partner is male."

Dillon poured Julia's beer into a chilled mug. "But when you get into group killings — and I think all the evidence points to three participants in the judge's murder — you have another influence. Some might call it 'mob mentality' or peer pressure. When two or more people get together to commit a crime, they're more prone to doing things they'd never consider doing on their own."

"Wasn't there a case out in Florida or Georgia about four teenage boys who killed a teacher at their school?"

Dillon nodded. "I read about that case. One of the kids was older, nineteen I believe, no longer a student. Two of the kids came from solid homes. There was no apparent motive. They went to the house of a music teacher and shot him dead."

"But wouldn't people like that already be predisposed to murder?" Julia asked.

Dillon tilted his head. "Perhaps. Or their leader could be so charismatic or threatening — or both — that they think they're doing the right thing. Consider cults. Most are relatively harmless, but Jim Jones convinced hundreds of people to kill themselves, most of whom probably would never have considered such an act without his influence."

"That would play into the Judson murder," Connor said.

"Judson?" Julia interjected, confused.

Connor explained what he learned from Billy Thompson about Wishlist and the e-mail from Emily.

"And you didn't tell me?" she asked, angry. "Isn't that what I'm paying you for? To keep me in the loop?"

"You're paying me to clear Emily. If you want more than that, go get it from your pal the DA."

"I would if I could," she snapped. "But I'm on administrative leave."

Both Connor and Dillon looked up, surprised. "What happened?" Dillon asked.

"I don't know. He didn't like that I hired Connor, and I don't think he liked that Iris brought you in before they could retain you." She gave him a wry smile. "We all like working with you on our big cases."

Dillon grinned. "Thanks. But Stanton's actions make sense, even without Connor or me working for the defense. The press are all over this case. He wants to separate his office from any impropriety."

"I had to turn over all my cases to another prosecutor."

Julia looked so forlorn that Connor found himself touching her arm. "I'm sorry."

She looked up at him, startled. Her lips parted and Connor stared, recalling the one incredible kiss they'd shared five years earlier. Would she taste just as delicious now as then?

He removed his hand. *Don't go there, Kincaid.*

"There are two theories that fit the evidence as we know it," Dillon said, thankfully interrupting what could have been an awkward moment. "First, that Emily planned the murder and had someone help her."

"No —" Julia interrupted but Dillon put his hand up.

"The second is that the killers are vigilantes."

"Vigilantes?" Julia asked, her brow furrowed.

"Possibly, though I'd go a step further." Dillon sat down and looked from Connor to Julia. "I think they're young. Teenagers or college age."

"They're damn smart criminals for teens," Connor said.

Dillon agreed. "These crimes are connected. In some way both victims had hurt a young person. A fellow teenager. The connection is the online group Emily and Billy were part of. Just like Emily's case, Billy Thompson is connected to Judson's murder, even though he didn't pull the trigger."

"Why can't we just subpoena the host company and find out who's involved?" Julia asked.

"We can't, but I'm sure the District Attorney's Office will," Dillon said. "I'm going to talk to Emily about the group and hopefully she'll give us information that we need, because we're not going to get it from the police department."

"I don't even know what kind of case they're building against Emily," Julia said. "But they still have a guard on her door, and it's not for protection. Iris is trying to get information, but it'll probably be easier for me. I have friends inside."

"If you can get the autopsy report and what they have that points to Emily, it might help in figuring out what's going on," Dillon said.

"I'll work on it tomorrow."

"Don't do anything illegal."

"I'll do anything I have to for Emily."

There was an awkward silence, and Connor finally said, "So Dil, what's the verdict on the killer? We were talking about a profile, something to go on."

Dillon looked at the closed file. Julia grew antsy the longer he remained silent. She glanced at Connor and found him looking at her. Staring at her, his dark eyes unreadable, his face hard and unyielding. But he didn't look away, he didn't have that edge of hatred she'd felt when she'd first talked to him this morning about helping Emily.

She turned away, picked up her mug, and drank. Still, his eyes were on her, his probing gaze unnerving. Anger and frustration, all rolled up in a tight, hard body.

Connor Kincaid might be a total jerk, but he was a damn sexy jerk. When they'd first met, she'd been a new deputy district attorney and had worked with him on a case that ended miserably. Two cops killed, one suspect dead, and one suspect beaten nearly to death. Connor resigned after testifying against the cop who took bribes, and two others had ended up facing prosecution for their crimes. It was a messy situation, but it wasn't the police department's responsibility to mete out justice. That was for the court system, the same system to which Julia had sworn allegiance.

But that case had disturbed Julia for a long time, and she'd quietly been pleased when the former district attorney had been forced from office in scandal and Andrew Stanton was elected to clean house three years ago.

She drank more beer and then caught herself biting her thumbnail. She put her hand down. Fidgeted.

Dammit, why was he looking at her so intently? What was he thinking? What were *they* thinking? Dillon Kincaid with his quiet, studious manner pondering the profile of a vicious murderer; Connor Kincaid, the younger brother, with his hard, dark eyes on her. Analyzing, probing, judging.

Five minutes later, Dillon spoke. It might as well have been five hours.

"The leader is the oldest and able to convince others of the rightness of what they're doing. Completely in control, focused, methodical. A planner. Thinks about the details. Thinks ahead. Does not fear being caught. Might even enjoy the limelight of being caught. Enjoys irony. Plays on people's emotions and is able to turn emotions on and off at will. Has little empathy for others."

"You said he's a teenager or young adult," Connor said. "Are you thinking college student? Maybe underachiever — smart but not living up to his potential?"

"I never said 'he.' "

"A teenage *girl?*" Julia asked in disbelief. "Andrew Stanton is not going to buy that."

"I don't know if I buy it," Connor said. "You said yourself that the leaders in killing pairs are men."

Dillon countered, "The leader could be male or female. Either way, this person was abused as a child by a male authority figure. It may or may not have been sexual abuse. Penile amputation — even if they were going off Emily's fantasy of killing her stepfather — is still a sexual and incredibly personal crime. It would be difficult to accomplish such a gruesome murder without additional motivation."

"But the other crime — Judson's shooting — wasn't sexual."

"The eyes — it was Billy Thompson who

174

said that Judson needed to get his eyes checked. But why did that draw out the killer or killers?"

"Maybe because the victim was easy to identify. Billy Thompson gave a personal connection to the victim, called him Jackass Judson, that maybe the other e-mails didn't do."

"Made it easy for them," Julia said.

"We need to learn more about this group," Dillon continued. "That's the key. And I don't think Dr. Bowen's involvement is a coincidence. I'm going to play a little give-and-take with Patrick and see if I can get any other information if we give up what we know. Patrick needs to dig deeper online. I can almost guarantee that they have more than two murders under their belt."

"You said the killers were young. Bowen must be in his forties," Julia said.

"The leader himself may be young or not, but it's definitely someone older than the others and in complete control. The killers themselves are under thirty. The leader's the key. Without him — or her — these murders would never have happened."

"Going through all the unsolved cases in the county will take hundreds of hours of manpower," Connor said.

"I'm going to write up an informal profile

for Chief Causey to give them a direction, but I don't know if they'll use it, considering they don't have me on their team."

"They'd be foolish not to," Julia said, "but is this going to jeopardize Emily?"

Dillon shook his head. "The police need to look at every angle, and I'm sure that they will. But there are only a handful of psychiatrists who consult with the police department, myself and Bowen are among them. They need to know that they have to stay away from Bowen. I talked to him today. I didn't like what he had to say."

"How far back in the files do we need to look for similar crimes?" Connor asked.

"Eighteen months. Two years, to be on the safe side. They have a taste for killing, so they're going to continue. They see themselves as meting out justice. Vengeance. They may have started with people identified on Wishlist, but they'll find their victims in the newspaper, anywhere. They've gotten away with at least two murders; they feel invincible."

"What else? Two years of unsolved crimes? That's a lot of man-hours."

"Look at unsolved violent crimes. Stabbings, shootings. Male victims. All ages."

"I'll do it. I have the time and I'm still a member of the bar, so I have access," Julia said. "I'm on leave, remember?"

Connor caught her eye and for the first time Julia felt something like protection from his gaze. "Don't do anything stupid, Julia. If this gets hairy, let me handle it."

Spoken like a true Neanderthal. Why had Julia even thought for one minute that Connor had changed?

"Come in, Cami."

His dark eyes pierced her, held hers, drew her toward him like a bitch to her master. Her breath hitched as she glided over to him. He took her hand, kissed it. So elegant, so refined.

"Tell me everything. Again."

She crawled into his lap and he stroked her hair. "Everything went exactly according to the plan."

"I want details. Leave nothing out."

"You were right about the judge."

"I'm always right, Cami."

"He protested at first, but not for long."

"Sex addicts never do."

"I turned his chair around so his back was to the door. I showed him my tits, and then I had him completely."

"You have beautiful breasts, Cami." He stroked them softly, then squeezed her nipples hard. Twisted them. It hurt but she pushed her breasts into his hand.

Pain meant she was alive.

"I got down on my knees and took out his cock. Sucked him long and hard. The others came in quietly. I slowly moved the chair into position and as he was about to come in my mouth, I pulled back and Faye cut off his erection."

"How did she do?"

"She didn't hesitate. Just one hard snap. The shears were really sharp."

"You did good recruiting her." He ran his hand up her skirt. She wasn't wearing panties, as he ordered. She spread her legs to allow access. His fingers played with her and she grew hot.

"Who put his penis down his throat?"

"I did."

"How did it feel?"

"Powerful. He was screaming when Faye cut it off. Blood shot everywhere."

"You changed shoes like I told you?"

"Yes. We threw everything in garbage bags, got out fast. Just like you said. We all wore gloves. I didn't touch anything until . . . after. We wiped down to be sure."

"You're not in the system."

"No, but Faye —"

"She won't talk if she gets caught, would she?"

Cami shook her head, enjoying his talented fingers, the line between pleasure and pain, the sensations that poured through her body, making colors brighter and sounds sharper. "Faye would never talk." Her breath was rushed, rapid.

"Do we have a problem with Robbie?"

"No."

He withdrew his hand.

"Please," she begged.

"Tell the truth, Cami."

"I don't know. He was high today."

"Take care of him."

"I told Faye if he used again she would have to take care of him."

A long silence. Then his hand returned between her legs. He shoved three fingers up her vagina while his thumb probed her anus and then he pinched hard. Her vision faded as the pain took over, every cell in her body alive and on fire.

"Good, Cami. Very good."

"Thank. You." Her breath was rushed as she spiraled higher, higher. Thoughts faded, all that mattered was being here, feeling the pain and pleasure, the need, the heat. She was not dead inside, no longer a hollow shell to be looked at, admired, envied. She was *real,* the pain proved it.

"The final execution will be Saturday. Are

you ready?"

"*Yesssss,*" she whispered.

He murmured in her ear.

"Release yourself to me."

After Cami left, he tidied up his office. He was hard as a rock, but didn't dare give himself over to Cami. He knew what drove her, what motivated her. She worshipped him, admired him, and he needed that to continue to control her.

He gave her the pain she craved, but not sex. Not with him. He could give her nothing of him. She manipulated everyone around her, everyone but him. Whether she thought she could was another matter, but he'd leave her to the boys and her fantasies. He gave her what she wanted and she always came back. He gave her lust and held back with the anticipation of more. Later, in the future, but that future would never come. He'd never fuck her. The thought sickened him.

Her desire for pain would be the death of Cami, but not by his hand. Not yet at any rate. He needed her. The victory and passion he saw in her bright eyes when she recalled her part in Victor Montgomery's execution, that was the highlight of a successful operation.

Cami enjoyed it for the control, the power, the thrill.

He enjoyed it for different reasons, but for one. It was on his orders, his command, who would live and who would die. The thrill of the hunt, of marking the sinners, elated him, kept him focused. He would fix the world one death at a time.

He couldn't fuck Cami, but he knew who would be waiting for him.

Faye Kessler had given him what he needed before, and he knew she hadn't told Cami. Cami was a jealous, arrogant girl, she wouldn't sit calmly on the sidelines if she knew he put his dick in Faye's cunt when he wouldn't do the same to her, no matter how much she asked or how much she was willing to do for him.

A woman with a closed mouth was a rarity, but one he would keep as long as it served him. Faye kept her mouth shut tight. He loved her for it . . . and for other reasons. There were things he could share with only her, because only she understood.

For a time, he'd worried about his attachment to Faye. After they were together, he was surprised to find himself missing her when they were apart. Her soulful eyes, her touch, her quiet understanding — he craved it. He didn't mind wanting her, but he

181

feared needing her.

These were thoughts for a later time. The game was still working perfectly, and he still had Cami and Faye completely under his thumb.

His girls would do anything for him. *Everything* for him.

And he didn't have to bloody his hands in the process.

In less than forty-eight hours, the hammer would come crashing down on the one who had wronged him. He was truly a god.

TWELVE

Julia was drunk.

If she hadn't been leaning so heavily against him on the way out of Dillon's house, Connor wouldn't have believed anyone could get drunk on three beers.

"You'll make sure she gets home safely and unmolested?" Dillon asked, raising his eyebrows.

"Very funny," said Connor. "I don't even like her. I'm not going to take advantage of her."

"I knew you didn't like me." Julia pouted.

"Like that's a big revelation," Connor muttered.

"And I'm *not* drunk." She hiccupped. "I just haven't eaten."

"Since when?" he asked as he slid her into the passenger seat of his truck. He and Dillon had eaten all the pizza he brought before Julia showed up.

"I don't know." She hiccupped again.

"Yesterday, I think."

"Great." He slammed the passenger door shut. Now it made sense. Three beers, empty stomach. And now the counselor was his responsibility.

He should have asked Dillon to take her home.

He started up the engine of his truck. He lived only a few blocks from Dillon, but he wasn't taking Julia to his house.

He glanced at the counselor. Her eyes were closed, but she wasn't sleeping.

"Tell me the truth, Connor," Julia said quietly, not opening her eyes. "Do you think Emily is guilty? Do you think she helped kill Victor?"

How could he answer that? He'd been a cop, cops looked not only at the evidence but used their experience and instincts to figure out who was lying and who was telling the truth. Leave the facts to scientists like Jim Gage; the truth was cops bartered lesser evils. So did prosecutors. That's why the two professions were usually tight. They needed each other. A prosecutor may have a solid case, but they might turn free a drug addict in exchange for testimony to nail the coffin shut on a killer.

"You do," she said when he didn't answer right away. "Take me home."

"You need to eat."

"I have food. I think."

"Julia, I don't think Emily did it, but you need to face the fact that she may have played some role in the murder."

A sob escaped her chest. *Don't cry. Dammit, Julia, don't cry. I can't handle tears.*

But she didn't cry. Instead she said, "The last thing my brother said to me before he died was 'Take care of Emily.' I didn't protect her, and she ended up being raped, running away from home, and possibly involved with a murder. I failed in the only thing I ever cared about: living up to my promise to Matt."

Connor glanced over at Julia when he stopped at a light. He instantly regretted it. She was looking at him, her face a mask of torment, her eyes dry but full of pain. "Matt gave me the world. He gave me *freedom* to do what I wanted to do with my life. He became the perfect son so I wouldn't have to be the perfect daughter. All he wanted, all he ever asked of me, was to take care of his daughter. And now . . ." She turned her head, looked out the window. "Emily is already going to pay the price of my incompetence for the rest of her life."

"That's alcohol talking," Connor admonished.

"It's the truth."

Connor drove over to La Honda, a restaurant owned and operated by his mother's best friend, Felicia, another escapee from Cuba. Though crowded, it helped being family friends. They were seated immediately.

Felicia, a small round woman, came over, hugged Connor, and smiled wide. "The usual?"

"Absolutely."

"You've never brought a lady friend in before." She beamed at Julia.

"We're not friends," Connor and Julia said simultaneously.

Felicia's smile only widened as she left to fill their order, coming back immediately with two beers, chips, and salsa.

"It's hot," Connor warned.

"I love salsa," Julia said, scooping a huge chunk onto a chip and popping it into her mouth.

Connor covered his mouth to keep from laughing out loud. As the heat from the habanero peppers reached Julia's sinuses, her eyes watered, her nose began to run, and he could almost see sweat form on her brow. He had to give her credit for chewing and swallowing, before draining her water glass, and then his.

"I warned you," he said.

"Next time, I'll listen."

They ate in silence, and Connor was surprised when the tension dissipated. Julia cleaned her plate, drank another beer, and lost the ghostly pallor she'd had since arriving at Dillon's earlier in the evening.

They stared at each other in silence. Connor asked softly, "What happened with your brother? I heard he died in a car accident."

She nodded, picked up her beer, and took a long swallow.

"Were you there?"

She nodded.

"And?"

Julia's face contorted in pain and anger. "I was driving the car." Softer, "I killed him."

"You didn't kill him."

"I know that road like the back of my hand. Every bend and turn. It was my car, my road, and —"

Connor regretted bringing it up, but he couldn't stop now. He didn't *have* to know the truth; he *wanted* to know.

"It was raining and I skidded. Crashed into a tree." Her voice was quiet, matter-of-fact, as if she were a witness on the stand. "I swerved, acting on instinct — self-preservation — and turned the car. The passenger side slammed into the tree trunk. We were going about forty. Matt —" her voice hitched, she took a deep breath, then said, "Matt was crushed. He died there, before the paramedics came. Before anyone came."

Connor took her hand. It was soft yet firm, feminine yet strong. "It was an accident."

Julia couldn't believe she was telling Connor Kincaid, of all people, about the night Matt died. Her chest tightened — is this what a heart attack feels like? The pain was real, hot, twisting and climbing, taking over.

"He was my best friend," she said quietly, not able to look at Connor. "My only friend."

And it was true. She'd distanced herself from her family; and by doing that, she had also separated herself from the friends she'd grown up with. If she could call any of the wealthy families her parents allowed her to associate with her *friends*. Matt was her only true friend, her brother, her mentor, her savior in so many ways. When he was gone, she had only her work. And Emily.

"I'm sorry about your brother, but it was an accident."

"So?"

"You weren't drinking — if you were, you'd have been disbarred and probably imprisoned. It was raining, but I'll bet if I went up to that road the posted speed limit would have been forty."

Julia stared at Connor. She remembered five years ago when he was a hot-tempered cop stuck in the middle of an internal investigation he wanted no part of. He was still hot-blooded, but age — and experience — had calmed him.

Or had it? What did she really know about Connor Kincaid's life since she told him his choice was testify or prison?

And for the first time in the last five years she wondered if she had made the right decision.

Connor had gone against orders and involved himself in the takedown of crooked cops he was ordered to stay away from. Not only that, but he broke more laws than Julia could count on both hands.

Laws must be upheld. They had to mean something. If they could be disregarded at any time, whatever the reason, wasn't that the first step toward anarchy? The law grounded Julia, gave her strength and purpose. But Connor Kincaid was a good man, and maybe she should have looked more into giving him a second chance than laying down the rule of law and lecturing him on right and wrong.

Julia had broken no laws when Matt was killed, but she harbored more guilt than most criminals. She didn't understand why her niece didn't confide in her about the rape, but she did understand why Emily didn't turn Victor in.

And for the first time, she began to understand the rocks Connor Kincaid had been wedged between when he broke the law for justice.

She was on the other side of the door. Connor hoped she wasn't naked, that she had the sense to sleep in her clothes.

He had locked his door. Not that Julia Chandler would step foot into his bedroom, but it would make him pause long enough to unlock his door and think about what he would be doing if he touched her. Stop long enough to remember.

He still couldn't believe he'd brought her into his house. He never brought women home. Of course, Julia wasn't really "a woman," someone he was dating or thinking of dating or sleeping with or thinking of sleeping with, or any other foolish thing like that. She was a district attorney and she'd hired him.

Yep, keep the facts firmly planted in mind. Don't think about her long legs or big eyes or silky hair or the way her head fell against his shoulder when she drifted off to sleep in the truck. Don't think about those lips and how much he wanted to kiss them. Don't think about Julia naked and underneath his body asking him to make love to her.

Damn, he needed a shower. Cold.

Remember that she forced you to give up everything you believed in, everything you ever wanted to be.

How could he forget? She'd manipulated him into an internal affairs investigation he wanted no part of. He wasn't going to turn on his own. He'd wanted to handle it his own way.

Two dead girls sealed his fate.

In the heat of the summer, Connor Kincaid had gone out on a call. He'd just taken his detective exam and was awaiting results, hoping to land in the gang resistance detail. He had hope for some of these kids. Not all of them, not most of them, but a few of them. That was all he needed. They were the consummate underdogs, kids whose fathers were dead or in prison and whose mothers worked two jobs or did drugs or plain didn't care. Many of these kids were in foster care, a system so broke that it would have to be destroyed completely before it could be rebuilt. Connor learned early on that he had a knack for working with these kids. But for now he was a street cop, one of the best.

The call came from the San Diego Mission de Alcalá, the first mission in the California chain and an active Catholic parish and tourist attraction. But it was now five in the morning and he was coming off graveyard shift, first responder to the tragedy.

The dead girls were huddled together in a pew in a small chapel off the main church. They'd broken into the church instead of going to the hospital or to the resident pastor who lived in a small bungalow on the far side of the Mission. One look and Connor knew why they hadn't sought medical care for their extensive injuries. They were illegals. They didn't want to be sent home.

The young priest had a long face, made more homely and sad when looking at the girls. "This isn't the first time."

"Excuse me, Padre?"

"The young girls — they bring them over the border every day to sell their bodies for a chance at freedom. When they don't perform, they are killed. Disposed of like garbage." He looked at Connor, imploring him with eyes so blue they seemed heavenly even surrounded by death. "But you know of this, don't you?"

"Me? I have nothing to do with this. I agree it's —"

The priest shook his head. "Your kind. The police. If you look where you don't want to look, you'll see the truth." Again, the priest stared at him and Connor, not a particularly religious man, felt for the first time that maybe someone with more authority than the priest was speaking to him.

"People believe what they want to believe. They see no evil because they don't want to. But evil is out there, and this is the result." The holy man gestured to the dead girls. "You might not see the evil, Officer Kincaid, but you can see its handiwork right here."

Quietly, Connor kept tabs on the investigation of the girls' deaths. Almost immediately they were put in the cold case file. Two illegal Jane Does. No one cared.

Connor couldn't stop thinking that but for his birth in the land of opportunity, he and his brothers and sisters would be fighting to come to America. Or dying under Castro's brutal regime like nearly everyone on his maternal family tree.

The dead girls were only fourteen. Beaten to death on the grounds of a sacred place, crawling inside to die in front of Jesus, the only sanctuary they had.

Then he learned that his mentor, Detective Wayne Crutcher, who had helped him with his exam and smoothed Connor's path into his move from street cop to detective, had been taking bribes to look away.

Connor didn't want to believe it.

"Who was that guy?" he asked Wayne. He'd been quietly following him for weeks, compiling evidence he didn't know yet how he was going to use. But he saw the exchange. He couldn't lie to himself anymore.

Wayne had been surprised to see Connor, though he hid it well. "A snitch."

"We pay snitches. They don't pay us."

As he said it, Connor realized he'd signed his death warrant. But he didn't budge.

He pictured his little sister Lucy's face superimposed on the dead girls. The dead girls deserved justice as much as anyone.

Wayne's face hardened. "Walk away, Kincaid."

Connor still didn't know exactly what it was that set him off. If it was the hard smirk on Wayne's face or the indifference in his bleak eyes. Connor struck him across the face. Once, twice, three times before the detective punched back.

The fight brought down Internal Affairs.

Both Connor and Wayne clammed up and called in their union representatives. Connor's direct supervisor, Lieutenant Todd, came to Connor at his house. "Crutcher has been transferred to the Northeast substation. He won't be a problem anymore."

"Transferred? That doesn't solve the problem."

"What do you suggest I do? Go to Internal Affairs and have them up my ass and yours? I've fixed the problem."

In the end, Connor couldn't walk away, even if he wanted to. Internal Affairs came to him. He turned over the documentation he'd compiled, thinking it would end there.

It didn't.

Connor was no longer a cop because of Julia. And yet the sexy counselor slept on the other side of his door, and he stood here with a semi-hard-on and thoughts of taking her into his bed playing with his mind.

For the second time in as many days he took a cold shower.

The stainless-steel blade had been sharpened to its maximum, the long straight edge curving slightly toward the deadly point. The shiny blade reflected the moonlight that filtered through the long, narrow windows of the Spanish-style mansion she'd lived in since her mother deserted her ten years ago.

Faye's father wasn't home, not that it would matter if he were — Blaine Kessler had virtually ignored her since her birth. *He* had come to her six times without a thought to being caught. Meanwhile, her father was usually in his own room with his own woman.

The one who came to see her was an angel. It wouldn't surprise Faye if no one could see him but her, because she was the one he'd chosen.

"Why aren't you with Cami?" she'd asked the second time he came to her house and made love to her under her father's roof. The night Skip had shot the teacher in the eyes and she had watched.

"Why would you ask that?" His fingers skimmed her breasts, her stomach, her thighs.

"She's beautiful." Her words came out a croak. The truth was ugly, like she was. Men wanted Cami because she was beautiful and sexy.

"Cami is selfish," he said. "Her own pleasure is more important than mine."

"I can't believe that."

"You think I'm lying?"

Faye shook her head.

He kissed her. That night, like tonight, had a near full moon. "You are precious to me. Cami is important, but you are my rock. I trust you. You would never betray me."

"Never."

"That's why no one can know about this."

"I understand."

"Even Cami."

"I didn't tell her last time."

"I know." He kissed her, touched her gently. "Do you trust me?"

Her lip trembled. "Yes."

He picked up her knife. "I trust you." He handed her the blade. She stared at it, blinded by the power of the steel. One slice and he'd be gone, she'd be gone. "Cut me," he whispered, his hot breath against her face.

He rolled over to his back, his arms outstretched. She straddled his naked body, slid onto him, gasping at the invasion within her. She lowered her hand, the hand wrapped tight around the blade's pearl handle. Showed him the knife, just as he told her the first time. He licked his lips, closed his eyes.

"Now."

She sliced his skin, a mere sliver, but the

pain of the sudden piercing made him gasp, tremble, and grow harder within her. The sight of the blood, dark in the moonlight, excited her and she rubbed her chest against his, his blood on her, the thrill that he trusted her with his life, that one slice too deep and he would be gone, his blood on her hands, in her body, staining her soul.

They rose together, peaked, and as he toppled over the edge she cut him once more and tasted his coppery heat.

Every time it was deeper, harder, rougher. The pain of the first night was nothing compared to today. When would it stop? Faye didn't want it to. But tonight he'd lost blood and slept in her bed, something he'd never done before. She had him all to herself and she lay awake and stared at him through the night. She touched his hair. He was real. When he woke, she apologized, she hadn't meant to go too far, they'd gotten carried away.

"It was heaven, my darling," he said. "I'm fine. Better than fine. You make me alive."

Faye had never felt alive. She stared at the blade. Just once. One more time . . .

Gently, carefully, she sliced her arm and watched, enchanted, as blood seeped out and dripped onto her sheets.

THIRTEEN

Julia sat up abruptly, disoriented. She wasn't in her own room. She wasn't in her house. Her head was thick with sleep and a dull fog. How many beers had she had last night?

She looked around, fearful she'd done something really stupid. Like sleep with Connor Kincaid. Alcohol stripped away inhibitions, and he'd been kind to her. She'd confided in him things she hadn't been able to share with anyone else.

And he was really, really nice to look at.

"Dumb," she mumbled. She'd handed Connor Kincaid ammunition to use against her down the road. Why did she feel she could trust him? He'd made no secret what he thought of her.

But he'd actually been *nice* last night.

She glanced around the living room. It didn't look like she'd done anything stupid. And she remembered the night before, talking with Dillon about Emily's case, eating Mexican food with Connor, him driving her home — but she wasn't home.

She'd fallen asleep in his truck. When he woke her up, she'd looked at his porch and said, "This isn't my house."

"I know. I asked, but you fell asleep. Where do you live?"

"La Jolla."

"That's thirty minutes from here. And I'm beat."

"Take me to my car," she said.

"You're too tired to drive."

"I have my second wind."

"Don't be ridiculous. Come inside, I won't bite."

He'd unfolded the couch and it became a bed. He tossed her a blanket and said, "Sleep tight." Then he went to his own room and shut the door.

She thought she wouldn't be able to sleep, but she was wrong. She'd slept surprisingly well, dreams of Connor infiltrating her thoughts. Betrayed by her subconscious.

"He's too sexy for his own good and you haven't had a man in —" How long? *Years?* "— a long time."

"Are you talking to me, Counselor?"

She jumped when Connor came out of the kitchen. His collar-length black hair was wet and slicked back, his face clean-shaven, and the smell of soap and a mild cologne wafted out to her. Had she spoken aloud? No. *Maybe.*

"Just thinking," she mumbled.

"You think loudly. Coffee's ready, then I'll take you to your car."

"Um, thanks," she mumbled, but didn't move.

"I don't do breakfast in bed," he said. "Unless I'm the one being served." He winked and crossed his arms.

She glared at him. All niceties from the night before went right out the window. Fine, if that's how he wanted it. She slid out from between the sheets and stood, hand on her bare hip. Her panties barely covered her, and she'd been told her legs were her best feature. She crossed the room to where she'd tossed her skirt the night before, Connor's eyes heating her back and everything below her waist. She blushed, but she wasn't going to give him the satisfaction of knowing his perusal had gotten to her. She stepped into her skirt, pulled it over her rear, zipped up the side.

She whirled around and was about to give him a lecture on manners when she closed her mouth. The raw sexuality and desire on Connor's face startled her. This predicament was certainly unplanned. She swallowed as his gaze moved up her body to her face.

Then he turned around and went back into the kitchen.

He was attracted to her, no doubt about it. But physical and emotional attraction were two completely different animals. They'd had a past, a brief past, but too much had happened since. He would never truly forgive what she'd done, and she couldn't be sorry for it. She was sorry he'd lost his career, but not that a bad cop had been stopped and the death of two girls avenged. Connor's career was collateral damage.

Ten minutes and a cup of coffee later, Connor took her to her car. "What are your plans today?" he asked, his first words since seeing her half-naked.

"First to my office to see if I can sweet-talk Frisco into getting me a copy of Victor's autopsy report. I gave him a huge case when Stanton put me on leave; he owes me one."

"Frisco?" Connor asked.

"He's a DDA, like me." Did Connor sound jealous? No. Her imagination. "Then to the courthouse. I'm going to pull all of Victor's recent cases and Garrett Bowen's court filings. It'll take all day, but it needs to be done. Especially if I can make any other connections to Billy Thompson or Emily." It sounded like a long shot.

"Dillon wants to see the files as well. Meet me at his house tonight."

It sounded like an order and Julia cringed. "And you?"

"I'm going to talk to Emily about her friends, then head over to her school."

"Maybe I should do that," she said.

"You know the court system better than I do," Connor countered. "It would take me weeks to pull those files. And Emily and I have a rapport. I promise I'll go easy on her."

Connor met Dillon at the hospital. "How did Emily do last night?" he asked.

"Very well. Aside from being underweight, she's healthy. Dr. Browne wants to discharge her, and I stalled. I don't know how long I can keep her here — Browne wants to move her to the criminal psychiatric wing downtown."

"You can't —"

Dillon interrupted Connor's admonition. "Of course not. She's here for at least thirty-six more hours. Hooper was here thirty minutes ago wanting to interview her, but I said she wasn't mentally ready. I can't put him off indefinitely."

Connor looked through the window. Emily was sitting up in bed, looking out the lone, barred window. She looked so much like Julia they could be mother and daughter.

"Let's get some answers about Wishlist," Connor said.

They walked into her room and Emily gave them a half smile.

"Good morning, Emily," Dillon said. "I brought an old friend with me."

Emily's pale face lit up when she saw Connor, then her eyes clouded. "Hi," she said sheepishly.

"How're you doing, kid?" He sat at the end of the bed. "Holding up okay?"

She sat up and touched his hand. Tears welled in her eyes and Connor hoped she wouldn't cry. He didn't handle female tears well at all. "Do you know . . . everything?"

He nodded, squeezed her hand. "Why didn't you come to me? I would have done anything to help you. So would your aunt."

Emily's bottom lip trembled. "I know. I just . . ." She didn't look at him or Dillon. "I just couldn't."

"She loves you, Em," Connor said softly, not wanting to push the kid too hard.

"I just wanted to be strong with her. She's

so smart and beautiful and perfect. I felt, oh, I don't know. Tainted."

Dillon sat on the chair next to the bed. "I told you yesterday that nothing Victor did to you was your fault. You were attacked. No one blames you, except yourself. You need to stop thinking this was your fault."

"I know, but —" She stopped, took a deep breath. "Anyway," she changed the subject, "you're here for something. What?"

Connor said, "We found an e-mail you wrote a couple months ago to a group called Wishlist. In it you described how you wanted to kill the person who hurt you the most. Your stepfather was killed in the same manner. Is that what you meant yesterday when you said you planned it?"

She nodded. "I never meant for it to happen. It was supposed to be just an exercise to get rid of the anger. And then . . . I saw." She closed her eyes and lay back on the bed. "I saw it all. I touched his blood. I was so drunk I didn't know what I was doing."

"You didn't kill him," Dillon said.

"No!"

"And you didn't plan it."

"No, but —"

"You didn't really *mean* for it to happen. Someone asked how you would get back at the person who hurt you the most."

She nodded. "Right, but isn't it my fault anyway?"

"No, it's not." Dillon made her look at him. "Emily, we need to know everything about Wishlist."

She frowned. "Like what?"

"How did you join the group?"

"Dr. Bowen recommended it. It's an anonymous listserv where we can talk about things that happened to us and what makes us angry and how we feel about it. At first, it sort of helped."

"But?"

"I don't know. It started getting weird. I don't know why I wrote that about Victor. I might have been wasted. I remember that day, though. Victor made me, you know, do that to him, and I felt sick and disgusted with him and me and my mother. But I couldn't tell Dr. Bowen — he tries to be all understanding, but it's an act. I'm a specimen to him, you know, like a bug under a microscope." She looked at Dillon, gave him a half-smile. "I know you're a shrink, but you don't make me feel like that."

"I'm glad."

She didn't say anything for a minute. "That day . . . I just lost it, totally. I was in the garage, thinking how to destroy his precious car. I picked up a wrench and came *this* close to smashing his headlights. Then everything cleared. He *wanted* me to react. He was pushing me to do something stupid again. Everything he said that humiliated me, the things he made me do, the way he made me feel, it was all to get me to be stupid so he could get control of my money. I realized then how truly evil he was, about how I'd love for him to be dead. I wrote that e-mail out of anger, and I think Victor was surprised that I didn't act out. It empowered me and I realized it wasn't that long before I would get my trust fund and could leave. I'll be eighteen the day before I graduate from high school. Thirteen months. And the day I graduate I'm flying to Europe with all my money and never setting foot in that house again."

She crossed her arms, cheeks flushed, eyes bright with determination, her inner fortitude revealing itself. She looked more like Julia now than before.

Connor asked, "Did you ever reveal your identity to the Wishlist group?"

She vigorously shook her head. "Never."

"Sometimes," Connor continued, "you reveal yourself in small ways. Not your name or address or school, but maybe some of your history. For example, vandalizing the courthouse. If you mentioned that in the group, someone might have figured out who you were."

"Are you saying that someone in my group killed Victor?"

"We don't know," he quickly said, "and you shouldn't talk about it. We're looking into everything right now."

"Are you a cop again?"

"No. Your aunt hired me."

"Jules?" Her eyes widened. "She must be worried."

"She's tough," Connor said. "She wants to make sure you're protected."

"She thinks I'm guilty," Emily said softly.

"No, she doesn't."

"Then why hire a lawyer for me?"

"To protect your rights."

Emily looked at Dillon. "Isn't that why you're here?"

"Yes," Dillon said, "but I'm not an attorney. Julia hired Ms. Jones because she wants to make sure no one can hurt you. Trust me on this. She doesn't think you had anything to do with Victor's murder."

"How can she not? I had everything to do with it. I'm the one who wrote the e-mail in the first place. I set things in motion." She looked from Dillon to Connor and said defiantly, "But I'm not upset he's dead."

"Emily, this is important. Has anyone

from Wishlist tried to meet with you in person? Either at your house or a public place?"

"No, never."

"You said Dr. Bowen put you in contact with this group. How?"

"He gave me an e-mail address and a code word."

"Do you remember the code word?"

"A Bible verse. Isaiah 35:4. I remember because he said I had to put in the colon for it to work. I wasn't going to because I really didn't want him knowing things about me, but he promised it was completely anonymous and he'd never bring it up in our sessions, that he didn't know who most of the people on the loop were and he wasn't the only shrink who referred people to the group."

Connor touched Emily's cheek. "You're strong, kid. We're going to get through this, okay?"

"What's going to happen to me? Am I going to be arrested?"

"We're doing everything we can to make sure that doesn't happen."

Dillon and Connor left Emily's room and Connor said, "I'll bet they have a Bible somewhere in the hospital. The verse might mean something."

Dillon shook his head. "Twelve years of Catholic school and you don't know the verse?"

"In one ear." Connor shrugged.

Dillon quoted, *"Say to those with fearful hearts, 'Be strong, do not fear; your God will come, he will come with vengeance; with divine retribution he will come to save you.'"*

Faye didn't mind playing hooky from school because she was always bored in class. Though she and Skip went to the same school — Robbie attended a different private school in downtown San Diego — they drove separately to the La Jolla beach. Cami was already there, but they had to wait for Robbie.

"He'd better be clean," Cami warned.

"He is," Skip said. "He has a twenty-minute drive. Give him a break."

Robbie was late but sober, and Cami went through the plan meticulously. Her excitement surprised Faye. She hadn't been nearly as excited about the previous murders. But Faye wasn't as sure about this one.

The victim was too close to home.

"Skip, you have the gun, right?"

"Check."

"Loaded?"

He looked at Cami, his mouth tight with

anger. "I'm not stupid, Cami. Don't treat me like an idiot."

"That's not what I —"

"Right." Skip rolled his eyes.

Faye interjected. "We can't start arguing. This is serious."

"Exactly," Cami said, crossing her arms over her ample chest. "This is the pinnacle of the plan. Once we execute it, we'll be truly free of him. It's perfect."

"No plan is perfect," Robbie said, speaking up for the first time.

"You're not using again, are you?" Cami asked, an undercurrent of anger in her tone.

"Not now."

"You have to stay clean. At least through tomorrow night. I can't have you screw this up."

"I won't." He glared at Cami. "I have it under control."

"You'd better." She turned away, but Faye didn't miss the anger in Skip's eyes. All directed at Cami. She feared he knew what she and Cami had discussed yesterday. At least Cami's part of the conversation.

She took Robbie's hand. She didn't want to kill him. She *really* didn't want to kill him. "It's okay," she said softly. "I'll handle Cami."

He softened a bit. "She's a bitch," he muttered under his breath.

Robbie didn't understand Cami like Faye did, but that was okay. Faye knew how to control her friend, that was all that mattered.

"There'll be a lot of security, so we ditch the gun."

"Why?"

"You don't want to be caught with it," Cami said as if Robbie was an idiot. "It's part of the plan."

"I still don't think it's a good idea to connect the judge's death with this," Skip said.

"It's a perfect idea. The police will never know what's happening. It's our *swan song,* as they say. And if anything goes wrong, you know the escape plan."

"It's risky."

"That's the thrill!" Cami stood and paced, kicking sand up with her bare feet. "If I can't trust you guys, I'll do it myself!"

Faye got up and touched Cami on the arm. "Cam, they're just getting out the fear. Remember what we talked about? If we go into it scared, we'll make a mistake. Talking purges the fear."

Cami nodded, frowning. "Maybe we should do it alone. Just you and me. *Alone.*" She glared at the two boys sitting in the sand a distance away.

Faye shook her head. "We need all four of us for the plan to work. You know that."

Cami sighed. "I'm just excited and nervous."

"It's going to work. But not if we start turning on each other." She frowned at Skip and Robbie. "That goes for you two as well."

If they looked at her with a sense of awe or wonder that she seemed to be taking over Cami's role as leader, Faye barely noticed. She was emboldened after being with her secret lover last night, especially since Cami didn't know about the relationship, or their history. After all, *Faye* had been his first recruit, not Cami. He had only sent Cami to "recruit" Faye in order to give Cami a sense of control and power.

But Faye held the real power. And after last night she now understood what her role was. The secret thrilled her. Cami thought she was the one in his confidence. Cami didn't know shit.

For someone as smart as Cami, she could be so dense about some things. Cami thought she had nothing to fear.

FOURTEEN

The guardian of the court records was a six-foot-tall fifty-year-old black woman with dreadlocks who wore jeans against the dress code, bright shirts that lit up the dingy basement archives, and hoop earrings so big Julia was certain she could have worn them as bracelets. Selene Borge didn't take shit from anyone, especially lawyers, but she had a soft spot for Julia Chandler.

Julia knew this had quite a lot to do with her quarterly "donation" to Selene of a Starbucks gift card. The woman lived on hot lattes from the Starbucks across the street.

Julia brought two double lattes to the basement at eleven that morning. Selene smiled, took one before Julia had even offered. "Good morning, Ms. Chandler." Her French-Jamaican accent was artificially exaggerated. Selene was from Jamaica and spoke fluent French — as well as Spanish and German — but she'd moved to America when she was four and could speak perfect "American" when she chose to.

"How are you today?" asked Julia.

They made small talk while sipping coffee. Julia saw two empty cups on Selene's desk. So she was no longer the only attorney who knew Selene's weakness.

Selene finally asked, "What is it you want from me today?"

"Your magic. A list of the case files assigned to a regular court-appointed psychiatrist."

She raised an eyebrow. "Word is you're on administrative leave."

She hadn't expected word to get out so fast. Julia said nothing.

Selene sat at her computer. She briskly typed. "Name?"

"Garrett Bowen."

She punched in some numbers and his name. In seconds, a long list of case files was displayed on the screen. She printed them. "I take it you need these files."

"Only the last two years."

Another few keystrokes and the list was shortened to about fifteen.

"These are all juvenile cases."

That meant she'd need a court order.

"I just want to look," said Julia.

"Juvenile files require the consent of a judge," Selene said as she slid the printout across the desk to Julia. "I'm sorry I can't help you."

"I understand." Julia folded the paper and slid it into her purse. "I also need a list of every case Victor Montgomery presided over for the last two years."

Selene frowned, fingers flying across the keyboard. Julia suppressed a smile. She'd seen Selene use only her index fingers in a painstakingly slow fashion when she didn't like someone. Julia was glad she was on the "good" list.

"Here." Selene handed her a three-page printout. "I take it you want to look at the files?"

"I'm happy to pull them myself."

"Good, because I need to take my lunch break. Union rules. Can you stay here until my replacement comes?"

"Sure."

"You're a doll."

Julia watched her leave and mentally thanked her. This was no longer a gray area. Julia was breaking the law. But she had to help Emily, and if this helped her, dammit —

All adult criminal cases were stored in the computer system, so she could access those from her office. Though she was on administrative leave, Stanton hadn't asked for her ID or keys.

The juvenile files, on the other hand, were not on the network.

The files were sorted by year, then case number. Pulling them was easy. Some were surprisingly thick. She went to the copy room and shut the door, locking it. Her heart beat too loud, the truth of her deception hitting her. It wasn't just her career on the line, but that of an overworked county bureaucrat and everyone else who was helping her, including Frisco, who promised a copy of the autopsy report in her desk drawer before the end of the day.

She fed dollars into the copy machine and quickly copied the pertinent pages, not spending too much time reading them because she needed to put them back before Selene returned.

One name caught her eye.

Jason Ridge.

Why was that familiar? She glanced at the summary page. Deferred Entry of Judgment — DEJ. Nearly two years ago after a juvenile court trial resulted in a guilty verdict, the judge issued a sentence of Deferred Entry of Judgment, which basically told Jason that as long as he behaved until he was eighteen his record would be expunged.

Jason had gone back to court the week after his eighteenth birthday and the judge wiped his record clean.

According to the records, Jason's psychiatrist, Dr. Garrett Bowen, testified on his behalf. But these were Bowen's records, not the court's, and there was no transcript. She needed to find out exactly what the court said, but it wasn't in this file.

Because it had been expunged already? She'd never get it if that were the case. Unless one of the attorneys involved still had a copy.

Jason Ridge. Now she remembered why she knew his name, even though it was a juvenile court case. Eight months ago, first game of the season, he had died on the football field for apparently no reason. An autopsy showed steroids in his system and the cause of death was heart failure. She remembered the news story only because it was another example of a young life cut short.

She copied his entire file, though it was much thinner than it should have been. She could ask around, find out who the judge and prosecutor were on the case, but that would get back to Stanton and her job would be in jeopardy. She had to find another way to get the information she needed.

She put the files back when she was done. Selene was at her desk working on the computer.

"Thanks," Julia whispered as she passed, the copies secure in her briefcase.

"Ms. Chandler, I didn't know you were here. Do you need anything?"

Julia was confused, then saw two of her colleagues at a table only feet away looking at files. "No, just returning a file."

"Thanks."

Julia practically ran out of the building, heart pounding. If Andrew Stanton knew what she'd done, she'd be severely reprimanded. Possibly fired. And the bar wouldn't look too kindly on her pulling juvenile files *and* copying them. She'd have her license to practice suspended. Or worse, be prosecuted.

She gathered her wits while sitting in her car. She pulled out her cell phone and called Connor.

His voice mail picked up.

"Dammit," she said, irritated. "Do you deliberately not answer my calls? I have the files and am going home. You have the address." She hung up. She shouldn't get angry with him, but she wished he would just pick up for once. He probably saw her number on his cell phone and ignored it.

First, she stopped by her office. Her secretary was still there. "Donnell," she said, "I have a favor."

Donnell glanced around, tucked her hair behind her ear. "Anything."

"Can you print out these files for me? I'll pick them up tomorrow."

Julia slid the list of Victor's cases across Donnell's desk.

"I'll bring them to your house."

"You don't —"

Donnell nodded. "Stanton ordered me to tell him if you came by."

"Shit." Julia ran a hand through her hair. "Fine, I'm here to get my address book. Tell him *that.*"

"I will. Oh, and Frisco came by. He didn't say why."

Julia went into her office and looked in her top desk drawer. There was a file folder with Frisco's small, perfect print. *Julia Chandler, Privileged and Confidential.*

Thank you, Frisco.

Dillon learned from Bowen's secretary that the doctor was having lunch at the La Jolla Country Club, but before he could head out there, his ex-brother-in-law Andrew

Stanton called him.

"I need you in my office now."

Dillon almost refused. "I'm heading out to an appointment. How about we meet — ?"

"Dillon, you've crossed the line. You brought Connor into Emily Montgomery's room knowing full well she's a suspect in a murder investigation who is only being stopped from a police interview because of her physician's order. You. And I can — and will — get a court order inside of an hour to have Emily Montgomery moved to the criminal psychiatric unit and put under another doctor's care if you don't explain yourself to me in person right now."

Dillon's hand hurt from clutching the phone so tight. "Don't threaten me, Andrew. And don't threaten my patient."

"You're playing a dangerous game."

"It's no game."

Dillon felt the tension through the phone.

"Ten minutes," Andrew finally said.

"In the rose garden." Dillon wasn't going to give Andrew the power to sit behind his desk. It was psychological, and Dillon wouldn't be deterred by Andrew's power play. Also, Andrew would be less forthcoming in his own office.

Dillon was already near the courthouse,

so he parked on the street, fed the meter a couple quarters, and walked to the small rose garden outside the justice building.

Andrew approached at the same time, dressed impeccably, with the aura of importance befitting a man of his position. Dillon saw the pain behind his eyes. Maybe he was the only one who saw it, and maybe that's why he was the only one in the Kincaid family who still had a relationship with his former brother-in-law. It wasn't that Dillon's parents and siblings doubted Andrew's pain at the loss of his son, it was what had come out about Andrew's life after Justin's murder that had turned the family against him.

Dillon harbored a lot of pain from his nephew Justin's murder — Andrew and Nell's only son. It changed him in ways he was still discovering now, eleven years later. But unlike Connor, he couldn't put all the blame on Andrew Stanton, however much he'd like to. The truth was no one was to blame. It was a brutal crime committed by a child predator who had most likely moved on to another city and state to minimize his chances of being caught.

Dillon regularly checked the FBI database for like crimes. He still hoped that, someday, justice would be served.

"I'm ready to deal," Andrew said.

And Dillon knew then the case wasn't solid.

"Deal what?"

"Plead her out."

"I'm not her attorney."

"You can get the message to Iris Jones."

"Andrew, do you honestly think Emily is guilty?"

"Yes."

"She couldn't have acted alone."

"She turns in her friends and we'll be lenient."

"She says she didn't have anything to do with Victor's murder."

Andrew sighed. "I have evidence that she planned it. Premeditated murder. I will try her as an adult."

"I know what you have and we can take it apart."

Andrew's jaw clenched. "Dillon, you don't know what's going on in my building."

"I have an idea. Judge murdered. You want to nail someone outside the justice system. You don't want your judges feeling the pressure of their actions, that a criminal, someone they put away, can get to them. What happened with Santos?"

"Detective Hooper is on his way to interview him. But it wasn't him."

223

"And you know this how?"

"Santos wouldn't have left that girl alive upstairs."

"If he knew she was in the house."

Andrew opened and closed his mouth, proving to Dillon there was additional evidence that either discredited the Herman Santos theory, or pointed to Emily.

But a plea? That told Dillon that the police didn't have a solid case against Emily, grandstanding notwithstanding. It had been less than forty-eight hours. Andrew was getting restless because it was a high-profile case. Pressure came from everywhere.

Dillon wondered whether Santos had in fact pulled off the judge's murder. On the one hand, the brazenness of the murder suggested payback, and Santos was both brash and arrogant. He could pull it off. But on the other hand, two members of Wishlist had their tormentor killed. Dillon didn't buy into that coincidence.

"I still have Emily for thirty hours. You're not getting to her."

"Dammit, Dillon, we're on the same side!"

Dillon hadn't yet trusted Andrew with the information that Victor had sexually abused Emily. The court would have the information soon enough, if the case got that far.

"Emily is innocent. I'm not giving her to you one minute before I have to." Dillon stared at Andrew. "I'll commit her myself if I have to, while the police work the case. There's much, much more to this than a simple domestic violence."

"Shit, Dillon." Andrew stuffed his hands into his pockets and paced. "We have blood evidence that she was at the crime scene. Her fingerprints were on his desk. The weapon — pruning shears — was found on the grounds. I can make a case against her. I want her accomplices."

"What if she's telling the truth?"

"How would I know? You've kept her under medical wraps, we haven't even been able to talk to her! You're making this harder on everyone involved, particularly Julia."

"Why did you put Julia Chandler on administrative leave?"

Andrew stopped walking. "She's going through a difficult time. She's getting paid. I just don't —"

"It's not because she hired an attorney for Emily. It's because of Connor."

At the mention of his name, Andrew reddened. "Connor is a loose cannon. You can't trust him, even if he is your brother."

Dillon took a step toward his former brother-in-law. They were the same height, so it was easy to get in his face.

He said in a low voice, "You hate Connor because he exposed your affair after Justin was killed. Nothing more, nothing less."

"That has nothing to do with it." But the punch was out of Andrew's words.

Dillon nodded. "You were in bed with your mistress when your son was murdered, and you'll live with that truth for the rest of your life. Now Julia is paying for your guilt because you feel better blaming Connor than looking into your own heart."

Andrew's mouth opened and closed.

Dillon softened his tone. He didn't hate Andrew, and he didn't want to hurt him. "Don't be so blinded by the past that you jeopardize this investigation. I won't let Emily be a pawn in your game."

"In thirty hours, she's ours."

"Don't push me, Andrew."

"You're jeopardizing your career."

"I'll let Emily talk to the police when I think she's ready. Not a minute before."

"When do you think she'll be ready?" Andrew barely restrained his anger.

"You'll be the first to know."

Julia passed the La Jolla Library on her way home. Jason Ridge was nagging at her. One Bowen client dead, one cleared of murder, and one suspected of murder.

Coincidence? She didn't believe it. She made a U-turn and pulled into the library parking lot. She couldn't help but remember that only six weeks ago, a young volunteer of the library was found dead right here.

She shivered, not knowing if it was remembering the brutal murder of Becca Harrison, or thinking about how Garrett Bowen creeped her out. Something about that guy was disconcerting. She'd met him several times in court, in particular when he was assigned to Emily's case. On the surface he was attractive, professional, and intelligent.

But Emily didn't trust or like him, and that held a lot of weight with Julia. Comparing Bowen to Dillon Kincaid, there was no comparison. She'd prefer working with Dillon any day of the week.

She walked in and found an available computer terminal to search the newspaper archives for Jason Ridge. She found several articles about his death as well as many about previous games he'd played in, going back to his freshman year. She printed every article she found.

The first article about his death on the field had a byline by someone she didn't recognize, but the second article's byline she *did* recognize: Grace Simpson.

Why was a crime reporter covering the drug-related death of a high school football star?

She read the article carefully.

Mystery Surrounds Football Star Death
By Grace Simpson

Saturday night's game between the La Jolla Rockets and the San Diego Sprints was interrupted in the third quarter when star Sprints quarterback, senior Jason Ridge, collapsed on the field. He was pronounced dead at the scene after a vigorous attempt to save his life by the league's doctor, David Mortimer.

A subsequent autopsy on Monday indicated the cause of death to be heart failure due to steroid use.

All varsity football players in public and private schools who play in public leagues are required to be tested at least once a season for steroid use, and can be randomly tested throughout the year. The school released Ridge's records showing he'd been tested two months before his death and was clean. In his high school career, he'd been tested a total of six times and all were marked "pass" with no traces of steroids or illegal drugs in his system.

The pressure senior Ridge was under this season was more intense than last year, however, according to his grandmother Evelyn Squires of Carlsbad. "Scouts are at every game watching him. It bothered him, the pressure."

Ridge's father, James, denied his son used steroids. "Jason loved football and he was naturally a star athlete. He'd never take drugs or steroids. There's got to be some mistake."

There was no mistake, according to the coroner's office spokeswoman Anita Ferrar. "The report is conclusive. Six to twelve hours before his death, Jason ingested four times the safe limit of an anabolic steroid popular among bodybuilders."

Dr. Mortimer said he'd never heard of an athlete overdosing on steroids. "Steroids cause death usually from repeated use," he explained. "I've known Jason for four years and he's the last person I'd expect to take steroids."

Steroid use has been under scrutiny nationwide and colleges are cracking down on players who use. "One strike, you're out," UCSD football coach Brian Kyak said. "We don't control the testing anymore, it comes from the league. They don't play favorites."

Jason's friends were shocked, but one high school junior who asked to remain anonymous said, "Jason was under a lot of pressure this year, especially after all the rumors about him and his girlfriend."

Jason's ex-girlfriend, Michelle O'Dell, refused to discuss their past relationship, saying only, "Jason had issues. He was getting help."

When asked, his father declined to comment about any issues O'Dell may have been referring to.

The police are looking into how Jason obtained the steroids. The selling of steroids without a medical license is illegal in California.

A memorial service will be held this afternoon at 4 p.m. at Good Shepherd Church in San Diego. A private burial service will follow. The Sprints head coach retired Jason Ridge's jersey, Number 10, in a somber school assembly Monday.

Grace Simpson, crime reporter. She knew more about the story, otherwise she wouldn't have been assigned to it. Maybe she thought she could get someone to talk about the "issues" Michelle O'Dell had mentioned. Was Michelle the girl Jason had been accused of raping? Or perhaps she knew what had happened.

Julia wondered if journalist Grace had been trying to get more information about the underground market for steroids.

Only one person knew for sure. Julia hesitated before picking up her cell phone.

"Grace Simpson. Talk to me."

"Grace, it's Julia Chandler."

A long pause. "You're just about the last person I expected to call me. Do you have a comment about Victor Montgomery's murder? Or maybe why you were put on administrative leave?"

How did everyone know about her leave? "No. I want to talk off the record about something other than Victor's murder. I'll buy you lunch."

"It's well past lunchtime. You're going to have to give me more. The judge's murder is my number one priority right now and I can't waste my time."

"I promise if anything comes of this, you'll be the first to know. And it could be really big. Please."

Julia could almost hear Grace weighing the pros and cons. "All right," Grace finally agreed. "When and where?"

Julia named a restaurant in La Jolla, far from where any of her colleagues might spot her talking to a reporter.

Julia hung up, far from certain she'd made the right decision, but her instincts told her there was something about Jason Ridge's death that seemed peculiar, perhaps related to the other two murders. She hoped Grace had information to share.

And she hoped it didn't cost her.

Dillon feared he'd missed Garrett Bowen at the country club, but saw him above an empty plate, drinking a cocktail at a table overlooking the golf course.

"Dr. Bowen." Dillon sat across from him.

"Dr. Kincaid. This must be important to track me down on a Friday afternoon. May I call you Dillon? 'Doctor' seems too formal among colleagues."

Dillon nodded. "It's about Wishlist, Doctor." Keep it formal. He watched Bowen's expression. Except for a tightening around his mouth, his expression didn't change. If Dillon hadn't been watching carefully, he'd have missed it.

"Yes?"

"Have you heard of the group?"

"Of course."

"How?"

"I created it."

Though Dillon knew he shouldn't be

surprised, since all the evidence pointed to Dr. Bowen's involvement in the online community, he was nevertheless shocked at the frank admission. "Why?" he asked.

Bowen cocked his head, looking at Dillon as if he'd asked a ridiculous question. "It's therapeutic, of course."

"How so?"

Bowen laid his hands on the table. His right index finger lightly tapped on the linen cloth. "Anger management is a difficult discipline, as I'm sure you well know," he began. "Especially with teenagers. Especially today. Young people mistrust their elders. They'd believe the word of a fellow teen — however ill informed — over the word of an experienced adult."

"That's nothing new," Dillon said.

"True, but with the additional pressures of a complex, sensory-rich society with every fantasy, every wish, able to be fulfilled, keeping young adults focused on their own health and safety — as opposed to the take-what-you-want-when-you-want-it attitude prevalent today — is an almost impossible task for parents. Add to that dilemma the situation of rich kids with distant parents, physically or emotionally, and you have a recipe for disaster. In my practice, I deal almost exclusively with teenagers who have problems with their parents and their teachers — in essence, those in authority over them. I realized this when I started taking cases from the court with youth who vandalized property, acted out against people in a rage, anything that stemmed from anger. And these weren't the underprivileged, but kids with means and education."

Bowen was on a roll. "Take the issue of cutting. You know what that is, correct?"

"Of course. When people, usually young teens, mutilate their bodies in order to feel pain."

Bowen shook his head. "Partly, but you're focusing on the *pain* when in fact it's the *feeling* and the *control* that they hold on to. That the feeling comes from pain is incidental. Cutting is about being in control. Some kids turn to drugs or drinking to dull the feelings — to give up control and responsibility. If under the influence, they become detached from themselves. Cutting is the exact opposite. In fact, in my practice, cutters often have a disdain for drug users. Cutters would rather die than give up their bodies and minds to drugs and alcohol. Cutting heightens their feelings, gives them control over their own destiny. Drugs take away control."

"I understand, but what does cutting have

to do with Wishlist?"

"Cutting is anger management. They can't release their feelings, or they don't know how to release them, so they turn inward. It's empowering. Just like yelling at your parents or vandalizing the school. They get a brief high. But each time, they need to go deeper, hurt longer. If they can't control it, they'll self-destruct." Bowen sipped his drink as the waiter cleared his dishes.

"So you started Wishlist for people who cut themselves?" Dillon said.

"Originally, several years ago I put together a small online group of cutters. I felt they would benefit from talking to each other. And I was right. The results one-on-one were far better after the anonymous group therapy. So I expanded Wishlist to include all teens with anger management or emotional control issues, which is really the same thing. A teen who lashes out in anger has the same basic problems as a teen who turns to promiscuity to solve problems. They don't feel as if they are in control of their destiny."

"There are a thousand underlying reasons for self-destructive teenagers. You can't put them all in the same category."

"I understand that, Dr. Kincaid," Bowen said, irritated that he'd been contradicted.

"But together they see that others have problems *like theirs* and they can try different methods to control their spontaneous destructive behavior and to develop sound coping mechanisms."

"Kids counseling kids." Dillon couldn't hide the disdain in his voice.

"I supervise the list," Bowen insisted. "I use the information in my practice and work with other teens experiencing the same problems. It's the same principle as group therapy."

"Except there's no professional supervision."

"It's anonymous."

"You've gone online. You've read the messages." It wasn't a question.

Bowen acknowledged the fact. "Just to observe or to provide prompts."

"Like how they would kill those who hurt them."

He shook his head. "You don't understand. It's about getting rid of the anger in a safe and anonymous environment in order to move on and heal."

Dillon said, "So when Emily Montgomery wrote that she wanted to kill Judge Montgomery by making him choke on his penis, that's healing?"

"I didn't know the message came from

Emily. It was anonymous."

"But you saw the message."

He hesitated. "Yes. But —"

"Why didn't you go to the police?"

"It's therapy. And there was no threat. It was a fantasy, nothing more."

"It's a secure server that you need a password to join and is monitored by a licensed psychiatrist who should know better than to put a group of mentally imbalanced young people into a group to talk about murder."

"That's not the purpose, Kincaid. You're only looking at one message out of thousands."

"And where would those messages be kept?"

"Nowhere."

"You don't retain them?"

Again, he hesitated. "Not for the long term."

"Any other messages you remember that you might want to make the police aware of? Any other threats?"

Bowen stood. Dillon had crossed the line. "I wasn't aware that I was the subject of a police investigation."

"I'm trying to help Emily."

"Hmm." Bowen looked down his nose, trying to use his height over the sitting Dillon to intimidate.

Dillon stood.

"What do you know about Paul Judson?"

"I don't know who you're talking about."

But Bowen wasn't looking him in the eye. Dillon knew he was lying.

Bowen went on the offensive. "Perhaps you're the one on the wrong side here. Have you thought that perhaps Emily acted out her own fantasies? She is a violent, emotionally distraught girl who has never recovered from her father's sudden death. She has a verbally abusive mother, and her stepfather was attempting to fill a role that emotionally she couldn't handle. You can't overlook her potential involvement."

"And do you believe Emily was involved in Paul Judson's murder as well?"

Bowen looked at him blankly, but Dillon didn't forget his original reaction.

"Do you have a list of everyone you invited into the group?"

"If I did, I wouldn't give it to you without a court order, Dr. Kincaid."

Dillon started to leave, then turned and said in a low voice, "You should have your license pulled. Giving your patients essentially the right to counsel each other. You've created a forum for anger to fester, not diminish."

"You're wrong, Dr. Kincaid."

"No, I'm not."

FIFTEEN

Connor parked outside Emily's private college preparatory high school in La Jolla. It was after two and the kids were still in class.

Emily had given him a list of her friends, surprisingly short for an attractive, smart girl like Em. The school wasn't large — maybe a thousand students in all four grades — but it was meticulously maintained and looked like a small version of an Ivy League university. A place rich parents sent their kids.

There were a handful of girls on the list, but the one Emily said she was closest to was Wendy Roper, whom she'd known since early childhood. Connor had a description of the girl and her car, and waited until classes let out at three. Ten minutes later he spotted Wendy, a dark-haired beauty, tall and lanky, and dressed impeccably. He followed her to the parking lot to verify her identity and as she was about to get into a sporty red compact, Connor called out. "Wendy?"

She turned, neither scared nor worried. "Yeah? Who wants to know?"

"Connor Kincaid. I'm a friend of Emily."

Wendy's round face relaxed. "Em's talked about you."

"Do you have a few minutes?"

She glanced at her watch. "Sure. Is Em okay?"

"She's going to be fine." He looked around, saw too many people walking around, curious about him. He pointed to a grassy slope with trees on the far side of the parking lot. "Let's go someplace private to talk."

They walked in silence, sat on a short stone wall near the grove.

"People are saying she tried to kill herself," Wendy said. "I tried calling the house, but her mother refused to talk to me. What a bitch." Wendy looked at the ground. "Em would never kill herself. She didn't try, did she?"

"It was an accident," Connor said. "She did drink too much, though. Had to have her stomach pumped."

"Ugh. I told her she had to stop."

"Do you know why she drinks?"

Wendy didn't say anything, and Connor

sensed Wendy knew more than anyone about Emily.

"Wendy? Emily told me to talk to you, that you were her closest friend. She needs your help. Tell me the truth."

"I know about Victor, if that's what you mean." Wendy didn't look at him, her hands squeezed together so tightly that her knuckles were white.

"Yeah, that's what I mean."

"She didn't tell me until a few months ago. I came over one afternoon and she was drunk. It all came out then. I told her she had to stop drinking and tell her mother what was happening, but she said her mother wouldn't care, that she would blame her for it like she blamed her for everything bad that happened in her life. Besides, Crystal's never around."

"Did you know whether Emily ever talked to anyone else about what Victor did to her, other than you?"

"No, and every time I brought it up she refused to talk about it. She was scared, I think. That she'd lose her inheritance if she said anything."

"She was worried about money?"

"You make it sound bad. If you had five million dollars sitting in a trust fund and only a year to go, would you make waves?

All she wanted to do was get the money and get the hell out of there. The other stuff, like the vandalism, she did when she was plastered. I really tried to help Em with that, but she needs real help, not me."

"Did Emily talk to you about Wishlist?"

"I don't think so."

"It's an online therapy group. Anger management."

"Oh, she talked about how stupid her therapy was all the time. The guy her mother sent her to creeped her out. But it was only once a week, and she said she had him wrapped around her finger."

"But she didn't talk about an online group."

"Not that I remember."

"Did she ever talk to you about wanting to kill Victor?"

Wendy stared at him, eyes narrowed. "Whose side are you on? I thought you wanted to help Emily."

"I do. That's why I need to know everything."

"She'd never hurt anyone."

"You didn't answer my question."

"The jerk made her suck his dick! Don't you think that's gross enough?"

"Wendy, please. The police are going to be talking to you and if you lie, they'll put you on the stand as a hostile witness."

Realization hit Wendy and she paled. "Do-do the police really think she killed him?"

"I don't know what they think, but I used to be a cop and looking at the evidence right now, chances are she's on the top of the suspect list."

"She would never."

"Did she talk to you about it?"

Wendy said nothing for a long minute. "It's not what you think. You know how people talk. They say 'I'll kill him' just as a part of conversation. Not because they really mean it. Sure, Emily hated him, she wanted to hurt him, but she didn't mean it."

"Did she talk about this with anyone else?"

"Absolutely not. I had to pull everything out of her. She never talks about it, even now. It's just one of those things we both know and talk around."

Wendy took Connor's hand. "Please, please help her. Crystal won't. She just wants Emily's money."

"Crystal's worth more than five million dollars."

Wendy laughed. "Emily's trust is worth a lot more than that. She gets five million when she turns eighteen. And a million dollars every year for the rest of her life. Last I heard, her trust was worth over fifty million bucks and growing."

Connor walked Wendy back to her car and wondered if somehow this was all about money.

"Sorry I'm late."

Grace Simpson slid into the seat across from Julia at Crab Catcher, a restaurant up the coast in La Jolla, far, far away from the courthouse.

"Thanks for coming out here."

"I only have thirty minutes, so what's up?"

The waitress came over before Julia could answer. They both ordered the Crab Catcher's excellent salads, then Julia said, "What do you know about Jason Ridge's death?"

Grace went through her mental catalog, then her eyes widened. "The football player from San Diego?"

"You covered it for the paper, which I thought odd considering you usually work the crime beat."

"How did he come to your attention?"

"You talk first," Julia said, "then I'll share what I know. *Off* the record."

"That's not fair," she pouted, but continued. "Basically, I took a look at it because that was when steroid abuse was all over the news, Jose Canseco had his tell-all book, the Bonds thing was coming down. Now the big guys can get steroids, but where do kids get them? Are they street drugs? Do their parents get them on the sly? Doctors? I thought it might be a great investigative report."

"But you didn't have any other follow-ups."

"I spent *weeks* on that case, talking to everyone about Jason Ridge, talking to the cops about steroids on the streets, even talked to a drug dealer down in the Gaslight district who dealt in steroids. Nothing on Ridge. Not one person even *hinted* that they suspected he was using. The detective in charge of the case, Ollie Grant, said the best he could figure is Ridge bought them on the black market and unintentionally over-dosed, but overdosing on steroids is virtually impossible. Still, there was a lot of pressure on him. I did learn that he was seeing a psychiatrist, though his parents clammed up about it. Said it was growing pains."

"Off the record, right?" Julia asked, raising her eyebrow.

"Yes." Grace pouted.

"Ridge got a Deferred Entry of Judgment after a rape trial in juvenile court. Part of the DEJ was a mandatory anger management class and community service."

"DEJ?"

"A slap on the wrist. The judge telling him essentially to not do it again and it'll all go away when he's eighteen." Julia squinched her face up in anger. "It happens more often than you think."

"Sounds like it might make a good story," Grace said, making notes.

"Yes, it would, and I would be happy to comment on the record."

"You would?"

"Yes . . . but not now. I have something more pressing. Bowen was Ridge's psychiatrist. Ridge is dead. Bowen was Billy Thompson's psychiatrist after Billy trashed his teacher's car and the teacher is shot to death. Bowen is Emily's psychiatrist and her stepfather ends up dead."

"Suspicious, but it's not enough. Bowen is a renowned child shrink. He's on retainer by the court. And Jason Ridge died of a heart attack attributed to steroid use."

"According to the article you wrote, he tested clean several times over the course of the year."

Grace nodded. "They have a fail-safe system. The team doctor watches them pee into the cup. No switching urine or bringing in your own."

"And the team doctor was clean?"

"I couldn't find anything on him. He was genuinely distraught about Jason's death." Grace paused while the waitress brought their salads. "You wouldn't be telling me this unless there was something important that I missed."

"I don't think you missed anything. The juvenile records are sealed and you wouldn't have been able to access the DEJ."

"But you did."

Julia didn't answer the implied question. "I need everything you have from that investigation. Jason's friends, family, doctors, everything you can get me."

"You leaving the DA's office to become a reporter?"

"Grace, you have no reason to trust me, but I need your help. Can I have your notes?"

Julia wondered if she sounded as desperate as she felt. Grace pulled out her laptop and turned it on.

"Do you have a pen?"

Julia dug a pen and notepad out of her purse. "Shoot."

Grace typed rapidly, pulling up a spreadsheet. "I have every contact for every article I write. You're lucky I'm a packrat, because this is old news."

"Thank you."

Grace gave her a list of contacts, all Jason's friends, and the contact information for his ex-girlfriend whom Grace quoted in the paper. "I have a note next to her name. *More.* She knew more than she told me. I'm a reporter, I can sense when someone's holding back. Usually people love talking to me — except cops, attorneys, and politicians. You'd think you all had something to hide." Grace laughed good-naturedly and shut down her computer. "But kids, the average person, they all want their name in the paper. Michelle O'Dell gave me a bone, but when I pushed she clammed up. I don't know if it was because she was scared or if it was really nothing. But you might want to track her down."

"Know where I can find her?"

"Sorry, once I gave up on the case I didn't follow up with any of the people involved. But it shouldn't be too difficult. Oh, one thing I remember: she didn't go to Jason's school. Either she had already graduated or went to another school. I don't have those notes anymore, sorry." She glanced at her watch, shoveled salad into her mouth. "So, what do I get?"

"An exclusive."

"Start talking."

"Not now, when I figure out what's going on."

"I can get an exclusive from Andrew Stanton. He loves me because I made him look good when he was running against that scumbag Descario."

"Anyone looks good next to Descario."

Grace laughed. "So an exclusive isn't going to hold much water with me. What more can you give?"

Julia sighed. "What about an interview?"

"You? An interview?" She smiled. "I've been dying to interview you for years."

"I know." She wasn't happy about it, but the information Grace had was valuable. "If you have anything else on this case, call me."

"Will do. And I'll call you about that interview after this thing with your niece is resolved." She stood up, then sat back down and asked, "One question. Off the record. Why is Connor Kincaid working for you?"

Julia would never cease to be amazed at how fast news traveled, even in a large city like San Diego. "He's the best. He knows Emily and can help prove she didn't kill Victor."

"That's not my question. Why would he agree to it after you forced him to testify five years ago?"

Julia didn't exactly know why. She didn't

want to think about it, or about her role in Connor's resignation. "Connor found Emily when she ran away three years ago. He cares about what happens to her."

"Hmmm. I don't know if I buy that, but if you believe it, I guess I can give it a pass." She jumped up again and waved her fingers at Julia. "Are you going to the art fundraiser tomorrow night?"

"What fund-raiser?"

"The Chandler Foundation is a cosponsor of some big art charity event."

"You know me well enough to know I'm not involved in the Foundation."

"Everyone who's anyone will be there, and since Jason Ridge's parents are big muckety-mucks in the arts community, you might want to check it out." She winked.

"Thanks for the heads-up."

"Ciao." Grace waved her fingers and sauntered off.

Julia picked up her cell phone and called her personal secretary. Sarah Wallace had an office down the hall from the Foundation and handled Julia's other life — the life of being a Chandler. Most of her job was sending regrets and managing the trust correspondence for Emily. Julia had no desire to be involved in Chandler business, especially since she had given up involvement in the Foundation for one day a week with Emily.

She asked Sarah to fax her at home with all the information about the art charity event. She didn't know if she would go, but she thought the information about Jason Ridge's death — and Bowen's involvement in his DEJ — was odd. There was definitely more to the story than what Grace had written, and Julia needed to find out what. It might have nothing to do with Emily, or everything to do with Emily. Jason's death was the third she could connect to Garrett Bowen, directly or indirectly, and that was two coincidences too many.

She paid the bill and stared out the window as she finished her iced tea. One thing Grace said bugged her: Why was Connor helping her? Why did she go to him when she had no one else to turn to?

The kiss.

No, she wasn't so shallow to think that he would even want to kiss her again after what happened. But she'd never forget the way she felt when he kissed her that night long ago, the night before she told him that if he didn't testify against a crooked cop, she'd put him on trial for manslaughter.

She'd been working late in her office. Working? No, she was torn. Stuck. Unable to figure out what to do about the entire screwed-up case. The two illegal immigrant minor females, still Jane Does, found in the chapel annexed to the San Diego Mission de Alcalá had started a task force that included the FBI, Border Patrol, and SDPD. But in the end, they couldn't stop the smuggling of sex slaves across the border. The girls wanted to come, they wanted a chance at freedom, and if they had to give their bodies, some felt it was a fair trade.

There was nothing fair about being sexually abused and used and then beaten to death when they started looking like the whores they were treated as. The men who bought the girls wanted them young and beautiful, not old and used. And if they tried to escape . . . she'd read the reports, seen the pictures of naked girls shot in the back and left for carrion in the desert east of the city.

But ultimately, after months of investigation, the only crime they'd been able to stop was the one within their own ranks, two cops taking bribes and turning their back on the sex slave trade.

The district attorney at the time, Bryce Descario, had come to Julia an hour before. "Have you talked to Kincaid?"

"Not yet." She'd dreaded it. Connor had made it perfectly clear he wanted nothing to do with the Internal Affairs investigation. But without his collaboration, the FBI said they couldn't proceed and take over the case, that it was an internal San Diego PD issue, not a federal issue. She disagreed, but she was one attorney in a sea of federal bureaucrats and special agents. She was definitely out of her comfort zone.

"I don't have to remind you how politically sensitive this situation is. I want it gone. The election is less than two years away, this needs to be old news. Kincaid will agree or you will file charges on the Suarez death."

"But —"

"I thought we were clear on this. The chief of police has agreed."

Only because you can't fire him, she thought with disgust. She hated politics. Hated this district attorney. Hated the mayor and regretted voting for him. What about the truth? Didn't anyone care about the truth anymore?

"We're clear."

"Good. Kincaid didn't do himself any favors. He set himself up for this. Now he has to sit at the table or leave the house. Do I make myself clear, Ms. Chandler?"

"Yes, sir."

Descario left and Julia reminded herself that Connor Kincaid had dug his own grave. Had he not gone after Suarez himself — without a warrant, without backup — he wouldn't have been under investigation. He shot an unarmed man. Suspected human trafficker, but armed only with a knife.

She'd read the report and statistics that a good knife thrower could have hit Connor with a clean throw, but politically — God, how she hated politics — politically, a knife was no match for a gun and they were twenty-five feet apart, clearly in the gray area.

Tomorrow. She'd tell him tomorrow. His entire problem would go away if he agreed to testify. If not, he'd have to take his chances with the charges. And probably lose his job in the process.

She packed up her papers. It was nearly midnight and she had an eight a.m. court appearance. Not that she would sleep well tonight, but at least she could soak in the bath and maybe work out some of the tension in her muscles.

A knock on her door made her jump. Who was still here this late?

Connor Kincaid came in without waiting for her answer. He was out of uniform, wearing jeans and a black T-shirt that hugged his broad chest a little too tightly for her comfort. They'd worked together closely for the last few months and she was attracted to him. Who wouldn't be? Hot cop in uniform. Piercing black eyes to match his black hair. Square jaw, long nose, and the muscles. God, his muscles were hard and sleek and she had often imagined what it would feel like to be locked in his arms.

She glanced at her desk, feeling a blush coming on. She acted like such a schoolgirl around Connor, and he'd made no indication that he thought she was attractive. He was more angry than anything. Angry about the status of the investigation, about how they found more dead girls in the desert just last week, how no one seemed to care.

She cared. But she wasn't in a position to do anything about it. An overworked twenty-nine-year-old deputy district attorney three years out of law school did the job she had to do, a job that two people could easily work full-time.

"The hearing is tomorrow."

"Yes." She shut her briefcase.

"Do you know anything?"

She wanted to tell him everything, but couldn't. Her duty to her office, her ethics wouldn't allow her to break the rules for him.

But she wanted to. It didn't seem fair. And for the first time, a little chisel hit the rock of justice in her heart, that maybe the law and the rules weren't always fair.

But they were all she had.

She came around her desk. "I heard about the girls in Calipatria. I'm sorry."

He tensed. "The bastards are going to get away with it. Trebone isn't talking." Trebone, a police informant who was tightly wrapped in the Crutcher investigation, had surrendered after Connor shot Suarez. And now Trebone had been scared silent.

She wanted to soothe Connor, to tell him someday justice would be served, but Julia couldn't get out the words. They didn't seem to mean what they had to her when she decided to go into civil service.

Instead, she touched his arm. "We'll figure it out."

He looked at her hand, then at her face. For the first time since they'd begun working together, she saw desire in his eyes. Connor didn't hesitate. If he had, she would have run away like a rabbit, avoiding the passion in his intense expression.

He put one hand on her neck and pulled her face to his. His lips locked onto hers.

He tasted of warmth and spice and a hint of hops. At five foot nine she never thought of herself as petite, but she felt remarkably feminine in Connor's arms.

She gasped, and he kissed her deeper, his tongue seeking hers. She responded, opening her mouth to him, her hands squeezing his biceps, holding on to keep herself from falling.

Connor Kincaid kissed like he did everything else in his life. Fiercely, passionately, without reservation or regret.

He walked her backward until her rear end hit the desk and he bent her backward. Her clock tumbled to the floor with a thud. Remembering where she was, she put her hands on his chest and turned her lips from his. "I'm sorry," she whispered into his ear, breathless.

He stepped back and she felt cold. "No, I'm sorry. I shouldn't —" Connor touched her cheek so softly Julia almost didn't feel it. "I'll see you tomorrow."

She watched him leave, then sat at her desk and cried.

Sixteen

Where the hell was she?

Connor Kincaid paced outside Julia's renovated Victorian house perched on cliffs along the coast outside of La Jolla. A small neighborhood was nestled below, then the highway, shops, and finally the beach and ocean, less than a mile as the crow flies.

He finally stopped pacing and leaned against a tree on the edge of her property, staring at the distant ocean.

He tracked down Emily's other friends but they had next to nothing to contribute. He attempted to talk to her teachers, but they refused to talk to him since he wasn't a cop. He called Emily's piano teacher, who had been advised by his lawyer not to speak to anyone, and the art studio downtown had no one on the premises who personally knew Emily. "The classes are run by the community college," the gallery owner told Connor. "You'll have to talk to the head of the art department, Anton Foster."

Connor took down the contact information and tried Foster, but only got voice mail. He left a curt message and slammed down the phone, reminding himself that this was the part of being a cop he never liked — following up on leads that went nowhere. But it had to be done.

Where the hell was Julia?

His cell phone rang: Dillon.

"What's up, bro?" said Connor.

"I thought we were meeting at my house."

"Julia isn't home yet."

"Why don't I meet you at her house? I have to make another stop. I'll be there in about an hour."

"You have news?"

"Some. I'll talk to you when I get there."

Connor hung up and sat down against the tree. At least the view was nice. Calming.

An orange-and-white tabby cat cautiously approached. Connor sat there, pretending not to notice. The cat came closer. Closer. Sniffed his hand, almost like a dog. Connor smiled. They'd had a cat when he was little, a black cat with a white chest who looked like he was wearing a tuxedo, hence his name, Tuxedo, given to him by Carina who was then seven. He'd been a stray, but the Kincaid family adopted him. They were in

Texas at the time. When they moved a year later for Virginia, they brought Tuxedo with them. He disappeared soon after the move, and they never found him. Nor did they get another pet that wasn't caged.

He wondered if the tabby belonged to Julia. He'd never pictured her as an animal person. A workaholic. A fierce prosecutor. A rigid attorney. Except around Emily, where she softened, became human, female. A woman he could picture with a cat on her lap and a fire in a darkened room. A woman like the one he'd kissed five long years ago.

He should never have kissed her, but she'd looked so beautiful, so vulnerable, so damn *kissable.* He couldn't resist. He'd been attracted to her from day one, but kept his feelings well tamped down. Back then when he'd kissed her, she'd responded with a fierce passion he'd never suspected was inside. He'd hoped that maybe, when things died down, he'd ask her out. Take her to bed.

It didn't happen. The day after their kiss, the cold attorney Julia Chandler was back with a lose-lose ultimatum.

He'd wanted to resign so badly and screw her, screw the case. But the truth was he couldn't see what would happen if he was tried for manslaughter. Even if he spent a day in jail, a cop behind bars was in jeopardy. He wasn't willing to give his life to protect criminal bastards who contributed to the abuse of underage girls.

He couldn't have been more shocked when Julia gave him the ultimatum. In the end, he did what they wanted and went back to work.

He'd tried to explain what would happen, but Julia refused to listen. She was so caught up in the rights and wrongs, she'd really had no idea what she was asking him to do.

The next six months were hell. The department was polarized. Ultimately, he resigned, refusing to be a lightning rod for controversy and anger anymore.

He shook the past from his mind. Five years was a long time, but remembering how he felt then brought back the old anger and resentment. Connor needed to put that aside so he could help clear Emily.

He heard the car's approach before he saw it. The cat beside him scampered off toward the house. Instead of bounding up the stairs to the porch, the cat went through a small hole beneath the stairs.

Julia's Volvo came into view. She parked outside of the detached garage and got out, looking at Connor's truck, then looking around for him. She wasn't in her attorney uniform. Instead, she was wearing a skirt similar to last night's, a flowing number in spring colors, and a tight little lacy white pullover shirt. Her hair was down and the light breeze played with it. He stood and approached her.

"Where have you been?" he said, focusing on the fact that she wasn't home when she was supposed to be, instead of how delicious she looked.

She frowned, her brows pulled in. "I didn't realize you were my keeper."

"You said you were coming straight here after the courthouse."

"I made a detour."

"And?"

"Let's go inside."

She led the way inside. She had three locks and a security system. "Scared of something?"

She shrugged. "Andrew Stanton suggested I get a security system after the Fione trial."

"I don't know that case."

"It was over two years ago. Fione raped and killed three women in the bay area. We had DNA, two eye-witnesses, and he kept souvenirs — the victim's underwear. We tried to plead it to life without parole thinking he'd go for it to save his life, but he refused to plead guilty, so we prosecuted special circumstances murder one and he got the death penalty. Of course, that costs us a hell of a lot more than the plea." She sighed. "I think that's why the bad guys go to trial, to cost us time and money. We had Fione easy."

"So he's away for life. Why the security?"

"He threatened me in court. I wasn't scared of him, he was going to prison for the rest of his life, but Andrew thought since I was handling high-profile cases it would be prudent to have security."

"Why are you shaking?"

"I'm not."

"Yes, you are." He touched her arm. She looked down, surprised that indeed she was trembling. "So what kind of threat did Fione make?"

"The usual. That he'd get out and cut my throat." She tried for a light laugh, but it came out a squeak. "That's water under the bridge, really. He's never getting out. Might not see the end of a needle in my lifetime, but he's secure in San Quentin."

"But he scared you."

"What he did to those women scared me and made me angry. He mutilated their bodies so badly they needed closed caskets. The second victim was discovered by her eight-year-old daughter. She didn't even recognize her mother. It was awful."

"Any more threats?"

"Here and there. I have a gun."

"Great," he muttered.

She glared at him. "I know how to use it. I went to safety training. I'm not stupid, Kincaid."

"I never thought you were. But you don't carry."

"It's for home protection. I'm safe at the courthouse. The security is tight."

"There's the parking garage, walking to lunch, driving home —"

She waved off his concerns and he couldn't help but grin. This was the Julia Chandler he remembered. The know-it-all professional prosecutor.

"What did you find in the archives?" he asked, following Julia through the wide foyer, down a narrow hall to the bright, country-style kitchen in the rear of the house. A partially enclosed sunroom with skylights on the roof had been built off the kitchen. The view was incredible.

"Nice place."

"Thanks."

She put her briefcase down on the kitchen table. "Can I get you something?"

"Whatever."

She opened her refrigerator and stared.

He looked over her shoulder. "It's empty," he said. "Have you been robbed?"

A laugh escaped before she could pull it back in. Connor was pleased that he'd made her chuckle. "I don't eat here much."

"Obviously."

"But I have filtered water. And ice." She pulled two glasses from a cabinet and pressed buttons on the door of the refrigerator for ice and water.

Connor picked up his cell phone. "Dillon's on his way. I'm having him pick up some food or we'll all starve."

Julia didn't know why she was nervous having Connor Kincaid in her house. Maybe because she'd been thinking about that kiss five years ago. Or maybe because she had unresolved guilt for what happened in the Suarez/Crutcher case and how it had affected him. But having Connor sitting at her kitchen table felt odd, so she started talking immediately about what she'd learned, just the facts, to see if he came to the same conclusion she had.

"You talked to Grace Simpson?" he asked, surprised.

"Off the record."

"She's a reporter. You can't trust reporters."

"I trust her on this."

"She's going to stab you in the back."

"No, she's not. Because I promised her an interview."

Julia didn't want to get into it. Grace had been hounding her for an interview since she'd become a reporter six years ago, why was a trust fund baby a civil servant, or some such nonsense.

"You know, I don't *have* to work because of my inheritance, why do I want to put in twelve-hour days working with scum, yada yada.

"Now can we get back to the business at hand?" Julia never felt comfortable talking about her family money.

"Jason Ridge."

"Yes. He was a patient of Bowen and he ended up dead. So we have Paul Judson — who wronged Billy Thompson, a member of Wishlist — dead. We have Jason Ridge — a patient of Bowen — dead. And Victor Montgomery — who wronged Emily, a member of Wishlist — dead, too."

"What if the girl Jason raped was a member of Wishlist?" Connor speculated.

"Don't you think that's a huge conflict of interest?" Julia asked. "That Bowen would be counseling both the rapist and his victim?"

"It seems a coincidence, but what else

would make sense?"

"Could Jason have been a member himself?" Julia wondered.

"Describing his own murder?"

Julia shook her head. "You're right. Sounds ridiculous. But there has to be some connection we're not seeing."

She suddenly jumped up.

"Oh! I called a friend and he's pulling the coroner's report on Ridge." She ran down the hall to her den, then returned. "It hasn't come in yet." She placed a fax on the table.

"What's this?" Connor picked up the paper. "It looks like an invitation. You going to a party tomorrow?"

"Maybe." Julia told him about the art fund-raiser. "Grace Simpson told me Jason Ridge's parents are big art supporters, and it might give me a chance to talk to them. But it's a long shot."

Connor put the fax down and tapped it with his finger. "Did you know this shindig is at Garrett Bowen's house?"

Julia's eyes widened as she read the invite. "What a coincidence."

"Somehow I don't think so."

In twenty-four hours, the game would be over. The players were in place, the plan formed, contingencies made. Just one more problem to solve.

He handed a shot of Chivas to his guest. "Don't go to the fund-raiser tomorrow."

"Of course I'm going."

"I've seen the guest list. You won't be able to control yourself, you'll blow it."

She stood. "I'm going. You can't keep me away."

"I can't protect you if you don't listen to me."

"Protect me?" She laughed. "I've never asked you to protect me. I wanted to kill him two years ago. You're the one who got in my way."

"I saved your life."

"I have no life." She let out a deep breath. "I'm not going to mess with the plan. It's perfect justice. The irony —" She swallowed, her jaw quivering, and for a brief moment he panicked. He couldn't have her fall apart on him now. He needed her strong, for just a little while longer.

Two years ago she had been fragile, on the verge of suicide. She'd had a gun, determined to kill the man who had stolen so much from her. He'd simply been in the right place at the right time and seized on the opportunity, not quite knowing how it would play out. Had he let the distraught and emotionally crippled woman kill the man she'd sought, he'd have been cheated out of *his* vengeance. A gun? Too fast, too easy.

His goal was not to simply kill the man who had wronged them, but to humiliate him before death. To destroy his lofty, hypocritical pedestal and watch him fall.

He hadn't known her before that day on the street when he stopped her from committing cold-blooded murder. A chance meeting? He didn't believe in luck. It was fate, giving him the spark to create such a brilliant operation. The aesthetics in each step of his masterful plan were glorious, harmonious with the overall goal of destroying injustice and restoring balance.

They were too close to victory to have her fall apart now.

He took a step toward her, touched her cheek. She leaned into his hand, closed her eyes. "You've been my rock. I would have been lost without you." She kissed his palm.

They'd never slept together, but now was the time. He saw her desperate need to cling to something, to give her strength to triumph over her adversary.

Only he could give that to her. He picked her up. She was surprisingly light. He took her to his bedroom, laid her on the bed. Her eyes were closed. Who was she thinking about? Her ex-husband? Him? Someone else?

It didn't matter. He would make her forget her weakness, give her the strength to get through the next twenty-four hours.

After that he didn't care. He'd walk away, untainted. He had a passport and a plan.

A plan for every contingency.

After Dillon arrived, they reviewed the files and the coroner's reports.

Dillon thought it as suspicious as Connor and Julia had that Jason Ridge had been Bowen's patient, too. "Bowen's name keeps popping up," Dillon said.

Connor looked up from the stack of paper Julia's legal clerk had printed that summarized every case Victor Montgomery had handled in the last two years. So far, the task was giving him a headache. "What happened with your meeting?"

"Bowen is a narcissist. Completely convinced that his opinion is not only right, but the *only* solution. He started Wishlist for cutters — teenagers who self-mutilate — and it grew from there. He sees himself as an almost godlike figure, certain he and only he knows how to cure these kids." Dillon rubbed his eyes. "He believes Emily broke down and acted out on her fantasy."

"Damn him," Julia muttered.

Connor squeezed her hand. "What a jerk."

"I couldn't get more out of him," said Dillon.

"Maybe he has something on his home computer we can use," Connor said.

"Breaking and entering is illegal," Dillon reminded him.

"Not if you're invited into his house."

"I don't think we'll be welcome."

Julia handed Dillon the invitation. "The Chandler Foundation is sponsoring a fundraiser at Bowen's house tomorrow night. I'm on the Foundation board, though I don't usually go to events. Not since Matt died. But I had Sarah, my assistant, RSVP for us."

"All of us?"

"I'd like you to come."

"I'd love to nail the bastard with conspiracy to murder," Connor said.

"It would actually be incitement," Julia corrected without thinking.

Connor growled. "Spoken like a damn attorney."

"I *am* a damn attorney."

Dillon ran a hand through his hair and cleared his throat. He held up a thin file. "Did you look at Montgomery's autopsy report?"

Julia nodded. "What do you think?"

"I was surprised, Montgomery didn't actually die from blood loss."

"Yeah, he choked to death," Julia said.

"On his . . . ?" Connor shook his head.

"Emily couldn't have done something like this."

"The prosecution has a compelling case," Dillon argued. "Her e-mail, her alcohol use, drugs in her system. With or without the sexual abuse, they can make a case. There have been cases of abused spouses who have pled to reduced charges because their story was compelling — they 'broke' from the abuse, killed because they felt they had no other choice. But Emily planned the crime, the prosecution has her Wishlist e-mail."

"But with the Judson case —"

"Andrew didn't mention it, and I didn't want to bring it up with him even though he has to know by now. Will Hooper interviewed Billy Thompson yesterday."

"You talked to Stanton?" Connor asked.

"This afternoon. And I got something out of him."

Julia was almost afraid to ask. "What?"

"They have blood evidence, and the weapon. Pruning shears found on the property."

Julia paled. Connor took her hand.

"Anything else?" she asked.

"It all matches what Emily told us Thursday morning," said Connor. "Her fingerprints on his desk."

"They're building a case against her," Julia said.

"I think we need to turn what we have over to Will," Dillon said.

"No," Julia said emphatically. "As soon as we turn it over, we can't follow up."

"We're already compromising the investigation," Dillon said.

"Good. The judge can throw out evidence right and left and Iris Jones can get the case dismissed."

"You'll be disbarred."

"Do you think I care?" Julia pushed her chair back, her hands on the table. "This is my niece! Someone is setting her up. I think it's Bowen."

"Why? He has no vendetta against her."

"Maybe it's not intentional. Maybe he's leading this little group of his, turning disturbed kids into a bunch of vigilantes."

"All the more reason for us to turn over the information to Will and let him get a warrant. And they want to formally interview Emily. They're going to, sooner or later."

"Not until after tomorrow night. Please,

Dillon." Julia turned to Connor, pleaded with him as well. "Let's see what we can learn tomorrow at the fund-raiser. And I'm going to track down this Michelle O'Dell who was Ridge's ex-girlfriend, see if she knows something more. Twenty-hour hours."

"One more day," Connor said. "If we can show doubt it'll be much harder for Stanton to build a case. It'll give us more time."

Dillon relented. "I have no problem keeping Emily under medical observation. I can stand by my diagnosis. But you both need to know you can lose everything. Connor, you could lose your investigator's license. Julia, the bar is unforgiving."

"I know." She turned to Connor. "You don't have to help, Connor. I don't want you to jeopardize your career."

Connor stared at her, and she didn't know what he was thinking. Finally, he said, "Dil, think Dad's tux will fit me?"

"Might be a little tight."

"Thank you," Julia said, and sat down.

"I want to arrange for Will to interview Emily on Sunday. That'll buy us time because they'll see we're cooperating. I can call Iris and have her set it up. That way it's on our terms. And we'll do it at the hospital." Dillon looked at Julia. "Okay?"

She nodded. "These stacks are still huge." She motioned to the files she'd copied. "We'll be up half the night."

"Do you have coffee?"

She shook her head. "I don't cook. Sorry."

"Coffee isn't cooking."

"I'm not home much."

Dillon jumped up. "I saw a Starbucks down the hill. They're probably still open. I'll be right back." With his departure, Julia and Connor were suddenly ill at ease.

Connor pulled Julia up from the table. "Let's go for a walk."

"Walk?"

"Stretch your legs. You're tense." He rubbed her shoulders as he ushered her out onto the porch.

"I'm worried, Connor. Emily's so young and vulnerable."

"Do you know her friend Wendy?"

"Sure. I've taken them to the movies, out for dinner. She's a good kid."

"Emily told Wendy about Victor."

Julia shuddered, and Connor continued to rub her shoulders. Julia rested her forearms on the porch railing and looked out at the ocean. The sun had long set, only a glimmer of fading light remained on the horizon.

"My own niece didn't trust me," Julia said.

"I don't think it had anything to do with trust. Not in the way you think about it."

"Then in what way?"

Connor thought about that. He'd worked with troubled kids for so long — not sexually abused kids, like Emily, but kids from broken homes, from the inner city. Kids with little hope, who chose gang life and crime because that was the only hope they had to get out of poverty. Problem was, they usually ended up dead or in prison.

Kids like Billy Thompson, with the world seemingly against them, who worked hard to accomplish something only to have their dreams dashed because of one misguided, wrong adult. Connor had given Billy no reason to distrust him, but it had taken Connor more than a year to earn the teen's respect and trust. Some kids never learned to trust anyone.

Julia hung her head. "I can't help it, Connor. I should have dug deeper. I should have seen something!"

A tear slid down Julia's cheek and Connor wiped it away with his finger. He tilted her chin up, forced her to look at him. Her sudden vulnerability hit him. Her bottomless green eyes filled with raw emotion and Connor's heart flipped. He'd never seen Julia Chandler stripped so bare, so needy.

He touched her full lips with his thumb, wiped away a lone tear at the corner of her mouth. She became a magnet and he moved closer, his chest touching hers, his lips only an inch from hers.

Connor kissed Julia.

Lightly. A feather of a kiss. A sign of support, of friendship.

Friendship? He didn't kiss women out of friendship. He kissed them because he wanted to take them to bed.

He wanted to take Julia to bed.

He stepped back. His body wanted Julia Chandler. His mind said *hold on.*

Shut up, he told his brain.

Julia stared at him, confused, her face flushed. The vulnerability disappeared, but she wasn't moving away. Wanting her was wrong. How could either of them forget everything that happened five years ago?

Something brushed between their legs and together, they looked down to see the orange-and-white tabby rubbing up against Julia. She smiled, bent down, and picked him up.

"Hi, Scruffy. Fits him, don't you think? He must like you. He doesn't usually come out from under the porch when people come over."

Connor scratched between the cat's ears.

"We met earlier."

"He was a stray, but . . ." Her voice trailed off. "A little boy, not more than six, had nearly kicked him to death. I saw and stopped it, brought him home, then tracked down the boy's parents. You know serial killers often start by abusing animals?"

"So I've heard." Connor gave her an odd half-smile, humorous but not ridiculing her.

She cleared her throat, stepped away from him. "Well, anyway, they didn't seem to think it was as serious as I did. So I kept Scruffy."

Headlights rounded the corner and Dillon pulled up next to the house. He got out of the car with a tray of coffee and a bag. "Dessert," he said.

"Time to get back to work," Connor said.

Dillon walked up the stairs. "I've been thinking about this. We're going beyond the gray area. We need to be cautious. If Bowen is somehow involved, we can't jeopardize his conviction with improprieties. We keep an eye on Bowen and play it by ear. Nothing bold."

"I'm not going to jeopardize this case. We're going to nail him," Julia said.

"No Fourth Amendment for you, eh?" Connor joked.

"If I thought every defendant sitting

across the courtroom from me was innocent, I wouldn't be doing my job."

"Bowen isn't in a courtroom yet."

It was three in the morning when they found a connection.

Having read Jason Ridge's thin file three times, Julia almost missed it.

SEVENTEEN

It took Julia three hours Saturday morning to track down Michelle O'Dell's parents, Richard and Gina. She debated phoning ahead, but figured she'd get more information if she came to their door.

The O'Dells lived in a modest San Diego neighborhood near the air force base, filled with post–World War II bungalows. As many houses as had been let go had been remodeled. Julia couldn't tell if the neighborhood was on an upswing or a downswing. The O'Dells' place hadn't been remodeled, but was tidy and well maintained. Flowers flourished in pots and in the ground.

Julia rang the bell. A woman answered with a cautious smile. "Mrs. Gina O'Dell?" Julia asked.

"Yes?"

Julia held out her card. "I'm Julia Chandler with the District Attorney's Office. I was wondering if you had a few minutes to talk about an old case I'm working on."

Mrs. O'Dell opened the door. She was a trim, attractive woman in her late fifties, but moved with the pain of arthritis. "Ms. Chandler, please come in. May I get you coffee? Water?"

"You don't need to go to any trouble. I won't be long."

Mrs. O'Dell waved her comment away. "Come into my kitchen. It's the coziest room of the house, and I have cookies in the oven."

"Thank you."

The short hall that led from the entry to the kitchen in the back of the house was filled with pictures, floor to ceiling. Half were old black-and-whites of ancestors; the other half were of a girl growing up. Julia stopped to look at a pretty girl in pigtails, this picture taken when she was eight or nine, her two front adult teeth too large for her face. Another picture showed a more mature, beautiful girl of about sixteen with long blond hair and exquisite blue eyes. Michelle grew from pretty girl to beautiful teenager. She could have been a model.

Mrs. O'Dell noticed Julia looking at the photographs and smiled. "That's Michelle, my daughter. Beautiful, isn't she?"

"Very."

"Smart, too. She's at Stanford."

"Impressive."

Julia sat at a fifties-style table, called "retro" today and available at stores like Ikea, but this was an original. The red vinyl on the chairs had been painstakingly cared for.

Julia sat in the chair Mrs. O'Dell indicated and didn't object to the coffee she poured. After her late night, she could use a cup. "Thank you for your hospitality."

"What can I help you with?"

"Do you remember a friend of your daughter's? Jason Ridge?"

Mrs. O'Dell shook her head slowly. "Poor boy. His death was so tragic, so sudden. She lost her two best friends the same year."

"You knew him well?"

"For a time. He and Michelle met at a dance, and he was smitten with her. A lot of boys were, but Jason seemed smart, too. Michelle didn't particularly care for boys her own age, much to my dismay. She said they were immature and dumb. When she brought Jason home regularly, we were pleased."

"According to the newspaper reports, Michelle and Jason were no longer seeing each other when he died."

"They'd broken up about four months

before that. But they were still friends. He came over several times after they broke up. I think he still wanted to work things out, but Michelle . . ." She sighed and smiled. "It was okay. Eighteen these days is too young to be serious. And Michelle had been accepted into a special Stanford program. She graduated a year early. Very smart, my girl."

"I'd like to talk to Michelle about Jason, but I couldn't find her number at Stanford."

"Can I ask why? Is there something wrong?"

"No, not at all. But I'm investigating another —" Julia fumbled. She hadn't expected to have to make up a story. "Um, another similar death and I wanted to ask people who knew Jason before he started using steroids if they saw a change in him prior to his death."

Mrs. O'Dell said, "It's a shame that young people today have so much pressure on them to succeed. Jason's father pushed him, harder than I felt was healthy. But I wasn't his mother, I couldn't very well tell the man to go easy on the boy. I think that's why Jason liked coming over here. The peace."

"You have a lovely home."

She beamed in the praise. "It's small, but we don't need anything more. We've been here for thirty-two years, since the day we came home from our honeymoon."

"Is your husband home?"

"He plays golf on Saturdays. He's retired military. Supply sergeant, not combat, but the pay and benefits were good. We could have moved, but why? Now that Michelle is in college, we can travel a little and afford to send her to a top school. We don't need a bigger place."

She rose and shuffled to a desk in the corner of the kitchen. She copied information from a Rolodex card onto a notepad and brought it to Julia. "Here is Michelle's phone number and address at Stanford. She lives in an apartment off-campus."

"Does she visit?" Julia wanted to meet with her face-to-face. She could better assess answers when she could look the person in the eye.

"Not as much as I would like."

Julia finished her coffee. "Thank you so much for the coffee, Mrs. O'Dell."

"No trouble at all."

Mrs. O'Dell walked Julia to the door. She was about to say her good-byes when she remembered something Mrs. O'Dell said when she first asked about Jason. "You said Michelle lost her two best friends the same year. Jason and who else?"

Mrs. O'Dell's face clouded. "Shannon. What a lovely girl. So sweet. She committed suicide. Devastated her parents. They ended up divorcing and moving away, they couldn't bear the memories."

Julia couldn't help but think about Emily. She'd been on the fast track to an early death as well. Though she believed Emily hadn't meant to try to kill herself, she still needed help and guidance.

"I'm sorry. It must have been devastating for Michelle."

"She hides her pain well. I sent her to counseling, though. When tragedy like that hits, you need to learn how to deal with it. And she wasn't talking to us, so I knew it bothered her more than she let on."

Julia thanked Mrs. O'Dell again and left. She drove around the corner, parked, and dialed the number written in Mrs. O'Dell's careful script.

"You've reached Michelle. I'm not in right now, please leave a message. Bye!"

Julia hung up without leaving a message. She'd try again later.

She debated going by the Ridge house, then decided she'd wait until tonight.

She went to the library and pulled every article she could find about Garrett Bowen and Jason Ridge. There were several articles about Bowen's psychiatry practice and she put those aside to give to Dillon. He'd probably be able to pull out the important information faster than she could.

One article about a teen suicide popped up. Julia expected to see Bowen's name, and was surprised to see Jason Ridge quoted.

"I don't know why Shannon would do that. She was so beautiful and nice and she did good in school," Jason Ridge, a junior at San Diego High said. Jason said they shared English and Biology classes together, and Shannon was a cheerleader for the football team where Jason plays varsity-level quarterback.

Nothing else in the article referred back to Jason, and it probably didn't mean anything. Julia skimmed the rest of the article. Shannon Chase had been sixteen and hung herself in the foyer of her house when her parents went out for dinner and a show one night. No one suspected foul play. She'd left a suicide note, the content not disclosed in the article.

Julia gathered up her copies and left when she realized it was getting late. Dillon and Connor would be picking her up shortly and she still needed to shower and change.

Connor. He'd kissed her yesterday. Could she even call it a kiss? No, it was more like sympathy because she was so upset about Emily.

It wasn't a kiss.

She could still feel his body hot against hers. His overpowering presence. The way his hard muscles and dark, probing eyes left her weak-kneed and wanting much, much more than a simple kiss.

Stop thinking about him.

Right. That was proving impossible the more time they spent together.

EIGHTEEN

Julia was too damn sexy in that dress.

She sat in the passenger seat of Dillon's Lexus on their way to Bowen's house in the prestigious Rancho Santa Fe area. Her hair done in a sort of fancy twisty thing with some loose curls hanging down and some pinned on top. Her makeup was impeccable, highlighting her aristocratic features and lush, red lips. But it was the dress that did Connor in, a green number that hinted at all her curves without showing a damn thing.

Connor didn't really like the fact that Dillon was playing Julia's escort. Their plan was solid: Connor would check in with them, then disappear and do his own thing — namely search Bowen's office for any material regarding Wishlist. Dillon and Julia would tag Bowen, identify Jason Ridge's parents, and work that angle in a diplomatic manner.

But Connor wouldn't mind having the beautiful counselor on his arm instead of his brother's. *They're not out on a date,* he reminded himself, though would he care if they were?

Yes.

He hadn't meant to kiss Julia yesterday. But today it was all he could think about.

"What do you think, Connor?"

"Excuse me?"

"Daydreaming, obviously," Julia said. "I *said* I couldn't reach Michelle O'Dell today. I talked to her mother, though, and she was very nice. Michelle attends Stanford. I tried her a couple times, her answering machine was on. I'll try her again tomorrow morning."

"Call her early, if she's a typical college student she'll have stayed up all night and be sleeping late on Sunday," Dillon suggested.

"Good idea, I'll do that."

"Yeah," Connor said, not exactly sure what he'd missed in the conversation. "What's this fund-raiser for, exactly?"

"It's a charity event for the San Diego Arts Foundation," Julia explained. "The Chandler Foundation is a major sponsor every year. I don't have a lot of the details because I don't follow Foundation business, but it's a worthwhile cause. The money raised goes to bringing big exhibits to town, as well as scholarships for underprivileged youth who show artistic talent."

"So how much does a major sponsorship cost?"

"I think we put in a half million every year."

Connor's chin almost hit the floor. He'd known Julia was rich — everyone in San Diego knew about the Chandler family — but knowing someone was rich, and knowing *how rich* someone was were two completely different things.

"And you're a public servant making what? Forty, forty-five thousand a year?" Connor said.

"Your point?"

She sounded pissed.

"I was joking."

"No you weren't. Did it ever occur to you that I like my job? Money doesn't buy everything. It certainly hasn't bought Emily happiness, and it hasn't been able to bring my brother back from the dead."

"I'm sorry."

And he was. He hadn't meant to insult her, and he definitely didn't want to hurt her.

"It's okay," she said quietly, staring

straight ahead through the car windshield.

Smooth move, Kincaid.

The show must go on.

Three days after her husband was brutally murdered and her daughter was put under psychiatric observation in the hospital, Crystal Montgomery had donned a long black gown, put on diamonds bought with Chandler money, and was attending one of the premiere charity events of the year. Julia could hardly believe her audacity.

"Are you okay?" Dillon Kincaid kept his voice low.

She glanced at his handsome face, gave him a smile. "I'm fine."

She wondered where Connor was. They'd checked in fifteen minutes ago and Connor had vanished. She hadn't meant to jump down his throat after he made that comment about her money, but she'd fielded so many insensitive comments over the years that it was a defense mechanism.

While she couldn't see Connor, she spotted Dr. Garrett Bowen right off, standing with an attractive woman in her forties wearing a long red dress. "Do you know her?" Julia asked Dillon.

"I don't get out much," he teased. "Haven't seen her before." He pointed to one of the paintings in the large gathering room. The party planners had brought in dozens of exhibits, large and small, on easels and stands, to fill Bowen's tastefully decorated home. But Bowen himself had numerous paintings and sculptures that he obviously owned based on their placement on walls, one of which Dillon gestured toward. It consisted of various vertical black lines of differing widths.

"Interesting," he said.

She turned her head this way and that, trying to figure out what it was meant to convey. She wondered if the painting would look different from a distance.

"I'm joking," Dillon said.

"Good. Now that one *is* interesting."

They walked across the room to a picture displayed above the fireplace. It was a watercolor with vivid colors. She wondered if there was some blending of mediums going on, perhaps watercolor traced in oil-based paints. Whatever it was, the image was spectacular. From a distance, the picture was obviously a woman sitting on a grassy knoll. But from close-up, several distinct images of children emerged.

"Definite talent there," Dillon said.

"Thank you."

Julia jumped, turning to face Garrett

Bowen. "You're a painter?"

"No, no. My nephew. He's very gifted. It's one of the reasons I am a patron of the arts."

Bowen turned from her to Dillon. "What brings you here tonight, Dr. Kincaid?"

Julia couldn't miss the hostility in Bowen's voice.

"Julia asked me to escort her, and I was happy to oblige," Dillon said formally.

Bowen didn't believe him, but didn't argue. "Crystal's here. Let me find her for you," he said to Julia.

"No need," Julia said, more curtly than she intended. It was then she realized Bowen's comment had been meant to throw her off balance. It had worked.

"Why are you here tonight?" Bowen asked Julia.

"Keeping my eye on you."

"I'm not under arrest, Ms. Chandler. I'm not guilty of anything."

"Guilt can be subjective, can't it?"

"What is it you want from me?"

"Nothing right now. I'm a firm believer that no crime is perfect. Evidence always talks. Sometimes we don't hear it right away, but it's there whispering."

"I had nothing to do with what happened to Judge Montgomery," Bowen said.

Julia hadn't meant to get into it with

Bowen, but she couldn't stop herself. "You didn't? You created that group, Wishlist. You brought vulnerable teenagers into an atmosphere where hate and anger fester, all under the guise of helping them. Does Emily look like she's been helped?"

Dillon put a hand on her arm.

"Emily is obviously a disturbed young woman," said Bowen. "Ask her mother."

He was baiting her, knowing about her history with Crystal. What else did he know? Did he use people's fear and anger against them? Had he manipulated Emily like this? Subtly jabbing, picking at old scabs?

"Let's look at the other painting," Dillon said to her. "There's food in the dining room."

"Garrett?"

The woman in the red dress who had been with Bowen earlier approached them, a cautious smile on her face.

"I hope I'm not interrupting."

"Not at all, Marisa."

Marisa smiled at Julia. "Nice to meet you, Ms. Chandler."

"I'm sorry, have we met?" Julia took her hand.

"Not formally. I of course know about the Chandler family. Garrett has been giddy as a schoolboy about the Foundation's support of Tristan's work."

"Tristan?" Julia asked.

"My nephew," Bowen said. "Ms. Chandler, Dr. Kincaid, please meet Marisa Wohler.

"Where's Camilla?" Bowen asked her.

"She's in the little girls' room," Marisa said. She smiled at Julia. "Cami is my daughter. Garrett is wonderful with young people."

Something tickled Julia's instincts. "Is that how you met?"

Marisa was about to say something when Bowen said, "Marisa, you haven't spoken with Tristan yet." He gestured toward the main living area where a tall, oddly attractive young man with a shaved head held court to a large group of admirers. "You'll excuse us," he said to Julia, avoiding eye contact.

Connor located some key computer files in Bowen's office, but he didn't have time just then to go through them. He hurriedly made electronic copies, then put the CD in his breast pocket. He made sure the desk was exactly as it had been when he walked in. He shut down the computer and started for the door.

The door opened when he was halfway across the room and Connor froze. Fortunately, he was no longer behind the desk.

"Who are you?"

Young and blond, she wore a skimpy dark-red gown that Connor wouldn't mind seeing the counselor wearing. On the teenager, the sexy dress made Connor uncomfortable. His dad would lock his little sister Lucy in her room before letting her out wearing something so revealing.

Connor felt old.

"A guest," Connor responded. "I was looking at the art in the halls and noticed the picture above the desk in here. Exquisite."

"Garrett doesn't like strangers in his office." The girl walked over to him, utterly confident in four-inch heels. Slits up both sides of the gown ended at the top of her thigh. She put a hand on his chest. "But I won't tell."

Connor tensed. "There's nothing to tell. Who are you?"

"Camilla Wohler. You can call me Cami."

"Maybe I should ask what you're doing upstairs."

She laughed seductively, leaned forward and breathed into his ear. "My mother is dating Garrett."

"How interesting." Connor took a step back.

She shrugged, a pout on her face. "I don't really care. I'm nineteen. If he makes her happy."

Her tone was off. It wasn't clear whether she really cared if her mother was happy, or whether she didn't think Garrett Bowen was good for her.

This was an opportunity Connor couldn't pass up. "Do you like Dr. Bowen?"

"I don't hate him." Cami touched his arm. "Nice tux. It's not yours, though."

Connor didn't know why the observation made him uncomfortable. It's not like he cared if he owned a tux or not. It was the girl's tone, almost derisive.

"And you know this how?"

"You're wider than the owner." She put her hands on his shoulders. "And a half inch taller, I'd guess." She glanced at his ankles.

True. The suit was his father's, and while Connor and Patrick Sr. were both built roughly the same, Connor was a little bigger all around.

"You're a fashion expert?"

"I'm an expert in a lot of things." Cami leaned toward him, her mouth inches from his.

He took her hands off his shoulders and

held her wrists. Instead of being shocked or hurt, Cami smiled. "You like it rough, don't you?"

"Not with nineteen-year-old girls." He took a step back.

She pouted, her bottom lip fuller, her eyes narrowing. "You don't know anything about me," she said.

"Nor you about me. We're even." He walked past her and to the door. He needed to get out of the room, not only before Bowen discovered him but to get away from Cami Wohler, who was very unlike the young women he was used to.

"Where are you going?" she demanded.

"Back to the party. I suggest you do the same."

He didn't wait for her to follow. He walked out and shut the door behind him.

Cami stared at the closed door. The arrogant bastard. How dare he call her a *girl.* She wasn't some giggling kid, she was a *woman* who knew more about what turned men on than they did.

The door opened and closed again. Skip came in. "Who was that?" he asked, angry.

"He was in here when I arrived."

Skip walked over to her, grabbed her arms. "Did you have sex with him?"

She laughed. "Right, I just got down on my knees and gave him head. I don't even know him."

"Like that's stopped you before."

"Are you jealous?"

"No."

Oh, was he jealous! She could play off that. Already the insults of the jerk who just left were fading. "I thought you might want to watch me fucking another man."

His grip tightened. *"No."*

She whispered, "You're going to leave bruises."

He jumped back, dropping her arms. He didn't like marking her, especially where it could be seen. His dark fantasies were deeply hidden — as long as he couldn't see the physical evidence of his anger, he'd do anything to her.

She walked toward him. "You love it. You want to put your mark on me. You want to draw blood and suck it like a vampire."

"You're sick."

She exposed her right breast, the one he bit three nights ago in the heat of climax. The red welt his teeth made had turned dark purple, the individual bite marks still prominent. "You liked it."

He shook his head. "I didn't do that."

"Of course you did. As you dug your nails

into my ass and fucked me."

"Stop it, Cami. Right now." He tried to cover her up, but she slapped his hand. Skip slapped her across the face.

She laughed. "Tonight, when this is done, come to my apartment."

"No." He pulled the dress back over her breast.

"Yes!" She pushed him in the chest. "Don't tell me no. We're in this together. I can't be here tonight to watch, dammit, I want to hear about it. Every detail."

"Want me to make a video?" he asked sarcastically.

"Don't be stupid. That would be evidence."

"Not if no one else was in the picture."

True. And she could always erase it after she watched it. The thought of seeing Garrett Bowen struggling for air calmed her down.

"You'd do that for me?" she asked Skip in her sweet voice.

He gently touched her cheek, where he'd slapped her, and said, "You know I'd do anything for you, Cami." He leaned forward and kissed her.

She didn't want to leave, but she had to. "Is Robbie okay?"

"Totally clean. I told you he would be."

"Good. And Faye?"

"She's in place."

Cami had unlocked the only window that wasn't visible to the external cameras. Now Robbie, Skip, and Faye just had to hide until the house was empty and Garrett Bowen was alone.

Julia had been monitoring James and Stephanie Ridge for the past thirty minutes. "Are you ready?" she asked Dillon.

"Let's go."

The Ridges were talking to another couple. Julia made small talk, not knowing who they were even though they knew her. It made her uncomfortable, but she was used to it. Finally, they left, and before the Ridges could excuse themselves, Julia said, "We haven't met formally, but I wanted to tell you how sorry I am about what happened to your son."

James's face tightened. "That was nearly a year ago."

"I know, but I work for the District Attorney's Office and another steroid death has been brought to our attention. Jason has been on my mind lately."

"Jason didn't use steroids," James Ridge said with complete confidence, or total denial.

"I'm sorry, I didn't mean —"

"I don't care what your idiot coroner found, Jason was clean. As Garrett can tell you."

"Garrett? You mean, Dr. Bowen?"

"Yes, he was seeing Jason. He'll tell you Jason worshipped his body and would never put alcohol or drugs into it. Jason's body was his temple."

"The autopsy report —" Julia was uncertain how to proceed.

"Mistakes happen, Ms. Chandler." James Ridge put his arm around his wife. She had tears in her eyes. Julia felt bad for bringing up their son's death.

Dillon saved her. "We wanted to talk to Michelle O'Dell, Jason's ex-girlfriend. In the initial investigation she seemed to have some information that may have helped —"

"Good riddance. She was no good for Jason." Stephanie Ridge spoke up for the first time.

"Excuse me?"

"I didn't like Michelle. He broke up with her after just a couple months. And that's when his problems started, and —"

"Stephanie," James said, his voice low and threatening.

"It's water under the bridge," Stephanie said with a half smile. "Jason was a good boy. He was."

"Excuse us," James said and steered his wife away.

"What do you think?" Dillon asked Julia when the Ridges were out of earshot.

"I think I want to talk to Stephanie Ridge without her husband."

They regrouped at Julia's house. Connor watched how Julia and Dillon played off each other as they shared their conversations and observations. Julia was relaxed and smiled at Dillon. He felt a pang of something odd in his chest. It couldn't be jealousy because, dammit, he didn't even *like* Julia.

He just didn't like the thought of Dillon kissing her.

He tried to convince himself that it was simply because the counselor had screwed him so royally five years ago. Dillon shouldn't be consorting with the enemy, so to speak. He knew damn well how Julia had messed with Connor's life. Wouldn't a good brother help keep her at arm's length?

But in the back of his mind, Connor acknowledged that it was the thought of Dillon intimately touching Julia that set him off. Kissing her lips . . . touching her breasts . . . making love to her.

"I think we're done," Connor said, jumping up. "Let's go."

"What about the disk you got?" Julia said. "I thought we were going to look at it."

Connor pulled it from his pocket and tossed it to her. "I assume you have a computer somewhere."

Julia frowned. She led the way down the hall to an office. It was perfectly furnished, with built-in bookshelves filled to the brim with legal, historical, and fiction books. Her computer sat on a large mahogany desk in the middle of the orderly room.

Parking herself in the leather swivel chair, Julia booted up the hard drive and put in the CD. Dillon and Connor looked over her shoulder. "So what did you get?" she asked Connor.

"I copied anything that looked potentially relevant, including e-mails."

"Hmmm." Julia clicked this and that and dragged the e-mail file into a program.

"He didn't use his home computer much, did he?" Dillon said, looking at the sparse information.

"No," Connor concurred. "There weren't a lot of files to download."

"Nothing about Wishlist," Julia said, disappointed. "Just messages from his nephew, his girlfriend, colleagues. And they're all recent, nothing older than two months."

"He may well have purged his e-mail file," Dillon said. "I do it regularly."

"Dammit. I really thought there'd be something here."

"It wouldn't be admissible in court anyway, Julia," Dillon reminded her.

"I know," she snapped. "I'm sorry. I'm just tired."

Dillon glanced at his watch. "It's late," he acknowledged, then said to Julia, "It's been a long couple days for you. Are you okay here?"

Julia smiled, nodded. "I'm fine, thank you for your concern. I talked to Emily earlier and am going by the hospital in the morning. She sounds better. I just — I'm scared about letting the police in to talk to her. Do you think she's ready?"

"Yes, I do. We'll prepare her in the morning. Meet there at ten? Will isn't coming until noon."

"What's going on tomorrow?" Connor asked, feeling out of the loop.

Julia said, "We're meeting at the hospital to talk to Emily about her police interview. I thought I told you."

"You didn't."

"I'm sorry," Julia began.

"I have a vested interest in this case, Julia. You hired me to help Emily. Don't keep me in the dark."

Dillon intervened. "I'll pick you up on the way," he said to Connor. "All right?"

Connor nodded. "Fine. Good night." He walked out. He heard Dillon mumble something incoherent to Julia, then follow him to the front porch. Behind them, bolts slid into place.

"What was that about?" Dillon asked. "Julia's been through hell this week and you just jumped all over her."

"I didn't."

"Yes, you did."

Connor slid into Dillon's passenger seat and drummed his fingers against the dashboard.

Dillon turned on the ignition. "What's with you?"

"Nothing."

When Connor didn't elaborate, Dillon said, "It's difficult for you to let go of the hatred you felt for Julia, isn't it?"

"Don't psychoanalyze me, Dil. I don't need it."

"She's beautiful and smart. It's impossible to hate her."

"So you're hot for her," Connor said, his jaw tense.

"I like her. I've worked with her on several cases over the years and have the utmost respect for her. I wouldn't say I was *hot* for her."

"Then what would you say?" Connor demanded, slapping his palm on the dashboard.

"I'd say that *you* were hot for her."

"That woman destroyed my career, Dil. I shouldn't have to remind you of what happened."

"No, you don't. And it was lousy. But it wasn't Julia acting alone. The case was bigger than her, bigger than you. I hate that you were pushed off the police force. You're a great cop with better instincts than anyone I've met. But sometimes things happen and they're no one's fault. Would you have wanted Crutcher to get off? To go back to pocketing an extra hundred thousand a year to turn his back on the murders of dozens of young women when they became too much trouble for their pimps?"

"Of course not. But it's the Blue Code. You don't turn on your own. I gave them everything they needed. They didn't need my testimony. I had already gone farther than I wanted."

"Evidently, they did need your testimony. And it worked. And just because some of your colleagues couldn't get beyond the Code doesn't mean you did the wrong thing."

No one outside law enforcement *could* understand. Being a cop was a different job from any others out there. On the other side of the shield, you were a family. Your brothers and sisters went through marriages because marriage was difficult enough, but as a cop they were almost impossible to sustain. You lost them to violence, to violent junkies pumped up on PCP or heroin. Good cops were sued by rapists and murderers who hurt innocent citizens, but who screamed brutality when they were slammed to the cement during arrest.

The cards were stacked against them. Criminals had no rules to follow, but cops were strangled by regulations, rules that sometimes got them killed or, if they broke the rules to save their life, got them sued.

When Connor learned about Wayne Crutcher's dirty dealings, he was physically ill. This wasn't a free Starbucks latte every morning when you walked the beat, but cold, bloody cash. Connor felt he had to do *something.*

He just didn't expect to lose everything he had, including his identity as a cop. He didn't expect to be threatened by a district attorney who'd never seen the world through a cop's eyes.

But Dillon was right. It wasn't just Julia he was angry with. The system had let him down, as had his former friends and colleagues who dropped him and forced him to resign.

Dillon said softly, "Doing the right thing isn't always the easiest thing."

"Tell me about it," Connor grumbled. His anger toward Dillon had dissipated. His brother had always stood by him no matter what. You couldn't buy that kind of loyalty.

"Are you going to cut Julia some slack?" Dillon asked.

"I'm helping her now, aren't I?"

"I guess that's a start."

"A start to what?"

"Forgiveness. Because I sure wouldn't want to hold a grudge against one of the sexiest women in San Diego, who also happens to have a sharp head on her shoulders."

"You *do* like her."

"Oh yes, I do. But not half as much as *you* do."

NINETEEN

The mansion on La Gracia in Rancho Santa Fe was empty. The housekeeping staff was gone for the night; Garrett detested strangers, even servants, living under his roof. The caterers had cleaned and packed up after the last guest left. Tristan's art was still displayed, to be picked up Monday morning by the new Art Center that was to benefit from this fund-raiser.

But it was more than his need to be alone. Tomorrow was special.

Monica. She died eight years ago tomorrow — no, today. Twenty-six minutes from now marked the true anniversary of her death.

Shaking his head, Garrett strode to the library and poured himself a drink. He knocked it back. It had not been murder. Monica had already been dead inside, her body black with cancer.

Garrett, please don't let me suffer anymore.

She would have been dead in months — or weeks. There was no hope for her.

The thick tumbler shattered in his hand. Garrett startled, stared at the blood dripping from his palm onto the white carpet.

He hadn't lost his temper once since that last time years and years ago. Before the cancer, before the murder.

Dr. Garrett Bowen taught people control because *he* was in control. That he hadn't felt his hand squeeze the glass to breaking point unnerved him.

He cleaned up the glass, then wrapped his hand in a small towel he'd found in the bar area and stared at the blood drying into his carpet.

Thump.

The sound came directly above him. He frowned. Could there be an intruder? Maybe a drunken guest who had gone to sleep in one of the bedrooms. He couldn't think of anyone off the top of his head, but over two hundred people had come in and out of his house this evening.

He walked upstairs and looked in all the bedrooms. Empty. The house was far too big for him, but it was an architectural masterpiece, an exquisite minimalist structure that had been written up and photographed in numerous magazines.

His wife had designed and decorated the house. It was a tribute to his long-dead wife Janine that he never moved. To their timeless love.

His den.

He'd seen Connor Kincaid earlier that evening. That Kincaid wasn't on the guest list, and he left before everyone else, but Garrett was certain he must have come in with Dillon Kincaid and Julia Chandler. Now, he wondered, how long had Connor been in the house?

Garrett opened the door to his office.

Nothing appeared to have been disturbed, but he smelled something . . . perfume. Marisa? No, it wasn't her scent and she would have no reason to come up to his office. Still, a lingering female presence hung about the room.

He booted up his computer. He wasn't savvy enough to be able to tell if someone had looked through his files or e-mail, but he could at least make sure he had in fact removed all hints of Wishlist on his system.

Everything was in order. He was okay. Not that he wouldn't be okay if everything came out. True, Bowen's approach to anger management wasn't yet accepted among his colleagues, but it worked. He'd been tracking the success of the program for over three years, and was documenting his findings to obtain needed funding and support to reproduce the program in a controlled university setting. He'd already been talking to the head of psychiatry at one of the most prestigious universities in the country, which was also affiliated with a top-ranked accredited hospital that specialized in mental health. Wishlist would catapult Garrett Bowen to the top of his field. Those who called him foolish and derided his theories would bow down to his brilliance. He'd turn every anger management program in the country into his model and finally receive the acknowledgment he richly deserved.

He needed to better assess prospective members, but he was working on the few glitches in the system. That's why he was doing this in the first place, to fix any potential problems before he took his theories to the industry.

He wasn't about to allow holier-than-thou Dillon Kincaid or his PI brother to stop him.

Except for the scent of perfume, Garrett was confident no one had gone through his office. Perhaps one of the guests had come in to powder her nose, or was just nosy.

Garrett left his office and walked into his former patient Faye Kessler, who was standing just outside his door.

"Faye?" Faye shouldn't be here. He hadn't been counseling her for months, and she'd always unnerved him just a bit. "What are you doing here? How did you get in?"

"Cami let me in," she said, her voice oddly flat.

"Camilla?" *Why?* He stepped back. A tickle of fear crept up his spine. *Call the police.* "Where's Camilla?"

"She left with her mother, of course," Faye said. "You saw her leave."

Faye's monotone troubled him, but it was her eyes — flat, emotionless, old — that increased Garrett's trepidation.

He tried to smile as he walked along the upper balcony overlooking the foyer below. Except for dim lighting in wall sconces perfectly placed twelve feet apart along the rounded hall, no lights were on in the house. Hadn't he left the foyer lights on? He generally did. Now everything was cast in odd shadows, and the foyer looked like a bottomless pit. "How have you been?"

She touched his sleeve. "Look."

He reluctantly stopped walking. He couldn't let her sense his fear. He was a trained psychiatrist, he told himself, if she planned on doing something, he could talk her out of it.

315

As he watched, she turned around and pulled up her shirt. Her back was covered with scars, old and new. *Her back.* Someone was cutting her. She was allowing it. He had thought she stopped. For the last year, he'd believed she was clean.

How could he have been so wrong?

She turned around and he caught a glimpse of her braless breasts, also defiled. Who had done it to her? Why had she allowed it?

"Who hurt you?"

Her laugh was borderline insane. "You never understood. You pretended to, and I let you think you got it, but you never realized the power." She pulled down her shirt, took a step toward him. Unconsciously, he took a step back and found himself backed against the balcony railing.

A door opened to his left, at the top of the staircase he was trying to reach. Skip Richardson emerged.

Panic hit Garrett Bowen head-on. Why were these two former patients in his house?

Now he didn't care whether they saw he was scared. He needed to get to his bedroom and lock the door. There he could hit the panic button that would bring the police and alert his private security company.

He ran down the hall, away from Faye and

316

Skip. Ahead, his bedroom door opened.

Robert Haxton held a gun, its muzzle aimed at Garrett's chest.

"What's up, Doc?" Robert grinned at his poor joke.

"What do you want? Money for your drugs? You're still on drugs, aren't you?"

"You should know. You got me hooked on them."

"I did no such thing," Garrett said, a new-found fury breaking through his fear.

"Oh, yeah. You're a fuckin' pusher. Ritalin. Then Wellbutrin when I turned thirteen. And the downers and the uppers and everything in between."

"You were depressed and ADHD," Garrett said. "You attacked your father."

"You never believed *me!*" Robert screamed, his voice echoing in the dark foyer below. "You believed that bastard when he said I'd thrown the first punch. Bull-*fucking*-shit."

"You were delusional when first brought to me, and —" but a tickle of doubt niggled in Garrett's mind. Robert's anger had been attributed to ADHD coupled by losing his mother at the age of eight. And George Haxton was a pillar of the community. He was mild-mannered and had defended himself when his son attacked him.

Hadn't he?

"Robert, we can talk about this."

"No talking. You didn't believe me then, you'll only lie to me now because I have the gun." He raised it and put his finger on the trigger.

"Stop!" He didn't want to die. "What do you want? Money?" That was ridiculous. Skip, Faye, Robert — they were all from wealthy families. "Drugs? I don't keep drugs here, but we can go to my office —" Anything to buy time until he could alert someone he was in danger. There were panic buttons in key parts of the house. His garage. The front door. His den . . .

"Drugs? Money?" Robert laughed. "And I used to be afraid that you *could* read my mind. The only thing that will make us happy is to jump up and down on your grave."

Garrett turned to run, away from the gun, heading for the stairs.

Skip was right behind him, his hand outstretched. He had a gun, too.

Not a gun. A Taser. Garrett ran right into it.

Deep electric pain radiated throughout his body as a powerful energy pulsed through his clothing, into his body, causing him to lose control of his limbs. Five seconds might as well have been five hours. Skip pulled the device away and Garrett collapsed against Faye. She was surprisingly strong and held him up. No. Not just Faye. Robert was there, too.

His body frozen, the pain made Garrett's teeth clench, his muscles tighten. He couldn't move. *Move, Garrett, move!* But he was paralyzed.

Faye whispered in his ear, her voice low and warm. "Cami cut me. And she sucked my blood."

"No," he tried to say, but he couldn't make his voice work.

The boys pulled something rough over his neck. The lights came on, too bright, and Garrett squeezed his eyes closed. Something scraped his neck, but the pain was minimal compared to the throbbing that radiated through his body. He was beginning to feel again.

He opened his eyes. The chandelier swayed in front of him. A rope was attached to the base.

He reached for his neck. *Noose.*

"No, please, no!" His voice was weak.

"Get his legs, Robbie," Skip said. "We need to do this fast, the shock is wearing off."

Garrett felt himself lifted up onto the railing. He flailed, kicked at the teenagers trying to kill him. He got Faye in the chest as he tried to grab on to the railing to steady himself.

"Bastard!" Robbie gave him a shove.

Then Garrett was falling, down, down, down. Flashes of light. He barely made out the three silhouetted figures at the railing above him. He tried to reach the noose around his neck, take it off, but everything happened too fast.

He couldn't scream.

He heard the snap of his neck breaking as his body jerked the noose tight. His vision faded, and his body swung back and forth, back and forth as his lungs fought for air that did not come.

"An eye for an eye, Garrett."

That voice! He was dying, he couldn't have heard her voice.

"Good-bye."

He'd wanted to be there when Garrett Bowen swung from the chandelier, but he needed an alibi, just in case, so he'd asked Faye to bring him back a visual.

She brought him four Polaroids.

"Excellent." Glee flooded through him as he stared at each subsequent picture.

Garrett falling. Swinging like a pendulum. Dying.

He stared at the last picture. "You took a picture of *her?* She wasn't even supposed to be there. What happened?"

Faye became defensive. "She showed up just as we were throwing him over the railing. Turned on the lights and we saw her. I didn't mean to take her picture."

He didn't believe Faye. She wasn't stupid. "These are the only pictures you took?"

Faye nodded. He didn't know if she was lying.

"Are you sure?"

Her face reddened. "You don't believe me?"

"Yes, of course, but —"

"You don't believe me." She turned away from him, hurt.

"Faye, I believe you. Come here."

Reluctantly, she came to him. "You did excellent work," he said. "But we have to protect her, if only to protect us. We can't do anything like this again. Garrett Bowen was the last. Now we let things die down. Skip planted the note on his desk, right?"

She nodded, still pouting.

"Then we have nothing to worry about. Come here. Closer."

She walked into his open arms and he

kissed her. He didn't want Faye to leave, but the bitch wanted everyone to split up for now. It was smart, but about this he didn't want to be smart. "One last time."

"What do you mean, last time?" Her voice cracked.

"We need to take a break until the police stop looking at Garrett's patients. I don't want you to end up in prison. I don't want any of you to get hurt."

"But —"

"Shhh." He kissed her again. Even though he had places all over the world where he could hide, he couldn't leave town now. Too many questions would come up. "Later, wherever I go, I'll take you with me, but for now we have to be apart. It won't be forever."

"Promise?"

He kissed her. "I promise. Come to bed." He handed her his favorite knife. "You're the only one I trust. You know that, right?"

Her confidence returned and he finally relaxed. "I know." She took the knife, stared at it. "Are you sure? Have you recovered?"

He nodded. "In your hands, I'm always sure."

When Faye left, he called the stupid bitch who was going to blow everything.

"How dare you show your face!"

"I had to see for myself."

"We agreed you'd be miles away. With an alibi."

She laughed humorlessly. "I have an alibi, darling. I'm no fool."

"We're so close."

"We're done."

"No, we're not. You're playing a dangerous game. You went to the party. What if someone recognized you?"

"I didn't get into any of the media photos. No one recognized me. I've changed a lot."

"Don't be so sure," he grumbled. He'd planned this for too long. Now he realized that he should never have brought her into the plan in the first place. What had seemed like a brilliant idea two years ago now was crumbling around him.

Maybe he should have let her kill Bowen back then and go to prison. Garrett Bowen would be dead either way.

But his game was *perfect*. It was the players who were flawed. Not him, not his idea.

"You worry too much," she was saying. "Payback is sweet. Now you can sit back and have everything you wanted."

She didn't know what he wanted. Sometimes he didn't even know.

"Can you be sure no one saw you at the party?"

She didn't say anything for a long minute. "Julia Chandler was there."

"Dammit! Julia Chandler! What were you thinking? You should never have gone —"

"She doesn't know who I am. I chatted with her very briefly, barely a word. Don't ruin this night. This was the best night of my life. Garrett Bowen is dead. An eye for an eye. I watched him die and enjoyed every minute of it. I had to be there. You don't understand. Sometimes I think you're just like him —"

"No. Stop." He squeezed his temples. "Okay, I'll take care of it."

"There's no need. Julia Chandler doesn't know . . ."

"But you can't know that. She's connected and smart. She's looking into Wishlist. If she makes the connection to Jason Ridge, then she might —"

"Don't say his name." Her voice was almost a growl.

"I'm sorry." She had become a liability, he realized. Maybe he'd always known it would have to end up like this.

He might have to dispatch his team one more time, to tie up loose ends.

But first, Julia Chandler.

He called Cami. "I need another job done. Call Robbie. If he balks, kill him."

TWENTY

Connor couldn't get her out of his head. Worse, in his thoughts, Julia was naked, laying on his bed doing things to him that left him needing a cold shower when he woke that morning at the crack of dawn.

When he got out of the shower, his cell phone was ringing. Seven in the morning? He glanced at caller ID and saw a number he didn't recognize.

"Kincaid."

"Hey, Kincaid. Billy Thompson."

"Billy, what's up?"

"I, um, am heading to the gym to play a little ball. I thought you might want to meet me. I haven't seen you there much lately."

"I'm sorry, I've been busy with this case."

"I have some information."

Connor glanced at the clock. He had time. "I'll be there in thirty minutes."

Julia tried Michelle O'Dell again when she

woke up early Sunday morning. Again, the answering machine picked up. This time, Julia left a message.

"Michelle, my name is Julia Chandler and I'm a deputy district attorney investigating a steroid-related death. I'd like to talk to you about Jason Ridge. Even if you think you have nothing to add to your statement, please call me." Julia thanked her and left her cell phone number.

She hung up, frustrated. She showered, then went downstairs to review her notes. She drew out a timeline.

Jason Ridge is given a Deferred Entry of Judgment in a rape case.

Was Michelle O'Dell the victim? If it was Michelle, her mother probably wouldn't have been so consolatory toward Jason.

Paul Judson is murdered.

Billy Thompson, a short-term member of Wishlist, had been investigated for the murder, cleared. He had posted an incriminating e-mail to the Wishlist loop. But he was innocent.

Jason Ridge dies.

Julia didn't know much about steroid use, but she had to imagine it was dangerous. But could someone overdose on steroids like other hard drugs? She didn't know and made a note to ask Dillon. The autopsy report said heart attack due to excessive steroid use. But what did that mean? Jason Ridge's psychiatrist was Garrett Bowen.

Bowen's name popped up everywhere. Everything connected to him.

Did Jason's death have anything to do with Bowen? Or Wishlist? What if Jason was part of the group?

What if Jason's *rape victim* was part of the group?

Stephanie Ridge.

After last night, Julia knew James Ridge wouldn't say a derogatory word about his dead son. In his eyes, the kid had been perfect. But maybe Stephanie Ridge could contribute some realistic insight into her son's death. And if it would help Emily, Julia would use every emotion at her disposal — guilt, remorse, anger if she had to — to find out the truth.

And where did Victor Montgomery fit in? The only connection, again, was through Bowen and the Wishlist — through Emily.

Julia went through the files, wondering if there was another connection. Something she'd missed. After all, she had over a thousand pages all over her kitchen table, most of them copies.

The judge who gave Jason Ridge the DEJ was Vernon Small.

Judge Small was dead. Julia hadn't attended his funeral, nor had she particularly liked him. He was too easy on the bad guys, too hard on the good guys.

And now he was dead.

Coincidence? She didn't remember how he'd died. He was old, that she knew. She'd assumed it was natural causes.

What if it wasn't?

Connor hightailed it to the downtown gym. Though early on a Sunday morning, there was already a sprinkling of kids lifting weights or playing B-ball on the blacktop.

"Hey, Kincaid, we need another man. Two on two?"

Looking around for Billy, he didn't see him. He glanced at his watch, realized he was ten minutes early.

"For a few minutes." Connor tossed his duffel bag under the bench.

Jesus was a tall, skinny, fast-on-his-feet Cuban American kid who played hard. Mitch and Travis were long and lean six-foot-five-inch brothers who'd been in a gang until Connor busted them for possession with intent to sell and a concealed weapons charge only months before he quit the force. They'd been twelve and thirteen. They'd managed to turn their life around for the most part, but had dropped out of high school. Both worked full-time in blue-collar jobs with little future. But they were clean and spent all their free time at the youth center helping Connor keep the younger kids out of gangs.

Every so often they saved one. Jesus was one such kid. He'd landed a scholarship to Berkeley.

They played hard for thirty minutes before Connor realized Billy hadn't showed. He called time and slapped the kids on the back. "You doing okay?" he asked.

"We're hanging," Jesus said.

"Keep it clean, bro." Connor wiped down and looked around for Billy.

Ten minutes later, when Connor was ready to just leave, Billy entered the basketball courts.

"Hey, you're late."

"I don't want to get fucked."

"I wouldn't fuck you, buddy."

"I remembered what you said. You know, the pay it forward crap."

Connor had tried to instill in the kids he met through the youth center that they always needed to do the right thing, even when they didn't get a direct benefit from it. Most kids, particularly those in the gang culture, couldn't see beyond their own wants and needs.

"And?"

"Well, I remembered something that might be important."

"I'm all ears."

Billy, to his credit, didn't hesitate. "Some fine young woman came up to me a while back."

"Does this gorgeous babe have a name?"

"She didn't tell me. She was a white chick, blond, hot. I thought she might have a thing for black guys, so I listened." Billy grinned.

"Yeah, you're all hung," Connor joked. "Nearly as well as Cubans."

"Shit, you wish." Billy laughed. "So Blondie comes up to me, all sexy and hot, and says she wants to talk to me about justice."

Connor's instincts hummed. The e-mail subject line in Emily's post on Wishlist had justice in it.

"When was this?" he asked Billy.

"A week or so before Judson was shot."

"What did you say?"

"I told her I'd listen. It was at the shop, after hours. She locked the door, got down on her knees, and gave me a blow job."

"In your dreams."

"I swear it, man." Billy held up his hand. "Got right down on her knees. Then she

331

tells me she has a job for me to do. A test."

"What kind of test?"

"That's what I asked."

"And?"

"She said I had to trust her. That she knew all about what had happened at the school, how I lost my scholarship. That there were other people like me who couldn't fight back."

"What did you say?"

"I told her I wasn't interested. Water under the bridge or some such shit. It creeped me out that she knew all about Judson when she didn't even go to that school, you know? I mean, it wasn't like in the papers or nothing."

"Yeah, sounds suspicious to me."

Billy seemed relieved that Connor didn't think he was a dope.

"I'm sorry I didn't tell you before. I didn't really think about it until after you left, and I didn't know if it was important. But . . . you don't think it has anything to do with Judson's murder, do you?"

"I don't know, buddy."

"I'd feel really bad if something I did or didn't do got him killed, even if he was an asshole. I didn't want him dead."

Detective Will Hooper stared at Garrett

Bowen's body hanging from the elaborate chandelier in Bowen's pricey mansion in the gated community of Rancho Santa Fe.

He almost couldn't believe it. It seemed too easy, too convenient.

For the past three days he'd been poring over Wishlist e-mails and came up with the theory that Bowen had used mentally unbalanced kids in his care to play vigilante. Will Hooper didn't think any teenager could plan and implement Victor Montgomery's murder. And while Judson's murder had the *feeling* of immaturity, the irony and vanishing act of the perpetrators gave Will the distinct impression someone was pulling the strings.

And until now, he believed the puppeteer was Garrett Bowen.

Jim Gage called from upstairs. "There's a note."

"What does it say?"

Gage held up the clear plastic evidence bag and read the note inside. " 'I didn't mean for it to go this far.' "

"That's *it?*"

"That's it."

Will didn't like it. Something was off, but just what he couldn't say. Had his call to Bowen the day before to set up a "friendly" meeting — letting it intentionally slip that he was interviewing Emily — set Bowen off? Will thought he had been playing the situation perfectly, but now?

What a mess.

He hesitated before calling Dillon Kincaid. He hated that Dillon was on the side of the defense on this case. A half dozen times Will had picked up the phone to ask his opinion about something, but then had to stop himself.

But he also knew Dillon had a heated conversation with Bowen the day before yesterday, and that he and the counselor had been at Bowen's fund-raiser the night before. That made them witnesses, and dammit, he was going to depose them and find out *exactly* what they'd been up to since Judge Montgomery's murder.

Will punched speed dial to reach Dillon's cell. "Dr. Kincaid."

"Dillon, it's Will Hooper."

"What can I help you with?"

"Bowen's dead."

Silence.

"You there?"

"Yes," Dillon said. "Garrett Bowen is *dead?*"

"Hung from his chandelier. Sometime last night after the party. We need to talk."

"I'll be at the hospital at noon, as we

settled yesterday."

"I need to know what you know."

"How did Bowen die?"

"I told you. He hung himself."

"No, you said he was hanging from his chandelier. Suicide . . . or murder?"

"He left a note."

"Is Gage there?"

"Yep."

"I find it hard to believe a man like Bowen would kill himself."

Will said, "I was looking at him, Dil, and he knew it."

"Looking at him for what? Killing Judge Montgomery?"

"No, instigating it. And that teacher, Paul Judson. I know you have the e-mails, so don't play stupid."

"I'm not, Will."

"You've been running your own investigation with Connor and the counselor, and it may have led to Bowen whacking himself. I need to know what you know."

"After you talk to Emily, we'll talk."

"What exactly does that mean?"

"It means I'll tell you everything I can without jeopardizing Emily's defense. You do think Emily was involved in Montgomery's death, correct?"

Will stared at Bowen's body. "I don't see

any other way it could have happened, but at this point, I don't know what the hell to believe."

"See you at noon." Dillon hung up.

Gage called from upstairs. "Will, I got something."

Will headed upstairs. "Better be good. I need a break right now."

"I don't know about *good,* but it's damn interesting." Gage pointed to the railing. "See those scrapes?"

"Barely."

"They're faint, probably caused by the buttons on Bowen's shirt as he leaned over the railing."

"Okay. So he puts a noose around his head and climbs over the railing." Will looked up at the chandelier. "How the hell did he get the rope secured?"

"That's easy. The chandelier is on a chain. It can be lowered mechanically through a panel by the front door, for cleaning."

"So he lowers the chandelier, attaches the rope, hauls it back up. Why not just put the noose around his neck and let the chain pull him off the ground?"

"The motor might not be designed to pull the additional weight. But that's not the interesting thing."

"Then what is?"

"There are no fingerprints on this railing."

"None?"

"Wiped clean. And I mean *clean.* Smell that?"

Will took a whiff. "Bleach?"

"Someone wiped down this entire banister."

"Maybe the cleaners came in after the party last night."

Gage pointed to the ceiling. "It cracked under the weight of Bowen's body. When we analyze the breakage, I think we'll see he came off the ledge here, like these marks indicate."

"Why didn't he fight back? I didn't see any marks on his hands."

"Maybe he was incapacitated. We'll be able to tell in the autopsy."

"This case just gets weirder and weirder."

"And another thing."

"What?"

"The paper the note was written on? I can't find any more of it in the house."

TWENTY-ONE

Connor was on his way to the hospital when Dillon called him. "Bowen's dead. Possible suicide."

"Possible?"

"He left a note, but I'm not buying it. Will is meeting us at the hospital at noon. Will's theory is that Bowen led some sort of vigilante killing team. I think we need to tell Will about the Jason Ridge connection."

Connor frowned, made an illegal U-turn, and headed toward Julia's house. "I think I'll go pick up the counselor."

"You don't think she's in danger?"

"I don't know, but she's been asking a lot of questions about Jason Ridge and pulled a bunch of files at the courthouse. She was all over the party last night. If Bowen *was* involved like Will thinks, that means the killers he created are free to do whatever the hell they want. If Bowen *wasn't* involved, someone is trying to make it seem like he is, and they wouldn't want Julia digging any further."

"You're right. Pick her up and we'll all meet at the hospital."

Connor sped through the streets toward Julia's, trying to reach her by phone.

No answer. Maybe she'd already left, but then he'd pass her eventually. Her classy Volvo would be easy to spot on the quiet Sunday-morning roads.

Julia loved her house and its ocean view soothed her soul. The road in front of her house had the opposite effect. It was the road Matt died on. She'd almost sold her house after his death, but couldn't bring herself to do it. This house was more than just a place to sleep, it was a symbol of her independence from her family and the Chandler name. It was her refuge. Matt had told her he saw her happiness etched in the fine woodwork she had herself lovingly restored.

So she kept the house and drove down the winding stretch like an old woman, slow and cautious. There were five other driveways off the road before it merged with a street leading to Highway 1.

Passing Mrs. Hutchinson's driveway, in her rearview mirror Julia saw a large black pickup truck pull out behind her. For a split second she thought it was Connor, then remembered his truck was dark blue, not black.

Mrs. Hutchinson's son must have gotten a new vehicle. He came by to check on her several times a week. Julia was about to wave in the rearview mirror, but the truck was now tailgating. She frowned, pressed the gas pedal down a hair more. Her heart suddenly started beating faster as she neared the spot where she'd gone off the cliff and slammed into the tree six years ago, killing Matt.

The truck was inches from her bumper. Julia didn't recognize the driver and couldn't make out details other than he had dark hair.

Hands clutching the wheel, Julia sped up. The truck bumped her hard. She swerved, compensated, and then he hit her again, even harder. Her head hit the steering wheel, her seat belt locked into place.

She could only think about survival as her tormenter sped from behind and pulled his truck parallel to her Volvo.

She braked as fast as she dared, hoping to let him pass, but he turned his truck into her car, though not enough to force her into the gully on the right. Had she not been braking, the impact could have forced her out of control and the drop on the left was precarious.

She'd gone off that rocky precipice before.

She was still half a mile from the main road, where traffic was steady. On this cliff-side stretch, cars were rare. Her quiet, small neighborhood used to make Julia feel safe.

Her heart pounded as the truck sped up, then turned and stopped. She swerved right to avoid hitting him and her right tire dropped hard into the gully, fishtailing her car. The sudden impact caused her air bags to explode.

She was a sitting duck here in the car. She coughed, could barely breathe. The chemicals from the airbag burned her throat and lungs.

She reached into her purse and fumbled for her gun, mentally thanking Connor for listing all the places she was vulnerable outside her house. This morning she'd packed her gun in her purse as a precaution. She'd never thought she'd need it.

She released the seat belt and opened the car door. The fresh air began to clear her lungs. She squatted behind the door. Her assailant was out of his car, about to walk around the front and toward her. What was in his hand? A gun? *A knife?*

Before she could get a better look at the guy, he ran back to the truck, jumped in, and floored it. Down the road.

Julia watched the black truck sideswipe a dark blue truck heading up the hill. *Connor!* He swerved and began to turn to go after the black truck.

A part of her wanted him to come comfort her. Julia was shaking, her gun — the gun she'd only fired on the range once a month — tight in her grip. She wanted Connor to hold her, tell her she was safe.

But the rational part wanted him to go after the jerk who ran her off the road.

She stood and waved at Connor to go after the truck. He paused, then completed the three-point turn and followed her attacker.

Her act of bravery was over. She walked away from the car, wiping her face to rid her skin of the stinging powder from the air bag. She found a spot ten feet behind the car where she could sit on a large, relatively flat rock in the gully. She sat, leaned against the crumbling, uncomfortable cliff, and closed her eyes.

Connor didn't feel comfortable leaving Julia alone and unprotected, but he had to trust she was okay when she waved for him to give chase. Unfortunately, he lost sight of the black truck once he hit Highway 1. Connor looked both ways and couldn't tell which way he'd gone.

Shit.

He dialed 911 and called in the description of the truck, sans license. Lot of good that did — black Ford 150s were a dime a dozen, and unless he got pulled over for driving without plates Connor didn't hold out much hope they'd get him today. Maybe the evidence at the accident scene would turn up something valuable.

As he talked to dispatch, he turned around, tires squealing, and hightailed it back to where he'd left Julia.

If anyone touched her, he would . . . what was he thinking? She wasn't his to protect. Still, he couldn't forget his gut feeling when he feared she'd been hurt.

He relayed their location and hung up after the dispatcher said a patrol was less than five minutes away.

Julia was leaning against the cliff behind her car, gun in hand. When she saw Connor's truck pull up, she visibly relaxed.

He rushed to her. "Are you okay?"

She nodded, but tears streamed down her face. "You didn't get him?"

"No. There were no plates on his car either."

343

"I noticed."

"I called nine-one-one," Connor said. "With any luck, someone will spot him. What happened?"

"I passed Mrs. Hutchinson's driveway and he drove out behind me. I thought he was her son, but he followed closely, then rammed my car twice. He forced me off the road, got out —"

Julia looked up at Connor, her green eyes bright with tears, a bruise already forming on her forehead. "I grabbed my gun. I didn't know what else to do."

He gathered her into his arms. She held on to his neck tightly, her body shaking with fear, relief, and sobs. They sat in the gully. She buried her face in his neck, her breath hot in his ear, her tears wet on his face.

Connor remembered their kiss all those years ago. He'd kissed a lot of women, but he'd never forgotten kissing Julia Chandler. He couldn't forget her lips, her taste, her scent. Now, Connor wrapped his hands at the base of her head, her hair soft and silky entwined in his rough fingers. Pulling her head away from the nook in his neck, he gazed at her beautiful face.

Connor pulled her lips to his and kissed her hard, hating himself for wanting her, hating himself for being unable to hate her.

He should, but she was too damn gorgeous. She made his head spin.

Dear Lord, she tasted like heaven.

Julia gasped when Connor kissed her, then her lips parted and she responded with an unexpected need for him. The light kiss the other day had whetted her appetite for more, had made years of guilt and anger wash away. She'd never been able to forget how good it felt to be held by Connor Kincaid, but even that exquisite memory was faulty. Being in his arms now, having his piercing eyes focus solely on her, was even better than she'd remembered.

"Oh God, Julia," he murmured as his hot kisses moved from her swollen lips to her neck. She quivered beneath his hands. With one hand she grabbed his collar-length hair, her other clasped in his. He kissed her neck and she arched back, wanting him to continue down, to give the same attention to her body as he had to her lips.

When his hand squeezed her breast through the thin material of her filmy sundress she gasped, and then his lips found hers again and she felt the hardness in his lap.

There were sirens in the back of her mind. She sat up, looked over the edge of the gully just as Connor took her hand and pulled her up. A police car came into view and she brushed the dirt and gravel from her dress.

Connor looked her in the eye. "We're not finished."

She just nodded and swallowed.

He handed her her gun, which she'd put down when Connor kissed her, then helped her from the gully. The police car stopped and an officer stepped out. San Diego primarily had one-man patrols, and Julia heard another siren in the distance.

"Shit." Connor raked a hand through his hair.

"What?" she asked.

He didn't answer. The officer approached. "Kincaid."

"Davies."

Julia felt the tension as the two men stared at each other. She took a step forward, extended her hand to Officer Davies. "Deputy District Attorney Julia Chandler. A man driving a black truck ran me off the road. I think he was waiting for me to leave because he came out of Mrs. Hutchinson's driveway — she's the first house after mine at the top."

"I know who *you* are," Davies said. His face was blank and his dark sunglasses hid his eyes. His voice dripped contempt.

She shifted, uncomfortable. She'd lost

some friends in the police department when she prosecuted Crutcher. Why couldn't they see that even though he was a cop he was no better than any other criminal she prosecuted?

But Davies's bitterness wasn't actually aimed at her. He stared at Connor, hand on the butt of his gun. Completely unnecessary, and it irritated Julia.

"Please drop the gun, Ms. Chandler," Davies said.

She turned the gun around and handed it to Davies butt-first. He took it, checked the ammunition. "I have a permit to carry, Officer. When the man ran me off the road, he stopped and got out. I didn't know what he had planned, so I took the gun from my purse."

"Do you have a description of him?"

She shook her head. "I didn't get a very good look. Dark hair. Six foot one or two. Not fat or skinny. Average."

"Would you be able to pick him out in a lineup?"

"I doubt it."

"Has anyone threatened you lately?"

"I often get threatened in court, but I generally don't take it seriously. Usually it's by someone on their way to prison," she added drily.

"What's your interest, Kincaid?"

"None of your business, Davies."

A half-smile turned up Davies's lips. "Chandler have you on retainer?"

Though the words were innocuous, the tone was combative. Julia had been around enough testosterone in the District Attorney's Office to sense these two men disliked each other. Davies was baiting Connor.

Connor said nothing. The tension grew.

Another car pulled up behind Davies. Connor looked over as the cop got out. "This just gets better and better," he said.

"You got a problem?" Davies barked.

"No problem," Connor said. "Ms. Chandler gave you her statement. Write up the report so we can get out of each other's face."

The second cop approached. Julia recognized him, and now she grew as tense as Connor. Rich Rayo had testified for the defense in her case against Wayne Crutcher and his cohorts. And she realized that's what this was all about — her prosecution of a cop for bribery and accessory to murder, and Connor testifying for her.

Rayo walked up and stood inches from Connor. "Turn around."

"No."

"I'll haul you in so fast your head will be spinning."

Julia stepped between them and put her hand on Rayo's chest. "You can't do that."

"Watch me, little lady."

"Excuse me. I'm an officer of the court and I will not have you inappropriately using your authority."

"Stay out of it, Julia," Connor said, his voice low and tinged with anger.

"Listen to your boyfriend," Rayo said. "You fucked with us once, Miz Chandler. We don't forget."

Julia didn't listen to Connor's warning. Her indignation peaked. "Officer Rayo, I did not *fuck* with you or any other good cop. I don't have to wave my credentials at you. I prosecuted a cop who watched two little girls die. Watched their pimps beat them to death. They were *thirteen!*"

Stepping forward, Connor put a hand on her arm. She shook it off. She was angry and upset. Everything that had happened this week — from Victor's murder to learning he'd raped Emily to the DEJ for Jason Ridge — made Julia's fight for the underdog that much more important.

She punched her finger in Rayo's chest. "Get over it. You have nothing to be proud about, standing up for men who victimized children."

Rayo growled. "Touch me again and I'll arrest you for assault."

She was about to jab him again in the chest just for spite when Connor grabbed her wrist and pulled her back.

"Davies has the information about the truck that ran Ms. Chandler off the road. File the damn report. We're going."

"But —" Julia tried to dig in her feet. She was sick and tired of the bullshit coming from these cops about a righteous conviction. Connor firmly led her to his truck.

"Get in."

"But —"

"Would you just do what I say this time without argument?"

Weariness clouded Connor's face and without another word Julia climbed into the truck. The adrenaline from this morning's attack, the kiss, the confrontation with the police, began to wear off. She slumped against the seat.

"I'm sorry," she mumbled.

Swearing under his breath, Connor started his truck. Passing the officers talking by the side of the road, he drove to Julia's house. So angry — with himself, with Julia, with Davies and Rayo — Connor didn't trust himself to speak.

At her house, he jumped from the truck and walked to the edge of the cliff, staring at the ocean. He took a deep breath, then another. Hands on his knees, head down, he finally felt his heart slow.

He rarely got into confrontations anymore. Half the force had been with him, quietly or publicly. The others had been quietly neutral or, like the cops today, blatantly antagonistic. Because his precinct had become so divisive, he had to quit. His boss suggested moving to another city, maybe up in northern California, but Connor couldn't leave his family. They were all he had left after the job. His parents, his brothers and sisters. He didn't want to grow into a bitter cop with nothing but a chip on his shoulder.

But that basically was what had happened over the last five years. He'd let his anger fester.

Turning against his own people had been next to impossible. He wouldn't have done it without Julia's ultimatum. And while he hated her for it, he realized that it was the only way those dead girls could have justice.

Only now did he realize that Julia had actually done him a favor by calling him as a hostile witness.

"I'm sorry," she said.

He hadn't heard her approach.

"I'm fine," he said, his voice clipped.

"I didn't realize how hard it had been for you after the trial."

"It doesn't matter."

"It does."

He turned, grabbing her by the arms. "I don't need you fighting my battles for me."

"I wasn't fighting *your* battle. I was fighting my own. We're on the same side."

"Are we?"

She looked stricken. "I thought so, but maybe I was wrong."

Connor dropped her arms and ran both hands through his hair. "Damn. Just forget it."

"I will. If you can."

Could he? She was offering him an olive branch, why did he hesitate to take it?

"I'll try."

She nodded, touched his face before quickly dropping her hand. "It's a start."

"We have more important things to worry about. The fact that someone tried to kill you is at the top of the list."

"We don't know that he tried to kill —"

He cut her off. "A stranger runs you off the road — a private road — and stops the car. I don't think he wanted to exchange insurance information. And I don't think it's a coincidence."

"But we haven't learned anything that helps us with Emily." She glanced at her watch. "We need to get to the hospital."

"You haven't heard the news."

"What news?"

"Bowen's dead. Apparent suicide."

"Apparent?" she repeated.

"Dillon's suspicious, and Will is hopefully going to be more forthcoming about their investigation. We need to talk about sharing what we have."

"No." She crossed her arms. "You can't give anything to the prosecution. They'll use it against Emily."

"Do you believe Emily is innocent?"

She looked like he'd slapped her. "How can you even ask that?"

"Well," he said, "I think she's innocent, and I also think the best way of proving it is by bringing the cops on board with what we know. Full disclosure."

"I can't do that."

"Yes, you can. Will's one of the best. He's not going to railroad Emily."

Connor pulled Julia into his arms and held her. Her body shook with silent sobs. "This is more about the past than it is about the present, isn't it?" he quietly asked.

She nodded against his chest, hands clenching his shirt.

"I will not let Emily go to prison or juvenile hall or a mental hospital," Connor said. "We will protect her together. I believe she's innocent, and right now I think Will Hooper will listen. Trust me on this."

"I trust you." Her voice was a mere whisper, but the words were powerful.

TWENTY-TWO

After Julia changed and cleaned up from the accident, Connor drove her to the hospital. It was already nearly noon.

In the observation room outside Emily's room, Dillon looked Julia over. "Are you okay? Do you need to see a doctor?" Dillon touched the bruise on her forehead.

"I'm fine. Really."

Fine physically, she thought, but worried to death about what they were asking Emily to do. She played with the rings on her fingers until Connor squeezed her hand. "Remember what I told you," he said.

Dillon said, "I just talked to Emily. She said she wants to talk to the police and tell them everything."

Julia released a pent-up breath. "I don't know what's the right thing to do anymore."

"Emily is going to be fine," Connor said. "You need to think about yourself. Someone just tried to kill you."

Will Hooper stepped into the observation room. "Excuse me? What's this about someone trying to kill the counselor?"

"Connor's exaggerating," she said. "Someone ran me off the road. We don't know that they were really trying to *kill* me."

Will opened his notebook. "Who were the responding officers?"

"Davies and Rayo," Connor said.

Will frowned. "Any problems?"

"Nothing we couldn't handle," Connor said. "They called in the crime scene so if there's any evidence they'll gather it. The truck had no plates."

"This just gets better and better," Will grumbled.

"What happened at Bowen's place?" Dillon asked.

Will said, "I don't believe Dr. Bowen committed suicide. He supposedly put a noose around his neck and jumped off the balcony, but his fingerprints were nowhere to be found. And get this. He cut himself with a glass downstairs — he'd poured himself a little drink. But there was no blood on the railing, not even a flake. He would have had to touch the railing someway to get over it. We found a towel with blood at the top of the stairs. And then the paper. Where he allegedly wrote his suicide note. It looks like his handwriting, but we couldn't find that paper anywhere in his house."

"An elaborate setup with amateur mistakes," Dillon said. "They didn't make those mistakes with Montgomery."

"Maybe, maybe not," Will said.

"What did you find?" Julia asked.

Will laid into them. "Why should I share anything with you? You've been running around investigating this case on your own without giving me even a courtesy call. I find out Connor talks to a potential witness, Billy Thompson, about another Wishlist murder. And before I can talk to Emily's friends, he's talking with them. And you —"

He pointed an accusatory finger at Dillon. "You're the last person I expected to be running around like a vigilante. Bowen filed a report against you Friday after you harassed him at the country club."

"I didn't harass him."

"I didn't think you did either, but it shows that he was getting nervous and you were in the middle of *my* investigation — yet denied me access to a key witness."

"I'm just trying to protect my niece," Julia said.

Will rubbed his face with both hands. "Right. I understand that. But we've now come to full disclosure time. I'm eager to talk to Emily."

Dillon nodded. "You can talk to her. But I'm still her physician and if I cut off the interview, no more questions."

"Fair enough," Will agreed.

"And you should know some other things."

Will sat down, took out his notebook. "Finally."

Julia told Will about Jason Ridge's Deferred Entry of Judgment and Bowen's role as his psychiatrist recommending the leniency.

"Who was the judge? Don't tell me Victor Montgomery?"

"No. Vernon Small."

Will stared at her. "Small? He never met a criminal he didn't like."

"He's dead."

"I guess I heard that, but how?" Will asked.

"I don't know. I assumed old age."

Will made a note in his notepad. "I wouldn't assume anything right now."

"And there's another thing, but I don't know how it fits in," Julia said. "Jason's ex-girlfriend is Michelle O'Dell. She's at Stanford now. But apparently they both knew a girl who committed suicide, Shannon

Chase. She hung herself."

Will straightened. "Hung herself? Just like Bowen supposedly did? Far too many co-incidences," Will concluded. "Now I need to ask Emily about these people."

Julia and Connor observed through the window as Dillon and Will went into Emily's room. For Will's benefit, Emily recounted her story, though it was now a much calmer version than on the day after Victor's murder. Still, she stayed true to the facts as she'd stated them before.

As Julia heard Emily recount Victor's rape and subsequent sexual abuse, a tear escaped. Connor wrapped his arm around her shoulders, pulled her into the nook of his arm. "She's going to be okay, Julia," he said. "She's strong, just like her aunt."

"Thank you."

Will asked about Jason Ridge, but Emily didn't know him. Nor had she heard of Michelle O'Dell or Shannon Chase.

Dillon took up the questioning. "How long have you been a member of Wish-list?"

"A couple years, I guess. Ever since the vandalism." She looked down, embarrassed. "I'm really sorry I did that."

"I know you are," Dillon said. "Wishlist is supposed to be confidential. So maybe you didn't know Jason by name. What about anyone who talked about football, someone who isn't around anymore?"

"I really can't remember. Some of the guys talk about sports, but I don't really pay attention to that."

"Do you know Judge Vernon Small?" Will asked.

Emily rolled her eyes. "What a weasel. My mother made me go to his funeral. He and Victor were great friends, but I thought he was creepy. He looked at me like . . . like Victor did."

"When was his funeral?"

"I don't know, before Christmas last year."

"Did anyone on Wishlist talk about Judge Small?"

"No, we rarely mentioned any names. But Judge Small is the one who put me on probation after the graffiti. I get three years for some stupid spray painting, but he lets some rapist off with a warning."

Dillon asked Emily, "How do you know about that?"

Emily frowned. "I-I don't know how I know." She leaned back and thought. "Something I read maybe?"

"Something on Wishlist?"

"Maybe. I really don't remember, but I know I heard it somewhere. And I remember thinking he was as big a hypocrite as Victor."

"Emily, have you ever been approached by someone who asked you to help them mete out justice?"

She shook her head. "No." Then her eyes widened. "But I did get a weird text message on my phone a couple months ago."

"What did it say?"

"Could I meet at Starbucks Wednesday afternoon."

"The Wednesday Victor was killed?"

She shook her head. "No. Long before. Like in January."

"Who sent it?"

"I don't know. I responded and asked who wanted to know."

"And did you get a message back?"

"Yeah. It said, 'A friend from Wishlist.' "

"Did you meet the friend?"

"No. This was right after I sent that message to the list about wanting to castrate Victor. It sort of freaked me out. I didn't think anyone knew me on the list."

"Why didn't you tell us before?" Will asked.

"Because I just remembered. Honestly, so much has happened this week, that stupid message wasn't on my mind."

■ ■ ■ ■

Outside Emily's room, Dillon handed Will a tape of Emily's first interview, the day after Victor's murder. "You'll see her comments today and her comments then are the same."

"Would you have given this to me if they differed?"

Dillon shrugged. "So now what?"

"I have a helluva lot of legwork in front of me," said Will. "I have Emily's cell phone records, and haven't had a chance to search through them further back than the last couple weeks. And I want to verify her statement." He shook his head. "This case is like an octopus of victims with no body. And what does this Jason Ridge have to do with it? He's dead."

"He was a patient of Bowen's," Dillon said.

"And he raped a girl and was given a Deferred Entry of Judgment by Judge Small, who's also dead," Julia said. "Ridge's slate was wiped clean so he could play football."

She turned to Dillon. "Did you ever get Montgomery's campaign reports?"

"They're in my office. I haven't had a chance yet to go through them."

"We should pull Small's, too. They're online through the county elections department," Julia said. "Small, Montgomery, Bowen, all dead."

"Montgomery didn't have a connection to Ridge."

"Not that we know about," Julia said.

Will slammed his notepad shut. "You need to look at the facts, not conjecture."

"The *fact* is that Small, Ridge, and Bowen were all involved in Ridge's DEJ and they're all dead," Julia said. "I don't know how Victor fits in, but he does. Maybe just as a smoke screen." She nodded, convincing herself as she said it. "That's it. A fakeout. To lead the police down the wrong path. What about Paul Judson? He was shot in the eyes after the Wishlist message from Billy Thompson suggested he needed his eyes examined."

Connor put up his hand. "Billy came to me this morning. I forgot about it when Julia was run off the road. But it's important." He told them about a girl, eighteen or nineteen, who had approached Billy, gave him a sexual favor, and asked him to become part of a special group. "Billy has solid instincts and walked away from the situation, but after I talked to him about Judson and Wishlist he remembered the girl and thought it might be connected."

"Are you suggesting that maybe someone in this group was trying to recruit him?" Will asked.

Dillon said, "It makes sense. They must have some method of recruitment. People in Wishlist are the perfect recruits. They all have anger management issues. Most probably have other mental problems as well — ADHD, sexual abuse, kleptomania — it's the perfect recruiting ground. And someone like Bowen who knows all their weaknesses, knows how to manipulate them, could turn them into killers."

"You believe that?" Will said.

"I do," Dillon said.

"But Bowen is dead."

"Maybe they turned on him," Dillon said.

"Or maybe," Connor interrupted, "he was one of their intended victims all along."

Will jumped up. "I need to meet with Bowen's next of kin. If we're on the same side again," he said pointedly to Dillon, "do you want to join me?"

"Sure, but why?"

"Bowen's son is a psychiatrist-in-training. And he stands to inherit a few million bucks."

"People have killed for much, much less."

■ ■ ■ ■

Eric Bowen didn't seem terribly distraught when Will and Dillon met him at the Coroner's Office.

"You don't have to identify the body," Will told him. "We've already made a positive ID from fingerprints."

"I just want to see him," Eric said.

"They'll arrange it." Will nodded to the coroner's assistant to prepare Bowen's body for showing. "Do you mind answering a few questions?"

"Not at all."

"Were you close to your father?"

Eric shrugged. "Yes and no. He was a hard man to get close to, but we had an okay relationship."

"Did he seem upset about anything recently? Did he seem different than usual?"

"At his party last night, he was his usual self."

"Which is what?"

"Arrogant, generous, and solitary."

Dillon asked, "What do you know about his online therapy group, Wishlist?"

Eric's jaw tightened. "I told him he was opening himself up to lawsuits. He didn't like my advice, so we never talked about it again."

"Do you know how the group started? Where the list of members might be stored?"

"There's no list. Dad wanted it to be truly anonymous. He kept no records of who said what. He didn't want people using their real names or talking about specific people. He intended it to be a forum for kids to talk to each other and learn that they're not alone with their fears and problems. Good in theory, I suppose, but Dad didn't want to see the problems. He only saw the potential for recognition. He wanted — needed — to be recognized in his field."

Sadness crossed the son's face.

"He told me he started the group for teenagers who self-mutilate," Dillon said.

Eric nodded. "Yeah, he did."

Will changed the course of the conversation. "Your mother died of cancer many years ago, before Wishlist."

"Yes." His voice cracked.

"I'm sorry, Eric," Will apologized. "I'm just trying to understand what happened to your father."

"When you called me, you said he committed suicide."

"Additional evidence has come to light

that indicates your father's death may have been made to look like a suicide."

"What does that have to do with my mother?"

"Today is the anniversary of her death, correct?" Will looked at his notes. "In your father's appointment book, it indicated that he planned to go to the cemetery this afternoon."

"My mom died in November," Eric said. "He was probably visiting his sister's grave."

"His sister?"

"Aunt Monica. She died of cancer seven years ago today."

"Was he attached to his sister or distraught over her death?"

"I always thought he was more upset about Aunt Monica dying than my mother, but maybe just because I was more upset about Mom than he was." Eric shook his head. "Dad kept his emotions buried. For a therapist who told everyone they needed to talk about their fears and anger, he never talked about his own."

Julia and Connor were in her home office. She was looking at contributor reports online and trying to make a connection between Montgomery and Small, other than their apparent friendship. She had all the files and articles stacked and sorted and went through them meticulously.

"Okay," she said to Connor. "Let's go through this step-by-step. Open up that cabinet. Over there, in the bookshelf."

He did, revealing a white board. She tossed him a marker.

"Here's what we know," she began. "Jason Ridge was arrested for rape, pled no contest, and was given a DEJ a few months later. This was nearly two years ago."

Connor made a notation. Then Julia's house phone rang. She picked it up.

"Hello."

"This is Tom Chase. Is Julia Chandler there?"

"Speaking, Mr. Chase. Thank you for returning my call."

He grunted. "What do you want?"

"I'm doing some follow-up on Jason Ridge's death and —"

"Who are you with?"

"The District Attorney's Office."

"And you have the audacity to call me about him?"

"I'm sorry, I —"

"Your office fucked up the investigation, gave the punk a clean slate, and because of that, my daughter killed herself. My daughter is dead and all you care about is this rapist? God, I can't believe you people."

Julia's face flushed. "I'm sorry for your loss, Mr. Chase, I'm trying to get to the bottom of something." She lied off the top of her head. "I'm doing an internal investigation on corruption in the judiciary and I believe the judge who let Jason Ridge off was bribed."

"Of course he was! But no one would believe me at the time. And after Shannon killed herself, I didn't have the will to fight. I had to take care of my family. My wife." His voice cracked.

"Anything you can tell me about Jason's case will help me."

"It no longer matters."

"It matters to me." She took a deep breath. "My niece was raped and I think there's a connection."

He didn't say anything for a long minute. "Jason Ridge raped my daughter. The boy I took into my own home for meals, who I thought was a good kid from a good home, the monster raped my little girl on the football field. She was so brave — pressed charges. She was ostracized at school. Humiliated by her friends. It was supposed to be secret, right? No one was supposed to know. But someone *did* know and spread the word, making Shannon feel like trash.

Then the damn judge gives him a deferred judgment! Why? Because he was the star quarterback. The team needed him. Needed a *rapist.*

"Shannon was so upset and became depressed. We were with her all the time. But — If I had known she was suicidal, I would have done something. Anything to save my baby girl."

"Is Mrs. Chase there?"

"I don't know where Laura is. She divorced me."

"I haven't been able to find her in San Diego. Do you know where she's living?"

It was as if Tom Chase no longer heard Julia. "You don't know. You don't know what it's like to lose a daughter. A beautiful, smart, sweet baby girl who had everything ahead of her. Because one evil creep wanted to get laid. She said *no.* She screamed it, dammit. No one heard. He hurt her so bad she couldn't walk for two days."

"Do you know where Michelle O'Dell is? She hasn't returned my calls."

"No. And I don't care. She knew what Jason did to Shannon and she still went to his funeral. She's a Judas as far as I'm concerned."

"And you don't know where I can find your ex-wife?"

"I already said no! I don't want to talk about this anymore." His voice was thick with emotion. "Don't call me again." He hung up.

Connor walked over to her desk. "You okay?"

"The system failed Shannon," she said.

"It's not perfect, but it's the best we have."

"Tell that to Tom Chase."

Her doorbell rang and she frowned. "Who's that?"

"Probably my brother."

"Dillon? I thought you said he was out with Will."

"No, Patrick. You need to beef up your security here."

Connor let Patrick in. "Thanks for coming."

"No problem. Thought you might want to know what I just learned. You know that e-mail sent to Emily that asked what she would do to the person who hurt her?"

"What about it?"

"Bowen didn't send it."

"Are you positive?" Connor asked.

"Absolutely. I've been through every message he posted to the group and he didn't send it."

Tom Chase couldn't imagine that after

nearly two years anyone would care about his dead daughter or the kid who destroyed her. He'd tried to figure out how a judge could do something like that — just let the rapist go — and when he learned how the system worked, he just walked away. He had no wife left — Laura had turned in to herself and was inconsolable. He couldn't concentrate on work. He could barely get out of bed in the morning.

Laura had been through so much he couldn't stand the thought of an insensitive government bureaucrat dredging all this up again. He'd lied, he knew exactly where Laura was. She was getting on with her life and he loved her too much to stand in the way.

I'll always be here for you, Laura.

He dialed her cell phone.

"Tom?"

Her voice was incredulous.

"How are you, Laura?"

"I'm fine. Why are you calling me? I thought I told you never to call."

She had. *Call me only in an emergency. A real emergency.*

"Some attorney called me and was asking about Shannon. And asking about Jason." He could barely say the boy's name without red rage blinding him.

Silence. "Who?"

"Chandler. Julia Chandler. I think she said she's with the District Attorney's Office."

"I have to go," Laura said.

"Are you sure you're okay?" he asked. "Do you need money?"

"I'm fine." She hung up before he could ask any more questions.

Of course she didn't need any money. She had half the money from the sale of his construction company and the house they'd shared for nearly twenty years. He had the other half collecting interest in the bank. He didn't need anything. He didn't want anything.

But he'd give every last cent for his old life back, to have Shannon alive and Laura happy. Together as a family. It wasn't going to happen.

He opened a fresh bottle of Jack Daniel's and sat on the porch. It was cold, even now in April, but he didn't care. And after a few shots of booze, he wouldn't feel a thing.

TWENTY-THREE

"You're secure," Patrick Kincaid told her after he checked out her security system. "It's a good system, though I improved it, of course." He blew air on his fingers and wiped them on his T-shirt.

Connor hit him in the arm. "Yeah, yeah, yeah, don't let your head get too big. Your hat won't fit."

"The system automatically dials your alarm service company when there's a break-in, but I now have it dialing the police department as well. Your address should already be flagged in the system since you're a DDA, but I'll double-check tomorrow morning."

"Thanks, Patrick, I appreciate your help," Julia told him.

Her doorbell rang — again. "I don't think I've ever had this many visitors at once," she said, joking, but the sad realization of her solitary life made the joke fall flat on her ears.

She let Dillon in.

"Julia, you were right to be suspicious about Judge Small's death," he said.

"He was murdered? Why didn't we hear about it?"

"It was ruled an accident. It was three in the morning and the police report suggests he fell asleep at the wheel. Nothing indicated foul play to them. But why was he out driving at three o'clock in the morning? He drove his car right off the Coronado Bridge."

"That wouldn't be easy," Patrick said.

"If he fell asleep and his foot was on the gas pedal, he could hit the edge and flip over," Connor said.

"They would have done an autopsy report to determine if he'd been under the influence of drugs or alcohol."

"Yes, and all the standard tox screens were clear," Dillon said. "The autopsy revealed an arrhythmia, essentially a minor heart attack. It could have caused him to panic, or perhaps render him unconscious."

"So why isn't this an accident?" Julia asked.

"Because it's the same type of arrhythmia found during Jason Ridge's autopsy. I compared the reports. No doubt in my mind."

"Do you want to exhume the body?" Connor asked, marking Small's death on the timeline he and Julia had created.

Julia said, "I don't see Stanton going for it. We don't have enough at this point. Especially since we haven't even a suspect."

"I agree," Dillon said. "But it makes me wonder if perhaps both Ridge and Small were given drugs to induce heart failure. In Ridge, the steroids would have been a contributing cause, not the primary cause, and in Small he went off a bridge. Died instantly of trauma."

"Do you know what drugs would cause an arrhythmia?" Julia asked.

"Several, but I'm not well versed in that area. If we can prove Jason Ridge was in fact murdered, I think Stanton will agree to exhume both bodies."

Dillon continued. "I have some other news about Bowen's murder. It turns out he was hit with a Taser gun."

"They don't leave physical evidence," Connor said.

"Not usually, but when fired they release microparticles with the gun's serial number etched in them. These particles were collected by the crime scene unit on both Bowen's body and the second floor hallway."

"And where did it lead?"

"The Taser was registered to Victor Montgomery."

He saw the first flaw in his plan.

He didn't expect anyone to connect Jason Ridge to Shannon Chase, yet Julia Chandler had made the connection. How? How did she even know Jason Ridge's name? What had led her down that path?

He would adapt. It saddened him that he would have to execute the contingency plan, but what choice did he have? If Robbie hadn't screwed up the hit-and-run, Julia Chandler would never have talked to Tom Chase.

Chase. Another idiot. But he was too far away to be effectively handled. He could always hope Chase would drink himself into oblivion.

After, they would disappear. He'd planned to stay in town, but it wouldn't be wise. He had a few loose ends to clean up, appearances to make, but in forty-eight hours he and Faye would be on an airplane for Brazil.

From there, they could go anywhere in the world.

Will Hooper knocked on Julia's door late

that night. She almost laughed. "You just missed Patrick Kincaid," she said. "He upgraded my security system."

"Can I come in?"

"What's wrong?" Julia tensed. Connor stood behind her, put his hands on her shoulders.

"Let's sit down."

Julia didn't like the secrecy.

"Emily's being released tomorrow morning," Will said.

Dillon frowned. "I thought we talked about that. You agreed we could keep her in the hospital for her protection."

"Stanton and Chief Causey have another idea."

"You can't arrest her!" Julia jumped up. "You told me you believed her!"

"I do," Will said. "We all do. But this is what we know. We know that three or more people killed Victor Montgomery. We know that Garrett Bowen's online list was used to incite people into planning, and likely executing, murders. I thought Bowen was behind it all, I was ready to serve him a warrant today, then he turned up dead.

"But as e-crimes proved, Bowen wasn't the one inciting people to talk about their killing fantasies. Someone else on the list is responsible — the same person who text-messaged Emily three months ago about meeting at Starbucks."

Julia shivered. "The killer knows who Emily is. They know how to get to her."

Will said, "What the prompts suggest is that someone was fishing for information. Someone was encouraging Emily and others to reveal as much information as they could. They wanted a *reason* to go after Victor."

"But where does Judson fit in?" Dillon asked. "There is no connection between Paul Judson and Emily — he didn't teach at the same school — no evidence that he knew Montgomery or Bowen or Jason Ridge."

"No one prompted Billy to share the information about Judson. He did it on his own. There were other similar e-mails and there may or may not be murders associated with them — we don't have enough information at this point. But as far as Victor Montgomery was concerned, someone was pushing Emily for information."

"So you're saying that maybe he was the target all along?"

"It was well planned and well executed, but I think Judge Montgomery's killers didn't expect Emily to come home when she did. What if they were already inside when Emily came home early?"

Dillon interrupted. "Judson was a red herring. Or a test."

Connor nodded. "This is a group of killers who maybe needed to initiate someone into the group, or it was a test to see if Billy Thompson would be arrested. Or to watch the police investigation and see if Wishlist was shut down. Whatever their reason, he's not connected with Montgomery."

"The only connection between all the victims — if Jason Ridge was in fact a victim — is Garrett Bowen," Julia said.

"And now Bowen's dead."

"We're back where we started," Julia complained.

Connor said to Will, "You said you had an idea."

"We have a plan to draw out someone in the group. Emily has been under wraps. No one knows what she knows, though the killer most certainly knows we have pegged Wishlist as part of the investigation. The e-mails have virtually dried up, according to e-crimes. Someone in that group knows Emily *personally.* Otherwise the information she gave online wouldn't have drawn the killers to her."

"Maybe someone had access to Bowen's records," Dillon said thoughtfully.

"Can they be hacked into?"

"Not easily," Will said. "How would they know if Emily was a Bowen client unless it was someone inside?"

"Because her sentencing was public record," Julia said.

"So anyone could find out that Garrett Bowen was her shrink," Will said. Glancing at Dillon, he added, "No offense."

Dillon shrugged it off with a half smile. "We need to follow up with Jason Ridge's parents. I can do that tomorrow morning."

"I need you at the hospital," Will said. "To approve Emily's discharge."

"I'll talk to Stephanie Ridge," Julia offered. "She'll be more forthcoming than her husband. I sensed that at the fund-raiser the other night. And I want to find out what Michelle O'Dell knows. She was friends with both Shannon and Jason."

"What's getting me is motive," Connor said, changing the subject. "What is this group of killers getting out of their game?"

"The thrill of the kill," Dillon said.

"Too simplistic."

"Is it? Some people kill simply because they enjoy hurting people. Some kill because they don't want to be left out. Remember what we talked about the other night? You get a group of seemingly normal kids together and they start committing crimes? Usually vandalism, petty theft, carjackings. Add a dynamic and homicidal leader to the group, and it's not a huge leap into murder. It's how cults work, it's mob mentality and how a group of normal people can band together to kill in extraordinary circumstances."

"But there's a pattern here," Julia said. "Outside of Paul Judson, these aren't random murders." She stood, looked at the timeline she and Connor had drawn out. "It all goes back to Jason Ridge."

Hooper was skeptical. "So what's the connection between Montgomery and Ridge? Montgomery doesn't fit," Hooper said.

"Yes he does." Connor held up a single piece of paper. "Victor Montgomery handed over a list of cases to Vernon Small when Montgomery went on vacation two years ago. One of them was 5CAG44563JV. We don't have the file because it was expunged, but we do know that was Jason Ridge's case number."

"Where'd you find that?" Julia hurried over to her desk and its towering stacks of paper.

"When you said there was a pattern, I started thinking about how Montgomery fit into the puzzle, so I flipped through the reports. It just jumped out at me, now that I know about the case."

"You mean because Montgomery handed Jason's case over to Small, he got killed?" Dillon said. "Because Montgomery went on vacation?"

"You could argue that if he *hadn't* gone on vacation, Ridge wouldn't have gotten off so easy. Victor had a reputation for giving first offenders jail time, but Vernon Small was notorious for leniency with first-time sex offenders." Julia sat at her computer and brought up the judicial contributor reports on the screen. "What if there's another connection between Montgomery and Ridge? A financial connection?"

"Montgomery was up for reelection three years ago," Will said.

"I was looking at these when Tom Chase called, and never finished going through them." Julia sat back at the computer.

Silence fell on the group until ten minutes later Julia said, "Bingo! James and Stephanie Ridge gave Victor Montgomery ten thousand dollars. And it wasn't in the election year, it was the *following* year. After Montgomery passed on their son's case to Judge Small. If the killer knew that, they might think it was a payoff."

"Well done, Counselor," Will said. "You

should have been a cop."

"Who has motive?" she asked.

"Shannon Chase's parents," Dillon said. "They lost their daughter. The system didn't work for them."

"Tom Chase lives in Maine," Julia said. "I called him there."

"But," Connor reminded her, "he returned your call. What if he retrieved his messages from elsewhere?"

"That's easy to determine," Will said. "I'll contact authorities in Maine and have them pay Mr. Chase a visit."

"What about Mrs. Chase?"

"I haven't been able to find her," Julia said. "Her last known address was in San Diego, the house where Shannon killed herself. The Chases sold it over a year ago and the father moved to Maine. Laura Chase didn't."

"I'll work on that one," Will said.

"What if there was another victim?" Connor suggested. "Someone else Jason attacked, after Shannon?"

Dillon nodded. "And because Shannon had been ostracized at school, the victim didn't come forward. Decided to take justice into her own hands."

"One person couldn't commit all these crimes," Will said.

"No," Dillon concurred, "we're looking for a killing team. And they're even more dangerous than we imagined, because they think their motives are pure."

"Or they just want to make it seem that way," Connor said thoughtfully.

"Then my plan is definitely going to bring them out," Will said.

"What plan?" Julia asked.

"We take Emily to the courthouse tomorrow. She goes into a judge's chambers. We have the press all over the place. She comes out and there's no comment. Chief Causey makes a report that she's a material witness and in protective custody."

Julia jumped up, almost knocking over her chair. "Absolutely not. You're making my niece a target for a killer."

"She'll be in protective custody. No one will know where she is."

"She's a child. You can't use her like that. I'm her guardian," said Julia. "I won't allow it."

"Julia, listen." Connor forced her to look at him. "We have to find a way to draw the killers out, to make them think they screwed up somewhere. We don't know that they don't have others on their 'wish list.' Bowen may not be the last."

"They're empowered," Dillon agreed.

"They've gotten away with murder. They may feel they can expand the scope of their actions. Enact more of their brand of justice."

Connor said pointedly to Julia, "Someone tried to kill you. They think you know something."

"Exactly! And they'll try to kill Emily, too!"

"She'll be long gone before we ever make the announcement to the press," Will said.

"You can't possibly agree to this!" Julia spun around, feeling like everyone was jeopardizing her niece. The people she trusted most. "What if someone wanted to use your little sister Lucy as bait?"

"Emily won't be bait," Connor said. "She'll be safe. We can get a policewoman to be bait in a known safe house. I would never jeopardize Emily's life."

Julia was torn. Her head saw the value in the plan, but anything that even suggested harm to Emily deeply disturbed her.

"Where would she be?"

"How about Montana?" Dillon offered. "Carina is still up there. We can have a deputy fly her up tomorrow and she can stay until we have this locked down."

Connor agreed. "Julia, Carina is with Nick, another cop. They would never let anything happen to her. She'd be out of the area, completely safe. I wouldn't agree to the idea if I thought there was even a chance we couldn't keep her safe." He touched her cheek. "You know that, right?"

Julia found herself nodding, but she didn't like it. Not one bit. But the thought that someone was going to get away with Victor's murder and let Emily take the blame made her physically ill.

Will stood. "I'll set it up. We'll bring Emily downtown and then drive her out of the garage in a windowless van. No one will know where she is. I'll call Carina, too, though if she balks about cutting her vacation short to play bodyguard, I'm blaming you guys."

Dillon and Will left, and Julia turned to Connor. She just wanted to go to bed, though she doubted she'd get any sleep. "What time are you going to pick me up tomorrow? I have a rental car lined up if you could drop me off —"

"Rental car? I'm not letting you out of my sight. I'm staying here. Security system or not, you're a sitting duck all alone. Someone could break in and kill you before the police are even dispatched."

"I'm hardly helpless, Connor," she said.

"Right, you have a gun." He rolled his

eyes, then walked through the house pointing out all the security flaws. She had no choice but to follow him. "Your house has more windows than walls. Anyone can see you. Take a sniper shot." He started pulling down blinds, then continued through the rest of the house.

"Connor, stop. You can't stay here."

"Why? This place is certainly big enough."

Not big enough for us to sleep under the same roof. She'd *never* sleep knowing Connor was in the room next to hers. Or on the couch downstairs. After that kiss this morning . . . "You can't stay."

Connor stopped checking the locks and turned to her. He was only a foot away, his dark eyes boring into hers. "Why not?"

"I . . . because . . . it's not . . ." Her face flushed.

"Because you're afraid I'll do this?"

He wrapped an arm around her waist and pulled her against his body. Before she could catch her breath, his lips were on hers, hot and hard, capturing her voice and eliciting a groan deep from her chest.

His body was solid muscle, his stomach flat. He held her with ease, she couldn't move if she wanted to. And she didn't. This was what she wanted. It was what she had wanted without knowing it for five years.

She groaned again and adjusted her head to kiss him with greater intensity. Her hands found his neck, his hair, held his head to her face, relishing his touch on the small of her back, the way his hands fisted in her dress, the way he nibbled on her lips, her tongue, trailing kisses down her jawline to her ear. When his heated tongue hit her earlobe, she gasped, the sensation full of promise, the heat penetrating her skin, setting her blood on fire.

She pushed Connor down on the couch behind him, hands on his shoulders as she straddled his lap and stared into his fathomless black eyes. His voice was low and gruff when he said, "Are you sure?"

She couldn't speak, so she showed him how sure she was. In a wanton move, she pulled her dress over her head.

Connor stared at Julia's breasts, barely restrained in a black lace bra. His hands went down to her ass — and found it, in the flesh. The conservatively dressed prosecutor was wearing a thong, and he couldn't help but smile. She smiled back and kissed him.

Connor had known from that first kiss five years ago that Julia had a core of passion waiting for the right man to tap. She'd now unleashed herself for him, and he relished it.

His hands molded her skin, all the way up her back to her bra, as she sucked his bottom lip, driving him to such total distraction that he couldn't figure out how to unclasp the darn latch on the bra. She laughed into his mouth — a low, sultry sound — then leaned back and reached between her breasts. With one hand she unclasped her bra and shrugged the piece of lace off her shoulders.

Beautiful. He took one breast into his mouth and she arched her back, a gasp escaping her lungs. He kneaded the other breast while he suckled and licked, bringing her nipples to full attention. Julia's skin was hot to the touch, a light sheen of sweat breaking out as he gave her breasts all of his attention. He switched sides, enjoying Julia's reaction as much as tasting her, touching her. She was a temptress hidden beneath a business suit and professional attitude. A beautiful, sultry goddess that he had wanted for so long.

There was no turning back. He brought his mouth to hers, tongues dueling, her breath tasting of lust and need as she moaned into his mouth and tried to push him down.

He grabbed her wrists and whispered, "Ladies first." He untangled their entwined legs — hers smooth and naked, his in jeans that he couldn't wait to get rid of. But first, Julia.

Julia wanted to make love *now*. Patience had never been her strong suit, and she'd always been the one to dictate the rules of lovemaking. She should have known Connor wouldn't comply, but she was in no position to complain. He lowered her onto the couch, staring at her body while sliding her thong down her legs.

He kissed her foot and she shivered. No one had ever kissed her foot before. She gasped when his hot mouth covered her toe and sucked. Then her ankle. Her calf. Her thigh. He gently pried her legs apart and settled his mouth firmly on her clit, his tongue parting her vaginal lips with the confidence of a man claiming his mate. She shuddered, trying to slow her reaction. Trying to savor his mouth, his tongue, the way his hands grabbed her ass and massaged it in rhythm with his mouth. In and out, squeeze and release, in and out. Soon she was gasping, unable to control herself, her orgasm washing over her before she could stop it.

Her body wet from perspiration and lust,

she might have felt embarrassed since she was completely naked and Connor completely dressed. But instead she felt sexy and wanted. He trailed kisses along her stomach, her breasts — oh, God, what he was doing to her breasts, his tongue wrapping around her nipples. Her neck, then her mouth. Hard and fast, he kissed her, his tongue going in and out, mimicking what he'd done to bring her to orgasm only a minute before.

Already, she felt herself spiraling upward again.

Connor stared at Julia, emotions churning inside, feelings he hadn't fully explored that he could no longer contain. Sexy lingerie aside, Julia wasn't the type of woman to jump in and out of bed with different men. Law enforcement was a closed community, and cops knew who slept around and who didn't.

Julia didn't.

Looking at her, at her half smile, her eyes that pinned him with their honesty, Connor couldn't give her up. He didn't know what would happen tomorrow, the next day, the next year, but he wanted her now and he had wanted her for five years.

Standing, he picked her up. He and Patrick had checked out the house earlier for security purposes, so he knew exactly where her bedroom was.

She gasped and held on to his neck.

"I'm not going to drop you." Then he pretended to let go and she grabbed on tighter. He laughed.

"Jerk," she said and laughed right back with him. She kissed his ear and he involuntarily shivered. "You like that?"

"Hate it," he said. She kissed his ear again, sucking on his lobe the way he had done to her, and he groaned. "Stop that."

"No," she whispered, lightly biting his lobe, sending additional shocks directly to his already-hard dick straining against his jeans.

He took the stairs two at a time, turned right, and pushed open the double doors that led to the master suite. He dropped her on the bed, which pillowed around her.

"What kind of bed is this?" He pushed onto the mattress that wasn't a mattress.

"A feather bed."

"Are you serious?"

"You're not allergic, are you?"

"We'll find out."

He must have set a world record stripping off his T-shirt and jeans. Finally, he lay naked next to her, hot skin against hot skin. He couldn't stop touching her, her round hips, her full breasts, her flat stomach, the wet spot between her legs just to hear her moan and tell him, "I want you, Connor."

He rolled on top of her, holding his weight off her as he kissed her. Again and again, bringing her back to the edge, holding her there. Holding himself off until he was going to lose it. His voice was heavy when he whispered, "Are you ready?"

"You know damn well I'm ready."

He grinned at her impatience. "Are you *sure?*" He kissed her lightly.

Julia was more than ready. She reached down and found his heavy penis and placed it between her legs. Then she arched her hips and took the tip inside her.

He groaned, all teasing and games over, as he thrust himself deep inside. She tensed. How long had it been since she'd had sex? A year? *Two?*

He stopped pushing. Kissed her. Her neck. Her ears. His hands were in her hair, rubbing the back of her head. Holding her tight against him. She squirmed, trying to bring him closer though they were as close as two people could be. Slowly, he pulled out, then back in. The friction, the pressure, brought forth a guttural response she was shocked came from deep within her. Connor's breath came hot and heavy onto her neck. She pulled her legs up and out as far as she could to give him as much as possible.

"More," she gasped, and he complied, holding her ass as he thrust deep inside her and held tight. Sweat coated both of them as they tried to slow down the race to the finish line, to force their bodies to draw out the ecstasy. She grabbed his head, pulled his mouth to hers, and as their tongues dueled, their legs entwined, she arched up against him.

"Julia, Julia." Connor kissed her, wrapping his arms around her back and pushing himself all the way in; hips rocking, bringing her up and over the top with a second orgasm. She cried out in response. He groaned as he came, kissing her over and over, their bodies still vibrating.

Connor held Julia close, unwilling to break the connection. He had his ear on her chest, her heart beating loud and fast. He listened to it as it slowed, a soothing, relaxing vibration. It lulled him into a half sleep, pushing from his mind all thoughts of how they were going to make this work.

TWENTY-FOUR

Faye sat on the end of the couch and stared out of Cami's bedroom window into nothingness. They had gathered here after midnight. Her father thought she was home in bed. Not that he would know. He was someplace else, in another bed, screwing his woman of the month.

Her stomach groaned uneasily. She didn't know if it was because she hadn't been eating well or if she was worried.

"You should never have tried to kill her," Skip said. He paced the room, worried. Frantic was more like it.

"It had to be done," Cami said. "Julia Chandler's digging too deep."

"Bullshit!" Skip shouted.

"We agreed —" Cami started.

"*You* agreed," interrupted Skip. "You're the one who's made all the rules, deciding who lives and who dies. Emily is in trouble because of your stupid idea to kill Victor

396

Montgomery."

"It was part of the plan."

"*Your* plan. One you haven't shared with us."

Cami's voice quieted, a sure sign she was ticked off. "The weak panic when the road gets rocky."

"The smart survive," Skip countered. "And you're not being smart."

"Don't start, Skip."

"Why? You going to try to kill me, too?" he taunted.

Cami's lips pursed. "You're treading on thin ice. All we have to do is lay low."

"We shouldn't have killed Dr. Bowen so soon after Judge Montgomery," Faye said, speaking up for the first time that night.

Everyone looked at her. She'd never contradicted Cami in front of Skip and Robbie. Cami looked betrayed. "Faye, you said —"

"I know what I said. But looking back I think we made a mistake. But it wasn't our mistake, was it? *He* wanted it done. There must have been a good reason. But I still think it was too soon."

"I want out," Skip said.

"There's no getting out," Cami shot back. "Don't even say it. Don't even think it. No one can connect us to Dr. Bowen's death.

No one can connect us to *anyone.*"

Faye's stomach clenched. She felt like puking. Skip had just signed his own death warrant. Nothing was working out like it was supposed to.

"I'm going to kill my dad," Robbie said. "By myself."

Cami jumped off her bed and slapped Robbie. "Don't you dare. That's not the plan. Just sit tight and wait. I promised you he'd be next, but we have to wait."

"I earned it. I did. I did what you asked me to do."

"Actually, you didn't. You didn't kill Julia Chandler," Cami said.

"We're all going to jail," Skip said. "Julia Chandler's a freakin' government lawyer!" He jammed his hand into the wall, wincing as the plaster cracked and blood seeped from cuts in his knuckles.

"Cami." Faye shook her head. They should never have told Skip about Robbie's failed attempt to kill the prosecutor. He was their weakest link. Even druggie Robbie was more reliable than Skip. Faye should have gone after Chandler herself. She would have succeeded.

Faye didn't want to kill Skip. She liked him. He'd been kind to her when he didn't have to be.

Skip stared at Faye and the realization of her duplicity sunk in. "You *knew* about trying to kill the lawyer lady?"

She nodded. Cami stared at her and Faye realized she had screwed up. Big-time.

"How'd you know?" Cami asked her.

"Robbie told me," she lied, looking at Robbie and pleading to him with her eyes.

Robbie shrugged. "What's the big fucking deal who knows? She didn't see me. She didn't see anything. I would have got her, too, if that other guy hadn't shown up."

"What other guy?"

"The one Cami was sliding up against in Bowen's office Saturday night."

Skip's fists clenched. He winced as his knuckles stung. "We're all fucked."

"No, we're not." Cami crossed to the center of the room, got their attention. "Everything's under control. The police have nothing. There's no way to trace any of us to Wishlist. We're covered. You have to trust me."

"You don't know the meaning of the word *trust.*" Skip left.

Faye walked over to Cami and touched her face. So enraged, Cami was shaking. "He's going to blow." Cami looked Faye in the eye. "We have to do it."

Faye shook her head. "No."

Cami now touched Faye's cheek. "Containment. We knew it might need to happen."

Faye nodded. A sob escaped her throat.

Cami turned to Robbie. He was half-asleep on her couch. He'd also been high when he'd hit the prosecutor's car. It's why he had screwed up.

"Hey, Rob, let's go take care of your truck," Cami said.

"Sure." He gave Faye a lopsided grin. "See ya tomorrow."

Faye watched them head for the bedroom door. Cami gave her a stern stare.

Faye knew what she had to do, but for the first time, killing didn't seem like fun.

Robbie dozed in the passenger seat of Cami's sleek sports car after telling her where he'd stashed his truck. The ride lulled him to sleep. He remembered Cami's warnings about drugs, but he'd only smoked a little pot. Okay, so it was laced with some primo opium, but it wasn't like he was on coke again. He wasn't a total idiot. Pot was nothing. It was just like smoking cigarettes. Better even, you didn't get cancer.

He dozed. Cami shook him awake when they arrived at the San Marcos quarry, in a part of it that hadn't been worked on for months. There had been an attempt at security, but earlier in the week Cami had taken care of it, and now, a couple days later, no one had noticed.

Robbie's truck was parked between two piles of half-processed rock — exactly as Cami had directed him after he'd tried to take care of the lawyer.

Cami said, "Robbie, wake up."

"Hmmm?" He'd been dreaming of Cami. Actually, he'd been dreaming of doing Cami and Faye together. He wondered if they'd be up for it. He knew they had something going. A couple lesbos. Okay, so they were bi. Whatever, it would be a treat. And he'd earned it, hadn't he? He'd done everything Cami had wanted. Even some things the others didn't know about, like taking those photographs she asked him to.

"Did you bring the pictures?" she asked now.

"Of course." Robbie pulled the folder from his jacket, handed it to her. "Your wish is my command," he chuckled.

She quickly flipped through the pictures. "The fucking liar!"

"What?" Robbie tried to look over and see what Cami was looking at, but she stuffed the photos back into the folder.

She handed him a sealed manila envelope

from under her seat. "Time to go."

"What?"

"Sorry, Robbie, but if the police are able to trace your truck, you have to be gone. Here's an airline ticket to Rio de Janeiro. And I got your passport from your father's filing cabinet last night — plus fifty thousand dollars."

"Fifty? But I have *millions* coming to me when I'm eighteen. Fuck if I'm leaving the country!"

"Well, a lot of good those millions will do you in prison," Cami said.

"I'm not going anywhere," said Robbie.

"*He* wanted me to kill you, Robbie, but I'm giving you life. I'm setting you free. But you *have* to go. The flight leaves in six hours. Park the truck in long-term parking. By the time anyone finds it and traces it to you, you'll be basking in the sun. I'll send more money, promise."

"No way. It's not fair."

She tenderly touched him on the cheek. "I've always liked you, Robbie. I want to help you. This is the only way I know how."

"It's the guy in the pictures, right? He's the one behind all this."

"Go, Robbie."

He didn't want to leave. He wanted to watch his father die. He still felt the lashes across his back from the last "lesson." The old bastard deserved to suffer.

"But if I run, they'll know I'm guilty."

Cami sighed, pulled out another folder. "I planted a copy of this in your father's office and am sending this one to the police. See how well I copied your handwriting?"

Robbie frowned and, shaking, took the folder and opened it. Inside was a photograph of him beaten black and blue. He looked small, weak, and stupid in the picture. But it was really him and it was unaltered. The negatives were also in the folder.

The letter did look like it was in his handwriting.

Dad:

You almost killed me last week. I was coughing up blood. Some day I think you will kill me. That's always what you wanted to do, right? Because you blamed me for Mom dying.

FUCK YOU! I'm sending these pictures to the police and to the newspapers. Ha! Ha. Deal with it. And if you think you can talk your way out of it, take a close look at the last picture. The negatives are going to the police. When you're in prison for raping your own son,

I'll come for a visit.

I'm so outta here, asshole.

Robbie

Hands shaking, he flipped through the pictures. Sure enough, there was one of his father standing over a young boy.

"That's not me," Robbie said, voice shaking.

"Doesn't matter. No one can see the face."

"He did that to someone?"

"I have the negatives."

"Why say it's me? I can destroy him with this alone." Robbie's stomach churned at the realization that his father was a pedophile as well as a child abuser.

"We will destroy him, Robbie. But it has to be you, to give you a reason to leave. Embarrassment, fear, whatever. Doesn't matter. You come back when everything dies down and no one will be looking at you for anything we did. I'll take care of the truck. Just leave the ticket in the glove compartment, okay?"

A niggling doubt tickled Robbie. Something didn't sound right. He wished he hadn't smoked that pot earlier. "I don't know about this."

"It's already done. The folder is on your father's desk. I mailed a copy to the police.

They'll have it tomorrow, or Tuesday at the latest. Go, Robbie. This was my solution, instead of letting him kill you. Please, Robbie, for me."

She leaned over and kissed him. She'd never kissed him before. He didn't think she'd ever even touched him.

Tears stung his eyes. He took the envelope, heavy with cash. "I'm going to miss you, Cami. And everyone."

"We'll miss you, too."

She took the folder from him and kissed him again. "I know where you are, Robbie. I might come down and see you if things get too hot here."

He smiled, kissed her back. Grabbed her breast. "I wish we had more time. Maybe —"

"We don't have time, Robbie. Please. For me, go."

He sighed and got out of Cami's car, walked over to his truck. He climbed into the driver's seat.

Cami watched Robbie from the safety of her own car. She had no remorse, feeling nothing but irritation that he had proved so unworthy and stupid. She flashed her lights once.

Everything had been set up earlier that afternoon. The woman in the quarry's control room pulled the switch. From above, three tons of rock fell on Robbie's truck. Whether he was crushed to death or suffocated, Cami didn't know.

He was now really stoned, she chuckled to herself.

She looked at the photos he'd taken for her, her anger raging. Someone would pay for this betrayal.

No one made a fool of her.

Skip had trusted Faye. And she'd killed him.

The light reflected off the blade. She watched herself stab him. He fought back.

"Faye, no!"

He held his arms up and she brought the knife down. Felt it cut flesh. Hit bone. Over and over. Up and down. He hit her once, then she got him in the eye.

She cut him even when he was dead. She couldn't stop. Didn't want to stop. She almost turned the knife on herself. Almost. Almost. Almost . . .

But in the end she couldn't take her own life, and she hated herself even more. She was weak. It would be so easy to slit her wrists and watch her life flow away to the nothingness she'd felt her entire life . . .

Faye stared at the bloody knife.

Skip had been her friend, and while she

killed him she almost felt as if she'd been outside her own body. She watched herself stab him over and over.

It got easier when his eyes stopped accusing her.

But what about the knife? And her own blood? The kill hadn't been easy. Skip hadn't gone willingly.

Cami was off taking care of the other loose end. Faye wondered if she herself was a loose end. If she went to him, would he kill her?

Maybe that would be for the best.

And she'd already put her life in his hands. He could decide whether she lived or died. Faye didn't much care either way.

Trembling, she approached his door, replaying the last forty minutes over and over. The knife. Skip's eyes. The way the blade had sliced his skin and muscle. The blood. Hitting bone, a hiss of air from a pierced lung. The kill seemed to have taken forever, but Skip was dead ten minutes after the blade first pierced his skin.

"What are you doing here?" His voice was angry.

She started crying. He ushered her inside. "Faye!" He shook her brutally, then slapped her. Blood got on his hands. She stared at it. Skip's blood or hers? "Dammit, you should never have come here like this. What's gotten into you? Do you want all of us to go to prison?"

She shook her head, but she didn't know what she was agreeing with. Or not agreeing with. She didn't know anything anymore.

"You were supposed to shoot Skip!"

"I don't like guns." Faye hadn't been able to shoot Paul Judson, so Skip had done it for her. He'd protected her, kept that secret from Cami and Robbie, told everyone she had used the gun as she had been ordered to do.

The knife was more real.

And Skip had been a friend. The knife made it personal.

He hustled Faye into his bathroom, putting her in the shower with her clothes on, mumbling. She only made out some of his words: "bleach" and "burn" and "bitch." She really didn't deserve him, she'd known it all along. She was an ugly and scarred freak, unworthy of love. She would be better off dead. She should have killed herself after stabbing Skip to death, something like Romeo and Juliet, except hate united them instead of love.

Skip's blood was washed from her body, down the drain, a whirlpool. Around,

around, and down, down, down. It was pink now, and getting lighter. She slid down to the shower floor, closing her eyes.

Someone stepped into the shower with her. She shook her head and tried to wake herself up. How much time had passed?

He was naked. He'd been so good to her. He had trusted her with his life. And with his knife.

"Faye!"

She looked up at her beautiful, naked lover. Had he slapped her? She touched her cheek. She couldn't feel anything.

"You cut yourself, Faye."

He was very angry, but he also sounded a bit worried. Maybe he did care about her. Could anyone care for her? No one had in her short life. They'd shared blood, they'd shared life and living and exquisite sin. They were soul mates.

She looked at her own body as he stripped her. She saw her blood this time. He turned off the shower.

She didn't remember cutting herself down her arms. Had she done that? Skip hadn't had a knife.

Lifting her bloody, wet form from the shower, he laid her on the tiled floor. She shivered.

He was looking through his medicine

cabinet, then opening and shutting drawers. He knelt next to her, with bandages, scissors, and tape. He sprayed something on her arm, but she didn't feel it. He brought out a needle and thread. She was a quilt he was sewing. She laughed. Was that her laugh?

"Faye, stay with me."

"I'm here." She thought she said it aloud. Maybe she hadn't. He could probably read her thoughts, though.

He taped over the gash he'd sewn up. Her arm felt numb. Maybe it always had. Her whole body was numb.

"Swallow."

He put a pill in her mouth. She trusted him and swallowed. He put a water glass to her lips.

She was in his bed, warm blankets all around her. But wasn't she just on the bathroom floor?

She tried to raise her arm.

"What happened?" she asked.

"You passed out."

He was wearing a robe now. She smelled bleach.

He sat on the edge of the bed, taking her hand. "No matter what you hear or see, you must always trust me."

"I will."

"Say nothing. Do nothing. Stay right here. No one can know you're here. Not even Cami."

Faye nodded.

He leaned over and kissed her. "I'll always take care of you."

"What's wrong with my arm?"

"You cut tendons. I fixed it."

"Thank you." She smiled. *He fixed me. That's what he does, fixes people.* "How long was I sleeping?"

"Sleeping?" His hand cupped her cheek and she felt oddly safe and loved. She'd never felt loved before, not like this. "You passed out from blood loss," he said. "You're still very weak. I have orange juice here. Vitamins. Some medicine that will help. You'll be fine."

"How long?"

"Twelve hours."

TWENTY-FIVE

After she finally convinced Connor that she needed transportation and he couldn't chauffeur her around all day, he reluctantly dropped Julia at a car rental agency Monday morning. "Be careful," he commanded, as she was about to get out of his truck.

"I will." She was surprised by the concern in his voice. *"I will,"* she stressed when Connor grabbed her arm.

But he didn't release her. He stared hard into her eyes, his own face animated, with conflicting emotions. He kissed her, long and passionate, his hands holding her head to his. Heat rumbled through her body, and when he let her go, Julia felt light-headed.

"Wow," she said, trying to lighten the mood. She swallowed, cleared her throat. "Is that a promise of what I can expect tonight?"

A half smile tilted Connor's lips up. "I'll meet you at the courthouse at noon," he said. "Don't be late, because I'll worry. We don't know what this killing group is planning, and they went after you once." He frowned. "I really don't want to let you go alone."

"Emily needs your protection right now. Please, I'll be fine. And I'll be seeing you in just a couple hours. Don't worry."

"Easier said," he mumbled.

She kissed him quickly, jumped from his truck, then leaned in through the window. "Think of it this way. They have no idea what car I'm driving."

"That doesn't make me feel better."

She blew him a kiss and watched him drive off.

Her first stop was the Ridge house. She'd made some calls earlier that morning and learned James Ridge was a CEO of a major corporation. He left for work before eight every morning. It was now nearly nine.

The understated house was in an expensive area of old San Diego. Its tree-lined streets were wide, and deep front lawns gave the community almost a New England feeling. Julia walked up the brick steps and rang the bell.

Stephanie Ridge answered the door. "May I help you?"

"Mrs. Ridge? I'm Julia Chandler. We met

at Dr. Bowen's house Saturday."

Recognition and suspicion crossed the woman's face. "What do you want?"

"A couple minutes of your time." Julia tried not to sound desperate.

Stephanie opened the door without a word. Though she didn't work, she was dressed in tailored slacks, a silk blouse, and simple gold jewelry. Her dark bob was sleek and styled, her makeup simple and elegant.

She led Julia to a formal living room. Above the elaborate fireplace mantel was a framed painting of Jason Ridge in his football jersey — number 10 — holding his football in both hands. He'd been a handsome boy with dark windswept hair and vibrant blue eyes. Julia suppressed a stab of guilt that she was dredging up the past with his grieving mother.

Stephanie Ridge didn't offer coffee. Nor did she offer Julia a seat.

"I know about Shannon Chase," Julia said.

Stephanie's face darkened. "You don't know *anything*. That girl hurt Jason deeply. She lied."

"Why do you think that?"

"Because I knew her and I knew my son." Her chin quivered.

"I read the police report she filed," said Julia. "I saw the medical report. There *was* a rape. There was DNA evidence."

Stephanie shook her head. "I don't care what any report said. Jason was a good son. He wouldn't hurt anyone. The poor boy was devastated when Shannon killed herself. Doesn't that tell you something? Doesn't that tell you that he had forgiven her for her lies?"

"She's not here for me to ask," Julia said. "Nor is my son."

"I've been trying to find Michelle O'Dell. She had been Jason's ex-girlfriend as well as a friend of Shannon's. By chance have you kept in touch with her? All I have is her number at Stanford."

"Michelle?" Stephanie blinked. "I'm surprised you missed her at Garrett Bowen's party Saturday. She was the one wearing a slutty little red dress."

"Michelle was in San Diego Saturday night?"

Stephanie frowned. "What is this *really* about? Why are you asking about a rape — something that didn't even happen — two years later?"

Julia changed the subject. "How well did you know Dr. Bowen?"

"Garrett? For years, but what — *did?* Has something happened to him?"

"He was murdered Saturday after the

party," she said. "I'm surprised you haven't heard. It was on the news last night."

"I don't watch the news. I need to call my husband."

"Dr. Bowen was Jason's therapist, correct?"

"I'm not going to answer any more questions."

"Why?"

"This is private family business! How dare you come in here, asking painful questions about our past, throwing out names right and left like you're on some fishing expedition. Leave now or I'll call the police."

At the door, Julia turned and asked one last question. "Was Jason a member of an online community called Wishlist?"

Stephanie slammed the door in her face. But not before Julia saw the surprised recognition in her eyes.

It surprised Julia how close the O'Dells lived to the Ridges, though the two neighborhoods had completely different flavors as well as income levels.

Gina O'Dell answered the door when Julia knocked. "Ms. Chandler, what can I do for you?"

"I was wondering if you have a recent photograph of your daughter."

The mother blinked rapidly. "Why?"

Julia didn't want to deceive her, but she needed the photograph. "The District Attorney's Office is looking into steroid use in high schools and we believe Michelle has information relevant to what happened to Jason Ridge last year."

"She's not in trouble, though," Mrs. O'Dell prompted.

"No, we just need to ask her some questions. She probably doesn't even know that she has information we need."

"I gave you her phone number. Why do you need her picture?"

"I haven't been able to reach her by phone, so a colleague in Palo Alto is going to stop by her apartment. He needs a picture to make a positive ID before he's allowed to discuss the investigation with her." The lies were rolling off her tongue easily now. It didn't make Julia feel good, but she needed to find out if Stephanie Ridge was right and Michelle O'Dell was in San Diego. And why.

"Just a minute." Mrs. O'Dell didn't invite Julia in this time. Three minutes later she opened the door and handed her a photograph. "This was taken four months ago, at Christmas, when Michelle came home for break."

Michelle had grown from a beautiful teenager into a stunning woman. Blond, blue-eyed, with the body of a Playboy model concealed in jeans and midriff top.

"When Michelle visits, does she stay here?"

"Of course," Mrs. O'Dell snapped. "We're very close. She tells me everything."

The kind, sweet mother from the other day was now replaced by the mother bear. Like Stephanie Ridge, Gina O'Dell would never believe ill of her child.

Julia couldn't blame them. She herself didn't believe Emily had any part in Victor's murder. And when she did have a tickle of doubt, she'd made excuse after excuse. The rape. The abuse. Anything to show that Emily wasn't responsible for her actions.

She hoped Stephanie Ridge was wrong about Michelle being in San Diego. It would break Mrs. O'Dell's heart if her daughter was in town, and had neither called nor visited.

"Thank you so much for your help," Julia said, and left.

Part of being a private eye was grunt work. Hell, most of it was, but it occasionally paid well.

Connor knew how to do the job, and missing persons — if there wasn't foul play involved — was often the easiest. He had friends, contacts, ins to track real estate transactions, bank transfers, credit cards, phone bills.

It appeared that Laura Chase had disappeared off the face of the earth.

While waiting for Emily to be discharged from the hospital, Connor managed to piece together the Chase family history.

Tom and Laura had been married for five years before giving birth to a daughter, Camilla Chase, who died six months later of sudden infant death syndrome. Less than a year later, Shannon was born. Months after Shannon committed suicide, Laura Chase filed for divorce. They sold the house and Tom moved to Maine but was living off his savings and the proceeds of the house sale and his construction business. He had no known job. Will Hooper had the local authorities drive by his Bangor address and everything checked out. As far as they knew, Tom Ridge hadn't left Maine — at least by airplane — since moving there eighteen months ago.

Laura Chase, on the other hand, seemed to have disappeared after the divorce. She owned no property in California and didn't appear to have a job in the state. Connor wondered if, like her husband, she had moved out of the area in grief over her second dead daughter. How devastating for the Chases to lose two children.

Connor understood grief. His nephew's murder eleven years ago had changed every member of the Kincaid family, himself included, but none of their pain came close to what his sister Nell suffered. When the killer wasn't caught, when the case grew cold and Nell knew it would be given less and less priority by the police, she left. She moved to Idaho to be alone.

Their mother insisted Nell would return home when her grief ran its course. But in the eleven years since, she had not set foot in San Diego. Connor hadn't even seen Nell since, though his parents visited her on occasion. If Nell didn't want to be found, Connor had no doubt she, too, could disappear as Laura Chase had done.

The one thing Connor couldn't access were bank accounts. When Will arrived at the hospital to transport Emily to the courthouse, Connor told him what he'd learned and Will called in for Laura Chase's financials. Connor hated the waiting game, but he had no choice.

He kept glancing at his watch as Dillon and Will went over the transportation plan for Emily.

"What's wrong?" Dillon finally asked.

"We're running late. Julia is supposed to be at the courthouse at noon. After yesterday's hit-and-run, I'm worried."

"I'm just waiting for the media to get antsy enough that they start speculating," Will said. "Causey will give a brief statement — something to the effect that Emily Montgomery has been released from the hospital, that she isn't a suspect in the judge's murder, but is being deposed because of information she has. While everyone thinks she's in the courthouse, we'll smuggle her out through the secure garage and get her up to Montana before the end of the business day. No one will know."

Dillon said, "Paperwork's done. Let's go."

Maneuvering on the highway past a car packed with young surfers, Julia left another message for Michelle O'Dell. She then called the Palo Alto District Attorney's Office and explained that she was trying to reach a witness and asked if they could check on her status. She gave them a physical description, her last-known address, and phone number.

Why was Michelle in San Diego? Julia had only wanted to talk to her about what happened two years ago between Jason and Shannon, and her cryptic comments to the press about Jason's "issues." Now she wondered if maybe Michelle was on a vendetta, if maybe she felt the system had failed her best friend.

But where would Michelle get other people to go along with her plan of revenge? And why would she go after Montgomery and Bowen? It didn't make sense. Jason Ridge, yes. Julia could logically make the connection — Jason raped Shannon, wasn't punished, and Shannon's best friend Michelle would want to do something about it.

But to carry on a vendetta for two years? She wondered what Dillon would say.

Whoa, Julia. Going from revenge to psychopath was a huge leap. And maybe Michelle had nothing to do with it, and her presence in San Diego the night Garrett Bowen was killed was a coincidence. Still, why would a college student of modest means be at a ritzy art fund-raiser?

The only way Julia would find out was if she talked to Michelle.

As if on cue, her cell phone rang. The number was "unknown." Julia answered. "Julia Chandler speaking."

"Um, this is Michelle O'Dell. I think you

left me a message."

Julia found a safe place to pull over so she could focus on the conversation. "Hi Michelle. Thanks for returning my call."

"What do you want?" the young woman asked.

"I'm looking into a cold case for the District Attorney's Office. Do you remember Jason Ridge?"

A long pause. "Yes."

"He died from steroid use. Had a heart attack on the football field. The District Attorney's Office has been investigating the illegal use of steroids by minors and since you knew Jason, I wanted to talk to you about what you knew of his actions before he died."

"Nothing. We didn't talk anymore."

"You were his ex-girlfriend, correct?"

"So?"

"He also dated a friend of yours. Shannon Chase."

"What does that have to do with Jason taking steroids?"

"Shannon's dead. I can't ask her about what she knew. She committed suicide, right?"

"Why are you asking me questions you already know the answers to? Why are you bringing all this up?" There were either tears or anger in her voice — maybe a little of both.

"I'm sorry to upset you, Michelle. You were close to Shannon."

"Whatever."

"It must have been awful to have your best friend commit suicide. It must have hurt."

"I never thought she'd do it." Michelle's voice was distant.

"Her parents divorced over it. When violence hits a family, it takes a toll on everyone."

Julia pushed. "Have you been in contact with Shannon's parents since they moved from San Diego?"

"No." Michelle's answer seemed to come too fast.

"Are you sure? Shannon's father moved out of state, but her mother is still in town."

Julia held her breath, hoping her fishing expedition caught something.

"I wouldn't know. I'm in college at Stanford."

"Oh, I'm sorry. Someone told me you were in San Diego this weekend."

"What? Who?"

"It must have been a misunderstanding. You've been in Palo Alto all weekend?"

"Yes. And you know, I don't have to answer your questions. I'm not in trouble, am I? I didn't sell Jason steroids. I didn't even know he was taking them. I had nothing to do with all of that. In fact, I hate drugs, and if Jason was experimenting with them, good riddance."

The phone clicked.

TWENTY-SIX

Julia still felt uncomfortable with the plan to use Emily, but she went along with it. Connor wouldn't jeopardize her life. Will Hooper was escorting her to the airport along with a female police officer who would be on the plane with her.

But she only had five minutes alone with her niece as they waited outside the judge's chambers.

"Are you okay?" Julia asked for what seemed like the hundredth time.

"I'm okay, Aunt Jules."

"Carina is nice. She's testified for me a couple times. You'll like her."

"Stop worrying about me."

"I can't help it. You've been through so much."

"I screwed up."

"No, you didn't."

"Yes, I did. I didn't tell you or anyone about what Victor did to me. If I had just said *something,* none of this would have happened. I hated him. I wanted him dead. But, you know what, I'm sorry he's dead. If that makes any sense at all."

"It makes a lot of sense to me." She hugged her niece. "When you come home, when all this is over, do you want to come live with me?"

Emily looked surprised. "You want me to live with *you?* I thought you were too busy."

"What gave you that idea?"

"Mom said you gave up the custody battle because you were too busy to be bothered with a little kid."

The pain in Emily's eyes brought tears to Julia's. "Damn her!" Julia swallowed. "No. After your dad died, I gave up the custody battle to protect your inheritance. That's why Crystal and Victor were never able to get their hands on your money. But I realize that was a mistake."

"Why?"

"Money doesn't matter. It's not worth the pain and betrayal that comes with it. But I thought you'd resent me if I fought for you and in the process lost everything your father wanted for your future. Matt wanted to protect you, to make sure you had everything you needed so you could create your own life." She touched Emily's cheek. She

427

was struck by how much Emily looked like a Chandler. Emily was Matt's daughter, through and through.

"I understand, Aunt Jules. Dad wanted me to have any future I wanted. Right now, I don't know what I want. I mean, I'll be seventeen next month, I *should* know. You did. Dad always told me you knew exactly who you were and where you were going."

Julia's heart swelled painfully. "Oh God, I miss your dad."

"Me, too."

Julia hugged her niece. She would never let her go again, even if it meant fighting Crystal in court.

The door opened and Connor walked in with Will Hooper, Dillon, and a female plainclothes cop Julia vaguely recognized. Will introduced her as Rachel Vasquez. She smiled at Emily, revealing deep dimples in both cheeks. "Ready to go hit on some cute pilots?"

Emily grinned. "Air force or marines?"

Rachel laughed. Connor squeezed Julia's shoulder as Will said, "It's a go. Chief Causey is giving his statement to the media. I'm taking Rachel and Emily to the airport."

"Emily," Julia said, "does the name Michelle O'Dell mean anything to you?"

Her niece shook her head.

"No. What about Jason Ridge or Shannon Chase?"

Emily thought, then shook her head again. "No, I don't think so."

"Jason was a football player who died from steroid use last year. He may have been on Wishlist."

"Why do you say that?" Will asked.

"I spoke to his mother today. It didn't go well, but she recognized the Wishlist name."

Will's phone rang. He excused himself and left the room.

Julia pulled Michelle's photo out of her purse. "Emily, do you know this girl?"

She looked at the picture. "No."

Connor grabbed it. "She was at Bowen's party Saturday night. She came on to me."

"She *hit* on you?" Julia asked, incredulous.

"Her name was, shit, let me think." He closed his eyes. "Cami."

"Cami?" Julia asked, frowning. "Was she wearing a red dress?"

"Yes."

Julia tapped the picture. "This person you call Cami is Michelle O'Dell. I spoke to her not an hour ago and she said she was at Stanford all weekend."

Will walked in and looked at Emily. "Do you know Dennis Richardson? Nickname Skip? He's a senior at your school."

Emily nodded. Julia took her hand. "Why?"

"He was stabbed to death in his bedroom sometime last night," Will said. "Gage is already on-site."

"It's all unraveling and it's your fault."

The bitch paced. He wanted to kill her.

His voice was calm. "It's under control."

"Where's that psychotic kid? What's her name, *Faye?*"

"I don't know," he lied. "I haven't seen her."

Damn if he was going to sic this bitch on Faye. Not when she was so weak. If Faye was at full strength, there'd be no contest. Faye would win. It's why he loved her. No matter what life threw at her, she survived. Damaged, maybe, but she'd go on. He'd kill himself before he'd let the bitch see Faye in her current weakened state, and there was no way in hell he'd kill himself.

"She butchered Skip. *Butchered* him. She's not right in the head. You'd better not be protecting her. She's our trump card. She'll do anything to protect you, even confess to everything. And with Robbie and Skip gone, it's all we need."

She stared at him. "Tell her that. To save you, she needs to confess."

"I told you, I haven't seen her."

She stepped toward him. "And I told you, I don't believe you."

Faye hadn't stayed put like he commanded. She was listening from the upstairs hallway. *He loves me.* He was protecting her, even jeopardizing his own life, his own freedom, just for her.

He truly loves me.

She knew what to do.

Creeping down the upstairs hall, she took two more of the pills he'd been feeding her throughout the day. Though she didn't know what they were, they made her feel better. She wished she had clothes. He'd burned the bloodied stuff she'd worn when she killed Skip. Now she searched his drawers and closet until she found an old faded T-shirt shrunk enough to fit her, and some running shorts where she could tie the drawstring tight around her waist. It would be enough to get her home. There, Faye could change before finishing the plan.

She went back downstairs and slipped out the back door.

But the bitch was right: Faye knew she had to confess. And she would, to protect him.

She only regretted that she wouldn't be able to say good-bye.

Two hours later, Faye Kessler walked into the police station and said, "I killed Victor Montgomery."

Twenty-Seven

Dillon Kincaid stared at the girl who had announced an hour before that she had killed Victor Montgomery and four others.

They were in an interrogation room. Faye Kessler was seventeen, and in a capital offense they didn't need parental permission to talk with her. They had, though, attempted to contact her father. Will had read Faye her rights and she clearly understood them.

"I'm not stupid," she said.

Not stupid, Dillon thought, but her eyes were dead. Staring into those dark orbs Dillon had no doubt that Faye Kessler was capable of murder.

Not only had Faye told them she'd killed five people, she had the evidence to prove it. In front of him, Will tapped the Polaroid photograph of Garrett Bowen hanging from his chandelier.

Dillon couldn't get over how pale and

slender Faye was, perhaps in the beginning stages of anorexia. She wore a long, thin sweater, its sleeves covering her hands. She played with the frayed yarn ends constantly. Her mousy brown hair was shoulder length, clean but limp. She wasn't an attractive girl, her face too long, nose too large, and forehead too high. But her eyes drew Dillon in, so deep and empty Dillon might have been afraid of this girl if they'd met under different circumstances. He wondered if she was on drugs. He'd get her a medical exam as soon as they were done, but for now a confession came first, especially since she appeared lucid and relatively healthy.

"Why did you come in today?" Will asked, their conversation being recorded.

"I told the cop behind the desk. I killed some people."

"Who did you kill?"

"Do you want to hear about the first one or the last one? Or the others maybe?"

"Why don't you start with this picture?" Dillon picked up the Polaroid in front of Will and showed it to her.

She stared at the picture, her face expressionless. "That's Dr. Bowen."

"Yes. Did you take this photograph?"

"Yes."

"Is this the only picture you took that night?"

"Yes."

"Why?"

"I wanted it to remember him by."

"And did you kill him?"

"Yes."

"Why?" Dillon asked.

"Because."

"Just because? You just felt like it?"

"We hated him."

"Faye, who else hated him besides you?"

"Skip and Robbie."

"Do you have full names for them?" Will asked.

"Skip's real name is Dennis Richardson Jr. No one calls him Dennis, though, not even his parents. Robbie is Robert Haxton."

"Where are they now?"

"Dead."

Dillon hadn't been out to the latest crime scene, but Will had described a violent and bloody murder. Skip Richardson had been butchered.

Faye showed no remorse, didn't even raise her voice. There was not a quiver of emotion in the timbre. She looked from Dillon to Will with no apparent concern about her fate.

"What happened to Skip and Robbie?"

Will asked.

"Robbie was a hothead. His father beat him, you know. All the time. I didn't understand why he took it since now he's bigger than George." She shrugged, as if telling an unimportant story. "Robbie tried to kill Emily's aunt. It was a stupid idea, but he did it all on his own. Just because he saw her at Dr. Bowen's party Saturday night. Skip and I decided he was being stupid, so I brought him out to that huge quarry near San Marcos. We put him in some part they don't really use anymore, so I didn't think they'd find him for a while. We told him he had to leave the country. Gave him some money. Skip rigged the quarry to dump some big rocks on him when he got in his truck. It took half the day to set it up, but Skip is really good with mechanical things and made it work."

"You and Skip killed Robbie. He was your friend?"

She nodded. Again, emotionless.

"So what happened to Skip?"

"I killed him."

"Why?"

"I wanted to."

Dillon had to work to refrain from showing emotion. Will was unsuccessful in hiding his anger and contempt.

"Because you *wanted* to?" Will asked, the words punching the air.

She nodded, waiting for the next question, casually rolling the edges of the sleeves between her fingers.

"Did Skip do something that upset you?"

"Not really. He was mad that Robbie tried to kill Emily's aunt. Really angry. I didn't like that."

"How did you kill Dr. Bowen?"

"Robbie, Skip, and I came into the house during his big party and we hid upstairs until everyone had gone. It's a big house, lots of places to hide and no one knew we were there." She smiled at the memory. "When Dr. Bowen came upstairs, Skip hit him with the Taser gun we stole from Judge Montgomery's house. Then we got the noose over his head and threw him off the balcony."

"Why did you hang him?"

"I'm not sure. It was Skip's idea. Or maybe Robbie's. Well, we were just talking about it and thought it would be fun to try."

Dillon had met hundreds of killers during his nearly eleven years as a psychiatrist. Never had he met someone as even-tempered and matter-of-fact as youthful Faye Kessler. Many killers had no remorse for the actual murder, but most didn't want to go to prison. They would lie, manipulate, yell, plead, cry, promise the moon, do anything to get a lighter sentence or convince anyone that the killing was justified.

Faye Kessler was either a brilliant actress or one of the few true psychopaths Dillon had met.

"How did you get the noose up the chandelier?" Will asked.

"There's a button by the front door. Skip knew about it because he has one in his house. It lowers the chandelier, for cleaning I guess."

She had definitely been at the crime scene.

"Why did you set up Dr. Bowen's death to look like a suicide, but then wipe down the banisters?"

"Robbie forgot to bring gloves." She sighed and shook her head, as if Robbie were simply a forgetful child.

"Why? Why did you kill Dr. Bowen?"

"We didn't like him. He was so snooty, always wanting us to talk about our feelings, why we did this or that, or whatever. He tried to have so much control over us."

"Control?"

"Yeah. If he didn't like something we said or did, he was going to file a report with the court and have us institutionalized. He did it before, you know."

"To whom?"

"I don't know, we just knew."

"Did you kill Judge Montgomery?"

"Yes."

"Why?"

"He hurt one of our friends."

"Who?"

"Emily. She goes to my school. She was on Wishlist with us."

"How did you know it was Emily?"

"Wishlist is supposed to be all secret and stuff, but Skip was a brainiac when it came to computers and stuff. Anytime someone new posted, he'd hack around and discover who it was."

"Do you have a list of everyone on Wishlist?"

Faye frowned. It was obvious she wasn't expecting the question.

"I don't."

"Did Skip have the list?"

"He might have."

"And you and Emily went to the same school?"

Faye nodded, more comfortable with this line of questioning.

"We had Western Civ together last year. She was nice to me. Not everyone is nice to me because I'm ugly."

"But you're not ugly, Faye," Dillon said.

Faye looked down at her hands, still worrying the fabric at the end of the sweater. "It's okay. I know I am. Emily was beautiful but she was so sad, too. We talked some. Found out we both saw Dr. Bowen. She told me about the vandalism, though I already knew about that. It'd been on the news and, well, everyone at school knew. So when she started posting on Wishlist, I was pretty sure it was her and Skip confirmed it. So then we just listened to what she had to say." Faye looked up. For the first time, Dillon saw complete clarity in her eyes. "No one listens to kids. Parents and teachers are too busy to be bothered. And Dr. Bowen didn't really care what we said, just cared if he could fix us for some magazine article or something. Some of us aren't even broken."

She looked back down. "But some of us are. And sometimes you can't fix what's broken, and you can break things that are just fine the way they are."

Dillon asked in a low, compassionate voice, "Why were you seeing Dr. Bowen?"

"I don't want to talk about that right now." She stared at Dillon, eyes narrowing. "You're a shrink, too, aren't you?"

"Yes, I'm a psychiatrist."

Anger flashed across her face, the first real emotion aside from compassion for Emily.

"You're all control freaks. Everyone has to fit in some compartment or category. Circles in fucking circles and squares in fucking squares. Why can't you just leave us alone? Why can't you just *shut up?*" Faye was working herself up, had risen from her chair during her tirade. The switch from complete calm to anger had been startling.

"Faye," Will said. "I need you to sit down."

"I want him gone. Out of here."

Dillon stood. "If you want to talk later, Faye, you can ask for me."

She spat in his face.

Dillon walked into the observation room, shaken. Julia handed him a tissue from her purse and he wiped off Faye's spit. "Are you okay?" she asked.

"I'm fine. Faye's not."

Dillon had always believed that troubled people could be helped. With the right combination of therapy — and drugs, if necessary — he thought most people could overcome whatever psychosis or chemical imbalance they had and go on to lead relatively normal lives.

He stared at Faye through the observation window, realizing that he didn't know enough right now to help her. But he wanted to. Something inside her was crying out for help.

He feared it was too late.

Will continued with his questions after Faye calmed down. Dillon, Connor, and Julia watched through the one-way mirror.

"Did you also kill Paul Judson?"

"Who's he?"

"The teacher from —"

She nodded, cutting Will off. "Oh, yeah, right. The principal. Shot him through the eyes. Skip did that. I was supposed to. Robbie and Skip didn't think a girl could do what we'd planned. But I don't like guns. That's why I used a knife on Skip."

Will asked Faye, "Why did you kill Jason Ridge?"

Faye shook her head, her face blank. "I don't know him. I didn't kill him. He doesn't go to my school."

"And you don't know Shannon Chase? Michelle O'Dell?"

"No."

"Do you know a girl named Cami? She was at Bowen's party Saturday night."

A brief flicker, then nothing. It might have been Dillon's imagination.

"No."

"What about Judge Vernon Small?"

Faye shook her head. She counted on her fingers. "Skip, Robbie, and I killed that principal because he cost that nice kid his

442

basketball scholarship, then the judge because he hurt Emily, then Dr. Bowen because we didn't like him. Then I killed Robbie and Skip. They were getting stupid."

It sounded logical the way Faye put it, but something was off in her statement. Dillon couldn't pinpoint what exactly was bothering him.

"Why did you turn yourself in? You killed the only two people who knew what really happened. You might have gotten away with it."

Faye sighed. And for the first time, Dillon believed she spoke the whole truth.

"I'm tired. I just can't do it anymore."

Observing in the back of the room, Dillon turned to Chief Causey and Stanton.

"This kid needs to be on a 24/7 suicide watch. At the hospital secure ward. Complete medical exam. Faye Kessler can't be alone, even to urinate."

The phone rang in the observation room and Causey answered it. Everyone watched his face harden. He hung up. "Faye didn't lie about Robert Haxton. The quarry manager checked the area on our request. He found the kid crushed to death in his truck."

TWENTY-EIGHT

He hadn't gone to Cami's apartment before, but now he was desperate.

"Where's Faye?" he demanded when she opened the door.

"You haven't been watching the news, have you?" Letting him in, Cami waved her arm toward the flat, wide-screen television on the wall above the fireplace.

A newscaster somberly gave his report. "The San Diego Police Department has made an arrest in the murder of Judge Victor Montgomery. There are no details at this time, but Chief Causey will be providing a statement at four-thirty this afternoon. Sources say the killer surrendered to authorities early this afternoon at the downtown precinct. Wait —" The attractive newscaster was looking at something off-screen. "We have just learned that the alleged killer is female, possibly a minor.

"To repeat this breaking news, an arrest

has been made in the homicide of Superior Court Judge Victor Montgomery. We'll be broadcasting Chief Causey's press conference live at four-thirty. Stay tuned to the station that brings it to you first, Channel Seven."

Cami hit the remote. "You see? It's over. We're safe and Faye will be happy in her padded room."

"Safe? You think we're safe?"

"Faye would never turn me in," Cami said with complete confidence.

He didn't think Faye would either. Cami had such tight control on Faye that the girl didn't even know it.

Had Faye heard what the bitch said this morning? Is that why she'd confessed? *To protect him?*

The thought of Faye being locked up disturbed him. She'd never survive imprisonment. She hated shrinks and doctors and anyone who poked at her.

He thought of her scars. They'd run test after test. Blood tests, psychological tests, medical tests. She'd sacrificed herself for him. Not for Cami, for him.

"To save you, she needs to confess."

Faye must have heard. He didn't need to hear the report to know she put all the blame on herself, Skip, and Robbie. Skip and Robbie couldn't contradict her. They were dead.

But he wasn't stupid. The police would verify everything she said. Julia Chandler had already spoken to Tom Chase, had been trying to talk to Michelle O'Dell. Could they put all of it together?

He could disappear tonight and no one would be the wiser until he was far beyond the reach of the U.S. government.

Faye wouldn't break. She would never give him up. She'd kill herself first. It was his fault. Cami's fault. They'd used her, used Faye's weaknesses and passions and fears to get her to carry out their plan for vengeance. Justice.

And in the end, justice no longer meant anything to him. Sure Garrett Bowen was dead, but the one person he loved was behind bars.

He had to find a way to get her out. If he had to spend every last dime, break every law, whatever it took, he was going to protect Faye.

"I know everything." Cami stared at him, eyes hot and narrow.

He should have seen her rage when he first came to the door, but he'd been too worried about Faye to fully take in how close to the edge Cami was.

"What do you mean?" he asked.

"You slept with her. You wouldn't fuck me, but Faye? You were all over that ugly bitch."

"Don't say that. Faye worships you. She did everything you told her to."

"Of course she did," Cami snapped. "She wanted to *be* me. She wanted my body, my face, and I thought she wanted my life. I see you preferred fucking the ugly duckling over the swan." She threw a pile of papers at his face. No, not papers. They were photographs of him and Faye in bed. Of her cutting him. In their rawness they were ugly, distorted, fuzzy. The crude images hardly conveyed the exquisite high, the perfect beauty he'd experienced in Faye's arms, under her knife.

"Why are you jealous? I never cared that you were screwing Skip. And who else? Probably every man who crossed your path. I heard about you throwing yourself at that guy at Bowen's party. You think you're the only one with spies?"

"Well, my spies are dead, and so are yours."

"Don't you lay a hand on her."

"I won't have to. One night locked up and Faye will take care of it herself."

■ ■ ■ ■

Cami paced, furious he'd chosen *Faye* over her. How could he? How could he even *touch* that bisexual cunt?

She made the call.

"It's me," she said. "He's going to cause trouble."

"Didn't you see the press conference? That little psychotic bitch confessed to everything, implicated Skip and Robbie and no one else. We're fine. Everything is done. Justice has finally been served."

"You need to do something about him."

"Don't be ridiculous, Cami."

"Don't call me that anymore! I hate that name."

"If anyone has become dangerous, it's you."

"Don't start. You were going to shoot Bowen in his office, in front of witnesses. You'd be in prison if it weren't for —"

"You owed me, Cami. You still owe me."

"I'm free. And if anything happens to me, you'll be sorry."

"Are you threatening me?"

"You bet I am. I learned from the best, didn't I, *Mother?*"

"I'm *not* your mother."

"If you harm a hair on my head, every-thing will come out. *Everything.* I want him taken care of. He's been fucking Faye."

A long pause. "Are you certain?"

"Very certain." Cami stared at the photos in front of her. Took one and began to tear it into tiny pieces.

"I'll do it in my own time in my own way. We need to let things die down a bit."

"Don't make me wait too long."

Cami slammed down the phone.

No one would make a fool of her.

She picked up another photo and slowly shredded it, making the pieces so small no one could see the paper had once been a picture of something.

Dillon admitted Faye Kessler to UCSD's downtown psychiatric ward while Connor drove Julia home. She'd insisted she was fine to drive herself, but didn't argue be-cause she was exhausted.

Connor turned off his truck's engine in front of her house. "Come here." He un-buckled her seat belt and pulled her across the bench seat and onto his side.

He held her tight against him. She released a pent-up breath, the tension beginning to work itself from her muscles.

She kissed him on the cheek. Then found

his lips. A gentle kiss, a hint of passion. "Will you stay the night?" she asked, her heart beating fast. Last night he'd been worried about her safety; tonight he had no reason to stay.

No reason except for her.

He held her face, kissed her. "I was hoping you'd ask."

They were walking toward the house when headlights rounded the curve leading to Julia's home. Connor frowned and stepped in front of Julia as a dark Mercedes squealed into the driveway, braking only inches from Connor's truck. "What the hell?"

"Crystal," Julia said.

Crystal Montgomery jumped from her fancy car and strode purposefully over to where Julia and Connor stood at the bottom of the porch stairs.

"Where's my daughter?" she demanded.

"She's safe," Julia said.

"She was released from the hospital and no one told me. She was transported *out of state* and no one told me until after the fact."

"I have temporary guardianship until Victor's murder is solved. You know that." Julia was not going to allow Crystal to intimidate her.

Crystal tried to push past Connor, but he

stood firm.

"Get out of my way."

"You're not wanted here," Connor said.

"It's okay," Julia said, but didn't invite her inside. "Let her talk." When Crystal didn't say anything, Julia put a hand on her hip and raised her eyebrow. "Well? Did you come here for any reason other than to yell at me?"

Crystal was surprised. Julia had always been gracious, almost formal, relying on etiquette and manners when she didn't like someone. But Julia had already resolved to bring Emily into her home, no matter what she had to do. Even take on Crystal Montgomery.

"I know what you're doing," Crystal said.

"You do?"

"You're trying to get Emily's money. Victor was right about you. You just wanted control of the purse strings, not what was best for Emily."

Julia should have been angry, but instead she laughed at Crystal's ridiculous accusation. "Victor came to me twice trying to gain control of Em's trust. I said no. I will not be bullied. Emily will have her money to do what she sees fit with on her eighteenth birthday. And you're just furious that your free ride is almost up."

"How dare you? I don't need Emily's money."

"Don't you? You've been receiving a sizable allowance from Emily's trust that will end in thirteen months. Then you'll need to live on your inheritance. And considering the lifestyle you've grown accustomed to, I don't think it'll last."

Julia stepped in front of Connor. "Did you know that Victor raped Emily? That he molested her?" Julia took another step toward Crystal. "He hurt her under your roof and you forced her to take his name. You never cared about her, never cared about anyone but yourself and Matt's money. It's over. Don't bother to return to the Chandler Foundation. I'm buying you out."

"You can't do that."

"I control the board, Crystal. I'm a Chandler. I can do whatever I want. I'll make it worth your while. You walk away quietly, without fanfare, without dragging Emily through the mud, and I'll match the inheritance Matt left you. Cash."

She saw the greed in Crystal's eyes warring with embarrassment and anger.

The greed won.

"I'll have my attorneys contact you."

"I want custody of Emily."

"No."

It was an automatic answer, without passion or pain.

"I'll continue your child support allowance until she's eighteen."

"Until she's twenty-one," Crystal countered.

"Nineteen. And you know it won't hold up in court if you push me. Do you want to spend your money fighting me for custody?"

"I'll think about it," Crystal snapped. "You're a bitch, Julia."

"So are you."

Crystal reddened, turned around, and left.

"Good riddance," Julia said.

"Are you okay?" Connor asked, taking her hand.

"For the first time since Matt died, I know I've done exactly the right thing for Emily. And me." She turned to him, kissed him. "I'm better than okay."

Holding her hand, Connor led her into the house. He kissed her again and again, her face, her neck, her shoulders. She pushed the door closed, reset the alarm, and dropped her purse and briefcase in the entry, wrapping her arms around him.

Connor's breath was hot on her neck, sending bolts of lightning down her spine, bringing a moan to her lips.

"Julia," he whispered in her ear, her name sounding so sexy coming out of his mouth. He walked her backward until she found her back up against the wall, Connor's body pressed full against hers, his erection hard against her stomach.

She rubbed against him, wanton and sexy, wanting him *now.* Without giving herself time to think, to change her mind, she unzipped his jeans. He gasped, buried his face in her hair when she touched him.

"Oh, sweetheart." He kissed her ear, her neck, her lips. Hard and driving, his lips pinned her against the wall, his tongue dueling with hers. His hands fisted around her skirt, pulled it up around her waist, his fingers grazing over her upper thighs.

She pushed his jeans down past his hips, stuffed her hands down his boxers, and squeezed his firm butt, her nails digging into his flesh, pushing him into her, trying to bring them even closer together.

"Now," she gasped, her voice sounding low and odd to her ears. "Right now."

Connor wanted to take Julia to her bed and make love to her properly, but more than that, he wanted to be inside her. Now. Her seductive order was all the permission he needed.

He pulled her thong aside, bent his knees,

and guided his hard dick into her. She gasped as he entered and he paused, his entire body quivering as he tried to maintain control.

Julia kneaded his ass and pushed, forcing him fully inside. She gasped, her breath coming hot and fast against his neck. Her athletic body writhed between him and the wall. As he eased back, she pushed him back into her.

"Oh, like that," she said. "Just like that."

Her demands turned him on; he'd do anything to give her pleasure. The wall was unyielding; every time he withdrew a fraction, she pulled him back. They developed a perfect rhythm that didn't last long. Her breaths took on a higher pitch as he moved faster within her. Sweat glistened on her perfect skin, mingling with his, the scent of sex and desire caressing his mouth and nose.

He dared to look at her, her eyes closed, her mouth open, cheeks flushed. She gave herself completely over to him, no inhibitions. He kissed her hard as he thrust into her one final time. She clutched him, her body shaking with her own release.

"Julia." He kept her there, holding her up, catching his breath while peppering her with kisses.

"Take me to bed," she whispered.

He picked her up. She wasn't expecting it and grabbed on to him, a shocked smile crossing her face.

He'd never laid his eyes on a more beautiful, sexy woman. Her hair had fallen completely out of whatever tie she had it in. Her skin moist, flushed, glistening. Those eyes — their dark green appeared black in the dim lighting. And he'd never get enough of that fine mouth. He paused while walking up the stairs just to kiss her again.

Julia almost melted from the sweetness of Connor's spontaneous kiss.

She'd never done anything like that before — sex up against the wall. But she hadn't wanted to wait. A primal desire, a *need,* had welled up inside her as soon as he touched her and she'd wanted him right then, right there. The wall just seemed like the right place at the right time.

Now they could go slowly and fully explore.

He laid her on her bed, looking at her with a mixture of awe, desire, and love. Love? No, she was misreading that. Maybe she was projecting her feelings into his expression. She'd loved Connor Kincaid from the minute they'd been thrust together during the Crutcher investigation five years ago. The way he'd kissed her then. The way he

touched her now. She hoped, over time, that they could fix their problems and create something special. But Julia wouldn't rush it, didn't even know if she dared dream it. For now, they had tonight.

She was still dressed, but Connor had lost his jeans before coming up the stairs. She started to unbutton her blouse but he pushed her hands aside.

"Allow me."

He bent down. With his teeth he unfastened the top button of her shirt. His tongue circled the tender spot between her breasts. She swallowed, her mouth dry.

He moved to the next button. Bit it. Pulled it from its hole. Used his tongue to push the fabric apart, his mouth feathering kisses along the edge of her lacy white bra. She breathed deeply, let out a sigh.

His teeth unfastened the third button. She arched her back, wanting to pull the shirt over her head and dispense with the teasing. At the same time, she wished she had dozen buttons so she could enjoy his exqui site ministrations. She reached for hi grabbing his hair in her hands, rubbing shoulders. She wanted to touch him eve where all at once.

He ran his tongue under her bra, missing her hard nipples. She squir

wanting to feel his mouth on her breasts, his hands on her hips, his penis deep inside her again.

Pulling back, he bit open the fourth button.

Connor was enjoying the slow torture. Julia's face glowed, her body responded, her hands never stopped moving. He kissed her stomach, circling slow, wet kisses down, down to her navel where he darted his tongue in and out to mimic lovemaking. She moaned, her hips moved off the bed, and he ran his hands under her shirt, undid the front clasp of her bra, and watched her breasts pop free.

The fifth button took a little too much time, his own breathing becoming labored as teasing Julia also gave him intense pleasure. He was too rough and the button popped off into his mouth. He moved up her body, kissed her, shoved the button in her mouth with his tongue. "Sorry," he whispered.

She spat out the button and laughed. She wrapped her arms around his neck and pulled Connor into a hot, wet embrace.

He pushed the blouse and bra off Julia's shoulders, his hands finding her full breasts, his thumbs circling her nipples in time with the kiss she lavished on him. The playful

moment soon transformed into a passionate need, the need to be naked, the need to be as close as possible.

Connor broke off the kiss and sat up, straddling her. He pulled off his T-shirt and Julia stared at his dark, hard, muscled chest. She reached up and touched the short, curly hair in its center, her thumbs rubbing his nipples with the same strokes he'd given her only moments before. His body tensed and he closed his eyes as her hands massaged his chest.

"Take off my skirt," she said, the material bunched up around her middle. He turned the material, found the zipper, and slid it down. The sound was nearly as erotic as what was to come. He pushed the skirt over her hips, taking her panties with it, and then his mouth was on her toes. Kissing, sucking, teasing. Slowly, too slowly, he kissed her ankle. Calf. Under her knee. His tongue trailed along her thigh, higher, higher, small circling motions giving her a taste of what was to come.

His hands kneaded her muscles, not leaving one inch of skin untouched, unloved. Between his mouth and his hands, Julia thought she was going to die of the most painful pleasure known to woman.

He blew kisses into her moist center and

she gasped, arching her back, physically begging him to taste her, to give her the pleasure she was on the verge of spilling.

But he barely skimmed his lips across her sensitive path, instead planting his mouth on her navel.

He moved constantly, touching, kissing, licking. She writhed beneath him, hands in his hair, his chest, his beautiful hard muscles. Being in bed with Connor was better than she'd dreamed, the reality superior to the anticipation.

Tonight they could forget the past, the lines they'd drawn in the sand five years ago. This night they could enjoy what they both had wanted for so long, what they'd waited for, what they needed.

For now, now, she had him, and she was going to show him how well they fit together.

Connor was ready to enter Julia for the second time that night, his body tight and hot, Julia moving beneath him. He kissed her, and she pushed him away.

For a split second he thought he'd done something wrong. But there was a half smile on her face, and she rolled over so she was on top.

In a sudden move, she slid onto his dick, fully sheathing him. He froze, fearful one move might set him off. She sat on him, her heavy breasts rising and falling with her own restrained passion.

She made love to him.

Her arms came down, one on either side of him. She controlled the pace — slow, steady, easy. Her lips were swollen from their earlier kisses, red and lush. He leaned up to taste them.

The light touch of lips on lips made Connor's heart flip. He grabbed her hands, held them tight on either side of his head. Julia's eyes stared into his, open, dark, full of lust and love, need and want. Their faces were mere inches apart; her eyes never left his. He swallowed, feeling a connection he'd never felt with another woman. With each easy, languid movement, Julia was drawing him in. Deeper, deeper, until he was falling into her eyes, lost, his orgasm building as his heart swelled. The quiet, unhurried lovemaking brought him to a level of sensuality he had never experienced.

It was the woman he was with, not the act of sex, that made this moment so incredible.

It was as if Julia saw the realization cross his face, because at the same time he knew no woman could fill his heart like Julia, she rolled over, pulled him on top of her, and whispered, "Make love to me."

He did. In and out, touching her, kissing her, never breaking eye contact. Her breath came in gasps, their hands entwined, and they were coming together, a long, languid release that left them satiated and complete.

Connor kissed Julia lightly, the same way she'd kissed him at the moment he realized there was something more between them than he'd accepted before.

He spooned her into his arms, held her close, vowing he'd find a way to keep her always with him, where she so obviously belonged.

TWENTY-NINE

Faye looked even worse than Emily had the morning after Victor's murder. Dark circles framed her pale blue eyes. Her hair was limp, her skin even paler than usual.

They observed her through one-way glass. Faye was in the hospital's locked psychiatric ward.

During her medical exam, the doctors discovered that Faye had been cut on her right arm. The wound had been sewed up with regular household thread, and Faye insisted she'd done it herself.

Dillon shook his head and said to Julia, Connor, and Will, "While it's possible she dressed her own wound — she's lefthanded — I highly doubt it."

"She looks like she's going through withdrawal," Julia commented.

"Looks like it, but her tox screen came out clean. The reason I don't think she sewed herself up is that she had Amytal in

463

her system, a prescription barbiturate given to patients when they go in for surgery or to reduce pain and lower blood pressure. How would she know about that? And where would she get it?"

"You mean a doctor prescribed it?"

"It can be found on the streets, but these were within normal limits and she has no signs of long-term drug abuse. We ran through the drugs Bowen prescribed for her — none of which she filled — and it wasn't on the list. But someone knew what it was for, or someone with access and knowledge gave it to her."

"Isn't Garrett Bowen's son a psychiatrist as well?" Connor asked.

"He's in med school, third or fourth year. I was thinking about him," Dillon agreed. "And he had some interesting things to say about his father when he went to view the body at the morgue. He was upset, but something was odd."

"I'll talk to him," Will said. "Connor, want to come along for the ride?"

Connor hesitated, glanced at Julia. She nodded. "Sure," he said.

"I'm staying to observe," Dillon said. "I'm still worried about Faye's mental health."

"Yeah, the poor darling," said Connor. He squeezed Julia's hand. "Be careful." He left with Will.

Dillon said to Julia, "The only person Faye wants to hurt is herself. You asked about withdrawal? Let me show you something." He opened the medical chart. Inside were photographs of Faye Kessler's back, arms, and legs. A multitude of scars crisscrossed.

Julia paled. "Who did that to her?"

"Mostly, she did it to herself. Except on her back. But she won't talk about that."

"She *cut* her own body."

Dillon nodded. "It's increasingly common among young people today. Even adults. A way to feel in control, or to feel something when they feel nothing. I think Faye is going through withdrawal because she can't cut herself. Watch her." Dillon cautioned Julia. "I'm right out here, and if I think either one of you is in any danger, I'll be through the door in two seconds."

Because Faye refused to talk with any doctor, Dillon suggested Julia go in and develop a rapport with the young killer. There were still too many unanswered questions. Julia entered the hospital room.

Faye wasn't restrained, but the room was bare, nothing accessible that she could use to kill herself.

Julia swallowed a tickle of worry that she

was going to do something wrong with Faye. She couldn't think that way. After all, the girl had killed in cold blood. She'd been messed up long before she came here, so how much damage could Julia do just by talking to her?

It didn't seem plausible that three teenagers could plan and execute such an elaborate set of murders. Dillon was right: someone had directed Faye and the boys. Maybe it was a brainwashing technique — Faye killed her partners and confessed in order to deflect attention from the person who'd put the whole thing in motion.

"Hi, Faye," said Julia.

"I know you. Are you prosecuting me?"

"How do you know me?"

"I saw you at the school, picking Emily up sometimes."

Julia shivered. This killer, who looked so small and frail in her hospital gown, had been watching her. She shouldn't be surprised. Faye had already told them she'd spoken to Emily at school, and knew what had happened with Victor Montgomery. In her own way, Faye was trying to protect Julia's niece.

"When we were doing research," Faye continued, "we learned all about you."

"Research about what?"

"Killing the judge. We needed to know your schedule, Emily's schedule, the judge's schedule."

"So why did you kill him when Emily was in the house?"

"She *wasn't* inside when we killed him. We heard her come in after. I hid under his desk while Skip locked the door. In case Emily came to his office on her own. But she didn't. When we were sure she was upstairs, we left."

Faye shrugged. Didn't take her eyes off Julia.

"Why did you jeopardize Emily? The police thought she was involved."

"I was sorry about that," Faye said, sounding contrite. "Emily was always nice to me. I didn't want her to get in trouble. But she's in the clear now, right? Is that why you're here? You want me to say she had nothing to do with it? Okay. Emily had nothing to do with it."

"That's not why I'm here," Julia said. "The police seem to think someone else is involved. Not just you, Skip, and Robbie."

"They're wrong," insisted Faye. "It was only the three of us. Now they're dead. Maybe I should have killed myself instead of coming here."

"You don't want to die," Julia said. "If you

wanted to die, you wouldn't have sewn up your arm." She pointed to Faye's bandaged right arm.

Faye looked at her arm, lost in thought, her blue eyes both blank and searching. "I hadn't thought of that," she said, incredulous. "Do you believe in love?"

Julia was only momentarily thrown by the odd question. "Yes, I do."

"Have you ever loved anyone? Not like your family, who you're supposed to love even when you hate them. But someone you met because of fate, who you let inside your body and your mind and you told him everything and he still loved you?"

"Have you?" Julia asked without answering Faye's question.

"Are you a shrink, too?" Faye's face reddened. "Shrinks always answer questions with questions. Trying to be smarter."

"I'm not a shrink. I'm an attorney. And Emily's aunt. I care about Emily. I care about you, too, Faye."

Faye laughed a low, sick cackle that twisted Julia's stomach into knots. "*You* care about *me?* Do you know what I did to Victor Montgomery? I took pruning shears and while Robbie and Skip held him to his chair, I cut off his dick." She moved her hands as if they were holding shears and made a chopping motion. "Sliced it right off. They were new and sharp and they did the job. I slammed it down hard, but you know the penis is really just muscle and flesh and blood. Kind of rubbery. He was hard. Still, I just sliced right through it."

Julia swallowed her revulsion. "Are you saying Judge Montgomery's penis was erect?"

Faye laughed. "Exactly."

"Did you have sex with Judge Montgomery?"

"No. I sucked him. Got him to the edge, then I sliced it off. Stuffed it down his throat, just like Emily wanted to do.

"Whatever. What's done is done. You can leave now," Faye said.

"Faye, we know someone helped you plan these murders. Tell me who and I can protect you."

"Protect me from what? No one's going to let me out of here. I'm okay with that. Really."

"Faye, you need to be completely honest with the police. Tell them who asked you to kill Victor Montgomery and Garrett Bowen and Paul Judson."

"A little bird told me," Faye said, and started laughing.

■ ■ ■ ■

After leaving Faye, Julia asked Dillon, "Do you think it's all an act?"

"Faye's protecting someone, no doubt about it," he said. "A man. Someone she's having sex with."

"She's only seventeen."

Dillon raised an eyebrow. "Not that I condone underage sex, but it's not uncommon."

"You know what I mean. It's not just her having sex, but killing without any remorse. Even killing her *friends.*"

"Like I said last night, she has no empathy for her victims. But there is one very unusual thing."

"What's that?"

"She's protecting someone, which means she *is* capable of emotion. You have to care about someone to go to prison for them. I certainly don't think Faye cares enough about herself or even whether she lives or dies."

Dressed as a nurse, and sporting a stolen security pass, Cami found it surprisingly easy to walk onto the secured floor of the hospital. She'd learned a long time ago that

470

when you acted like you belonged somewhere, people accepted that you belonged.
A form of psychology.

She ducked into a room when she saw
Julia Chandler walk from Faye's wing with
a tall, handsome man. Cami recognized
him. He'd been at Dr. Bowen's fund-raiser.

Who had spilled her identity? It had to
have been Jason's parents. They were the
only ones who knew who she really was,
but it hadn't occurred to Cami that anyone
would have a reason to talk to them.

Again, the two-timing asshole was wrong.
He said they'd never make the connection
with Jason Ridge. Well, hotshot, they had.
And now they knew Michelle O'Dell also
went by the name of Cami.

Cami watched them walk past. As soon as
they were out of sight, she strode down the
hall. A doctor gave her a double look, but
she just nodded curtly and kept right on
going, chart in hand. Cami had a purpose.
Don't hesitate, always look like you know
what you're doing, no one will get in your
way.

A guard stood at Faye's door. He checked
her ID, but fortunately didn't look too carefully. It looked enough like her on the
surface, though the woman in the photo was
much older. Cami had stolen it from the

nurses' locker room.

After signing in with the guard, Cami entered the room. Faye was lying on the bed, staring at the ceiling.

"Hello, Faye."

Faye turned her head, surprised. "What are you doing here?"

"He wanted me to thank you for sacrificing yourself. It was such a noble thing to do, Faye."

"I don't want him to go to prison."

That confirmed it. Faye had been fucking him, and was in love with him, and had never once said one word to Cami. Never even hinted.

He'd never made love to Cami. Sure, they'd done things, but he was always in control. He never gave it up. But the photographs Robbie had taken proved he and Faye were more than intimate. And the knife . . .

Walking over to the bed, Cami pretended to check Faye's vitals, held her wrist as if taking her pulse. She then slipped a small, sharp knife between the sheets.

"You know what to do."

The pain and uncertainty on Faye's face rivaled her need to cut herself.

Cami tried to smile. "Here, I took over for the nurse on duty. You're supposed to get these meds. Make it look good for the cop."

Faye nodded, took the pills, and swallowed.

They were anticoagulants. Cami knew Faye well: she'd cut herself.

The pills assured that Faye wouldn't survive.

Connor stared at the "apartment" where Garrett Bowen's son lived near the UCSD campus.

"Apartment" didn't do Eric Bowen's three-story town house justice. Connor could fit two of his houses inside with room to spare, and the rear doors opened to a golf course, making the entire living area look even bigger.

"What can I do for you?" Eric Bowen asked. He looked like a younger version of Garrett Bowen.

"Thank you for agreeing to meet with us," Will said as they walked in. Connor noted a huge painting taking up most of the largest wall of the living room. It was unrecognizable for the most part, black and white with some odd splashes of color. He'd seen a similar painting in Garrett Bowen's house.

The town house looked lived in, though it was clean and tidy. Eric was comfortably dressed in slacks and a polo shirt. He escorted them to the dining room in the rear of the main floor, off the kitchen. "Coffee? Water? Soda?"

"I'm fine, thank you." Will sat down.

"You said this was about my father's death. I heard on the news that a young woman confessed to killing him and making it look like suicide. Is that true?"

"We're inclined to believe the witness," Will said. "But there are some inconsistencies in her statement that we were hoping you could help with. The person who confessed was a patient of your father's. We believe she was part of the Wishlist group that you indicated had been originally set up for people who self-mutilated."

"That was ages ago. It evolved into something different."

"What do you know about the group?"

"My dad had a couple of patients who wouldn't open up. He wanted to give them a safe and open forum to discuss their situation."

"And you thought it was a good idea?" Connor asked, thinking about Dillon's derisive comments about the group.

"At first. But then he broadened it and included practically everyone. I couldn't imagine it succeeding. I asked him about it a couple times, but he told me to stay out of it. My father loved attention. He loved when people came and told him their deep, dark secrets. He loved to play God, cure all the ills in the world. Maybe his goals were noble at the beginning, but he lost it somewhere down the line."

"You two didn't get along, I take it."

Eric stared out the window, his mouth a tight line. "I used to be close to my dad. But after Mom died he worked nonstop. I didn't see much of him. Aunt Monica moved in, but she was sick, too. And then two years later, *she* died."

Will flipped through his notes. "Monica was your father's sister, correct?"

"Right. She'd gone through a divorce or something — I never really knew what happened — but shortly after my mom died she needed a place to live with Tristan."

"Tristan?"

"My cousin." Eric swept his hand around the room. "He painted most of these." A cloud crossed his face.

"Where is Tristan?"

"He travels a lot, but he's been in town the last month or so because of Saturday's fund-raiser. The studio which has been exhibiting his work benefited from the event."

"Do you know where we can find him?"

asked Will.

Eric got up, sorted through a Rolodex, then copied an address and phone numbers onto a Post-it note. Will took it with a "Thanks."

"Do you know who's in Wishlist?" Will asked.

"No. I helped him construct the messaging system, but that's all. My dad didn't have the technical skill to put it together, but, like I said, that was it."

Will changed the subject. "My understanding is that you just inherited a few million dollars."

Eric sighed. "I guess all cops have to think that way. I don't care about the money. My mother was independently wealthy and I received most of her estate. That was worth three times what my dad was worth. The only thing he got from her estate was the house."

"What about anyone who threatened your dad? Was he scared? Angry about something?"

"Dad never got angry, even when mom died. He was unique."

"What happened to your cousin Tristan after his mother died? Did he continue to live with you?"

"Let's see, he was eighteen at the time.

He moved out almost immediately. Tristan and Dad didn't see eye-to-eye about a lot of things, and —"

He stopped.

"What?" Will prompted.

Eric frowned. "Tristan is the reason Wishlist was created in the first place. After Aunt Monica died, Tristan started cutting himself. He refused to talk to Dad about it, but agreed to the anonymous counseling. It seemed to work wonders. Tristan stopped self-mutilating, focused on his art, and now, seven years later, he's a rising star in the art world. I got to hand it to him, he's done well."

Connor stared at Tristan's painting across the room. At first he only saw swirls of pink and red, jagged lines fading toward the edges. Other, darker colors seemed randomly thrown onto the canvas. But from this distance, Connor made out the hint of a female shape. And the jagged lines were shadows. The fading out was drip marks.

The skin crawled on the back of Connor's hand. Tristan's paintings were creepy.

Faye kept the knife under the blanket. She rolled it between her fingers. Back and forth, back and forth. It nicked her once and she jumped in pleasurable surprise. She liked being surprised. It was why she liked being cut on her back. She could anticipate it, but not know the moment when it would come. Then the sting was far more exquisite.

She was going to miss her angel. For a moment, she wondered if she'd done the right thing. Maybe somehow they could have run away together.

But she had to take the blame. After all, she had killed.

Faye didn't want to go to prison. And she damn well didn't want to talk to any more shrinks. Playing with your mind while pretending to be your friend. They didn't know shit, only wanted to live vicariously through you because they had no lives of their own.

She remembered one session with Dr. Bowen. He wanted to know all about her sex life. He was probably getting off on her description, so she made it as lewd and lurid as possible. She described how her lover had cut her breast, then he sucked her blood. She then did the same to him. They came together as the pain and the feelings peaked.

She smiled. Bowen never even guessed Faye was talking about his own flesh and blood.

Taking the knife in hand, she cut deeply

from the inside of her right elbow to her palm. The instant, burning pain almost stopped her. She almost called for a nurse.

Instead, she bit her tongue and watched the blood spread, seeping through the sheet, through the cotton blanket, spreading . . .

THIRTY

"Faye's dead," Cami said.

His hand shook as he held the phone to his ear. "Wh-what?"

"I was watching the hospital, just to see what they were going to do with Faye, and Julia Chandler went into her room. Right after she came out, a nurse went in and then called for doctors and an alarm went off. I saw them take Faye's body from the room."

Didn't Faye know how much he needed her? That they were a team? He was empowered with her at his side, knowing and understanding his dark needs. Offering him her trust and faith.

Now she was dead.

"Why would Chandler hurt her? She has no reason."

"I don't know. Maybe it wasn't something Chandler did, but something she said. Threatened her. You know how those prosecutor types all think they have the authority to do anything they damn well please. Maybe she told Faye she'd be locked up for life, or put on Death Row, or that they were going to put her on drugs to force her to talk. I don't know, but I think she was driven to suicide. Faye is dead and I just know Julia Chandler is responsible."

That made sense. Julia Chandler had been talking to everyone. She'd made the connection to Jason Ridge. She had been a problem and he should have done something about her earlier, but he never thought it would go this far. He didn't think Faye would end up dead, or that Chandler would push her to kill herself.

Didn't they have any propriety in that hospital? Didn't they have doctors who cared about their patients?

What was he thinking? There was no Hippocratic oath. Doctors did whatever the hell they wanted. They had all the control.

Like Garrett Bowen. He decided to be God for a day and stole the only solid thing in his life.

"Are you there?" Cami's voice grated on him.

"I'm here." He squeezed his eyes closed, surprised to find he was crying.

"What are you going to do about Julia Chandler?"

There was a knock on his front door. "Hold on."

Cautious, he glanced out his bedroom window, then pulled back.

"I'll take care of it." He hung up.

In her office, Julia released a long, pent-up sigh. She'd spent the last hour being reprimanded by Andrew Stanton for interfering in an investigation. She justified her actions without emotion, the entire time scared to death that he'd fire her.

In the end, he put a reprimand in her file and took her off leave effective next Monday.

She planned to flip through messages, talk to her legal assistant, and wait for Connor to call when he was done talking to Garrett Bowen's son. Her cell phone rang.

"Is this Julia Chandler with the San Diego District Attorney's Office?" the voice said.

"Yes."

"I'm Harriet Jameson from the Palo Alto Police Department. I spoke with you yesterday about a student at Stanford, Michelle O'Dell."

"Right. Did you talk to her?"

"No. The address you gave me is a mail drop, not a residence. I ran the phone number and discovered it's a cell phone forwarded to another cell phone with a six-one-nine prefix."

"San Diego," Julia said.

"I talked to the dean of students first thing this morning. He went through the student records and said that a Michelle O'Dell of San Diego, California, is a registered student in an independent study program."

"Which means what?"

"She only has to meet with her counselor once a month and turn in her assignments. The last meeting was two weeks ago and she is current with her assignments."

"Thank you, Harriet. I appreciate your following up for me." Julia hung up the phone.

Michelle O'Dell wasn't at Stanford. She was most certainly the mysterious "Cami" Connor had run into at Garrett Bowen's house. And she was also probably the "Cami" that Faye had responded to, but denied knowing, during her interview, as well as the lascivious blonde Billy Thompson said had tried to recruit him.

Michelle O'Dell had been Shannon's best friend. Had Shannon told her everything that had happened with Jason Ridge? Maybe Michelle blamed herself in some way for Shannon's suicide, that she hadn't helped her friend after Jason had gotten just a slap on the wrist.

But why such an elaborate plan? What did Michelle hope to gain from this string of murders?

She was just leaving to walk to the parking garage down the street when her cell phone rang, again.

"Chandler," she said, walking down the hall. It was after six and there were a few people in the building, but it was mostly empty.

"Julia, it's Dillon Kincaid. Faye Kessler committed suicide."

"I'll be right there."

Garrett Bowen's nephew, Tristan Lord, lived in a converted warehouse on the edge of the renovated cultural district. The three-story loft stood on a short cliff near the ocean, up the hill from the Art Center where his paintings were shown. Will knocked on the metal door.

"What are you thinking?" Connor asked Will.

"Maybe Eric Bowen was leading us down the wrong path. Did you really see something in that picture?"

Connor sheepishly admitted it. "A woman cutting herself."

"Huh. All I saw were bright splotches."

Will called dispatch and learned that the loft was owned by Garrett Bowen. All utilities and taxes were paid by him. Tristan Lord had no record, not even a parking ticket. He had a driver's license and a passport. Will had another detective looking into his travel history. "And while you're at it, put a hold on his passport. I don't want him skipping out on us before we get a chance to talk to him."

They knocked again, but heard no movement inside. They walked around the side. The cliffs went straight down thirty feet to a rocky beach. Connor glanced up at the deck above them; no one was there.

"Why don't you put a BOLO on him?" Connor suggested.

Will put in the be-on-the-lookout order as they walked back to the car. "Questioning only. I don't want him totally spooked."

They drove down the hill to Tristan Lord's art studio. Tristan wasn't there either, but they went in and looked around.

"They call this art?" Will said. "I can't tell what anything is supposed to be."

"You're supposed to use your imagination," Connor said.

"I'd never have taken you for the arty type," Will said.

"And I always thought you were."

While Will talked to the studio's art director, Connor looked at the paintings. One in particular disturbed him, and he didn't know why.

"Haunting, isn't it?" The curator approached. "Tristan Lord is immensely talented. His work is displayed at the Washington, D.C., Museum of Art and we're honored that he opened a studio here. His presence will help build our center."

"Hmm." Connor didn't want the small talk. He wanted to figure out why this particular painting bothered him.

Like the painting in Eric Bowen's town house, this was predominantly red, pink, and orange, with dark slashes at random intervals. Slashes, but maybe not random. He tilted his head. Saw something. He couldn't figure it out. Maybe it was his imagination and there was really nothing there.

"Tristan's uniqueness comes from perspective," the curator continued as if Connor hadn't been ignoring him. "From one angle you see one thing, from another you see something completely different."

Connor glanced around. The art studio was a three-story open warehouse with multiple levels that displayed different works of art under premium lighting conditions.

Connor ran across the floor, almost knocked over a statue, and ran up a spiral staircase that led to the third-floor balcony.

The distance brought clarity. The dark slashes made up another female body, naked, this one hanging from a chandelier. An eye had been drawn into her back. In the corner was a football with a faint number 10.

Jason Ridge had been number 10.

Another layer coated the painting. Connor changed perspective by moving several feet to the right and saw the hanging image was now a man. He also had an eye in his back.

An eye for an eye.

Vengeance. Revenge. Garrett Bowen for Shannon Chase.

Who would care about the suicide death of a young cheerleader? They'd already ruled out her father, three thousand miles away in Maine with an alibi. But her mother was nowhere to be found. And what about that Cami he'd encountered at Bowen's house?

But where did Tristan Lord fit into this? He was a mere relative, the son of Garrett's sister.

Was it Connor's imagination that saw something in the paintings, things that wouldn't be admissible in court?

"Hey, Kincaid!" Will shouted from the bottom floor. "Get your ass down here." He was animatedly talking into his cell phone.

Connor ran down the stairs two at a time. "What?"

"Faye Kessler. She's dead. Someone smuggled in a knife."

Julia pictured the scars all over Faye's body, scars the girl had put there or allowed to be carved into her skin. Faye had been self-mutilating for years; she had problems long before she got wrapped up with Michelle O'Dell and the others, long before she killed.

Julia pulled up in front of the hospital at a vacant meter and glanced at the hours of operation. It was after six, but the meter ran until seven p.m., so she fumbled for a couple of quarters. She knew how the meter maids worked — wait until five minutes before the meter day ran out and ticket everyone. Julia had gotten a half-dozen tickets that way.

She was about to put two quarters in when she sensed someone rapidly approaching her from behind. Before she could turn around, scream, or run, one hand covered her mouth while the other jabbed something

sharp into her neck.

She kicked violently backward, but then her limbs grew suddenly heavy as her head grew light.

THIRTY-ONE

"What the hell happened?" Dillon arrived at the hospital just as Connor and Will ran up the stairs to Faye Kessler's room. Connor could see his brother was extremely upset.

Officer Diaz looked distraught. "I-I don't know how she did it."

"Tell me everyone who went into that room after I left."

"Only two nurses!"

"*Two* nurses?"

"One nurse about fifteen minutes after ou left. Her ID checked out. She was in ere for about seven minutes, then left. She ned the log here."

And the other?"

er," Diaz nodded toward the nurse sit- in the nurses' station, her head in her s. "She came in thirty minutes ago and Miss Kessler."

Klein, RN, was shaken. "I make my

rounds every two hours. No patient is left alone for more than two hours. We check their vitals, talk to them. We have everyone on 24/7 surveillance."

"Where are the tapes kept?" Will asked.

"At the central security desk in the basement."

The three men went down to the basement. The security chief was already there, expecting them.

"I have the tape from Ms. Kessler's room."

"Run it," Dillon said, tight-lipped.

He started the black-and-white tape from the time Dillon and Julia left. There were three angles of tape into the room. One showed the view from the observation area, which showed most of the room plus the patient. The second was above the patient, showing only the bed. The third focused on the door.

The door opened and a young nurse came in.

"What did her ID say?" Will asked.

"Isabel Younger," said Officer Diaz. "But I found out Younger's supposed to be off-duty today."

"Pull her employment files and photograph."

The security chief nodded to an assistant, who scurried off.

On the videotape, words were exchanged between patient and nurse. The nurse picked up Faye's wrist and looked at her own wrist, as if taking Faye's pulse.

"The nurse is not wearing a watch," Connor said.

"And her fingers aren't on the pulse point," Dillon added.

The woman on the video wrote something down on a chart and handed Faye a small cup, then the water from the side table.

"She drugged her," Will said.

"We'll run a tox screen for psychotics and other drugs," Dillon said.

More conversation. Then the "nurse" left. Faye lay there.

Connor watched the second camera. Faye had something in her hand under the blanket. She was moving her hand back and forth. For the first time that Connor had seen, Faye's face was peaceful. Almost joyous. She rolled to her right side. Pain crossed her face, but she just lay there, eyes half closed. Sleeping? No. Darkness spread under the blanket. Blood. It looked black on the black-and-white video.

"Why didn't anyone see this?" Dillo demanded.

"We did and called the nurse. But it was too late."

"Why?"

Nurse Klein had come down with them. "The blood wouldn't stop. She was bleeding for less than ten minutes. She shouldn't have died. But maybe with her other injuries and her anemia . . . I don't know." The nurse was obviously pained. "I couldn't staunch the blood."

They reviewed the tapes again. Connor stopped it at the profile of the unknown nurse. He tapped the screen. "That's Cami, the woman I encountered at Bowen's house."

After Nurse Klein left, Will put an APB on Michelle O'Dell a.k.a. "Cami" while Connor filled Dillon in on what they'd learned about Tristan Lord.

In the basement room, Dillon sat down and contemplated what Connor had said.

Connor added, "He's involved — you should see the paintings, Dil. It's like they tell a story, almost like a confession."

"Almost impossible as far as evidence that will stand up in court," Will said.

"What I don't understand is *why*," said Connor. "What's Tristan Lord's motive?"

"Sunday was the anniversary of Bowen's sister's death," Dillon said. "Tristan's mother, Monica. You said Tristan's mother was ill and they moved in with Garrett and

Eric Bowen. What about his father?"

"Eric didn't know much about Tristan's father, other than that he hasn't been part of Tristan's life since he'd been a young child. Monica Lord traveled a lot, and Tristan went with her."

"So his mother dies, Tristan starts self-mutilating, and Garrett Bowen created an anonymous group to help his nephew." Dillon thought more on it.

"There's something there — the anniversary of Monica Lord's death, the use of Wishlist, killing Bowen. It all circles around Tristan Lord. But why? What did he have against Bowen? And why the elaborate plan to kill Paul Judson, Jason Ridge, and Victor Montgomery? And there may have been others. Faye denied knowing anything about Jason Ridge's death, but that could be to protect this 'Cami' — Michelle O'Dell — who ended up killing her."

"We're looking for Lord and O'Dell," said Will. "It's only a matter of time before we pick them up."

"Unless they've already left the country."

Will said, "I have flags on their passports and we've alerted airport security."

"They could drive over the border and disappear, especially with enough money,"

Connor said. "I need to call Julia, fill her in."

"She's on her way here," Dillon said. "I talked to her when Officer Diaz called Will."

Connor glanced at his watch and frowned. "That was over an hour ago." He pulled out his phone and dialed Julia's number. Her voice mail picked up immediately. He left a message, hung up, tried her home number. Her answering machine came on after four rings.

Worry, and a deep-seated fear, hit Connor as he dialed her office direct line. Her voice mail picked up once again. "It's not like Julia to not check in or be unavailable," he said. "Where was she when you told her about Faye?"

"Her office."

Will said, "I'll put all-units on the lookout for her. What rental is she driving?"

"A white Ford Explorer from Enterprise." Connor walked to the elevator, pushed the button. "I'm going to find her."

"I'm coming with you," Dillon said.

When the elevator didn't come right away, they ran up the stairs. In the parking lot, they jumped into Connor's truck and peeled away. "We'll go back to the DA's office and retrace her steps," Connor said.

As they drove in front of the hospital, from

the corner of his eye, Connor saw a white Explorer. He slowed down and gave the vehicle a closer look. On the back bumper was an Enterprise company sticker.

Hitting his hazard lights, he pulled parallel to the SUV and jumped out. Looking in the window, Connor saw Julia's briefcase on the front seat.

"This is her rental car." Connor pulled out his phone again, dialed her number. Again, voice mail picked up immediately.

He walked around the car, stopped next to the meter. Two quarters reflected the falling sunlight. Squatting, he studied the ground next to the car, but there was nothing to see on the cement.

Dillon phoned Will. "We found Julia's rental out front. Has she come up there? Maybe we missed her."

Dillon shook his head when Connor caught his eye.

Dammit, where in the hell was Julia?

When Julia woke, her body was physically drained, but her mind was instantly alert. She remembered being attacked as she fed the meter outside the hospital, but she hadn't seen who'd grabbed her.

Her neck hurt, and she put her hand on a sore spot that stung something fierce.

She blinked open her eyes, saw a familiar man leaning against the doorjamb of an unfamiliar room. The walls were covered with paintings, some half complete. The only light came from small spotlights over a few of the pieces.

She glanced behind her. She was leaning against a railing, at least three stories up. Paintings and art hung everywhere. Most she couldn't make out in the shadows. One huge painting, however, hung in the middle of a brick wall, the streetlights casting a dim glow into the vast room. As she stared, an image emerged of a woman hanging. A man stood beyond. Julia blinked, and the image seemed to change.

The drugs in her system — whatever it was that had knocked her out so completely — were still messing with her mind. She slowly sat up. Feeling nauseous, she leaned against the pillar, willing her body to get it together. She would need all her strength to figure a way out of here.

Julia stared at the figure in the open doorway. It took her a minute to recognize Tristan Lord, the young artist, Bowen's nephew, whose studio had benefited from Saturday night's charity event. She'd only seen the tall, slender artist briefly at the party, but his shaved head and arty tunic were distinctive.

But the quietly confident, almost ethereal appearance of the man Julia had seen at the fund-raiser didn't match the wild-eyed, vicious glare of the monster staring down at her.

There was no doubt in Julia's mind that Tristan meant to kill her.

She unconsciously scooted back, but had nowhere to go. Below her was a three-story fall. She was in his studio. It was late. The sun was down, the shops on the street were closed.

If she screamed, who would hear?

"Why?" he said to her.

"Why what?" Her voice was hoarse.

"Why did you give Faye the knife? She was no harm to you."

"I didn't give Faye a knife." Julia swallowed.

"I saw you." A woman's voice came from her side. "Just like you saw me. Loose ends."

Julia hadn't been able to see her from her position on the floor, Michelle O'Dell had been hidden by a large metal art object. But when Michelle stepped into view, there was no doubt this was the same girl who told Connor her name was "Cami."

"Why would I give Faye a knife? She's a suspect in a murder investigation."

Michelle laughed. "Does anyone need a *reason* to kill?"

Julia stared at her. "Yes."

Michelle crossed her arms and looked at Tristan. "Ms. Chandler here gave Faye the knife because of what happened to her niece, Emily."

Michelle held a gun.

"Emily has nothing to do with this."

"But the police thought she did," Michelle said. "It could have easily gone the other way."

"Were you trying to frame Emily?" Julia asked, incredulous. "Were you trying to make her seem guilty?"

Tristan interrupted. "Of course not. Emily was an innocent."

Julia wondered if Michelle felt differently than Tristan. She wondered who was really in charge.

"What do you want with me? With all Tristan's money, the two of you could have escaped, been halfway across the world by now."

Tristan shook his head. "You're an example of the corrupt system, one of the twisted people who decides who lives, who dies, who goes to prison, who goes free."

Julia shook her head. "I'm doing my job.

Trying to get people the justice they deserve."

"Bullshit!" Tristan grabbed a manila file from the top of a desk near the door and threw it to her feet. A few papers — they looked like court documents — slipped out. "When we were researching you, we pulled all your cases. Your plea agreements. Your prosecutions. When you asked for the death penalty and when you asked for minimal time."

"Every case is unique," Julia said. "I look at them based on the evidence and what I think a jury will convict on. And my boss —"

"Stop. Don't offer some lame justification. We're not buying it."

"But none of this has anything to do with me." Julia was grasping at straws, hoping one would hold. "It's Faye, right? You think I hurt her. I didn't. I didn't bring her a knife. I swear to you, I had nothing to do with her suicide."

Tristan looked torn, and Michelle interjected. "Shut up. We don't believe you."

Julia glared at the girl. "You were there? Why? What reason did you have to go to the hospital? You must have known the police were getting closer."

"You wouldn't have figured it out in

time," said Michelle. "And I'm on my way south. *Way* south."

"You'll never make it. We know all about you. Your mother must have told you about my visit, that I have your picture. You changed your appearance a little — lightened your hair, changed your clothing style — but anyone who saw you would realize that Cami and Michelle are one and the same."

"None of that means anything," Michelle snapped, "and it doesn't matter what you know because you're helping me get out of town."

"Just tell me how you killed Jason. I'm curious." Julia was trying to buy time. By now, Connor would know she was missing and be looking for her. They knew about Michelle; had they figured out Tristan Lord was involved?

"Don't you want to know why? Why is much more interesting than how."

"I know why."

"Really?" Michelle stared at her with disbelief. "Why?"

"He raped your best friend. This elaborate plan of yours was a way to seek justice because the system failed Shannon." Julia stared at Tristan. "I don't understand why you're involved."

But Tristan wasn't looking at her. He stared at Michelle. "Who are you?"

"Don't listen to her."

"You're Shannon's sister."

"We were *like* sisters." Michelle turned her head from Tristan to Julia.

Julia remembered something in the back of her mind, from Garrett Bowen's party.

"Where's Camilla?" Bowen asked his girlfriend.

"She's in the little girls' room."

What was her name? Marisa Wohler. The triangle took shape. "Marisa is Laura Chase."

Tristan turned to her, an edge of panic in his expression. Michelle just laughed. "Give the lawyer a prize."

"They've been lying to you," Julia said to Tristan, trying to find a way to turn the two against each other. It might be her only hope to find a way out of here alive.

"Cami is Shannon's sister," Tristan said, his confidence waning.

Julia said, "I can positively identify this girl as Michelle O'Dell. I spoke to her parents, got her photograph. It's in my purse. Go look."

Tristan didn't move.

Julia continued. "She was *friends* with Shannon Chase. She also dated Jason Ridge

502

before he raped Shannon. I'm sorry the system failed Shannon, I really am, but why do you care, Tristan? What's in it for you?"

Tristan wasn't paying attention to Julia. He was still staring at Michelle. "Laura isn't your mother? Why'd she bring you in?"

"You saw how reckless she was when she tried to kill Garrett two years ago. She was a disaster. I convinced her she needed my help. You're the one who assumed I was Shannon's sister. We just let you keep thinking that. Camilla died when she was a baby, before Shannon was born."

"Then why?" Tristan asked the same question Julia was thinking. The bonds of friendship didn't go so deep as to kill, did they?

Michelle didn't answer his question. Instead, she turned to Tristan, hand on her hip. "Go ahead, tell her all about your master plan to restore truth, justice, and the American way."

Tristan shook his head. "You never understood. Faye was the only one who saw the aesthetic beauty in my plan. Revenge means little if you don't use the wicked against themselves. Garrett deserved a fate worse than hanging. In destroying his reputation, his image, his own ego, I found justice for my mother. Everyone else was part of the game, the chessboard. It was balanced."

He looked at Julia as if pleading with her to understand his reasoning. "Laura and I met outside of Garrett's office. She was going to kill him. I stopped her. Each kill led back to Garrett. I never expected you to go as far back as Jason Ridge."

"If I hadn't," Julia agreed, "we wouldn't have figured it out so quickly. But everything's public record. You just have to know where to look."

"Let's go," Michelle said, motioning toward Tristan with her gun. "Go help her up. We'll drive across the border and if anyone tries to interfere, we have a hostage."

"Why did you stop here?" Julia needed to buy more time. She couldn't get in a car with them.

"I had to get money," Michelle said as if the question was stupid. "You fucked up my timeline, I hadn't planned on leaving until tomorrow." She glared at Tristan. "What are you waiting for?"

He stared at Michelle with an intensity that scared Julia. "Why did you help Laura? If you weren't Shannon's sister, what hold did she have over you?"

"She had no hold over me," Michelle snapped. "You're wasting time."

"There was no reason for you to get involved. You told me a long time ago that you couldn't save Shannon in time. What did that mean?"

Michelle let out a long, exasperated sigh.

"Look, Tristan, it was just a game. It was never supposed to go that far. Jason broke up with me to date my best friend. And she went out with him! I couldn't believe it. The traitor. She slept with him, was all goo-goo-eyed. If she only knew how down and dirty he could be, but she was so fucking *romantic* about everything."

"He raped her," Julia said before she realized she'd spoken.

"Funny what a little mixing of Rohypnol and Ketamine will do to a man. I thought they were just used on women," Michelle said thoughtfully. "Anyway, I screwed it up, okay? I just wanted Shannon to see how rough Jason *really* liked it. I didn't think he'd hurt her, and I didn't think she'd go all batty and tell everyone he raped her. I figured she'd dump him and he'd come willingly back to me. And I certainly didn't think she'd go off and kill herself! Who does something that stupid? Only whack jobs like Faye."

"Shut up! Don't talk about Faye like that —" Tristan began.

"Faye was as crazy as they come and you know it." Michelle's eyes hardened. "I know what you did with her. How could you?"

"You know nothing about Faye."

Julia saw her opportunity. "Faye was alive and well when I left her."

Tristan shook his head, his hands rubbing his scalp. "Just stop!"

"I want you to know the truth," said Julia. "Michelle gave Faye the knife." It became clear to Julia then. "You loved Faye, didn't you?"

"Don't talk about her," he said.

"You loved her and Michelle was jealous. She found out and used Faye's weakness against her."

"Faye was too good," he said. "She'd never have cut herself deep enough to die. She knew what she was doing."

"Not if someone drugged her or manipulated her. Faye was taking the entire blame for all the murders. We knew someone else was involved, but we didn't know about you. We knew about Michelle, though, and we were looking for Laura Chase. Tristan, you would have gotten away with it, at least long enough to disappear and leave the country.

"Michelle feared Faye would turn *her* in. That's why she got her to kill herself. Michelle did it to protect herself."

"Don't be ridiculous," Michelle spat out

viciously. "By the time the police figured anything out, I'd be as far away as Tristan." But Michelle's eyes kept darting to the man who, until now, had barely moved from the door.

"You killed Faye?" Tristan stepped toward Michelle.

"She was going to destroy you," said Michelle. "Destroy all of us."

Tristan shook his head slowly back and forth. "Faye *worshipped* you. She turned herself in to protect *you* just as much as to protect me."

"Bullshit," Michelle said. "Faye would never have raised a finger to save my ass. When I saw those pictures, I realized the truth. You used me. You and Faye must have had a grand laugh at my expense."

"You know nothing of my relationship with Faye."

"Relationship? You call that little sex-and-vampire act the two of you had going a *relationship?*"

While Michelle and Tristan were focused on each other, Julia began to scoot along the railing toward the spiral staircase at the far end of the loft. She gritted her teeth at the sharp stabs of muscle pain as her body regained sensation.

Tristan glared at Michelle, his hand reaching inside his pants pocket, eyes sharp with wild intelligence. "You know what? I recruited Faye. I brought her in from the very beginning. Then I told you to recruit her. But she was already on board." He barked out a laugh. "Faye had as much control over you as you thought you had over her."

Michelle's face contorted with rage. "You're as crazy as she was. I didn't kill Faye. She voluntarily used the knife I gave her on herself. Why? Because I told her *you* wanted her to."

Tristan pulled a butterfly knife out of his pocket, the *click-click* of metal on metal as he flicked his wrist to unsheathe the blade. Julia bit her tongue to stop a yelp from escaping.

He brought the knife up without hesitation.

"You bitch!" he screamed.

Michelle raised her gun and fired.

Tristan's body slammed back against the wall, a smear of bright red blood blending with the black ink of the painting behind him. His knife dropped to the floor.

"Perfect," Michelle said. "I'll have time to get away after all." She turned to Julia and smiled.

Julia's blood ran cold.

THIRTY-TWO

"There are at least three people inside," said SWAT team leader Tom Blade from his command post in the rear of Tristan Lord's warehouse/art studio. There were no windows on this side of the building — it was all brick — but Blade had a team up on the roof using an amplified infrared imager to detect body heat inside.

"Let's go," Connor said impatiently. Julia had been missing three hours.

"Wait." Will caught Connor's eye. "There's no way to get into the building undetected. They're on the third floor. They can see the whole open space below them."

"We can't just sit here and twiddle our thumbs!"

Blade motioned at the blueprints. "There are skylights here and here. We have men on the roof already and they're working on unsealing the windows. We can get in here"

— he pointed — "on the far side of the third floor."

Connor stared at the plans. "Why not go in here, on the bottom floor? This doorway is under the third floor. They can't see anyone, and we've already disabled the alarm."

"There's no easy way to get to them," said Blade. "A metal staircase going up. No way to get up there undetected."

Connor wasn't sure. "But if they come down, we'll have the element of surprise."

Blade thought about it. He was a sharp cop, but had been promoted to the position only six months ago after his boss was killed in the line of duty. Connor suspected Blade was uncomfortable in his role as leader.

Will leaned over and told Connor, "We've found Laura Chase."

"What does she have to say?"

"I should have said we've found where she's been living. Under a new identity: Marisa Wohler. The police in Maine talked to her ex-husband and got her phone number. We traced the number to a Marisa Wohler, then e-crimes traced Wohler. She miraculously appeared eighteen months ago. There was no record of her in San Diego, California, or in the rest of the country prior to November 2005. Get this,"

Will added, "she's been living around the corner from Garrett Bowen's mansion in Rancho Santa Fe."

Connor stared at the rear door of the art studio. Two SWAT team members framed the exit. He said to Blade, "Let me go in."

Before he could answer, a gunshot sounded in the building.

Blade was on the com with his team on the roof. "Do you have a visual?"

"Negative."

Blade glanced at Connor, then told his team. "Possible hostage situation. Proceed with caution."

Connor drew his weapon and followed the SWAT team inside. As soon as the door opened, another gunshot sounded.

Julia!

"God, I really hated him." Michelle was looking contemptuously down at Tristan. Her face showed no emotion, nothing but a mild irritation.

Stumbling, Julia scrambled for the staircase as soon as Michelle turned her back.

"Stop or you're dead."

Julia stopped.

"Sit down, against the railing."

Julia hesitated.

Michelle fired the gun into the ceiling.

Dust rained down on Julia and she sat back against the railing. She'd been so close!

"Move back to your original position, Ms. Chandler."

Reluctantly, Julia did as Michelle commanded.

"Good." Michelle smiled as if Julia were a prize student.

"The police know everything."

"Like I care? I'll be so far gone they'll never find me. Let's make this fast." Michelle popped out the cartridge of the 9mm and Julia recognized it as her own gun. Michelle pressed the gun into Julia's hand, then put it on the floor next to her. Michelle put on gloves and picked up the knife Tristan had dropped.

"What are you doing?"

"It's perfect. He stabs you and as you lay dying, you shoot him. The police will figure it out, but it'll take them a couple days, and by that time I'll be on some beach far, far away."

There was no doubt in Julia's mind that Michelle would go through with her plan without hesitation or remorse.

Julia reached for the gun. The cartridge was gone, but there was a round chambered. She had only one shot.

She put the gun behind her back and

slowly stood, shaking off the nausea sweeping through her.

Michelle whipped around. "Sit down!" She strode over to Julia, knife in hand, irritated.

Julia swallowed nervously. "Michelle, let's figure out a solution to this. No one else needs to die. I have —"

"Shut up."

"— lots of friends in the —"

"I said shut up!" Michelle stomped her foot hard on Julia's shin and Julia winced, biting her lip.

Michelle was listening. Something downstairs had caught her attention.

Julia didn't hear anything unusual, just her rapidly beating heart vibrating in her ears.

"Someone's downstairs," Michelle said. "Change of plans."

"You won't get away with this."

Michelle laughed. "You sound like a stupid television show. Get up."

Julia sagged. "I'm not going anywhere."

"Then you'll die here."

"So will you," Julia said, pulling out the gun from behind her back.

Michelle's face contorted in anger as she brought the knife up in her fist. Julia pulled the trigger. The one bullet hit Michelle in the upper abdomen. Reflexively, Julia pressed the trigger again, even though she knew there were no more bullets.

Michelle's blue eyes reflected shock and disbelief. She raised her hand, the knife still clenched tight in her fist. Her body shook violently as blood seeped from the wound.

Michelle lunged forward, the sharp blade coming down fast toward Julia's face.

Julia grabbed Michelle's wrist. The momentum brought the knife to Julia's cheek.

Julia winced at the sudden sharp pain, but didn't loosen her hold on Michelle's arm. She dropped the empty gun and used both hands to hold Michelle's knife hand away from her. Michelle fought back, her mouth soundlessly opening and closing, her left hand reaching for Julia's neck.

Julia squirmed from the woman's grasp, but Michelle was above her, gravity aiding her momentum and fury.

They struggled for control of the knife. Julia lost her grip. She tried to roll away from the blade, but it cut deep into her shoulder. Pain shot down Julia's arm and she screamed, clutching her bloody left shoulder.

Michelle used that moment to push Julia to the railing, pulling her up with unusual strength. She bent Julia backward, trying to throw her over the edge. Julia's vision blurred with the strain of keeping Michelle from killing her. Pulse racing, Julia fought the dying girl. But Michelle had nothing left to lose and wanted to take Julia with her.

"Bitch," Michelle spat in her face. "You bitch!"

Michelle still grasped the knife, now dripping with Julia's blood. Julia blinked, fear and panic making her heart race and her head swirl. Michelle brought the knife down again, but Julia moved to the right, grabbed the woman's wrist, and slammed it hard against the metal railing.

Michelle screamed, but didn't relinquish the knife.

All Julia wanted now was to get away, but Michelle kept her pinned to the rail, trying to push her over.

Julia's mind clouded; her vision faded. She swallowed and tasted blood.

"You'll die with me," Michelle spat in her ear, the knife inches from Julia's neck.

"No. I. Won't."

Julia didn't want to let go of Michelle's wrist, but her instincts told her she had to.

She released Michelle. The killer's momentum kept her falling forward and over the railing.

Julia reached for her, but missed. The body hit the cement floor a moment later.

"Julia!"

Connor had found her.

"Oh God, Julia." Connor stripped off his T-shirt.

She reached for his face, but her hand fluttered back down. She had no strength.

Connor's training took over. He immediately applied pressure to the wound. "Medics!" he shouted. "Are you hurt anywhere else?" He examined her body, saw blood everywhere.

She shook her head, closing her eyes against the pain.

"Hold on, sweetheart, the ambulance is almost here." He heard sirens approaching. "We'll get you sewed up in no time."

SWAT team leader Tom Blade came over. "Two dead. Male, twenties, over there." He gestured against the back wall of the studio where Tristan Lord lay, his blood splattered on the wall behind him.

"Downstairs, female."

Connor demanded, "I need the medics up here, ASAP."

"Right here." Another SWAT team member came in. SWAT had their own field medics.

Connor moved over to give him room, one

hand on Julia's wound and the other grasping her hand.

"What's your name, darlin'?" the medic asked.

"Julia," she whispered.

"Julia Chandler," Connor said, swallowing his fear. There was so much blood.

"Looks like a nice clean wound. Kincaid here is just going to keep pressure on it while I clean up these little nicks, see if we have anything else we need to be worried about."

"She's going to be fine, right?" Connor asked.

"I am fine," Julia said, but her voice was faint. And she was so pale.

Connor panicked, staring at the medic. "Tell me."

"She's lost a lot of blood. Keep that pressure on. I'm doing all I can."

"Connor," Julia said faintly.

"Shh, don't talk." His own chest burned with suppressed emotion.

"I love you."

Connor's breath caught. "Oh, Julia. I love you, too, babe. Stay here, okay? Just hold on."

Her eyes closed. "Julia?" She'd lost consciousness.

There was commotion outside the door as

two paramedics came up with a basket. "We can't get the stretcher up here."

"I typed her blood. A-positive. She needs plasma ASAP."

The SWAT medic tied a tourniquet tight above the wound and the paramedics strapped her into the basket. Connor ran downstairs with one medic while the other two hoisted the basket over the railing. The art studio was full of crime scene techs and cops, but Connor barely registered the commotion. All he could think about was how pale Julia looked, how much blood she'd lost.

And how much he loved her.

"I'm with you," Connor said as they strapped Julia onto the stretcher.

THIRTY-THREE

Connor paced the emergency room while Julia was in surgery.

They needed to repair extensive muscle and arterial damage, and sew up the wound. The knife had gone in between the subclavian and pulmonary arteries. Had it been any higher on the shoulder, Julia would have bled out in minutes. Connor's heart jumped into his throat and he squeezed back the moisture in his eyes. He shuddered at what could have happened, that but for a half inch, Julia would have died in his arms.

"She'll be fine," Dillon was saying. "They stabilized her in the ambulance. She's going to make it."

"I know. I'm just worried." He ran a hand over his rough face. "Did Will arrest Laura Chase?"

When Dillon didn't say anything, Connor stared at him. "Where is she?"

"They're out in full force looking for her.

Her house was empty," said Dillon.

"She wasn't at the art studio?"

"No. And her car is missing. We know she's driving a silver Mercedes registered under the name Marisa Wohler."

"Why? Why all . . . this?" Connor asked in exasperation.

"What we've been able to piece together after talking to Tom Chase is that Laura was devastated and inconsolable after Shannon's death. She'd lost one daughter, Camilla, as an infant. She immediately got pregnant again and her entire life revolved around Shannon. She'd likely had an untreated psychosis already, and Shannon's suicide flipped a switch."

"So, kill the kid who raped her daughter, but why kill Bowen? Or Montgomery?"

"Will's still trying to figure out how Tristan Lord and Laura Chase hooked up, but we know from records in Bowen's office that the good doctor had an appointment with Laura Chase nearly two years ago that she never showed up for."

"Where does Tristan Lord fit into this?"

Will Hooper walked in. "I think I can answer that."

"Did you find Laura Chase?"

He shook his head. "We have the airports, trains, ports all covered. Border patrol is on

the lookout as well."

"So why did Tristan want to kill his uncle?"

"The station brought in a forensic artist to look at his paintings. The gal said each painting tells a story, that Tristan Lord was a master of perspective. From different angles, primarily from above, you can see something completely different from looking at it head-on." Will grinned wryly at Connor. "So you weren't wrong when you saw the number ten and the girl hanging."

"And Bowen?"

"We know that Tristan's mother died of cancer when he was eighteen. A painting in Bowen's own house shows a man with a needle over a woman lying in bed. Under a microscope and ultraviolet light, you can see that some lines are made up of microscopic letters. They spell out 'Mother was murdered' over and over. Thousands of times. Sounds obsessive to me."

"Tristan thought his own uncle killed his mom?" Connor asked.

"Tristan was probably right," Will said. "I just came back from Eric Bowen's house. He said his aunt Monica, Tristan's mother, had breast cancer. Bowen's wife died of breast cancer several years before. He watched her waste away, in pain, and even-

tually die so drugged she didn't remember her husband or son. Monica Lord was in the final stages of cancer but was still mobile. Her medical records indicated that she had three to six months to live. Her doctor suspected she may have committed suicide — she was adamant about not wanting to 'waste away' like her sister-in-law."

"And you're thinking that maybe Bowen helped her."

"Why wasn't there an autopsy?" Dillon asked.

"Her doctor signed off on the death certificate without one. Her medical history showed invasive cancer; there was no reason to think anything but cancer killed her. And Dr. Bowen didn't want her family to think she killed herself. There's a matter of some insurance money."

"Insurance money?"

"Bowen and Tristan split over eight million dollars from Monica's estate."

The surgeon came out of the operating room. "We're done."

Connor asked, "Can I see her now?"

"She's in recovery, still sleeping. I'll let you know when she wakes."

"But she's going to be okay, right?"

"She won't be able to use her left arm for a while, but yeah, she's going to be fine."

■ ■ ■ ■

It was over.

Laura Chase slowly walked to the grave of her daughter. Her beautiful, perfect daughter.

An eye for an eye, a tooth for a tooth. Vengeance is mine, saith the Lord.

Vengeance? You don't know the meaning of vengeance, God. The wrath of a mother is far greater than yours. You let them hurt my baby, my little girl. And nothing happened. No lightning bolts, no earthquakes, no floods or famine.

I didn't want to wait for them to burn in Hell.

Hell. She'd been living in it for nearly two years, but now it was over.

She sat against the headstone that read *Shannon Marisa Chase, 1988–2005.*

Across from Shannon's grave was a smaller one, for an infant: *Camilla Christina Chase, October 12, 1986–April 13, 1987.*

Tomorrow marked the twentieth anniversary of Camilla's death. Six months old and died in her crib. The doctors said it was sudden infant death syndrome. Laura knew different.

For years she'd suppressed the guilt. It had been an accident. No one knew, not even Tom. Shannon, perfect Shannon, was Laura's chance to make everything right again.

She closed her eyes. Took out the bottle of pills she'd stolen from Garrett long ago. Swallowed them two by two.

Two by two.

Two by two.

Her head spun, but she kept taking the pills. She felt heavy. Heavy. Of course, they would put her to sleep. Forever.

But Shannon was dead. Vengeance, perhaps, for Laura's own sins.

Connor sat with Julia as she woke from surgery. "You're back."

"How long?"

"You skipped a day. It's Thursday morning." He glanced at his watch. "Five-fifteen."

"Wow. I didn't think — Did Michelle fall over the railing?"

"Michelle's dead. So is Laura Chase. They found her body near the grave of her daughters. Suicide."

"I could almost feel sorry for her."

"Dillon said Laura Chase was psychotic. She snapped. She managed to hold it together for a while. There's a twisted logic to all the victims. Except for Paul Judson. Dillon thinks he was a test, to bind the four

524

kids to a common goal, as well as keep them in line."

"Skip, Robbie, Michelle, and Faye."

"Tristan Lord accessed his uncle's files and learned the identity of all his online patients. Then it was just a matter of matching up the so-called anonymous e-mails with real people."

"Like Emily." Julia frowned. "Michelle's parents were of modest means. How did she hop back and forth from Palo Alto and San Diego? How did she live?"

"Will's still digging into the finances and timeline, but the penthouse apartment Michelle lived in was paid for by Laura Chase. In the divorce, the Chases split a substantial pot of money. Laura changed her identity and bought the house near Garrett Bowen. There's evidence that Michelle had a room there as well as the apartment."

"Maybe to keep the act going, that 'Cami' was 'Marisa Wohler's' daughter." Julia reached for Connor's hand and he squeezed it, bringing his lips down to her fingers. She asked, "All this in an elaborate plan to kill Garrett Bowen because he helped Tristan's mother commit suicide and testified for Jason Ridge. It's amazing that Laura Chase and Tristan hooked up in the first place."

"Not that amazing," Connor said. "E-crimes is still putting together a timeline of Wishlist and it looks like Michelle O'Dell was on the list long before Shannon committed suicide."

"She said something that disturbed me," Julia said. "She said she drugged Jason so he'd hurt Shannon, thinking they'd break up. She thought it was all one big game."

"Michelle was one sick young woman."

"Sick? No. She knew exactly what she was doing and she enjoyed it." Julia paused. "Maybe James and Stephanie Ridge would like to know their son had been drugged. Give them some closure."

"Will is going to be talking to them and the O'Dells," Connor said.

He took Julia's hand and brought it to his lips. "It's over."

"Emily can come home now?"

Connor nodded. "She's coming back from Montana with Carina on Sunday. I hope that's okay. She seems to be having a good time up there, and you need a couple of days to recuperate before a teenager moves in."

"I'll call her later. Thank you."

Connor played with her palm. "Are you really okay?"

"Just tired. And sore."

"I can get you some pain medication —"

He started to rise.

She squeezed his hand. "No. Stay."

He sat back down. "I was worried. You lost a lot of blood." His voice cracked.

"Did you mean what you said at the studio?"

"I always mean what I say." He stared at her. "I love you, Julia."

A single tear rolled down her cheek.

"Don't cry," he said.

"I'm not. I just — I was worried about the past. What I did to your life."

"We don't live in the past, Julia." Connor leaned over and kissed her lightly on the lips. She was still too pale, but time, sun, and lots of love would bring back her old self.

"We were both in a different place then," Connor said. "We were both right, and we both made mistakes. In the end, though, the dead girls were avenged through the system, not outside of it. And *that* was the right thing to do, even if it hurt like hell at the time."

"I think I've always loved you," Julia said, her emerald eyes bright with emotion. "Do you think we can find happiness?"

Connor kissed her again. "As long as we're together."